$\mathcal{P}$RINCESS

$\mathcal{S}$HANYIN

The Complete Obsession Saga

LILIANA LEE

Book 1: The Obsession

PROLOGUE

History will not remember me kindly, nor do I want it to. The book of our dynasty will say many things about me: that I was cruel, that I was decadent and depraved. They will claim that my pleasures were perverse in nature. Let me tell you that these things are all true...and not true...

It is hard for me to say exactly what I found so arousing about Yuan. From the very first moment I saw him, I wanted him in every way, more than any lover before or since. He was standing in a sea of bureaucrats and retainers assembled before the Emperor, though it was he alone who caught my eye.

Yuan was buried among the midlevel officials, yet he stood so tall and proud that it was impossible not to notice. He was young for such a position as well, perhaps only a few years older than myself. Fire shot through my veins at my first glimpse of him. As he watched the proceedings in the imperial hall, I detected a hint of defiance in the set of his jaw. His eyes were black and hard and my sex flooded when he glanced in my direction.

I leaned forward in my seat to address the Emperor on his throne. "Who is that?"

Several pairs of eyes fixed onto me from down below. I was one of the few in the empire allowed to address his Imperial Majesty so directly. The ministers of the court feared and hated me for that alone, imagining how I must whisper political schemes into his ear. But the Emperor was my younger brother and the things we said to each other were usually for our own amusement.

This time, Ziye actually looked impatient at my interruption. He took the throne when he was only sixteen years old after our father passed away. He was seventeen now.

"Who?" he asked me.

I gave a quick gesture with my hand. My brother knew immediately who I was interested in. And why.

"Lord Chu Yuan," he answered with a smirk. "You're shameless, Elder Sister."

Our conversation held up the entire court. Ziye turned his attention back to the elder official standing at the foot of the dais and I did as well. I had little interest in affairs of government, but when Ziye summoned me, I could hardly refuse.

The gray-haired bureaucrat was reading from a long sheet of paper.

"Continue," Ziye commanded.

As the official read, his voice began to tremble. I tried to recall the details of the situation. My brother had called this man to the front to read from a letter one of the imperial eunuchs had intercepted. I listened with a touch more interest—oh, the letter mentioned Ziye and it was not very flattering. The assembly grew deathly quiet.

My attention wandered once more to the handsome Yuan. For a moment, his gaze rose to the throne and my heartbeat ran wild. Such fire in that look! I couldn't wait to get him alone.

"So you question my ability to rule," my brother was saying.

His voice rang to the very back of the audience hall. Tension rippled throughout the assembly when he stood. "Does anyone else agree?"

Of course no one did. Most lowered their heads in

supplication, afraid to meet the glittering eyes of this boy who was barely a man. Ziye had only been on the throne for a year, but his courtiers had learned quickly. Even I held my breath as he descended the dais.

The official prostrated himself, pressing his forehead to the hard floor. He rambled an apology: this humble servant was mistaken, he was sorry, he was worthless.

"Tell me Minister He, who do you think should be on this throne instead?"

The official was given no chance to reply. Ziye's foot shot out and the sickening crack against Minister He's skull could be heard throughout the hall. My stomach lurched, but I froze. The entire assembly remained deathly still while Ziye kicked the old man again and again, as if the minister were no more than a dog.

"Who was this letter intended for?" he demanded.

My brother's personal bodyguards gathered at the edge of the dais, but not to stop the brutal beating. They were ready should anyone try to interfere. I winced as Ziye's foot snapped into the minister's ribs.

"Imperial Majesty!"

Mine was the only voice in the hall and Ziye stopped immediately. I rose to my feet to descend the steps, but my knees were water. My chest constricted so tight I co hardly breathe.

Ziye's face was so contorted with rage, I could barely recognize it. Yet his eyes glowed. His face was alight.

I glanced downward as I took his side. "Look, there's blood on the Emperor's shoe," I complained.

Ziye followed my gaze. "Right," he said after a pause. "We must keep up appearances."

The offending minister was dragged away and the court adjourned immediately after. As the ranks filed, I sought another glimpse of Lord Chu Yuan. His jaw was clenched.

His eyes were shuttered and unreadable and the tight fist in my chest slowly unfurled. The sick feeling in my belly faded to be replaced with a low, throbbing ache.

Outside in the courtyard, I sent one of my eunuchs to him while my pulse raced. Usually I would just issue an official summons and wait in my personal palace, but today I watched as my messenger approached.

Yuan shook his head with a harsh curl of his lip. The look of disdain on his face made my blood run so hot that it boiled in my veins. I swore by my very last breath that I would have him; I would have that strong body beneath me, undone and throbbing inside me. In every way under heaven.

They tell stories of how insatiable I was in the bedchamber. My bed itself was legendary. Carved from rosewood, it was said to be spacious enough to accommodate my entire harem. That fable wasn't true, but I did have ten join me once, surrounding me as if I were the center of a lotus flower. Closing my eyes, I lost track of hands and mouths and tongues as they worshiped my body.

So many at one time was entirely too cumbersome. I found that two suited me quite well. Perhaps three at times. Which one, or two, or three I chose each night depended on my mood.

Each of their names was listed on a tile. Every evening, I turned over the ones I wanted to summon to my chamber the same way the Emperor did in his harem.

Tonight, I didn't look at the names as I made my selections. There were times I preferred they remain nameless so I wouldn't be distracted from my pleasure, but there was a particular reason I didn't want any names or even faces this evening. Yuan occupied my every thought and desire.

My maidservants undressed me and let my hair down

before departing. I lay on the magnificent bed face down with my head resting on my hands. A sheer curtain hung around the frame, dimming the glow of the lanterns.

Then I closed my eyes and waited.

My lovers would come to me, sometimes one at a time, sometimes all at once. They would never keep me waiting too long. Just long enough to make my skin tingle with anticipation.

I sensed a presence in the chamber before I felt the touch on my body. The first contact was upon my back. It was a gentle, soothing stroke that traveled down my spine, then up again to round my shoulders. Strong hands. I sighed and arched into them. My muscles had begun to grow lax and my flesh warm when another hand circled my ankle. A thumb ran down my instep, making me flinch. *Insolence.* I hated being teased in such a way. I was about to turn around when the perpetrator pressed his lips to my heel in supplication before stroking his hands up my calves.

He was being bold, this one. I accepted it for now. He was doing it to make my pulse rise and to heighten the moment. A few of my concubines occasionally showed some initiative. I had to admit, sometimes willfulness had its advantages.

The myriad of hands were stroking me in broad circles, over my neck, my shoulders, my back. Slowly they worked my legs apart to massage my inner thighs. My breathing slowed and grew deeper. I could hear the men breathing heavy all around me as they readied me.

There was one more. He hadn't yet made his presence known and I wondered when he would join us. I didn't have to wonder for long. There was a shifting of weight on the bed and then a hand moved between my legs. Gentle fingers parted my sex and then the touch—oh, that first perfect touch. Not too soft and not too rough.

I imagined Yuan's long fingers there, caressing me for the

first time, and a flood of wetness poured from me. The fingers slipped through to explore deeper while the other hands continued to knead over my limbs. My body was being soothed as well as primed for sex at the same time.

One finger entered into me, curving upward as it penetrated. Yuan again. He would know how to pleasure a woman, wouldn't he? In my mind, I saw his face and imagined the hard set of his jaw as he glared at me in disapproval, which only made me hotter.

I would have him and it would be all the sweeter because of his initial resistance. I imagined him pleasuring me now with that look of disdain and condemnation. He didn't want to do it, but he had no choice.

I moaned. The sound was muffled by my arm, but my lovers had heard me. The hands turned me over and my heart pounded. The mouth that covered my breast was also Yuan's. As was the one kissing a line down my stomach. Another mouth was at my neck, nibbling then biting. They were becoming more insistent. They were slaves summoned for my pleasure, but they were still men and subject to their own needs as well.

When I was feeling wicked, I would hold them off and take my own pleasure while tormenting them. But I had been in a fever since Yuan had refused me. I lifted my hips to urge my lovers on.

A tongue flicked over my nipple and my body pulled tight, all sensation concentrating on that single point. I pressed myself to the source of the pleasure, demanding more. Whoever he was, he gave me what I wanted while his hand squeezed my other breast. I reached out to seek another concubine and dragged him down, kissing him hungrily. I wanted the intimacy of mouth against mouth tonight. I wanted everything.

Right then, someone wrapped his hands around my thighs

and held them open. Instead of lowering himself to me, he lifted me up to him. My sense of balance was disrupted right before his mouth closed over me and his tongue penetrated my sex. *Yes.* He licked upward to search out the apex of my desire, the small knob of flesh that was throbbing for attention. He found it and circled with just the tip of his tongue, filling me with waves of pleasure.

Yuan was with me again; as haughty and beautiful as he'd been in the Emperor's court. I squeezed my eyes shut. In my mind, my male concubines were holding him by the arms, pressing Yuan's head down between my legs to force him to taste me. That image and the quick flutter of a tongue over my pearl was all I needed to reach my climax. It shot through me like lightning and I had to bite down to keep from calling out Yuan's name. The name of the one man I wanted, but had yet to conquer.

When I opened my eyes there was a shadow above me. I couldn't see his face, but I could hear the strain in his voice.

"Princess!" he pleaded.

Instead of speaking, I curved my legs around his hips and he sank into me, stretching out my already sensitive flesh. The penetration almost reached the point of pain before he retreated, moving back and then forward again in a shallow thrust. He found a rhythm and I lifted toward him in approval.

They all knew what I liked. The entire harem would be punished if I was disappointed. Sometimes I had them punished even after I'd fallen asleep sated. It was good for them to not become too complacent.

I felt him quicken above me, his muscles straining to hold back. I wouldn't come again so soon, but I still enjoyed the rush of passion that overtook a man in the moment right before release. There was a rawness, a desperation to it that I loved. I looked into his face, enjoying the strain, the look there that bordered on pain.

With a groan, the slave pulled out of me and spilled upon the pallet. I hadn't given him permission to lose his essence inside me.

Another moved to replace the first. His organ slid into me in a long stroke that made me gasp. He was larger. Thicker. I might have recognized this one by the feel of him alone. Rather than thrusting deep, he ground his hips in a circle that made wonderful things happen inside of me. I closed my eyes and let my head fall back decadently. He would bring me to another climax, I willed it so. We strained toward it together, my nails digging deep into his shoulders until I was overcome.

My body was exhausted when the last organ entered me. He tried to please me as best he could, but I was no longer interested. I pushed him away and he withdrew without protest. I dismissed all but one, the one with the talented mouth who had brought me to my first climax.

He licked me slowly, lovingly, as I fell to sleep. He was able to bring me once more to a peak, but it was only a small release, a whimper rather than a scream. I should have been satisfied. My concubines had performed well that night, but I was unfulfilled.

I was still agitated, my mind churning from my confrontation with Yuan. He was what I wanted to remember from this day. Not the blood, not the violence in the imperial assembly. Instead, I thought of Yuan's strong body and his proud, handsome face while I plotted how to make him mine. This was the final thought I took with me as I drifted away. Even while I slept, I continued to dream in fits and starts, my mind refusing to let me rest.

CHAPTER ONE

People like to tell a story about me and my imperial brother, and how I came to possess a harem. I lamented to Ziye once, after he took the throne, about the hardships of being a woman.

"Though our genders are different, we have the same father," I pointed out. "Yet you have more than ten thousand woman in your palace for your pleasure, while I am only allowed one husband. That is hardly fair."

Amused by my audacity, the Emperor gifted me with thirty male concubines, my cherished and skilled harem of lovers.

Oh, what a wicked, immoral woman I am. And how perverse my brother was for indulging me.

Seven years separated my brother Ziye and me, though we were both born of the same mother; my father's Empress. Our lineage is an illustrious one. Our father became Emperor after killing his own brother who had previously taken the throne by assassinating their father.

My brother had always been a pawn because of that piece of flesh between his legs. Our father's enemies pondered over whether they should have him killed as easily as they pondered over what to have for dinner. He was a son, capable of ascending the throne, seeking revenge, waging war and beheading their sons. No one is more dangerous to royalty than our own families.

Ziye, after surviving so many plots, gained a rather twisted perspective on how fleeting life was as well as how he should make good and frequent use of his male organ while he was still able. After all, the treacherous thing had caused him to be a target all his life.

Am I being kind by trying to explain his obsessions? I am rarely kind, but I've witnessed how many times my brother was dangled before death. When he was a child of six and I thirteen, I held onto him in our dark prison cell while our uncle decided whether we should live or die.

I should tell you of another time, shortly after our father had claimed the throne, when I slipped into a senior official's bedchamber and removed my silk robe. I extinguished the lanterns and climbed onto his bed, allowing this stranger's hands to roam over my breasts and his thick organ to penetrate me. All so he would say a few choice words of praise for my brother in court.

So Ziye would then be named as crown prince. So we would be protected from our uncles and cousins and the other heirs who would destroy us.

Before you pity us, let me remind you that we survived. Now my brother is Emperor and I am Princess Shanyin. Once my brother ascended the throne, he remembered those indignities brought upon us. Like many emperors before him, he went on a killing spree, executing traitors and would-be traitors and powerful ministers who tried to tell him not to behead so many people.

Ziye also takes who he wants, whenever he wants. When he's bored, he strips his palace women naked so he can chase them about the imperial garden. If a pretty daughter of some functionary catches his eye, he'll summon her immediately to his bed and insist to her family they should consider it an honor that the Emperor had shown them favor.

Palace gossipers claim Ziye harbors an unnatural attraction to me, his very own sister by blood. They've observed how his eyes wander lewdly over my body as he brags to me of his sexual exploits.

If this were true, what better way to shield myself from his attentions than with thirty young, strong, virile lovers? I couldn't very well ask for thirty armed guards against the Emperor, could I?

My handsome concubines sleep in my chamber. They surround me whenever the Emperor makes an excuse to visit me in private. I make a show of thanking him for his generous gift of my infamous harem, which ensures that I will never have to sleep alone.

And each night as they pleasure me, I take back every sexual favor, every touch I ever bartered away.

I have no illusions about Ziye's perverse tastes or how power has made him corrupt and obscene. My brother is absolutely depraved.

But so am I.

"Thirty lovers aren't enough for you?" Ziye asked with a laugh when I made my request the day after seeing Yuan in court.

Though striking, Yuan was not the most beautiful man I'd ever seen, but since he'd refused my invitation I was unable to think of anyone else. I had to have him.

"It would amuse me, brother, if you sent him to my palace."

"Lord Chu Yuan is not some lowly retainer. He's of noble birth," Ziye replied.

"As are some of your favorite concubines," I countered. "Don't you tire of sleeping with slaves?"

My Emperor brother chuckled at that, and I knew he would indulge me.

"And I can give you my full report on his loyalty to the throne. Most men can't keep a secret in bed," I added sweetly.

Ziye regarded me unblinking. "I will grant him to you for ten days," he conceded finally. "Just so you can tire of him faster."

There was a raw edge of jealousy beneath his breath, but I didn't let it worry me. Ten days was more than enough to satisfy my curiosity for any man. Ziye was right, I would probably tire quickly of Yuan. For the moment, I was elated.

That evening, I couldn't swallow a single bite. I waved away dish after sumptuous dish as my stomach fluttered like a bird in a cage. Sleep wouldn't come, yet I passed by the row of harem tiles more than once, not turning a single one.

What had come over me? I was nervous, fearful, vibrating with anticipation of the moment Yuan would appear before me. The thought of it stole my breath. Every inch of my skin ached with yearning.

I wouldn't feed this hunger gnawing inside me. Not tonight. For once, I denied myself all the pleasures and comforts I'd come to expect as if they were air and water. I wanted to be empty and wanting when the object of my infatuation came to kneel before me.

Infatuation; that was it. I was besotted like a fresh-faced young scholar. A lovesick maiden.

Yuan was an infection inside me. I lay awake, thinking of the hard line of his jaw and the only slightly softer curve of his mouth. The breadth of his shoulders. His hands. Had I truly looked at his hands? Were they as well-formed and strong as I envisioned them now? All this from a single look and now I was filled with a raging hunger, rendered trembling and weak.

Just past the second hour, in the deep darkness of the night, I called for a bath. Maidservants attended me and I let myself sink into the steaming water anointed with oils of cinnamon leaf and rosewood. The heat of the bath was another scourge upon my skin, cleansing me for my awaited visitor, as if I could be rendered pure and empty to be filled.

Afterward, I reclined in my bedchamber, anointed with perfume oil. The sun had not yet risen, yet my body was awake. The womanly cleft between my legs was swollen and damp and I clenched my hands into fists to keep from touching myself.

The sweet pain of waiting! I reveled in it. It would make the union of our bodies so much more powerful.

I summoned Yuan to my Eastern Palace at the fifth hour. He didn't appear before me until well into the next double hour, sauntering into the audience hall with the same haughty air I remembered.

He stopped at the prescribed distance from the dais to bow. Every movement appeared outwardly correct, except he dared to meet my eyes briefly before his head lowered. A challenge. Defiance radiated out from him even as he remained on his knees.

We were alone. I had sent all my attendants away and my guards awaited outside the chamber, ready to storm in should I require them. But why should I? Yuan was merely a lowly subject and I was Princess Shanyin.

"Do you always answer an imperial summons with such lack of care?" I asked coolly.

His head remained bowed, hands to the ground. "This subject responds to all important matters with haste."

"Then my command carries no importance to you?"

I expected at least some mockery of an apology, but Yuan's lack of even a show of obedience angered me to no end. Heat rose up the back of my neck and I had to force my tone to remain light.

As light as the touch of a razor blade.

"I deemed the princess's request was not the most urgent task needing attention at the time."

"What does it matter if it was urgent?" I straightened on my seat. "There are over a thousand subjects within the imperial palace, each one the same as the next. An adequate number of servants to handle whatever else you deemed was more worthy of your attention."

"This subject humbly accepts whatever punishment the princess chooses for him."

His words weren't humble in the least. Yuan spoke as if he didn't take me seriously and that he was the one in command.

I was in an ill mood. The sheer insolence of his manner had cooled my desire. This wasn't how I had envisioned our meeting, bickering at each other with petty complaints.

Unknown to him, he had taken me in countless different ways since our first brief encounter. In my fantasies, he had brought me to my climax time and again until I wept for mercy. His thick organ had filled me like no other. I had imagined his face on all of my lovers while I bit down hard on my lip to keep from crying out Yuan's name. And yet here he was before me. Unaffected.

I was ashamed of the power he had over me when he had yet to lay a finger on me.

"Take off your clothes," I demanded, feeling the need to exert my authority.

With only a moment's hesitation he reached for the belt at his waist, tugging it free in two harsh movements. I reclined in my seat, head thrown back to watch with my arm draped lazily over one knee.

He didn't disobey, but there was defiance in the very manner with which he complied. Tension rippled along his shoulders. His black eyes remained on me as he disrobed, layer by layer. He let the clothing fall away where he stood and my mouth went dry watching him, though outwardly I remained impassive.

His torso appeared before me, cut from stone and bronzed to perfection. I let my eyes roam over the hard contours of his shoulders, the width of his chest. He reached for the ties of his trousers, still watching me as I was watching him. Did I catch a hitch in his breath? The knot in his throat lifted and lowered as he pulled at the strings, the muscles of his arm flexing just so with the movement.

I stood. Yuan's jaw hardened as I approached and the cords on his neck pulled so tight they could snap. I could see how much it shamed him to undress before me. His fury was barely contained beneath the surface.

With that, my frustration dissipated and my blood heated again. Yuan was no longer unaffected. Fury and passion were close cousins.

He let the trousers fall, sliding past his hips to pool at his feet. His organ drooped heavily toward the ground, half-erect. I said nothing. He knew I could see it all, the evidence of his stirring desire. I raised my hand, stroking my fingers lazily beneath my chin as I openly contemplated him. It would be a lie to say I found him lacking.

Was his breathing growing deeper, against his most valiant efforts? Surely I'd only imagined it. Yuan couldn't be making this so easy.

I realized I had gone too long without issuing the next command. What would I do with all this masculine strength and beauty? I longed to take his sex in my mouth and feel it harden to its full potential, but what good would that serve? Me, a princess, servicing him as if I were a harem concubine?

"Come forward."

He did as I asked, his jaw set in that same defiant manner. How I wanted to see him beg and weep to please me.

"Now follow me."

I led him naked from the hall, not once glancing over my shoulder to check for his compliance. I was confident in my authority. Insolent with it.

Heavy footsteps behind me told me he obeyed my command without question. I paraded him through the corridor, past the grim-faced guards and female attendants who immediately fell into a bow at my approach. I could hear their hushed murmurs as we passed.

Normally I would have frowned upon such gossip, but today I delighted in it. I knew Yuan could hear their whispers as well. He could feel their curious gazes upon him and know that it was I who was subjecting him to such indignity.

I pushed open the double doors to my private apartments and wove through the chambers to my bed. My personal maidservants scrambled to their positions, bowing obsequiously. I had come in unannounced, with a virile and handsome man at my heels.

The girls were young and untried, but they were far from innocent. They were *my* maidservants after all and the sight of a man at my heels was hardly strange. They stood to await my command, but I had none for them. Accordingly, they flitted away to the various nooks and corners as fast as they had appeared.

Inside the bedchamber, I strode directly to my notorious bed. It was nearly the size of a small pavilion and I arranged myself in a relaxed pose at the center of it, making the expanse of the bed appear obscene. Yuan stood at the edge, staring at me with his fists clenched at his sides. There was a flush beneath his skin that I attributed to anger rather than desire. His cock lay limp, supporting my conjecture.

"How will you be able to perform your duties in such a state?" I teased, with a glance slanted downward at his manhood.

Yuan didn't flinch. He really was a proud, proud man.

"With her vast experience, I assume the princess must have the means to remedy the situation." His jaw ticked. "Whether the subject is willing or not."

"I assure you, no man has been unwilling in this bed."

"Perhaps not in body."

I smiled then. "I know your kind. Righteous. Upstanding. *Moral*." The last word slid acidly off my tongue. "So full of control and self-denial. Yet in the dark, when no one is looking—those men fuck like demons."

He swallowed, but his expression remained rigid. Too rigid.

"So you're here against your will," I prompted, bored.

"I will do whatever is asked of me, Princess."

"Upstanding *and* self-sacrificing. Here to be corrupted by imperial decree."

"It is indeed only the Emperor's command that brings me here," he said through his teeth.

I rose up on my elbows, regarding him with interest. "Are you married, Yuan?"

A muscle ticked along his jaw. "I am not."

"Then are you harboring some great love in your heart? A young and innocent beauty you're devoted to?"

For just a moment, there was a break in his impenetrable surface. There and gone.

"No," he said finally.

"I know that you are only here on the Emperor's insistence, yet you're a man. I don't truly believe you find this duty—as you call it—very distasteful. But go on denying it. Deny it while you spill your seed upon this bed. It will only amuse me more."

"As I said, my body can be made willing—"

"But not your mind," I finished for him with a sneer. "I won't force myself onto you, Yuan. What a chore that would be!"

He frowned at me, his fists unclenching. "Then I can go?"

I laughed outright. "No, you cannot leave. You are at my service for ten days. That is more than enough time to persuade your mind as well as your body—if they are truly as separate as you claim."

"I will never give in to you," he declared.

It was perfect. A challenge. Though I had my willing and devoted harem, it was still a special thrill to seduce a man to his knees. To see him surrender to his baser urges.

"Come here," I commanded softly.

He ducked beneath the canopy, going onto his hands and knees to approach me. I could see the sleek contours of his muscles as he moved, at once graceful and fierce. A sense of power swelled within me to have Yuan naked and crawling toward me while I was fully clothed. He hated every moment. I loved it.

"Undress me." I laid my head back as he came up beside me. When I looked up, I felt suddenly vulnerable as he leaned over me. Such was the precarious balance of sex; whenever a lover pushed himself inside me, whenever I took pleasure from another's body, it was both power and subjugation at once.

As Yuan reached for my robe, the lightness of his touch surprised me. The contrast of our positions had confused him as well. For all his proud anger, for as much as I repulsed him, he was the sort of man who looked at a woman and couldn't help but see softness. I knew that merely by how he untied my sash; carefully, with none of the brusque anger with which he had undressed himself.

To avoid looking at my face, Yuan stared instead at my body as he parted my robe. He didn't even undress me fully, instead only pulling the silk aside to reveal the embroidered bodice beneath.

"Touch me," I urged, the words scratching against my throat. My breath came shallowly and all my anticipation in the dark of the night returned to me, warming my skin and pulling my nipples tight beneath the undergarment.

Where would he touch me? The first moment of skin against skin carried meaning. A touch to my face or neck would signal tenderness. Certainly there would be none of that. A touch to the hand would seem too affectionate. The feet, sensual. Intimately erotic. My shoulders—my breasts?

Yuan hesitated. His fingers still grasped the edge of my robe and suddenly I feared his decision. I shouldn't have given him so much power.

After a moment's pause, his hands lowered to the skirt that covered my legs. With his head bent, he pushed the thin material upward. There would be no slow, sensual exploration. He chose to serve me in the most expedient way possible.

I could hardly argue with that. Relaxing my limbs, I let my head fall back to await his hand.

The touch never came. I glanced up at Yuan and saw he had spied something on the bed. Reaching to the side of my pillow, he lifted up the smooth, elongated object carved from jade.

Ah, the jade phallus I had brought to me during my long hours of frustration the night before. I had left it by my pillow unused, choosing instead to prolong the wait. The phallus was intricately carved, with a broad, smooth tip that tapered down with a slight curve.

He finished pushing up my skirt and lowered the jade between my thighs, his face a mask above me. So this was his game—he loathed to touch me with his hands at all. No matter. The jade phallus was one of my favorite toys and I would still emerge triumphant, regardless of what game he tried to play.

I locked my gaze onto his face, but Yuan refused to look at me. The first touch of the cool jade against my sex sent a shudder through me. My legs opened of their own accord, my hips tilting upward. I had been waiting for this for so long.

Yuan directed the smooth tip over me and I bit down to keep from moaning. The jade slid easily along my flesh which was slick and swollen. I had expected his ministrations to be rough and laced with spite, which would have satisfied me regardless. Instead, the phallus moved in a slow, circular pattern, gathering moisture, making my hips churn with restless need.

So Yuan knew how to touch a woman. He knew the gentle rhythm that would render me weak and trembling. Each time the jade tip glided against the small pearl of my sex, a ripple of pleasure shot through me. My limbs grew rigid as I lifted my hips even higher.

Through slitted eyes, I searched out his face once more. His head was still bent, his expression focused and determined. His brow glistened with sweat and I could see his breathing had quickened. I couldn't resist glancing down, but with his legs bent as they were, his male member was hidden from me. It didn't matter. Every other sign showed that he was caught up in his task.

"Inside me," I whispered.

Another telling moment. Yuan knew how to perform this crucial act as well. The tip of the phallus centered onto me before easing slowly into my silken passage. I had expected to have to guide his hand, to show him exactly what I needed to be brought to climax. Instead I closed my eyes and concentrated on the feel of the smooth, hard stalk penetrating my flesh.

Yuan shifted positions, leaning closer to drive the phallus deeper. I imagined it was his cock thrusting into me instead of unyielding jade. Stone would never be as satisfying as flesh and blood, but for now it would do. It would do wonderfully.

Then he twisted the phallus inside me as he pulled outward and I did moan. Another twist as he pushed back in and I was in heaven. The ridges on the phallus teased against my inner walls, pleasuring me in ways no real organ could.

My hands had been clenched into the silk of my robe, but I reached out now to clasp Yuan's wrist. I don't know why I did it. I just needed some part of him to hold on to, but I regretted it immediately.

He froze, ceasing all that glorious sensation when I was at the edge of climax. My eyes flew open and I saw that he was looking directly at me, jaw clenched. Fighting against himself. I wanted to beg for him to continue, but instead I let my hand fall away. I squeezed my eyes shut.

After a moment, the phallus thrust deep into me and it wasn't long before my body found its rhythm once more. With a sharp cry, I shattered with pleasure, my hips rolling to prolong the moment.

Satiated, I let my body fall back onto the bed with loose limbs. A soft sigh escaped my lips.

Yuan moved beside me. I could feel him brush against me as he stretched himself out. All at once, my pulse quickened. Had this lover's service aroused him? Would he lower himself over me now and replace the jade with his own flesh?

The phallus remained inside me, though Yuan's hands were no longer guiding it. I felt his hot breath against my cheek before he spoke into my ear, his voice low.

"Is that all it takes, Princess?" he taunted.

My eyes flew open to find him close. Close enough to kiss me, but that was clearly not his intention.

"I believe that was no more than three minutes. Three minutes to make you sweat and scream."

I sat up, which only made me more aware of the weight of the carved stone still embedded in my sex. My robe hung partly open around my shoulders.

"How dare you—"

Yuan rose from the bed. It didn't matter that his cock was half-erect. For a moment, his words had filled me with shame, but I forced it out with anger.

"You bastard," I seethed. "You worthless slave."

His black eyes glittered at me and his smug expression said it all. I could call him whatever I wanted. He was the bastard, the demon, the beast that had rendered me helpless with desire. No matter that it was only for the space of a breath. No matter that this was the natural way of yin and yang and he didn't get to claim such superiority. No matter that it was exactly what I had demanded of him.

I dragged the phallus from my body and threw it at him. It missed his head and thudded against the wall behind him.

"Get out! *Get out!*"

I didn't care who heard me. This was my palace. There were my attendants and Yuan was here as my puppet to command. *Mine.*

If he had deigned to affect a bow, I would have torn him apart with my own hands. Instead Yuan said nothing and left as he had come. It was no consolation to me that he once more had to parade himself past the attendants naked. The glow from my orgasm had faded, stolen away by that bastard. And Yuan had dared to insult me. To turn what was my privilege and my triumph against me.

I wanted to order my guards to haul him back so I could have him flogged, but if I saw Yuan again at that moment, I would have probably had him killed. Instead I summoned the most well-endowed of my male concubines and worked him to exhaustion, taking what I wanted without a trace of shame.

CHAPTER TWO

I woke up the next morning to the stroke of hands soothing over my skin like water. My desperate hunger of the night before, fueled by my anger and humiliation, had been temporarily sated and now I rested languidly in the center of the spacious bed.

The hands on me became more insistent. Not to the point of roughness, just firm to the touch as they massaged over my legs, my arms, my breasts. I sighed, closing my eyes as I luxuriated in the flush of warmth.

Why had I allowed a few crude remarks from some underling to upset me? Yuan was exactly that. A lowly servant who had been granted temporary favor—favor that he chose to spit upon.

Strong arms lifted me from the bed and I smiled as I was laid back, my shoulders resting against a firm and muscular chest. It was my same lover from last night. Tai Jin was what I called him, or usually just Tai. The supreme. The most highly valued for how well-endowed he was and how well he pleased me.

I could feel the rise and fall of his breathing against my back as Tai took me by the hips. I did nothing more than lie there like a doll as he positioned himself beneath me. A moment later, I felt the thick head of his organ pushing into me from below.

With a sigh, I tilted my hips to urge him to enter me fully. He did so, stretching me once more until the sense of fullness brought me fully awake. By then, we had been joined by another from the harem. I didn't need to open my eyes to know who it was. Jiyi. Skill. I had bestowed that name upon him and skilled he was. His tongue swirled endlessly over my pearl while Tai's cock thrusted gently in and out of me.

The two of them often paired up and I suspected they were lovers. The days and nights were long while sequestered in the harem quarters and no other women were allowed there. There was an unspoken communication between them and they moved as if they were of one mind.

By the time Yuan was brought into the chamber, my two morning lovers had found the perfect rhythm, one thrusting into me from beneath while the other licked over me in long strokes.

The moment I sensed Yuan's presence beside the bed, my heart began to race. I slitted my eyes open to see him watching impassively, with his hands clasped behind his back. He was fully clothed in a dark robe without any adornment. His expression was a cool mask.

I said nothing to him. Instead, I stretched like a cat and concentrated on the soft, wet rasp of the tongue on my sex; the penetration of a hard cock inside me. And Yuan, forced to watch it all. I could see the pulse beating at his throat and the way his chest rose and fell. All the while, he granted me a hard, cold stare that was meant to rob me of any pleasure, but all it did was arouse me more. I let my head fall back against my lover's shoulder while keeping my gaze fixed on Yuan, letting my enjoyment show on my face. Tai's arms closed tighter around me as he deepened his penetration, rocking me toward heaven.

It was a long time before my climax took me over. I made sure to prolong it. To make Yuan stand there and witness every moment. My toes curled when the pleasure blinded me and I shuddered, sighing. Content.

Afterward, I took my time dismissing my darling

concubines, and a maidservant brought a robe to drape over my shoulders. I cast a glance over at Yuan as I tied my sash. He was still standing beside the bed with his statue-like expression. How tiresome.

I breezed past him and felt a hint of satisfaction when he turned to follow obediently.

Out in the parlor, tea had already been set. The leaves steeped inside an ornate porcelain bowl. I beckoned for Yuan to sit across from me even though there was only one setting. His movements were stiff as he lowered himself onto the seat.

"Are you well in mind and body this morning, Yuan?"

"Was that display meant to tempt me?" he returned with disdain. "It had quite the opposite effect."

"Fool. I don't care about your pleasure or enjoyment. The only one I care to arouse is myself." I lifted the lid of the tea cup to take a sip, but not before I delivered an important message. "And I should inform you that if you ever make a petty attempt to insult me again as you did yesterday, I will simply have your tongue cut out."

I smiled, flushed with a heady mix of sex and power. Beneath the silk robe, sweat pooled on my skin and dripped between my breasts. The scent of my two lovers still lingered on me and I wondered if Yuan could smell them.

There was no reply, which I took as acceptance. What choice did he have, really? With that, I took my time sipping tea and nibbling lotus seed cakes while he watched me. With every moment that passed, Yuan became angrier and I more gleeful.

"You really do despise me," I remarked, darting the tip of my tongue over a fingertip to catch a crumb.

Again, no answer, but I could see the fierce glint in his eyes.

"I thought about having you whipped last night for your insolence. Hearing you beg for mercy would have put me in a better mood, but I realized the worst punishment I could bestow upon you was an entire day in my presence, with all my wickedness."

"Whatever you wish, Princess."

Stubborn, frustrating man. I shouldn't have promised not to force myself upon him. Then I could have him tied down and aroused before riding him until he shuddered and spilled his essence into me. That would take away that smug superiority of his. I could guarantee he would take less than the three minutes I had required.

I reached for my tea. The corner of my robe slipped from my shoulder as I drank and Yuan's gaze flickered to my bared skin before shifting away, as fast as the beat of a butterfly's wing.

His sense of modesty amused me greatly. As did his effort toward restraint.

"I want a bath," I declared, rolling my shoulders so the silk slipped further downward. "And you shall attend to me personally."

A haze of steam hovered over the bathing pool as I stepped into it. I sank down and reclined against the ledge until the water rose to my neck. Then I laid my head back against the edge of the pool, turning to meet Yuan's gaze expectantly.

He stood fully dressed in the damp, tepid air of the chamber, as if preparing for an audience in the imperial court. The steam had turned his dark blue robe to black. If he removed his shoes or official cap, he would be more comfortable, but he did none of those things. Instead he rolled up his sleeves, folding the material back in crisp movements.

I was fascinated by the muscled contours of his forearms as he reached for the washcloth.

"How did you get your appointment to the inner court?" I asked when he knelt beside the pool.

"I was promoted by Emperor Xiaowu for valor in service to the empire."

"Ah, a general in my late father's rebellion?"

"My father was the general. I merely followed his lead."

A soldier then, a former one. He looked to be perhaps four or five years older than I. Nearing thirty.

Yuan picked up a cake of pressed soapbean and concentrated on rubbing the soap into my shoulders and arms. His touch was rough, but I didn't mind.

"You fought against my uncle, then."

"Liu Shao was a usurper, without rightful claim to the throne," Yuan said.

Ziye had mistaken him for just another aristocrat. My brother hadn't known that Yuan's family had helped put us where we were now. It didn't change my plans in the least.

I was momentarily distracted as the washcloth ran down my arm, grazing the side of my breast. With an appreciative murmur, I closed my eyes and let myself sink deeper into the water. For the next few moments, all I could hear was the lap of the water against the side of the pools as Yuan washed my shoulders and arms. The cloth skimmed over my collarbone, deliberately avoiding my breasts.

But his hands were wonderfully strong and capable. His palms were slightly calloused, not the soft, pale hands of a courtier. It wasn't the first time I wondered how a pampered bureaucrat maintained such a physique, but now I knew he'd once been a soldier.

"It would be easier if you came into the bath," I suggested lazily.

Turning so I now faced the edge of the pool, I folded my arms over the side and rested my head on them. The new position exposed my back and I waited for Yuan's ministrations to continue. After a moment's pause, a ripple in the water told me he had come into the bath as he was told.

Opening one eye, I saw that Yuan was still fully clothed as he submerged himself.

With a snort, I closed my eyes once more. Let him be a fool. I had no care for his comfort.

Soon Yuan was beside me in the water, reaching for my shoulders. As his hands began to work at the knot of muscles in my neck, a shiver of unadulterated pleasure ran down my spine. The tension drained from my body and I went limp beneath his touch, luxuriating in the heat of the bath and the skilled workings of his hands.

I don't know why I ever considered that I needed to seduce Yuan to bed me in order to enjoy his services. I could have him attend to me like a slave, seeing to all my trivial needs. There was plenty of satisfaction that could be had.

"You know how to touch a woman," I murmured.

His hands hesitated upon my skin. I wondered if he'd remove his touch just to spite me.

"You're certainly no pale-faced youth," I went on. "Unsure of what to do with a woman's body."

There had been no hesitation yesterday when he'd pleasured me with the jade phallus. Even though he tried to shame me afterward, I knew how the act had made him hard.

Yuan continued my bath as if I'd said nothing. He ran the cloth along my spine, following the curve of my back down, but then returning up again before dipping any lower. It could have been modesty, but it could have also been a tease. My breath came in shallow pants as I waited for him to run those miraculous hands all over me, over all the parts that were womanly and forbidden. In my palace, nothing was forbidden. At least not to me.

"Who was the first woman you took to bed?" I asked him.

I thought he would refuse to answer, but his reply came easy enough. "A courtesan."

That was typical for a young man of aristocratic blood.

"So she took *you* to bed," I teased, the corner of my mouth turning up wickedly.

"So she did."

Did I detect a hint of wistfulness? The washcloth traveled once more down my spine and followed the curve of my back to glide over my backside and thighs. I was kneeling in the bathing pool and I pulled my knees apart to give him access. Unfortunately, Yuan didn't take the invitation. He washed the back of my legs and then once more returned to my shoulders. By the end of the bath, my shoulders would gleam like polished ivory, they'd received so much attention.

"And then who else?" I pressed on. "Did you fall for your first lover or were there many others?"

"There were others. Courtesans…prostitutes."

He only hesitated for a moment before admitting the last part. Perhaps he had figured that the more easily he yielded to my smaller demands, the less I would antagonize him. He was being surprisingly accommodating—except for not allowing me to bed him.

I turned in the pool to face him. Yuan was soaked to the skin while still dressed in his robe. His official's cap had been removed and his hair hung long and damp against his face. There was a flush beneath his cheekbones that could just as easily be attributed to the heated water as it could be to other…things.

"Those women must have been very beautiful," I said.

"I hardly remember their faces."

Such restraint. The muscles of his jaw were pulled tight, his shoulders rigid just above the water. This conversation took more out of him than any sexual act I had demanded so far.

My eyes narrowed on him in challenge. "But there must be someone whose face you do remember."

Otherwise why would he be so determined to resist? Why

not bed me like all of those other courtesans and prostitutes? I wouldn't even mind the comparison. Not when I considered him a plaything for my own desires.

He hesitated before replying. "There is no one."

I let his reply hang between us in the weighted air of the bath chamber. As I approached him, his breath hitched. Reaching for the front of his robe, I pulled him toward me, keeping my eyes locked onto his the entire time. Silently, I dared him to look away, but he wouldn't. He stared right back at me, his pupils black and hard.

His belt was also soaked through and difficult to work loose in the water, but I managed without too much delay. I wasn't inexperienced either.

"You'll need new clothes," I said, pulling the robe open to expose his chest before releasing him. "Even I'm not cruel enough to have you walking around all day like a drowned rat."

For the rest of the morning, I had Yuan follow me about and stand by waiting while I performed the most mundane and inane of tasks. I strolled through my garden, which I visited every morning. It was summer and the flowers were in full bloom, filling the air with sweet perfume. I proceeded to inspect and touch every blossom while Yuan waited on me. My garden was my pride and joy; proof that even I could create something pure and beautiful.

Afterward, I had Yuan sit quietly and watch while I completed a brushwork painting I dedicated to the Emperor, may he live a thousand years. I visited the palace temple to light incense for every single one of my ancestors. Every single one, though I cared little for the lot of them.

Throughout these tasks, I barely spoke to Yuan. I was content to have him following at my heels, ensnared and unable to escape like he was my shadow.

So he despised me? Let him spend every waking moment of the day by my side.

When it was time for my midday meal, we returned to my chamber where I had course after course brought to me while I reclined upon the bed. Yuan sat cross-legged opposite me, watching silently while I drank my wine and picked at my meal with silver chopsticks.

"He must be a very trusted servant," Yuan remarked as he watched the food taster take a morsel from each dish before the delicacies were placed before me. The taster and all of my other attendants immediately retreated to the far corners of the room, behind various screens and walls to give me a semblance of privacy.

"It is a very privileged position," I pointed out. "A taster dines on the most expensive of wines and the best food in the kingdom. In return, he faces danger on my behalf."

"There is little danger if one is tasting for someone who is well-loved."

I smiled acidly at him. "While I am well-hated?"

He didn't deny it. I decided not to take offense.

"The Emperor's taster faces much more danger than mine," I said. "There is little political gain in assassinating a princess. Certainly one who has not given birth to any potential heirs."

My brother was overly protective of me. I was the one who was closest to him, after all. He didn't trust his Empress or any of his other imperial consorts. Certainly not any of our treacherous family.

The thought made me uncomfortable. Our pasts had linked Ziye and me inextricably together.

I took a sip of wine and lifted a slice of roasted duck to my lips. For the first time, I noticed how Yuan's eyes followed my every move.

"You're hungry," I realized.

Yuan shook his head.

"You haven't had anything to eat all day."

"I'm fine, Princess."

I held the slice of meat out to him, a wicked smile touching my lips. "Here."

"I'm not hungry."

Of course he would deny it. If he wanted to eat, he'd have to take it from my hands and proud Yuan would do no such thing.

"Come now." I leaned closer, waving my chopsticks toward him, taunting.

"*I'm not hungry*," he repeated firmly.

His fingers had just taken hold of my wrist when we were interrupted by the cry of an imperial messenger.

"The Emperor summons Imperial Princess Shanyin to the inner palace!"

The command echoed throughout my apartment. There was no questioning an imperial summons. I was to go immediately.

"Don't starve while I'm away," I said to Yuan with a sly look as I placed the chopsticks back onto the serving tray.

I left him then to go to my brother.

A litter was waiting for me outside as a journey from my palace to the Emperor's residence could take nearly an hour on foot. Four carriers lifted the litter onto their shoulders and began their trek through the imperial grounds while I sat inside the curtained transport, shielded from the sun.

Tension coiled along my neck and shoulders, removing all the wonderful work Yuan had done in our bath this morning. What could my brother want?

When I reached the imperial residence, the guardsmen and servants and cronies who attended to the Emperor all kowtowed and swung aside to allow me entrance. It was well known that I was the most trusted of my brother's confidants, more so than the highly ranked ministers and eunuchs who hovered about, seeking favor and recognition.

Ziye was in his private quarters in a state of undress that was far from royal in appearance. His robe was open and his hair disheveled. I could hear the sound of weeping in the inner chamber.

"Elder Sister. I'm beginning to believe that to be Emperor is to be constantly disappointed in those around me."

He sprawled onto one of the long benches in the antechamber. Sometimes I forgot he was merely seventeen years of age. Old enough to officially rule in his own name, but prey to the whims and impulses of youth. The weeping continued on the other side of the silk screen that divided the room. I spared a glance toward the inner chamber before going to stand over Ziye.

"Is it not late for the Son of Heaven to still be in his private quarters?" I asked gently. "Is the imperial court not waiting for him?"

His black hair was unbound, falling down to his shoulders. He regarded me from behind a long section that had fallen over his eye. "So dismiss the court."

I imagined the rows of ministers and secretaries waiting in the audience hall for his appearance, their foreheads pressed to the floor.

"Ziye—"

"You go and listen to them," he said with a shrug. "Tell them you're there on the Emperor's behalf. Their complaints make my head hurt."

He knew I would do no such thing. As a rule, I didn't involve myself in court politics. The schemes and workings would go on with or without our involvement, but Ziye as Emperor needed to at least make an effort.

I took an empty seat across from him. "What is troubling you, Brother?"

Something had put him in a foul mood and it was obvious the woman sobbing in the far corner of the room was involved.

"It's Sparrow," he said with a toss of his head. "She's become tiresome to me."

Sparrow. One of his newest concubines. I only knew the name because he'd mentioned her more than once.

"Why Ziye! She remained your favorite for nearly the entire summer," I said with a knowing smile.

Usually he found my wry humor amusing, but today he scowled. "She's become willful, abusive of my favor. Thinking she has some hold over me."

"Then be rid of her," I suggested, which brought on a fresh wail from the screen. Apparently Little Sparrow was eavesdropping on our conversation.

"Women are all the same, with their lying eyes and the stink of perfume wherever they go. Pretending to be flowers and gems and flittering birds," he spat, but then a wistful look crossed his face. "Except for you, my dearest Shanyin."

Shanyin wasn't my birth name, but the name he'd given me to indicate my status. Much like I bestowed names upon my harem. The pinnacle of femininity, the title proclaimed. The ruling lady of this imperial court.

I didn't quite like how he looked at me now, almost worshipful. My younger brother needed to find goddesses to worship and he did so repeatedly, in a beautiful face or the graceful sway of slender hips or perhaps a pretty singing voice. He would be utterly fascinated until he took her to bed and immediately learned that she was no goddess after all. Then he'd smash her to pieces like a false idol.

"If they could only be more like you, Sister."

He reached out to touch my cheek, but I stood and slipped away from the contact. "Well, let me see this disobedient concubine of yours."

I stood before the screen and stared at the vague shape behind it. My stomach sickened when I thought of what state the girl must be in. At least she wasn't too broken to make a sound.

"Come out, Little Sparrow," I called softly. "Dry your tears. Your song no longer pleases the Emperor."

Ziye didn't counter my command, but I could hear him sitting up on the bench. Gradually, the sobbing grew silent and a slender girl appeared from behind the painted silk. She was no older than fifteen herself, a frightened little thing. She had a handkerchief pressed to her lips to muffle her cries. Though the layers of her silk robe were wrapped around her, I could see the welts on the side of her neck and even over her hands where she had tried to defend herself. Perhaps that was what had enraged the Emperor; such a willful, disobedient concubine, raising her hands to him.

I took hold of the girl's chin, tilting it gently upward. Her face was streaked with tears and there was a fresh gash across her cheek. The streak of blood appeared stark against the paleness of her skin. Two large eyes darted to mine before quickly looking away.

"A pity," I declared. "She's quite pretty."

Behind me, Ziye snorted. "I thought her pretty once too, but now the sight of her disgusts me. My manhood can barely stay hard long enough to fuck her."

His cruel words brought fresh tears to Sparrow's eyes. The poor creature. Not too long ago, she had probably been certain of the Emperor's love for her and the bright future that would come with it.

"Perhaps you should give her to me, then," I suggested lightly. "So that I might educate her in the ways of men and women."

Ziye's mouth twisted into a sneer. "Aren't you occupied with your newest infatuation?"

Once again his tone took on an edge of jealousy when he spoke of Yuan. I glanced over at him, watching his expression carefully.

"He certainly is entertaining," I replied with a shrug. "But only useful for the first quarter of an hour or so. His stamina leaves something to be desired."

My brother laughed sharply and stood, finally righting his robe. "Take her. I'm interested to see if you can make any improvements."

I took my leave and strode away from the imperial apartments, leaving Sparrow to shuffle behind me. When we reached the litter, she needed assistance to climb in and I noticed how she winced when the attendant took hold of her arm.

"Show me," I commanded as soon as the curtain fell. Outside, the carriers lifted us to start the journey back to my palace.

Sparrow froze and stared at me. How did my brother ever have any interest in such a meek and shrinking creature?

"No one can see you. Show me what he did."

Slowly she turned away and let the edge of her robe slip from her shoulders. Red welts crisscrossed all along her back and shoulders. He'd taken a bamboo switch to her.

I told her she could cover up. She did so gingerly, but there was no avoiding the welts. A fresh sob escaped from her lips and she bit down hard to keep from crying.

"What happened?"

"I didn't mean any offense! You must believe me, Princess."

I let out a sigh. "I believe you, but he is the Emperor. If he takes offense then you are at fault."

I wasn't trying to be cruel, but the girl had to know that there was no understanding some of the things my brother did. And she needed to stop her damn crying as if it would gain her any sympathy from him.

"The Emperor summoned me from the women's palace in the middle of the morning," Sparrow began, her voice trembling. "By the time I arrived, it seemed his Imperial Majesty was upset about something. Nothing—nothing I did seemed to please him. The Emperor then commanded me to get on my knees and he pushed his…pushed himself into my mouth—"

"There is no need to give me all the details," I interrupted with a roll of my eyes. "What made him so angry?"

Sparrow blushed bright red. "I wasn't prepared. I could barely breathe and when he pulled out my teeth scraped onto…onto his…"

"Dragon?" I finished for her.

Not noticing my mocking tone, Sparrow nodded. "He became furious. He struck me across the face and then started beating me. I was so frightened. So humiliated."

I inspected the cut across her cheek once more where my brother's ring had marred her face. "You are fortunate the Emperor summoned me before he did any worse."

I knew my brother was often immature and impulsive. But the worst was when he was trying to prove his power. Then he transformed from a self-serving and selfish youth to a tyrant and then nothing could sway him. Certainly not a few soothing words from me, his elder sister.

"I am most grateful, Princess. I'll do anything, anything you ask of me."

I nodded, accepting her thanks without reply. There were things I could do, if I were intent on weaving an intricate scheme. I could tutor Sparrow back into my brother's good graces. Then I could have her be my eyes and ears in the women's quarters so she could pass me information about Ziye's wife. I was certain the Empress was plotting my death.

But I had swum in the infested waters of palace politics all my life. All I wanted now were simple pleasures as my reward for surviving. Wealth, comfort and beautiful men in my bed to attend to my every desire.

When we reached my palace, I summoned a physician to tend to Sparrow's wounds. I didn't see any other signs of lasting damage, but I wanted to be certain. After that, I needed to act fast. As impulsive as Ziye was, he might have already decided he wanted Little Sparrow back beneath his thumb. I left the palace to make arrangements and didn't return until evening time.

Lanterns glowed around the perimeter of my private quarters and I entered to see Sparrow curled up asleep on a raised bench in the parlor. She roused as soon as I came inside and fell to her knees.

"Princess," she greeted, pressing her forehead to the ground.

I bade her to rise from the floor and then sank down myself onto one of the seats. My head pounded from having to deal with so many unpleasant details.

"You have a decision to make, Sparrow. And you must make it tonight before the Emperor comes searching for you."

Her eyes lit up and I wondered whether it was out of anticipation or fear at the thought of seeing my brother again. I would soon know the answer.

"There is a temple at the far edge of the province where I can send you. It is a quiet place, located near a lake. You can live out the rest of your life there as a Buddhist nun. Your head will be shaved. Your days will be filled with nothing but prayer and meditation. Your food will be bland, but you will be fed. Consider that existence, a life of abstinence, rejecting all earthly pleasures. Then consider the life you have led: a lover to the Emperor, sleeping on the finest silk and dining on meat with every meal. But know this." I regarded her with the most serious expression I could conjure. "You might be able to return to a life of luxury as an imperial concubine and even hope to be elevated in rank should you give birth to a son. But it is inevitable that one day you will displease the Emperor again, through no fault of your own. And he will be angry enough this time to really hurt you. Perhaps even kill you. He may regret it later. He may even finally profess his love, but only your spirit will hear it."

I didn't have long to wait for an answer. "The temple," Sparrow said. "If the Emperor won't ever find me there, then that is where I wish to be."

"I will make certain that he doesn't."

Sparrow bowed, kowtowing to me three times to display how grateful she was. Then I sent her off with an armed escort to take her away from the palace and to her new life.

By then I was tired, too tired to bother summoning any of my harem to me. As I wove around the screen into my sleeping chamber, I was startled to see Yuan still there. He'd moved off of the bed and was seated with his back against the wall, arms folded as he regarded me curiously.

I blinked at him. "You're still here."

Yuan rose to come toward me. "I was never dismissed."

He had waited here all this time. I glanced at the bed. The tray of food was exactly as I'd left it, untouched.

"Then you heard everything." My chest tightened. I didn't want anyone seeing me like this, my nerves strained and pulled thin.

"Enough to figure out the story. How exactly do you plan to keep the Emperor from reclaiming his concubine?"

"Easy." I waved my hand casually, as if shooing away a fly. "I will tell him of the dreams that plagued her. Then I'll tell him how the court astrologer declared those dreams were visions and that Sparrow was fated to become a nun. It was her destiny—no wonder she couldn't properly satisfy him in bed. My brother has always been very superstitious."

"And you are not," Yuan observed.

"It's all fable to me, but it occasionally serves my purpose."

"A heretic, then."

I shrugged away the insult. "If I had known you were here, I could have given Little Sparrow to you to corrupt instead. With your vast experience in the ways of love, you would have been the perfect tutor."

I meant to rile him, but I was so exhausted that the taunt came out flat. Resigned, I waved him away, but Yuan remained where he was.

"You gave her a choice," he remarked. "And moved mountains to do so."

"Hardly mountains."

"Why?"

"No one questions me," I said exasperated, but Yuan waited for an answer.

"It was my mood today. If it were yesterday or tomorrow, who knows what might have happened?" I went to lay down upon my bed, still fully clothed. "Now, are you going to stay and strip me naked, or will I see you again tomorrow?"

His gaze lingered on me for a second before he bowed and took his leave.

CHAPTER THREE

I am beginning to adore the way Yuan appears each morning. His robe is impeccable, his long hair tied back. He stands with his shoulders straight and his jaw set, awaiting whatever whim I might have. He's foregone with the bowing and the customary kowtows. I should probably reprimand him for that, but I do love the way he stands there waiting for me. He's stiff, like a granite statue. His expression remains blank as if the night has cleansed him all of the intimacies and vulgarities of the previous day.

How will he appear when he wakes up in my bed, with no chance to wash away such wrongs?

"I want to see what you look like when you come," I told him. I hadn't thought of it until that moment, seeing him standing so rigid and controlled before me.

Yuan didn't flinch when I stood to approach him, but I saw how hard he fought against the impulse. I opened his robe for him while he continued to stand still, staring beyond me rather than at me.

"It is only fair." I pushed the edge of the cloth aside and then worked the tunic beneath loose to expose the plane of his chest. He would be such a pleasure to explore with my hands, but there would be time for that later. "You have seen me at my most vulnerable, after all."

His eyes had been fixed onto me while he brought me to climax. No matter how he denied it, the sight had made him hard. I wondered if he was hard now.

I met his gaze and for a moment I saw something flicker

beneath the cold stare. It was the same look I'd seen last night when he'd asked me all those meddlesome questions. I realized that the moment I'd felt most vulnerable before him wasn't when I was writhing naked in my bed. It was when I'd been fully clothed and Yuan had seen inside me.

Looking away, I reached for his trousers. My hand paused before undoing the ties. "Shall I perform the act or shall I call one of the maidservants?"

I tilted my head up. From there I could see the sculpted angles of his face. His throat worked as he swallowed. "You," he said finally, his voice hoarse.

I had been hoping that would be his answer. Anticipation warmed my skin and pulled my nipples into peaks. "So you don't despise me after all."

He finally looked down to meet my eyes. "The Princess has already seen my body. I don't wish to corrupt anyone else."

My laughter rang throughout the parlor. With my hand planted against his chest, I pushed him back, directing him onto one of the benches in the sitting area. It had a wide seat, long enough for me to recline, but I left Yuan sitting in the center of it. I took the spot next to him, my body curving over his while he remained wooden beside me.

I raised myself to whisper in his ear, my breasts pressing against his shoulder. "Proud and upstanding Yuan, afraid of corrupting young maidens with his naked body."

A shudder went through him. I wanted to sink my teeth into his neck and taste the salt of his skin. Instead I kissed him, very softly, just below his ear. I don't think he liked it. If he were a horse, he would have flicked his ear at me in annoyance, but I didn't care. I was enjoying myself too much.

As I reached into his lap, I had a full view of his thighs. They were well-muscled, like the rest of him. Between them, I could see a bulge forming as his body responded to having a woman so close.

Instead of untying the trousers, I cupped my hand between his legs and heard a hiss of breath as his sex stirred against my fingers.

"I know what you're thinking," I murmured against his ear in a sing-song. "You're telling yourself that this means nothing. That your body is responding, but your mind, your pure and honorable mind, is unmoved."

I pressed the heel of my hand downward and rubbed slowly. Yuan clenched his hands into fists by his side but his organ swelled beneath my touch, straining upward to seek release. I undid his trousers quickly and his hips lifted to accommodate me when I pushed the material down over them.

He sat now with his robe parted and trousers lowered, sex exposed. Otherwise, he remained fully clothed. He appeared more vulnerable this way; his clothes in disarray, clinging desperately onto the vestiges of civility.

I filled my hands with him. He wasn't as large as the most well-endowed of my harem, but he wasn't smaller by much. His organ was long and thick and perfectly formed. The blunt head had darkened in color like a ripe plum. I longed to swirl the tip of my tongue over it, but I also wanted to watch his face as he released. I moved my thumb in a small circle over the tip, sliding through the bead of moisture that gathered there.

"Yin is yin and yang is yang," I said.

His flesh tightened even further in my grasp. I think he liked it when I spoke to him even though he was gritting his teeth now, fighting an invisible foe. I wanted him to try to hold back. It would make the torture all the more exquisite.

Lightly, I stroked my hand down the length of him while I watched his face. He shook his head sharply, denial in every inch of his body except for the part I had in hand. Meanwhile his cock twitched to seek out my touch. I rewarded it with another stroke, firmer this time.

So that was how he liked it. Hard. His hips churned as he forced himself back against the seat. Why fight so hard? It was only release. Orgasm. As natural and necessary as breathing.

I couldn't take my eyes off of him. Selfishly, I dragged my hand along his cock twice more, purposefully not providing enough pressure to take him to his peak. I loved watching how he burned.

By now, he was so hard that it must have pained him. His expression was caught between agony and ecstasy and his breathing was shallow, quick and uneven. He gasped when I squeezed him harder. The skin of his shaft was velvet smooth and pulsing with life as his heartbeat increased.

"There are men who feel they lose something of themselves when they surrender to a woman like this. Spilling their seed into the cold, empty air. It doesn't have to be that way." My hand never stopped moving. His entire body was drawn tight like a bowstring, every muscle vibrating for release. I had found a rhythm that suited him.

I was fascinated by the sight of Yuan struggling beside me. His body was begging for me even if he would never admit it. If I poured oil over him, he would slide hard and fast through my hands. It wouldn't take long to give him the release his body so desperately needed. If I let him into my mouth, he might go even faster with my lips and tongue urging him to new heights. But I wanted to watch him as he lost himself.

What I really wanted was for him to take me with him. I could feel my own wetness between my legs, my body readying itself for a man. Yuan was fiercely beautiful as he writhed beside me and my body was not used to being denied.

"It would be so good," I whispered to him. "You know it would be."

I pressed my lips against Yuan's bare collarbone and his cock jumped. He liked it when I touched him and not only with my hands on his cock.

"It would be so easy," I urged. I was no longer taunting him. I no longer had the will. If I straddled him now and lowered myself onto him, he would penetrate me with hardly any effort at all. I was swollen and empty, needing him to fill me.

"No."

He insisted on gritting out his denial. A moment later, his muscles locked and his seed erupted out onto his lap, spilling hot over my hand in the process. His hips jerked in a sporadic rhythm which continued even when his peak had come and gone.

At the last moment, before he'd come, his eyes had squeezed shut and his head had fallen back. It was the moment he knew his release was inevitable and had surrendered to it. It was also a moment of agonizing beauty. The sight of him was branded into my memory.

His sex gradually softened, desire spent. When I removed my hand, he immediately turned away.

"Let me—" His voice came out ragged and he had to start again. "Let me clean myself."

I directed him to a basin of water in the corner, dipping a cloth so I could wash my hand before returning to the center of the room. Yuan worked quickly, his back turned to me. I granted him this silence.

I felt no particular triumph in seeing him unmanned. It was merely for my own selfish pleasure. I was still flushed from the feel of his powerful body shuddering against mine. If only he could have been on top of me, his organ pushed deep inside. I would have wrapped my legs around his hips to absorb every last thrust. As it was, I was left hungry, the lips of my sex swollen and unfulfilled.

"It's just sex," I said lightly. "Neither sacred, nor profane."

He didn't answer.

"There is no need for shame."

"I'm not ashamed by what happens between a man and a woman," he replied, still turned away. His tone was cold.

Heat rose up the back of my neck. "Then it's me you find objectionable."

Once again, Yuan fell silent. He soothed a hand over the front of his robe and then moved to the window to stare out into the garden.

"Answer me!"

He turned only partway, refusing to face me directly. "I do not wish to have my tongue cut out."

I should have called in my guards to drag Yuan outside and carry out my threat. Instead I wanted him to drag me to the floor and take me then and there. In anger, if that was what he needed. I imagined how that anger would fuel his passion, pushing him deeper and harder into me.

But Yuan composed himself quickly. By the time he was following me obediently to the polo grounds, the flush was gone from his face and his expression was as dispassionate as ever. I could almost believe he was unaffected by me, but he froze whenever I "inadvertently" brushed against him. He tried to keep his distance as much as possible. Yet when my fingertips grazed over his knuckles, his breath stuttered.

It was only a matter of time, I told myself, grinning inwardly. I had seven more days.

The men of my harem had assembled for a polo match. They had been separated into two teams and rode astride horses from the Emperor's stable. Those who remained on foot served as handlers.

"This should be very entertaining. I promised the winning team a special reward," I explained with a coy glance over my shoulder.

Yuan followed behind me and had to dodge away from the

sweep of my parasol as I turned. Without warning, he reached out and took the bamboo handle from me. He held the parasol overhead, shielding me from the sun as we continued toward the playing field. The action brought him closer to my side. Ah, gallantry.

An awning had been set up on the grass with seats beneath it fashioned from rattan. I took a seat in the shade with Yuan at my side, pressed close by the width of the bench. We were surrounded by my retinue of attendants and bodyguards, but the polo match was purely for my entertainment.

The players assembled in a row before me to bow and pay their respects. I hadn't called any one of them to my bed last night, which always made them particularly competitive. There was more than one sharp glance directed at Yuan.

"You are fortunate this is not an archery match," I teased, squeezing his arm.

Surprisingly, Yuan didn't stiffen or draw away from the touch. It made me feel outright affectionate toward him. And why shouldn't I be feeling fond? The sun was shining. I was the most powerful woman in the empire and surrounded by my doting harem as well as one stubborn, challenging quarry who didn't despise me nearly as much as he claimed.

"Little do they realize they have no need to be jealous," I went on. "You've never had me beneath you whereas every one of them has taken me at least once a month. Sometimes twice," I added, staring at that granite profile.

Yuan folded his arms over his chest. "We're surrounded by others."

"I'm always surrounded," I replied, unfazed. "The concubines think I have a new favorite. An outsider who isn't one of them. It must make them furious."

He glanced at me and then away. I loved how agitated I made him. "It's dangerous to play a man's passions against him," he warned gruffly.

"There is always one favorite or another. They are quite accustomed to it."

"I don't wish to be called a favorite."

"I did no such thing," I countered sweetly. Then I leaned close, close enough my lips could almost graze his ear. "We haven't even kissed, my darling."

The polo match had started with the team in green making a drive toward the opposite field. Yuan made a show of watching the exchange of the ball from one player to the next. I settled back in my seat, deciding to behave for a little while at least.

"No man would tolerate his woman being possessed by someone else," Yuan said, staring directly ahead.

I was surprised to hear him speak. It was the first time he had initiated conversation.

"They are just slaves," I dismissed. "I don't belong to them. They belong to me."

A sense of pride filled me as I scanned the field. Thirty able-bodied young men, beautiful in face and form and mine to command. The captain of the yellow team raised his stick and swung hard, driving the ball away from his goal and back into enemy territory. He looked to the awning and caught my eye. I smiled back at him with an encouraging nod. Yao, handsome by name and by face. He shot a poisoned glance at Yuan before galloping down the field.

"That is not how they think of it," Yuan said, his point made.

I knew he was right in part. These men were my concubines, but once in a while, they held a princess in their arms and made her cry out in pleasure. When I surrendered to any one of them, he became prince for a night.

But Yuan wasn't a slave. He was an aristocrat with a good name who held rank within the court.

"Would you feel differently if you were the only man in my

bed?"

A cheer rose from the yellow sashes which saved Yuan from having to answer immediately.

"Nothing would change between us, Princess," he answered.

He was insufferable. He was also as unmoving as the mountains and it made me burn for him all the more.

"You do realize the sooner I have you, the sooner I'll tire of you."

I don't know if I said it for his sake or mine. One part of me hated having to negotiate at all, but the other part of me was dying to have him. The same part of me that was getting frustrated with all the toying and teasing.

"How about this proposal? We'll gather the clouds and the rain tonight until the lanterns burn out and then I'll free you in the morning?"

I pressed against his side as I spoke, soft curves against hard angles. My hand slid over his knee suggestively. His thighs were hard beneath my palm.

He raised an eyebrow at me skeptically. I was surprised to see his lips twitch with amusement. "The clouds and the rain?"

"I thought such poetic imagery would appeal to your prudish nature," I said with a smile. Then I pressed closer, my arms circling his neck. "Fuck me," I said into his ear, my voice low so that only he could hear. "Fuck me all night and I'll let you go."

I regretted the offer the moment I made it. I had been promised ten days and I didn't want to let him go, but my stomach also fluttered with the thought that he might accept. That would mean I could have him tonight in every way I had imagined. I didn't think he would give in to me yet, but it was possible. He hadn't drawn away from me. We were practically entwined upon the bench.

The polo match continued before us, but I hardly cared what was happening. My focus was completely on Yuan, whose pulse had quickened when I told him to fuck me.

"You'll likely be a disappointment," I goaded silkily.

A fierce light sparked in his eyes. That barb certainly got his attention. No man could tolerate his woman in the embrace of another, and no man would allow his manhood to be challenged without taking up arms.

He took hold of me with his hands on either side of my hips. The movement caught me by surprise and I thought he meant to push me away, but his grip tightened on me, his thumbs pressing into the indent of my waist.

His gaze smoldered hot enough to burn me to ashes, but that touch...that touch told me things. It told me exactly how he would hold me down, how he would command my body as he pushed into me. It also told me how I would melt beneath him until there was nothing left of me but heat and a deep, endless spiral to oblivion.

I almost wished he would be a disappointment in the end. He had become idealized in my mind, an incredible lover who frightened me as much as he enticed me. Yuan would take me a hundred different ways until I fainted from the pleasure, unable to take any more. If he were half that good, I would be the one enslaved. I had already revealed more of myself to him than any of my lovers.

A thundering sound filled my ears and I thought it was the rush of blood through my head, but the pounding grew louder. I looked up to see one of the horses rampaging toward us. His rider was struggling to pull back on the reins.

Screams shattered the air as my entourage scattered. The great steed filled my vision, his hooves lifting until he reared up on his hind legs. His great eye seemed to fix onto me and my limbs turned to stone. A scream stuck in my throat as the hooves came crashing down.

Rough hands grabbed me. I could hear my silk robe tearing as I was thrown onto the grass. Stunned, I turned my head to see Yuan standing between me and the enraged animal. From where I lay, Yuan towered over me, but the horse was even more massive. His hooves hovered dangerously close to Yuan's head.

Yuan held out his hands, palm out. Rather than backing away, he moved toward the steed. I dug my hands into the grass, trying to drag myself up. He would be crushed!

The horse's front legs came plummeting down, but Yuan stepped smoothly out of the way, taking position by the animal's shoulder. Yuan took hold of the reins and the horse made an agitated sound, shaking his head. Shortly after, the creature seemed to calm down. By then, the stable hands came forward to take command of the horse.

"We shall have the beast punished, Princess!" the head groomsman promised.

"Better to punish the rider," Yuan growled. "And all of you who were responsible for handling the horses."

The groomsman shrank back. Handsome Yao had been the rider. He had been unseated and remained sprawled in the grass on his hands and knees, his face pale. Whether he was shaken from being thrown or afraid of retribution from me, I couldn't tell. I was still shaken myself. My arms and legs couldn't seem to work. When I tried to stand up, I staggered back onto the ground.

Several of the men had dismounted to rush toward me, but Yuan reached me first. His arm closed around my waist to lift me to my feet. I clung to him, not caring who saw me in my moment of weakness. Not caring was one of the privileges of being princess.

As Yuan barked orders to the attendants, I saw how he was undeniably an aristocrat. Despite how I treated him, he was not a servant to be overlooked or ignored. My attendants must have realized this as well as they scurried to do his bidding.

My palanquin was brought to transport me back to my quarters. When the attendants moved to lift me from the carriage, I pointed to Yuan who had accompanied the procession the entire way.

"You," I insisted.

Without batting an eye, he bent to lift me, carrying me in his arms to my bedchamber. With each step, my heart beat faster. He was the one who had pulled me out of danger. He had put his person between me and a mindless beast, a creature who could not be negotiated with.

He laid me down onto my bed and methodically began to check me for injuries. His capable hands massaged along my arms, my ankles, testing for broken bones I assumed.

"You could just ask if I'm hurt," I said, surprised at how violently I was still shaking.

"You're in shock," he said impatiently, holding me still when I tried to move. "You wouldn't be able to tell."

His head remained bent as he tested the joint of my knee. Warmth pooled low in my belly, melting away the numbness that had set in. I liked how his hands felt on me when he touched me of his own free will. I liked it very much.

He shifted up alongside me and skimmed his palms upward over my ribs. My chest heaved with each breath and my heart felt as if it would burst out of my chest. His inspection stopped short of my breasts, his fingertips just grazing the soft skin underneath.

Oh, I was not wide-eyed and innocent enough to believe all of this was unintentional. Curling my fingers into the front of his robe, I dragged him to me, my mouth pressing against his in a sigh of breath.

His lips were yielding, warm; but only for a moment. Yuan wouldn't allow my kiss for any longer than the blink of an eye.

"I would have done the same for anyone," he insisted after

pulling away.

I didn't push any further. The fleeting touch of his mouth was enough to sustain me for the day, which was odd, considering it sometimes took the earnest efforts of three men for me to find any sense of satisfaction.

That night I ordered Yuan relocated to one of the chambers nearest to me. I didn't want to have to wait for him to answer my summons every morning. Not when my time with him was growing short.

CHAPTER FOUR

My concubines secured Yuan's arms the moment he set foot in my bedchamber. They shoved him toward the bed while I finished my morning tea in the corner.

Yuan fought them, as I knew he would, but my lovers were not like the pale and fleshy eunuchs who attended to the Emperor. They were tall and strong, as strong as Yuan was. Five of them were more than enough to subdue him and strip away his clothing while he flailed and kicked.

"Shanyin!"

No title. No honorific attached to my name. He could be punished for that alone, but being overpowered by my men was likely punishment enough. I watched while they used long strips of silk to tie his arms and legs to the posts of the bed. I had put much thought into the design of this legendary bed, as you can see.

When they were done, Yuan lay completely naked at the head of the bed with arms and legs stretched wide. I appreciated the flex of his muscles as he continued to struggle. He was masculine and well-formed and my stomach fluttered just looking at him. Even tied down, he didn't appear helpless.

The men had been rougher with him than I had anticipated. Tai Jin stood back and looked down at Yuan with an air of satisfaction. Then my former favorite looked to me expectantly. A few mornings ago, Yuan had stood by the bed while Tai and his partner had pleasured me at the same time. The concubine probably thought I would require his services now, but he was mistaken. He would be a distraction and I wanted to focus on one man alone.

With a flick of my hand, I sent the concubines away. A look of relief flashed over Yuan's face, but it was quickly replaced with a combination of fear and desire. I knew both well.

"Princess, this is unnecessary." He tugged at the silken ties. There was enough slack in the bonds to make some movement possible, but he was held securely in place and at my mercy.

"Oh, it is necessary, darling." I loosened my sash to let my robe slip from my shoulders.

Silk pooled on the floor at my feet. I stepped over it to stalk toward the bed. Yuan's eyes couldn't help but roam over me, darkening as they lingered. For the first time, we were both disrobed and naked at the same time. There was no hiding how my breasts were swollen and heavy, the nipples dark and peaked. And there was no hiding how his cock thickened as I came near.

There was no coyness or flirtation in my approach. I climbed onto the bed and straddled his hips, my thighs spreading wide to settle down onto the bed. The tip of his sex nestled against my slit and Yuan gritted his teeth as I slid myself back and forth over the smooth head of his cock, letting him know I was wet and that I was ready for him.

I lowered my hands to his shoulders to press him down into the pallet. "You need to be held down, don't you? You need to say that you don't want this."

"I don't—"

I silenced him with my mouth over his. The fight drained from him the moment our lips met and he returned the kiss with the same hunger as I. His tongue slid inside my mouth; the mere touch of lips and mingling of our breath not enough after how long we'd waited.

He tasted like tea with a spicy tang of cloves. My stomach

fluttered and my body liquefied as the kiss grew deeper.

With a groan, he broke away. "My hands," he growled.

It wasn't a plea. He would never beg me, but I wanted him to. I wanted it very much.

I shook my head and captured his mouth again, letting my hands roam down his shoulders to his chest. The flat of his stomach. He tensed and bucked as I reached his thighs, but the silk held him fast.

He moaned something incoherently. Whatever it was, the words were cut short when he exhaled sharply. I had taken hold of his manhood, gripping him gently as if he were fragile. I knew he wasn't. I wasn't the only one who appreciated a rough touch.

"I want you to tell me yes." My tone was hard, but my hand soft as I stroked him from tip to root. "Your body is already telling me everything I need to know, but I want to hear it."

He shook his head and his eyes squeezed shut. I took hold of his bottom lip between my teeth and bit gently.

"*Yes*," I insisted against his mouth.

It was the sentiment in my own heart. As my hips moved restlessly over his sex, my body grew more damp and swollen. Hard over soft. I pressed my mound down over him, shifting to find the right angle of my hips.

Yuan's hands clenched into fists over his head. The silk was pulled taut and his body had nearly raised off the bed in an effort to escape. He was not accustomed to being used in such a way, but he still wanted it. I could tell by the way his organ hardened even more between my thighs. If I guided him to my entrance and pushed forward, he would slide inside me. The thought made my knees week.

"Tell me to do it," I said, breathless.

"No," he insisted. "Never."

Insufferable man. I was caught in my promise to not force

myself upon him. I realized then that even if I hadn't made that promise, I would still be caught in a trap. I didn't want to take, I wanted to be taken. Hard and repeatedly. I wanted to be drained of all desire and fucked until there was nothing left inside me but him.

I climbed up along his body, letting him feel me sliding over him until my nipple was at the level of his mouth. Yuan needed no instruction here. The moment the soft curve of my breast touched him, he knew what I wanted. His mouth opened and clamped hot over my breast, making my toes curl in response. Before I could find my breath, the tip of his tongue slid back and forth over my nipple. Gently at first and then harder as I squirmed against him. A deep, spiraling sensation built in my womb, threatening to take me over. I was possessed by the need to climax and by the need for him to bring me there. Him. The only man who had ever dared to refuse me.

I fed my other breast into his mouth and he sucked me greedily. Beneath me, his body strained upward. There was no doubt what he wanted. What we both wanted.

"Now," I moaned, fitting my hips to his. His stiff organ was trapped between our bodies and I could feel the heat radiating from his skin.

"Untie me," he rasped.

So he could use his hands to escape? "Never."

I fisted my hands into his dark hair, pulling back hard enough for him to exhale sharply. His organ swelled and I shifted my thighs so the tip of it pressed against my sex. I was slick, aching and ready for him and I knew he could feel it because he stopped breathing altogether.

"This is what you want," I panted. I circled my hips, bathing the head of his cock in my fluids. The sensation was incredible, like nothing else I'd known. And it was only the beginning.

But Yuan shook his head. The lying bastard!

I cried out in frustration, a sob lodging in my throat. It would be so easy to reach down and guide his manhood into me. I would lower myself onto him, bit by glorious bit. Savor and torture him for every moment he'd made me wait.

Yuan's head was thrown back and his face caught in a mask of exquisite agony. If I rode him until we both climaxed, he'd say I'd claimed his body while his mind rebelled.

I raked my nails over his torso and his eyes flew open. "Tell me," I demanded.

He shook his head. "I can't. I won't."

I bit him then, sprawling over him to sink my teeth into his shoulder, making him cry out. I couldn't take him, not the way I wanted to. This was our game, our covenant, but my body wanted his so badly. I wanted him so much that taking merely pleasure from him was not enough. I wanted his will, his pain. And I wanted to know what this mysterious force was that kept him from me.

I ground my hips into him, rubbing my throbbing sex over his cock. A waste, my soul lamented. But it didn't matter. The sensation was enough to make my insides tighten. Desperately, I repeated the motion, closing my eyes at the lurid pleasure of it. I was mindless now, sliding his cock between my slick folds. Inelegant. I didn't care.

My back arched to press our bodies one precious breath closer. Below me, Yuan groaned, full of both ecstasy and frustration. He could only feel me sliding over his head and part of his shaft. The rest of his manhood was sorely neglected. His choice.

His arms strained against the silk bonds and his face was a grimace of denial and unwanted pleasure. I closed my eyes while my hips circled with abandon. I didn't want to see his expression. I only wanted to concentrate on how his flesh felt against mine. Hard against soft and heat, so much heat.

Yuan choked out something. It sounded like my name, but he would never admit it. A moment later, a hot splash of fluid coated my belly. Apparently my ministrations were enough to bring him to climax after all. He hissed as I continued to grind. I was too greedy, mindful only of my own needs to stop.

Suddenly, the muscles of my back seized. My insides clenched tight and bright spots swam beneath my eyelids. I was there, shuddering and lost in orgasm.

When I could move again, I opened my eyes to see Yuan looking up at me. His expression was unreadable. Unapologetically, I sank into the crook of his arm, resting my head against his shoulder. He had no choice but to let me, tied down as he was.

"Bastard," I accused, suddenly sleepy.

There were easier, more satisfying ways to achieve release and I was still angry at him for denying me.

"Untie me," he rasped.

His heart was still pounding and his skin damp with sweat. Mine was as well. I could see where my nails had left scratches across his chest. I traced one red line with the tip of my finger and ignored his request.

No man could possess such restraint. It had to be soon. Six days was more than enough time to tempt a man who was already not quite unwilling. *Soon*, I promised myself silently. And it would feel like nothing else I'd ever experienced. My mouth went dry imagining the moment I would finally have him inside me.

I didn't release Yuan until my pulse was no longer racing and the heat from my climax had faded.

CHAPTER FIVE

"Look, Elder Sister. I have a gift for you."

The hairs on the back of my neck stood on end as my brother gestured for the doors to be opened. We were standing before the grand banquet hall, but there was no feast laid out today. In the center of the floor were three iron cages. A lone figure crouched in each one, still dressed in court attire.

My stomach sickened. Ziye had locked up our uncles like animals.

I tried to be as soothing as possible. "Imperial Majesty—"

"The traitor He Mai wouldn't reveal who his co-conspirators were, but it has to be one of these pigs," Ziye said, running a bamboo switch against the iron bars.

Somehow, I had managed to forget that unpleasantness in the assembly hall. My head started to pound as I tried to figure out what to say. "As satisfying as it may seem, we cannot lock up everyone who displeases us—"

"Don't you remember how they imprisoned us?" Ziye interrupted, his voice cracking. "They threatened to have us killed, Shanyin."

He was in no mood for lectures from me or anyone else. There was a petulant whine to his tone that would have made him seem childish, if I didn't realize how dangerous his tantrums could be.

I bowed my head. "I remember."

He broke out into a grin. "Now we have imprisoned them. Traitorous dogs."

"Have mercy, Son of Heaven!" the oldest uncle begged while his hands grasped the bars.

Ziye lashed out at the exposed fingers with his switch and he fell back. The other two echoed his entreaty and I could see how much Ziye enjoyed seeing them grovel, which meant he wouldn't release them any time soon.

"Don't they look like pigs in there?" Ziye asked gleefully. "Fat and useless. Which one shall we slaughter first?"

"Don't be foolish!" I hissed.

My brother's eyes flashed at me and I realized I'd made a mistake reprimanding him in front of his enemies.

"The uncles aren't worth the trouble," I amended. "Let them remain in cages for your amusement. Then strip them of their rank and confiscate their holdings."

His eyes gleamed as he nodded. "Yes, a good thought. Pigs cannot hold rank."

The uncles tried to meet my eyes, silently begging. They hoped I would be more merciful than my brother, but when Ziye was in a mood like this, no one could sway him. I fled from the inner palace as fast as I could.

It took the rest of the day to gather the required bodyguards and maidservants and eunuchs to journey out from the palace. I sent a message to the Emperor that my elements were misaligned and my *qi* was out of balance. I needed a trip to the hot springs to soak in the curative waters.

I didn't wait for a reply. Even though it was already dark outside I gave the order for the caravan to move out. I couldn't bear to remain in the palace for another minute.

"You'll have us travel through the night?" Yuan questioned.

He alone accompanied me in my palanquin while the concubines of my harem had been left behind.

"The servants have lanterns to light their way," I replied.

The face he made indicated that my answer was somehow

inadequate. That was the danger of showing too much continuous favor to one man. He began to take liberties.

Though the rest of the entourage would remain awake late into the night, the litter was large enough for Yuan and me to lie down and sleep whenever we wished. Not that I had any plans to sleep just yet.

I reclined back onto the pillows while the litter swayed beneath us. "Come here."

I wondered if he would defy me, but he came willingly. Yuan remained on his knees, but somehow didn't appear to be kneeling before me, even from that position. He wore a plain robe, dyed in the deep blue-black color of midnight. The quality of it was evident in the fineness of the material and workmanship rather than any adornment. He had ceased dressing in court attire or any other clothing denoting rank since being sent to me, but he certainly didn't look like a slave.

With a lazy hand, I reached for his belt. Inside, my belly curled tight with anticipation, but I didn't want Yuan to think he had any hold over me. Even though I'd forsaken all of my other lovers to keep only him by my side.

At the last moment, he lowered his hand over mine. "Allow me."

His voice was deep, thick with desire, and it sent a small thrill down my spine. Gently he drew my hand aside and laid it beside my head on the pillow. For a moment, my wrist was pinned while he hovered over me, large and imposing. I could barely breathe.

He removed my robe and undergarments and laid me back completely naked against the pillows. I wondered if Yuan had had a change of heart about resisting my advances, but he remained fully clothed while I was exposed.

Just outside, the carriers bore the litter at a steady pace. The caravan continued toward the hot springs, oblivious to what was transpiring inside the curtain. Or perhaps not completely oblivious. I was the immoral and lascivious Princess Shanyin. Rather than being embarrassed at the prospect of being discovered, it excited me all the more. What wicked things did Yuan intend to do to me? I couldn't wait to find out.

Reaching into his sleeve, he took out a small porcelain bottle painted with orchids. It was the perfumed oil I produced myself from the flowers in my garden. Had Yuan planned for this? My heart beat faster, and through no will of my own my shoulders fell back, lifting my breasts as if in offering.

Yuan's look was one of determination, a look I knew well. He poured a tiny pool of oil into his hand. I lay transfixed as he rubbed his palms together, spreading and warming the fragrant liquid. His first touch was at my waist as he'd done not too long ago after rescuing me from the polo field. For a moment, his broad hands did nothing but hold me, molding and framing my hips. My belly fluttered as his oiled palms slid along my ribcage, thumbs stroking over my midsection on an inevitable path.

He reached my breasts and I pushed myself into his hands, shuddering when he stroked his thumbs directly over the hard points of my nipples. A sharply pleasurable sensation traveled from his fingers down to my sex and I moaned, not caring if the servants could hear me from outside.

But Yuan didn't linger over my breasts like I wanted him to. His hands continued on their path up to my shoulders and then my neck, teasing and working at the knots there. I was torn between directing him toward the places I wanted most to be touched, and enjoying each new sensation along with the mystery of not knowing what would come next. As skilled as my harem was at bringing me to climax, they had become routine in their attentions. Cannily efficient at reading my moods and knowing how to satisfy me in the quickest way possible.

Yuan was a riddle. I never knew what would happen between us. I didn't know if he would ever give me what I truly wanted. Each time I reached a new height of sexual pleasure with him, he held something back to taunt me that there was more, so much more to come.

His hands now roamed over my entire body, paying loving attention to parts that were often neglected. My ears, elbows, wrists. There wasn't an inch of me that was undeserving, that wasn't an object of desire.

He applied more oil when he reached my legs. As he drew broad circles over my thighs, they parted of their own accord. I could feel the wetness filmed over the lips of my sex as I opened myself. I imagined the oil combining with my fluids when his clever fingers finally found their target.

But my sex wasn't his destination. He stroked lower, down my legs, to take hold of my feet. I would have groaned with frustration if the feel of his strong hands massaging my toes wasn't a thing of pure luxury. His thumbs pressed into my soles and I thought I might come just from that.

When he turned me onto my stomach I moved willingly, my body limp. There he seemed to hesitate, perhaps to gather more oil, before the exploration continued. His touch was firmer on my back side. Maybe he had become more confident. Maybe it was because I couldn't see him, he no longer had to look at my face…I didn't want to question it.

As Yuan's hands rubbed over my back, the sensual massage was no longer enough. He had awakened every pulse point and nerve ending on my body and I was primed and ready. I had been relaxed and compliant before, but now my muscles were tense and waiting. My hips churned against the pillows underneath me, demanding he finish what he started.

Just then, I felt Yuan's body lower over mine to plant a kiss onto the small of my back. Then he stretched his length over me, placing another kiss on my bare shoulder before reaching the crook of my neck where he laid his head against mine.

Then, with his weight pinning me from head to toe, I felt him slide his fingers into me. I gasped. His fingers were long and I was so slick and swollen the penetration felt endless.

The position was intimate and yet it wasn't. I was held beneath him, every writhe and twist of my body captured against his hard form, but I couldn't see him. Yet he was inexorably present. Surrounding me. His fingers were working me steadily toward orgasm as I panted, helpless.

His breath teased against my ear. "I can pleasure you, Princess. In all the ways there are to pleasure a woman," he offered.

Except that one final act.

I wanted to argue with him but my body was caught in an upward spiral. Any thought of protest fled away when his thumb curved to touch the apex of my sex. That tiny bud where the entirety of my being became centered. He flicked lightly over it, teasing the very tip and sending indescribable sensations to every part of my body. My toes curled and my hips bucked against him.

Yuan didn't completely deny himself. The hardness of his cock pressed against the cleft of my buttocks, grinding downward. The thumb over my soft pearl was replaced by his finger which worked me with a feather-light touch, faster and faster until I was sobbing.

I wanted his hard cock inside me so badly, but I would take this. I would take this.

I bit into the corner of a pillow as I came. It wasn't enough to muffle my cries completely and I whimpered as Yuan's hand slowed but did not stop. He circled my flesh gently now, soothingly, absorbing the tremors of my body against his.

"Again," he murmured against my ear, a command that allowed no room for denial. Gradually Yuan increased the tempo of his fingers, working me to another climax. I gritted my teeth as the tide crashed over me once more, not as sharp as the first time, but more prolonged.

My inner muscles clenched around his fingers, spasming without rhythm. He'd brought me twice to the peak, one orgasm immediately after the other, yet something kept me from being fully swept away. His insistence on taking care of my pleasure was only a ploy. A strategy on his part to maintain control.

I rolled over and reached beneath his robe. My hands closed around his erect member, squeezing hard enough to make him groan. He didn't retreat, but after one long stroke, all the pleasure he would allow himself, Yuan once again closed his hand over mine to stop me.

"She must be very beautiful for you to keep yourself for her," I challenged.

A ripple of tension traveled through him. He said nothing.

"I suppose I never give any thought to luring a man with my appearance," I went on. "With my concubines, it doesn't matter if I'm pleasing to the eye. I command and they obey."

"I've always thought you were beautiful," Yuan interjected. "That isn't the issue."

I waited for him to add something about how the prettiest of flowers were the most poisonous or how beauty was just a façade, a thin shell painted over a rotted center, but he didn't say any such thing.

"You have scars," he said instead, causing me to blink at him, not comprehending. "The scars all along your back," Yuan explained with his jaw tight.

"Those? Those are hardly worth mentioning," I replied airily. At the same time I reached for the robe crumpled beneath me and pulled it over my shoulders.

I hardly thought of those marks anymore. As I told him, it didn't matter what I looked like to my harem of lovers.

"Someone hurt you."

I was surprised he actually appeared angry.

"Don't you know?" I affected a laugh that felt thin even to my ears. "Such marks are nothing but souvenirs from a lover's game. You have a few on you from yesterday morning, if I recall."

When I tried to turn away he stopped me. "Those are merely scratches. Nothing that would leave a scar. Or so many."

I forced a smile. "My chivalrous and honorable protector. Don't you know that some games are played harder than others?"

The corners of his mouth turned downward, far from satisfied with my answer. "Just a game?" he echoed in disbelief.

I preferred the familiar look of disdain creeping back into his eyes. It was better than protectiveness or pity. Yuan refused to stick his cock into me, yet he insisted on prying into my secrets.

"Yes," I told him, averting my eyes. "Everything is merely one elaborate game."

CHAPTER SIX

We arrived at the springs before dawn and my attendants set about occupying the mansion that had been built upon the grounds. The complex had been there since the last dynasty, a favorite retreat of many an emperor.

Yuan was situated in the chamber adjoining mine and I dismissed him to get some rest. The oil he had rubbed over me had seeped into my skin, imbuing it with the scent of flowers and reminding me of how I'd writhed in ecstasy while trapped beneath him. From now on, I would always be reminded of that when visiting my garden.

I left my robe on as I sank onto my bed, wanting the memory of Yuan's hands to linger a little longer. Next time, I vowed, his fingers would be replaced with something harder, bigger and ultimately more satisfying. He would penetrate me deeply while I lay pinned beneath him, and I would be powerless to do anything but take all of him as he thrust into me.

My lustful thoughts kept me from being able to fall asleep even though I had barely slept during the journey. As I tossed about on the bed, one that was much smaller than the bed in my palace, I wished that I had brought at least a few of my male concubines along, just to ease this restless tension.

Agitated, I went to the wall that separated Yuan's sleeping quarters from mine. There was a spyhole cut into the painting of a dragon and I raised myself onto my toes to look into the opening. Hazy morning light drifted in through the windows of the other chamber. After my eyes adjusted to the dimness, I saw Yuan sprawled onto the bed with all of his clothing removed. My heart skipped a beat and my throat went dry. I was being granted a gift.

His legs were parted. Between them, his organ stood as straight as a pillar, flushed and suffused with blood. His fist was closed around it, pumping hard up and down the shaft. The muscles of his forearm flexed and bulged and his head was thrown back, eyes closed. In his other hand, he held a length of golden silk to his nose.

I reached to feel around my shoulders. My shawl was missing.

Yuan had the material clutched to his face, inhaling deeply as he worked his fist in an increasing rhythm. My tongue cleaved to the roof of my mouth and my throat went painfully dry as I swallowed. Down below, the muscles of my sex squeezed tight.

Stubborn, impossible man. I wanted to fly through the doors and straddle him, sinking myself down onto every last inch of him. I would become the dream lover he was imagining in his head as he desperately inhaled my scent. *Mine.*

Why settle for five fingers when I was right here in the flesh?

But he was too far gone for that, even if he would have accepted. With a strangled sound, his hips jerked upward and pale fluid erupted from his organ, spilling over his knuckles. Gradually, his body relaxed into the bed. The gold shawl remained against his face as he slipped away into unknown dreams, finding the peaceful slumber that had eluded me.

For a thousand years now, as long as can be remembered, hot water naturally seeped up from the earth at this place. Originally, the water had collected in small mud holes, but over time the ponds had been dug out and widened until there were a series of connected pools, each of varying temperatures. An elegant garden with flowering trees and rock structures encompassed the bulk of the hot springs.

Yuan accompanied me to a bath house which sectioned off two of the bathing pools into a private oasis. A constant haze of vapor rose from the waters to envelop the chamber. The larger of the pools maintained the temperature of a comfortably warm steam bath for soaking, while the water from the smaller cleansing pool was just below scalding. Perfect for awakening and purifying the body.

I slipped off my robe and lowered myself into the hottest pool. The walls and bottom were lined with rock, and large, smooth stones were arranged beneath the water to serve as benches. I let my head fall back against the edge where wooden pillows had been placed as neck rests. The tension drained from my muscles as the steaming water surrounded me, flowing around me like an embrace.

The water level rose as Yuan entered the pool. His muscular leg brushed against mine as he settled into the water. I kept my eyes closed and my breathing even, reveling in the moment of quietness.

I had come here to get away from the imperial court and the treachery and danger that always gathered when men came together to vie for power. If only the hot springs could wash away the things I'd seen. The sight of my uncles huddled like animals inside iron cages. The look of sheer delight on my brother's face. As if it were all a game. A game…

When I opened my eyes, I found Yuan watching me, his gaze shuttered. He had his arms thrown back as he reclined against the stone edge. The position accentuated the muscles in his shoulders and he appeared at ease, as if offering himself to me. I knew it wasn't the case, but desire pooled hot and liquid in my belly. He had sought his release this morning, but I hadn't and it didn't take much to reawaken the dull throbbing of my sex.

It was much more enjoyable focusing on Yuan's inevitable surrender than the power struggles of the imperial court.

I smiled, remembering how he'd thrust into his fist while inhaling my scent. Immediately Yuan's heavy-lidded expression was replaced with a frown.

"It's only a matter of time, darling."

When he raised his eyebrow in question, I traced my toe along his calf. He didn't pull away. Such a move would seem cowardly, of course. Instead, his lips twisted into a half-smile of his own. "It's been six days, Princess."

Such insolence! I'd watched him spill his seed over silken sheets only hours earlier.

"I have strong evidence that you're far from indifferent to me, Chu Yuan," I purred.

I rose from the pool, not caring to cover myself as water dripped from my skin onto the slate tile. I could feel his gaze on me as I sauntered to the main bath.

The water in this pool was cooler and the shock of it pierced into my skin like tiny pinpricks, further awakening my senses. I had the added pleasure of watching as Yuan rose to follow me. His manhood stood half-erect already and it was all I could do not to close my hands around the length of him the moment he lowered himself into the water beside me. The lips of my sex clenched around emptiness. It had been too long since I'd been properly filled. Properly fucked.

He had chosen to seat himself close, I noted. Yuan wasn't one to shrink away like a coward. That was one of the reasons I was so hungry for him.

"Is there something you can show me in four days that I haven't already seen?" he asked, his voice rougher than it had been only moments earlier. Could that possibly be anticipation I heard?

"Four days is plenty of time," I declared, though inwardly I was starting to despair. We had wasted so much time. "Perhaps I'll simply ask the Emperor to extend your services to me for a while longer."

His expression darkened at that, but mine was an empty threat. My attraction to Yuan had already awakened my brother's possessive nature. If I pleaded for any more than the ten days Ziye had given me, he would begin to think I'd become attached.

Had I become fixated? Yuan was a diversion who both challenged and amused me, but I was getting frustrated at his hardheadedness. I let none of that show as I glided through the water to him, my eyes narrowed coyly.

"Come now." I turned around and settled onto his lap, his front against my back. "Isn't this more enjoyable than long, boring days reviewing petitions and issuing decrees?"

His legs parted to allow me access and he lowered his hands beneath the water to grip my hips. Far from the denial I expected. His thick cock nestled into the cleft of my buttocks.

Seducing men, in my experience, had never required such plotting. I was a woman and willing. I was princess and in a position to offer power. But I didn't want to peddle influence to win Yuan over. I wanted him to burn for me the way I did for him.

With a sigh, I laid my head back against his shoulder. From there, I could look up at him. He regarded me with an expression that was certainly not as impassive as he intended. His eyes smoldered with heat.

"I know you think of it," I said breathlessly. "How perfectly our bodies will fit together."

I ground myself against him and he hardened further. The smoke in his gaze turned to pure fire.

"By nature, all men and women's bodies complement one another," he replied stiffly.

With a sly look, I pushed my shoulders back and saw how

his attention strayed toward my breasts as they lifted just above the surface of the water. The head of his organ teased against my opening, finding its rightful place of its own accord. I couldn't resist rounding my hips in a small circle, nudging him between my swollen lips.

The heated water was slippery with natural minerals. It would be so easy to push myself onto him and let him impale me. He would have me at his mercy, shuddering with ecstasy, with barely any effort on his part.

"You're shameless," he said in a low voice. There was no insult there, only a hint of awe.

"You like that I have no shame."

Yuan wasn't fighting. I could feel his thighs enclosing me like a vise and his breath came out in a shallow, broken rhythm.

I didn't want his passiveness, his mute acceptance. I wanted to feel him thrust into me so hard that I screamed with the pleasure of it. I wanted to squeeze him tight and spill his essence deep into my womb. Then there would be no doubt that we both wanted it.

But he was still resisting, even though I could feel his heart beating like a drum against my back.

"Perhaps my forward nature offends you," I suggested sweetly. "I can kneel at your feet. You can pretend I'm your concubine."

Groaning, he rested his forehead against mine, eyes forced shut. It made me want to devour him. I lowered my hips and the broad tip of his cock just entered me. The swollen flesh pulsed within my sensitive opening, making my knees go weak. *Now*, I urged him silently. *Please now.*

He dug his fingers into my hips, halting my movements, but doing nothing else to rebuke me. We were locked on a knife's edge of decision.

The entrance of one of my maidservants broke the

impasse, at least for Yuan. He shifted away from me like an eel in water, leaving us once again side by side. I glared up at the girl, who was blushing too prettily and avoiding his gaze.

It agitated me to no end. Was she the sort of innocent, fresh-faced young thing he typically preferred?

"What is it?" I demanded.

"Chancellor Wu is here to see you."

At the mention of the high-ranking official's name, Yuan straightened even further.

"Well, it must be urgent. Bring him in."

Yuan's muscles coiled as if he were preparing to spring away, but there was no escape. Within moments, a middle-aged official dressed in an indigo robe arrived at the entrance. Wu was tall in stature and well-spoken by reputation. He was also known to despise me.

"Princess Shanyin." He bowed low, making all the prescribed gestures. His eyes fixed onto my face as if he couldn't see that I was soaking in the bathing pool naked or that Yuan was beside me, equally bared.

"What brings you here, Chancellor?"

"I am concerned for the wellbeing of the Emperor, most honorable Princess."

I snorted. "Then speak to the Emperor. You're a member of his inner court."

Wu had served in the court for over thirty years. He had witnessed the overthrow of my usurper uncle as well as the early death of my father. A man didn't survive such monumental power shifts without being uncommonly fortunate or clever.

"He has imprisoned the princes of Jian'an, Shanyang and Xiangdong in a matter unfitting for their stations," Wu continued.

My eyes glazed over at the mention of titles. "I know about my uncles. My brother is right to consider them potential enemies."

Wu bowed once more. "The princess is of course wise in her judgment."

Already I was tiring of this unwanted guest. "The Emperor will have his way with them and then let them go—or he won't. I have no say in his decisions."

"There is another incident the princess may not be aware of. Something troubling to myself as well as anyone concerned with the welfare of the empire. I'm certain the princess would want to be informed about it."

Wu couldn't keep from sounding condescending when he spoke to me.

"What is it?" I asked, irritated.

"At the same time his uncles were imprisoned, the Emperor had their wives and daughters brought from their homes and installed within the palace."

A sick feeling snaked through me. "And why is this of any interest to me?"

"You know what your Emperor-brother is capable of. Have you not any sympathy for these women and children?"

"And you wish for me to intervene on their behalf," I remarked coldly. My chest had squeezed so tight I could barely breathe.

"You were born a woman, Princess. I beg of you to use your influence over the Emperor to guide him the ways of justice and mercy."

"Of course. We women are all kind and soft, full of justice and mercy." My tone was soft, then sharp. "Did you not tell the Emperor that I was a corrupting influence? Did you not urge the other ministers of the court to petition for my removal from the imperial palace?"

Wu bowed deeply. "That was long before this servant became aware of the princess's virtuous nature. I beg of you, in these circumstances, we must be willing to look past such disagreements. For the sake of the empire."

Willing? Even now, the chancellor's attitude remained disdainful and superior. He wanted my assistance despite looking down at me as if I were no more than dust beneath his heel. He wanted to put this burden on my shoulders.

"You appeal to my womanly mercy," I replied with a sneer. "Where were all these princesses—my aunts and cousins—while I was being held captive? And who had the audacity to call me virtuous? As you can see, I'm no more virtuous than you are."

Keeping my eyes fixed on Wu's face, I reached between Yuan's legs to take hold of his manhood. It had reduced in length and size, but still remained firm to the touch. Yuan jerked as my hand closed over him. Slowly, I stroked the length of Yuan's impressive manhood beneath the water, taking my time while I smiled at the chancellor, challenging him to spout more of his drivel at me. Wu finally glanced away, embarrassed.

"I'll consider your request," I said, full of enough insolence to match Wu's disdain.

The chancellor nodded and ducked away. The moment he was gone, Yuan shoved me away from him and rose from the pool, not caring that he gave me a full view of his naked physique.

"Are there no limits to your immorality?" he growled.

"Immoral?" I snapped back. Normally, it would have amused me to taunt and ignore the insults, but with Yuan my every nerve ending was pulsing and raw. "Men like Chancellor Wu have blood on their hands from a lifetime of treachery and intrigue, yet I'm immoral for taking men to my bed?"

Yuan stared at me, his eyes cold and jaw hard. Despite the warmth of the bathing pool, a chill ran down my spine.

"I am not your slave. Never use me like that again or you will regret it," he warned, storming from the chamber without bothering to don his robe.

My personal chamber was empty when I returned to it, but I didn't question where my attendants had gone. My hair was still damp and I had nothing covering me but a sheer layer of silk. There were too many things on my mind. Despite what I'd told the chancellor, I was thinking of my aunts and cousins. More importantly, I was thinking of Ziye. Killing his enemies was one thing, but their wives and children? Even I wasn't that much of a monster.

I searched through the desk in the corner, producing a writing box from one of the drawers. A message sent by fast horse would reach the palace long before my caravan, but what was I to say to the Emperor to penetrate the black shell of his madness?

My dearest brother, I would write. Do not make any grand gestures until your trusted sister is once more by your side, when I can share in both your sorrows and triumphs.

I lifted the lid from the lacquered case to reveal the calligraphy brushes and inkstone nestled inside. As I reached for a brush, strong arms took hold of me. The contents of the case scattered over the floor as I was thrown down and my legs pinned by an immoveable weight.

I fought. Or I tried to fight. The wind had been knocked out of me by the impact and I gasped, unable to find breath. A man straddled my hips, holding my wrists in an iron grip. For a moment I didn't recognize him, and his features took on the twisted visages of my nightmares, one face blending into another and then another above me while I was held down.

"No one will come for you, Princess. I told them you didn't want to be disturbed."

The hold on my wrists loosened momentarily, but not long enough for me to break free. He held both of them just as easily with one large hand as he did with two. With his free hand, he tugged the sash from around my waist.

My heart beat frantically and my throat clenched with fear, but the voice cut through the nightmare darkness. It was familiar. The shape of him above me and even his touch, as rough as it was, wasn't completely foreign. And the smell of his skin...

"Yuan?" I choked out.

I blinked through the momentary haze and saw it was indeed him, but his expression was one I'd never seen before. His eyes were dark and his teeth bared. He was seething with anger and utterly, completely focused on his task.

The length of silk looped around my wrists; once, twice, before Yuan knotted it tight. I tried to struggle once more when he secured the other end to the foot of the desk, stretching my arms over my head. The heavy rosewood refused to move when I tugged against it. Yuan merely looked down at me, watching with cruel interest as I writhed and fought to no avail.

He was naked still, not having bothered to clothe himself after leaving the bath house. I was also barely dressed, my thin covering falling open in the skirmish. His organ pressed against my sex as he straddled me and it jerked luridly when I twisted my hips to try and unseat him.

"You can even shout for them and they wouldn't come to your aid," he said, his tone cold. "Because your servants believe I am your little plaything and the louder you scream, the more you are enjoying all the things you are having me do to you."

Despite his words, he produced another length of cloth— my gossamer shawl he'd used while pleasuring himself—and gagged me with it. The material cut into the corners of my mouth, muffling my words.

"But I think I like having you like this more," he finished.

I was completely helpless beneath him, unable to move, to taunt or tease or command. Was this how it would happen? I had wanted him to take me, but not in anger. Not forced against my will.

Yuan lowered his hands to my breasts while I could do nothing but watch, sobbing in protest. I jumped at his first touch, but as he cupped the soft weights in his palms, I was stricken by the same sense I had of him the first time he'd undressed me. He could have been rough with me. Or cold and impersonal—everything else about his demeanor spoke of his intention to treat me like I'd treated him. But there was both a sense of care and mastery in his touch.

My heart thudded against my ribs and I knew he could sense it as he kneaded my flesh, testing the feel of me in his hands. His thumbs passed lightly over my nipples, both of them at once. Pleasure, pure and raw, raced through me. My heart beat even harder, but with more anticipation than fear.

I had no idea what he intended to do with me, but I knew he was still enraged by how I'd flaunted him in front of the chancellor. I stared into his face to search for some answer, but there was none as his endlessly black eyes fixed onto me. He merely repeated the slow caress of his thumbs over my nipples, forcing them into painfully hard points as he watched me; face blank, but eyes blazing hot.

"This is what you wanted, isn't it, Princess?" he asked in a dangerous tone.

I shook my head, the gag preventing me from anything more than a mewl of protest. It pleased him, my resistance. His cock was now hard and hot between my thighs and my head swam with confusion. Should I resist or not? And if I did resist him, would it only provoke him more?

And was that exactly what I wanted to do?

His lips lifted grimly when I shifted my hips away from his member. But he didn't thrust himself into me. That would have been too easy, the demon. Instead he reached for one of the brushes lying on the floor and held it up so I could see it.

It was finely made, with a long elegant stalk fashioned of bamboo. The head was made from rabbit hair and shaped to a point for delicate precision.

"You commanded me to touch you, did you not?"

Yuan swiped the brush over my cheek, then down the bridge of my nose. Squirming, I tried to duck away. It tickled.

After a pause, he touched the brush to my lips which were distended beneath the gag. This caress was completely unexpected, making my chest squeeze tight. The look in his eyes was both wicked and playful, but it shifted darkly as the instrument feathered down over my throat and collarbone. Watching my face intently, Yuan brought the tip down over my left nipple, drawing a slow circle over the pebbled flesh.

I closed my eyes as my back rose off the floor. Yuan was relentless, circling, then teasing in a never-ending pattern. As I squirmed and writhed, my sex flooded to demand more. When I thought I could take it no longer, he moved the brush tip over to my other breast. I cried out against the gag as Yuan tormented me, circling and stroking while I shook my head violently from side to side, trying to thrash free but failing.

The delicate stroke of the brush was tantalizing at first, each caress of the tip over my breast echoing down below in my sex. But the arousal quickly became overwhelming until every inch of me was on fire and I wanted to scream.

I did scream. "Stop!" I shouted against the gag, but it only came out as a muffled grunt. "Stop, stop…"

Each word was both a plea and a moan. I sobbed with relief as the brush moved away to feather over the underside of my breasts, then to my stomach. My skin tingled all over and I flinched whenever the brush found a particularly sensitive spot.

My relief was short-lived. The brush continued in slow strokes down an inevitable path over my hips and then lower still. He wouldn't dare—

Yuan had my lower body pinned while he straddled above me. He shifted now and took hold of one of my legs as I tried to kick at him. With a hand set at the crook of my knee, he held my leg against his side, bent at an angle which naturally opened me to him.

"Why fight me now, Shanyin? You've made your desires clear from the start."

The brush moved over my mound, lingering to prolong my torture. The moment stretched out into eternity and I could hear the sound of my ragged breathing. The thunder of my pulse filled my ears.

I did fight him. I fought him hard. The thought of what he was going to do to me was unbearable. There was nothing I could do to stop it.

The very tip of the brush slid over the pearl of my sex and I jumped, but Yuan used his weight and strength to anchor me to the ground. His gaze bore into me.

The sensation was delicate, almost elusive, yet I could feel it everywhere. My nipples, already worked to a point beyond pleasure, throbbed endlessly. My chest squeezed tight. Down below, my inner muscles clenched and pulsed, unfulfilled.

He leaned in closer, widening my legs as he positioned his shoulders between them. I felt his fingers on my outer lips, parting them wetly with a soft, slick sound. The brush head stroked over my slit, dipping into the well of moisture gathering there. Then it lifted to stroke directly over the hard bud of my sex.

It was as awful and as incredible as I'd feared. He repeated the movement, soft bristles dipping into my slit and then flicking over the small nub. I thrashed against my bonds and bit hard against the gag, making incoherent sounds like a wild animal. My knees fell open of their own accord now; mindless, blind with pleasure.

Please. Please, I moaned against the gag. The tip of the

brush became soaked with my fluids, making each stroke sharper, the sensation more acute. But the fine rabbit hair was too delicate to deliver me. Even when I strained my hips upward, begging silently, the pressure wasn't enough to give me the release I so desperately wanted. *Needed.*

And through it all, Yuan lorded over me, watching my descent into madness. I didn't care. I was at his mercy. I would do, would *become* whatever he wanted. His whore. His slave. If he would just let me come.

The motion of the brush stopped and I sobbed out loud, tears flooding my eyes. I had never been so aroused. Brought to the edge only to be denied.

"What was it you threatened?" Yuan asked. His voice was thick, saturated with desire. His cock lay heavy against his thighs. "You said you would cut my tongue out?"

He bent his head and granted me the soft, wet stroke of his tongue over my aching sex. I sobbed once more, but this time in gratitude.

"This tongue?" he taunted, his breath hot against my sex before he worked me with his lips and mouth.

My hips strained upward. My legs trembled and I tried to close them around Yuan to clamp him to me. If he stopped now, I would die. But he didn't. Thank heaven above and earth below. He flicked his tongue in small circles, lighter as my flesh became more sensitive. My cries blended together into one endless moan as he took me higher, easing me with the flat of his tongue when it became too much, then using the tip with unerring precision.

The orgasm shattered through me and I was gasping, crying, undone. I thought wildly that it would finally happen now. Yuan had demonstrated his dominance over me and now he would take his own pleasure.

Instead he pinned my hips down with his hands as the last of my shudders began to subside. He continued to lick at my flesh, but the touch became gentle, loving. Even so, it was too much. I tried to close my legs, turning my hips away and curling my knees toward me. Yuan wouldn't allow it. His hands exerted more force as needed, just enough to keep me trapped.

Soon the soft strokes became harder, deliberate. He worked me once more toward climax and I tried to shake my head no, but I went unheeded. I could see the top of his head dipping low as he pulled me closer, his hands sliding beneath me to grasp my buttocks and lift my sex to him. He dipped his tongue just inside my folds and then pushed deeper, spearing into me.

I came again. I had no choice.

Afterward, my muscles went slack and I lay in a pool on the floor, drained and exhausted. I tried to close my eyes, but Yuan wasn't done.

"But this isn't what you really want, is it Shanyin?"

My eyes flew open at the hardness of his tone. The two orgasms had left me sated, sapped of all will, but Yuan hadn't yet found release.

He slid up my side, dark intent in every movement. I became alert once more, my pulse racing. He stopped once he was crouched beside my head and reached down to untie the gag around my mouth before taking hold of the base of his manhood with one hand. His shaft lifted in anticipation.

"This is what you want." He leaned down and his voice was a rumble in my ear. "You want this cock deep in your cunt."

The stark words sent a dark shiver through me. My mouth was still sore from the gag and I ran my tongue over my lips and swallowed. Yuan watched every movement with interest. His other hand curved around the back of my head, his touch almost gentle.

"If you want me inside you, then get me hard, Princess.

Suck me so I can fuck you."

I'd never heard that growl in his voice before. Or the language of the gutter from his lips. He was already hard, but he pressed his organ against my lips regardless; not roughly, but insistent. The hand at the nape of my neck tilted me toward him and my lips parted of their own accord. He slid his length inside my mouth, forcing my lips wide. I was rendered hot and helpless at the feel of him filling my mouth until he was all I could taste and smell.

I moaned around his thick member and Yuan stiffened, his eyelids growing heavy. I could feel the shudder that ran through him against the walls of my mouth.

"Suck me hard," he urged.

Tied up as I was, there was little I could do but close my lips around him and draw him deeper into my mouth. I had taken men this way before, both larger and smaller than Yuan. Each one was different, but in some ways the same. I worked my tongue against the underside of his cock where I knew men to be particularly sensitive. Yuan's organ twitched, hitting against my teeth as he grew impossibly thicker.

Up until then he'd been patient, not moving while I became accustomed to him. But that moment was brief. Yuan's hand tightened in my hair and with a small pull of his hips, he withdrew. I breathed shallowly around the space created before he pushed back in, pausing to readjust the hand at my head. Then he pulled back and thrust again, in and out in a slow rhythm.

At first I licked my tongue over the head of his cock whenever he withdrew, but soon it was impossible. His thrusts became faster, harder as his breathing quickened. Though he was on his knees, I was the supplicant. My mouth, my body was nothing but an instrument for him to use.

I moaned around him as he pushed deeper, both in pleasure and protest. His hips continued thrusting as he grasped my head with both hands now, one cradled against my cheek, the other still at the nape of my neck to hold me exactly where he wanted me while he took his pleasure. The head of his cock butted against my throat and I flinched, gagging. Yuan didn't stop, but he seemed to thrust more carefully even as the rhythm increased.

By now, my jaw was aching and my neck stiff from being held at an odd angle. I knew he had no intention of fucking me now—if he'd ever intended it in the first place. He was too far gone for that. His entire body tensed, every muscle rigid. His face was fixed in a mask of agony and ecstasy.

He shifted closer, repositioning his knees so he could thrust into my mouth in shorter and faster strokes. It was difficult to breathe, but I knew it wouldn't be much longer. I willed his release to happen soon. Every moment of his pleasure now was traded for my pain, but I gave it willingly.

Suddenly his muscles locked and he went utterly still except for the pulse of his cock as he released his fluids into me. He tasted of salt and bitter tea as I swallowed. I could feel his hands shaking on either side of my face as he spent the last of his essence down my throat.

Then he let go of me abruptly and withdrew his organ from my mouth, still half-erect but softening quickly. He turned away and sat on the floor, knees raised and head lowered as if in meditation. His chest heaved as he fought to catch his breath.

I licked my lips, catching a trace of the salty-bitter taste of him as I waited for Yuan to find his voice. It didn't happen. Several long minutes later, he was still turned away from me, shoulders bent.

"Yuan, untie me," I said firmly.

When I repeated the order, his head whipped around. His eyes flashed with anger. "Maybe I should keep you there and torment you for the rest of the day," he snapped. "At my mercy now."

It wasn't too long ago when our situation had been reversed, with him tied to my bed. But here was the difference between us. Yuan had taken control. He'd given pleasure and taken it while I was helpless and writhing beneath him, yet he was the one broken.

My hands were still bound over my head and my mouth sore from being used. Between my legs, I could feel the wetness where his tongue and my juices had mingled.

"Untie me now," I commanded in a tone that said I was Princess Shanyin and mere men did not deny me. "It will take us all day to return to the imperial palace and I need to go to the Emperor as soon as possible. Before it's too late."

CHAPTER SEVEN

Yuan rode outside the litter on the journey back to the imperial palace and I didn't protest. Instead I slept.

My dreams. What did I dream about in the aftermath of being tied up and tormented to multiple orgasms? One would think it would be wild orgies and beautiful naked men, lining up to take their turn with me.

It was nothing like that.

As the transport rocked me with its swaying motion, I dreamed about flowers. The flowers in my garden which always looked so pure despite growing from dirt and decay. I ran my fingers across the cool petals and touched the tips of the green leaves.

One bloom in the center looked withered, but I merely plucked it and tossed it aside so it wouldn't mar the beauty of the rest of the garden. But then I found another so I plucked it as well. Soon everywhere I looked, every plant was black and shriveled, eaten through with worms. Dying.

Soon, I was no longer searching for wilted ones to remove, but for a single fresh flower. There had to be one left and I had to find it.

I woke up still searching and wishing I'd dreamt about orgies. Or at least about Yuan finally giving into his desires, though he was starting to confound me as much as the dream. I opened the curtain and peered outside to see the sun dipping below the horizon. Yuan sat tall astride his horse, set against the orange sky.

I didn't call out to him and he very pointedly did not turn

to look at me. The sight of his silhouette was enough to make my insides flutter.

Was Yuan still angry with me? I remembered how he'd bound my wrists, rendering me helpless. Perhaps I wanted him to be angry. Men who had no control over their emotions were easily blinded by rage. Those men became unpredictable and violent. They were monsters to be feared, but for a man like Yuan, anger aroused all sorts of passions.

He was slipping through my fingers like water. Selfishly, I wanted him to feel something for me when he was gone. Anger had a way of worming its way deep into one's heart and lodging there. At least anger wasn't indifference.

Whether or not Yuan succumbed to my demands, I only had four days left.

Our arrival at the imperial palace was met without circumstance. Evening was upon us and the guardsmen managed a cursory inspection before allowing the caravan inside. I immediately sent a message to my brother by runner to announce that I had returned.

I held the curtain of the litter open while I gave the command and I saw Yuan regarding me with a dark stare. The memory of his hands clamped around my head assailed me. I could almost taste him on my tongue. I let the curtain fall back in place while my heart continued to pound.

The moment already felt a lifetime away. While Yuan and the rest of the entourage returned to my palatial estate, I alone went to see the Emperor.

I entered the gates of my brother's inner sanctum and was met by the warm glow of red lanterns swinging from the eaves. A soft, haunting melody floated through the empty garden, presenting a tranquil scene that was at odds with the lawlessness and debauchery Chancellor Wu had warned me of. Perhaps my brother had found some peace while I was away. I could only pray it was so.

A hulking ox of a man blocked the doors to the bedchamber. My brother Ziye chose to surround himself with fearsome bodyguards of whom Bataar was likely the most menacing, at least by appearance.

As the story was told, Bataar had survived a wolf attack as a youth and the animal had taken half his face before he killed it. The ragged scars were still visible with one cruel gash cutting directly over his left eye which had been blinded in the attack. It was useless, covered by a milky film.

The brutish guard bowed gracelessly at my approach. He kept his head lowered as I approached, as was proper, but I could still see his face as he was so much taller than I. It was a difficult face to look at, as ruined as it was.

I wondered why Ziye chose to keep him in such a prominent place when it was tradition for the Emperor to choose the most attractive of attendants. I suppose he did it to ward away any would-be assassins. I myself had selected my concubines and maidservants for their physical beauty. Why surround myself with any reminders of the ugliness of the world?

Without slowing my stride, I aimed for the door. Bataar stood aside, but appeared to hesitate as if he wanted to address me. That would have been highly unusual—there was little reason for so lowly a servant to speak to a princess.

The moment passed and the guardsman pushed the door open for me. I entered the sitting room to find two ladies, one older and one young, playing a duet involving a stringed pipa and bamboo flute. Ziye was nowhere in sight, though he was expecting me.

The musicians continued uninterrupted and their song shifted to a sentimental, almost melancholy mood. I waved them into silence just as a figure stepped through the curtain that separated the sitting room from the bedchamber.

I halted to stare. The woman was a handful of years older

than me, though still youthful in appearance. The pins in her hair had come loose and her robe was in disarray. The vermillion tint on her lips had been smeared, but she made no effort to clean it.

As she reached me, the woman paused and I saw recognition flicker in her eyes before she ducked her head and hurried from the room. Ziye came out a moment later, sauntering through the curtain with a self-indulgent smile. His robe was open in front and his trousers haphazardly tied.

"Elder Sister," he greeted. "Did you enjoy your tryst at the hot springs with your new lover?"

I pressed my lips tight, refusing to be deterred. "That was Liu Shang's wife."

His grin widened. "Ah, but I'm learning the benefits of an older, more experienced woman. She sucks me like a goddess. I almost wanted to fall on my knees afterward, to thank her."

My frown deepened. "She's our aunt."

Ziye made a face and pointedly turned his shoulder to me as he stared at the musicians. The women kept their head bowed and eyes averted, though I caught a few nervous glances exchanged between them. My brother remained silent, appearing to weigh some decision for a long time before shooing them away.

"No man will tolerate another man claiming what's his," I scolded when we were alone. "You'll make a bitter enemy of our uncle."

"Liu Shang has no say in this matter!" my brother retorted. "He's still locked up in a cage, like a pig awaiting slaughter."

He made pig-like noises in his throat which would have seemed childish were I not completely chilled by his demeanor. He was becoming more aggressive and moodier by the day.

"And besides, I'm not another man. Am I not the Son of Heaven, powerful and god-like?"

Instead of seating himself on the benches and pillows in the room, Ziye went instead to the raised dais where his throne stood. There was one in every room where the Emperor might choose to have an audience. He sprawled onto it, one leg raised insolently.

"And when did you become so uptight, sister? You never answered me about Lord Chu Yuan. Does my latest gift please you? Are you so satisfied that you've forsaken all your other lovers for him alone?"

I didn't like the sharp edge to his words. I would not play this game, the one where he blamed me for his degeneration. With a deep breath, I went to stand at the foot of the dais.

"I know our uncles are our enemies and our greatest threat," I began soothingly. "But they have armies and factions behind them. Outwardly, we must keep the peace."

My counsel sounded hollow in my own ears. What did I know of politics? My arguments were thinner than paper, but Ziye's shoulders sank and some of the edgy restlessness drained from him.

"I hate them," he said, appearing lost and exhausted. "They still try to pull strings in court, forcing my hand."

"Then we won't let them," I assured.

I convinced him to release our uncles, but to send them into exile. I urged him to release their wives and families as well, keeping only one heir from each household in the palace as hostage, just as our uncles had done to us. Over the next hours, I wrote out the decrees myself and put them in front of my brother to sign and stamp with the imperial seal.

Ziye's hand paused over the decree that would release Liu Shang and his wife. It had to be the excitement of besting an enemy that had him so fixated with the woman. He had enjoyed her favors for only a day and, though far from elderly, she was past her spring years.

Firmly, I tapped the space at the bottom of the scroll and

my brother affixed his seal.

This is how one goes about wresting power, I realized with a heavy sense of dread as I watched the jade chop press down on the document to leave its red imprint.

The thought was ridiculous. There was no way I could act as regent for Ziye. I was a woman and only seven years older than my brother, without any knowledge of how to rule. When our father had taken over the throne, my only thought was to drown in excess and pleasure to make up for all the years of living in fear.

After the decrees were complete, I sent for retainers to have them carried out immediately. Then I had a sleeping elixir of mimosa bark steeped in green tea brought in for Ziye and put him to bed.

"Will you leave me now?" he asked as the herbal brew made his eyelids heavy.

"Once you're asleep, Imperial Majesty."

"No, Sister." His eyes flashed fiercely. "Will you leave me for Chu Yuan?"

I laughed. "Hardly."

"You're obsessed with him," my brother insisted stubbornly. "I've seen you."

My stomach turned on the last part. I didn't dare ask him what he meant. "Do you think any one man could enchant your sister?"

"I can smell him on you," he accused, his tone more hurt than angry.

"That's absurd."

"You're going to ask to be wed to him. You'll belong to him and not me."

His jaw clenched and the look of hatred in his eyes made my blood run cold. Ziye was fighting the elixir to stay awake and I willed for him to go to sleep.

I stroked his hair back from his face, something I had not

done for a long time. Despite the affectionate gesture, my chest felt as if stones had been placed upon it to slowly crush the air from my lungs. I looked into his eyes, searching for the boy I once knew, but found no trace of him. For the first time, I was as frightened of Ziye as I was frightened for him.

"Didn't we always say our fates were linked, you and I?" I asked gently.

Finally Ziye nodded drowsily and let his eyes fall closed. "You and I," he echoed, the last part trailing off. "I trust no one but you, Shanyin."

Like everyone else, I had learned exactly what needed to be said to please the Emperor. In doing so, I'd become just like all the other cronies and sycophants, kowtowing for his favor.

I remained there, staring at him while he slept. They say that in sleep all men look innocent and vulnerable. My brother did look young once more, with the harsh sneer wiped from his face. But I couldn't see past what he'd become in the year since he'd taken the throne.

He was a tyrant. A hateful, vengeful creature who struck out like a storm, with no consideration for what it destroyed. But as far as I could see, he was no worse than any emperor who had come before him, including our father.

When I left the imperial quarters, the bodyguard Bataar was still standing like a guardian lion at the entrance.

"Princess Shanyin," he called after me, his tone rough around the honorific.

I turned. "Yes?" I asked, perhaps a bit brusquely. It was late. Very late.

"Has—has the princess been to the Bamboo Hall?" he asked haltingly.

His hesitant manner was a contrast to his frightening appearance. While he averted his one good eye, the blind one seemed to stare directly at me. I had to bid him to speak before he would continue.

"There's blood everywhere," he told me. "Blood was shed there this very day."

Yuan's room was dark when I slipped inside, carrying a small oil lamp with me to light my way. The windows were open and the night air was just starting to cool. He wore a pale under-tunic and trousers to bed and lay on his back without any covers. Blankets were unnecessary during the summer months.

I placed the oil lamp on a side table and left it burning as I climbed into bed beside him. His hair had been let down from its topknot and fell about his face. In the eerie flicker of the light he appeared even more beautiful and more unattainable.

"Yuan," I murmured softly.

"Princess," he responded.

"Were you asleep?"

"No," he admitted and I was glad. I wanted him to lie awake thinking of me as I did of him.

I curled myself against his side, fitting my curves to the hard, solid frame of his body. Tension traveled through him as I did so.

"You have thirty lovers in your harem at your service." Yuan kept his eyes closed and I could see him swallowing as he spoke.

So this is the game he wanted to play; me the sex-starved fox demon and he the steadfast, righteous hero. Even though he'd had his tongue thrust inside me just this morning. The thought made my sex clench.

"Thirty-one," I corrected.

But not for much longer. I could feel a sharp pang in my chest as it constricted around my heart.

I ran the flat of my palm over his chest, finding where the beat of his heart was strongest and resting there. I had to stretch over him to reach his throat. With my chest against his shoulder, I kissed the side of his neck gently like a rain of flowers. Then I scraped my teeth lightly over the sensitive skin, reveling in the small shudder that ran through him.

"Imagine I'm your long lost love, if you have to," I whispered against his ear before taking the lobe between my teeth.

His hands came up to settle around my waist, but he didn't push me away. I reached down to undo his undergarments and push them aside as much as I could before mounting him. I was still clothed. Selfishly, I wanted him to undress me. There was something about undressing myself during sex that felt too much like I was doing a servant's task.

I felt his cock hardening beneath my pelvic bone before he spoke. "She's no longer alive."

I stilled while straddled above him. An odd sensation curled tight in my stomach. I didn't know if I was more bothered by him revealing such a personal detail to me or by his admission that he did indeed have a long lost love.

"Does this remind you of her too much?" I ran my hands along his arms, an innocent enough touch, but a sensual enough one to make my meaning clear. Was this truly why he refused to give in to his desires?

"We never kissed or touched. We rarely even spoke."

"Oh. You were arranged to be married, then."

"Last spring, but it was not meant to be."

I didn't push further, surprised that Yuan had revealed something so personal to me at all. It was more intimate, more invasive than having his cock thrusting into my mouth.

Bracing my palms, I lowered myself so I could lie over him. I liked the warm feel of him pressed to me from neck to toe.

"Do you think of her to help you resist me?" I asked shamelessly.

It was a tactless and deplorable question to ask, but I was the immoral Princess Shanyin. I was also one woman jealous of another, even if her rival was only a ghost. Heartache had the potential of lasting a lifetime, even into the next life.

"I wouldn't dishonor her memory by bringing her into your bed," he replied bluntly.

I should have been insulted, but I was already too numb by all that I had seen and learned that night to be wounded. Bataar had taken me to the Bamboo Hall, where my brother regularly cavorted with his palace women, to show me the bloodstains on the floor. He described how my brother had brought in a row of princesses, our aunts and their daughters, and ordered them to lie down on the floor so his attendants could have their way with them. When one of our aunts refused, Ziye had the woman's children dragged in and publicly executed before the gathering. She was then beheaded right there in the hall.

I sank against Yuan, my head resting on his shoulder. He was warm and undemanding, but it wasn't enough. I needed something to chase away the demons. The thought of summoning my harem to satisfy me left me cold.

"I don't want to sleep alone tonight," I confessed and immediately regretted it.

I sounded weak. Sentimental. Princess Shanyin took what she wanted.

Once again I laid my hand on his chest. I explored the expanse of his torso and the plane of his abdomen, my hands roaming at leisure. I dipped lower to round over the curve of his hip.

"Does this tempt you?" I asked quietly, as a matter-of-fact.

There was a long pause before he answered, his voice deep with a rasp of desire. "You know it does."

"But you'll fight it."

"Yes."

I knew he would and he'd likely succeed, but I didn't care. "Then fight it."

I explored his naked body with my hands and mouth, taking my time. Not an inch of him was neglected except for that selfish cock of his which twitched hungrily as I ran my hands over the strong muscles of his legs. I planted a kiss high on his inner thigh to make his breath catch, purposely letting my hair fall to tease over him. But I left his organ untouched.

Let him keep that part to himself. Tonight I wanted everything else.

I needed this more than I needed him embedded inside me right now. Sex by its nature was a crash of lightning and thunder that shook the foundations of the world before quickly dissipating. He'd spill over the sheets and be done, slumbering away, while I would be left awake and alone.

Instead I awakened every part of him and claimed it for myself. Yuan shuddered as I sucked his toes into my mouth and I was filled with pure, wicked pleasure. I turned him over to explore his backside and he was a willing puppet in my hands.

His shoulders were a joy to behold. I imagined what pursuits he engaged in to keep them so strong. Archery, most likely. A favored pastime of the aristocracy. Or perhaps wrestling, his body naked and oiled. I straddled him and dug my thumbs into the hard muscle, feeling his body relax and sigh. I could be kind as well as cruel. Didn't he know that?

I climbed off him and my hands followed the curve of his spine to his buttocks. I gave the hard globes a squeeze before raking my nails lightly over them. He groaned and his hips jerked against the bed.

But I was here for my pleasure and not his. I wanted to tease him to the point of pain, but do nothing to release his suffering. By the time I turned him onto his back, his hands were clenched around air and his breathing ragged.

I snuggled once more into the crook of his arm and took hold of his hand. It felt heavy in mine as I brought him between my legs.

"I'm here," I told him, directing his hand into the dewy wetness of my slit.

His eyes were squeezed shut. His expression was one of agony and his member was engorged with blood, stabbing straight into the air. Let him revel in his bitter triumph.

I couldn't resist circling his finger over my aching bud, slippery with my juices. His hands were so much rougher than mine, providing the perfect pressure over the slick, soft flesh. A delicious shiver ran down my spine.

"Come find me," I whispered, leaving his hand drenched in my sex before curling against him to fall asleep.

CHAPTER EIGHT

I half expected to wake up with Yuan moving deep inside me, unable to restrain himself. Instead it was the morning sunlight that woke me. Yuan was turned away on his side. My only consolation was that his hands were curled into tight fists, telling me that at least his sleep wasn't a peaceful one.

Irritated, I rose from the bed to return to my chamber. As I walked, I could feel my sex still swollen and unfulfilled from the night before. Why was I being so indulgent of him? Teasing him, even gratifying him with my hands and mouth, which only rewarded him for resisting. I turned to look over my shoulder at him once more before straightening.

The worst of it was that I had shown Yuan how weak I could be. How much I yearned for the attentions of someone who wasn't a servant or a slave. Someone I didn't completely command.

He continued to lord that over me and I was done with it.

I summoned Tai and Jiyi. It had been six days since I'd requested anyone from my harem and they were eager to see me. The moment Tai came to the bedchamber, he caught me up in his arms and kissed me, not waiting for my command. He held me eagerly against him while his mouth moved hungrily over mine. Normally I would have frowned upon such a display of possessiveness, but it was hard to fault such open enthusiasm.

"Don't be greedy! The princess summoned both of us, you ox."

Jiyi's taunt was delivered with his typical good-natured

charm and I smiled as he swept me into his embrace. He was leaner in build than Tai. His features were also more fine-boned while Tai was roughly cut, but they complimented each other perfectly. My eye never tired of looking at the two of them. There were so many differences and nuances to appreciate.

I had always thought the two of them combined would be the ultimate lover. Now I didn't know if such a man existed any more.

"We missed you, Princess." Jiyi nibbled my neck flirtatiously. I confess, it felt wonderful to touch and be touched so freely. "We were afraid you were still angry at us for that incident on the polo field."

"I *am* still angry at you." I affected a cross look while lifting his chin with the tip of my finger. "Your princess could have been trampled to death."

"I can't bear to think of it! We would have been entombed with you," Jiyi insisted.

I slipped from his embrace to sit back onto the bed, glancing from Tai to Jiyi. "Come here and regain my good favor, then," I said with a look that was full of smoke and fire.

Jiyi's clothes were already half off when he tackled me. I fell onto my back, giggling. Tai was more deliberate in his movements. He stood at the edge of the bed, presenting a lovely spectacle for my pleasure as he disrobed. All the while, Jiyi had his arms around me, deftly peeling my own robe from my shoulders.

"We took it upon ourselves to punish Feng for what happened on the field," Tai reported, quite serious. He stripped away his trousers last to reveal his already hardening member, which jutted upward proudly.

There was a reason they were my favorites. Tai and Jiyi were capable of being teasing, bawdy, wicked. Shifting to whatever suited my mood so that I rarely tired of them.

Tai was certainly the most striking of my concubines. They were all selected for their beauty, but he was a natural leader among them. I had seen it from the start. He had tried at times to take command of me as well, but that was when I'd put him in his place. We had an understanding, but at times like these, when he looked at me with such fierce hunger in his eyes, I knew he would always push at those boundaries. My heart pounded as I waited for him to approach. I loved the element of danger he provided, though I knew in the end he was completely mine.

Jiyi was different. He was honey-tongued in every way, able to gauge my moods and soothe away dark thoughts with clever words and good humor. His hands were equally skilled at discovering the hidden and secret nuances of my body. He could send me to heaven within minutes with his mouth, licking and sucking until I begged for more. Then he'd hold me afterwards and shower me with pretty words, making me smile, making me laugh.

I'd missed them, I admitted defiantly. For the last week I'd allowed myself to become fixated on one man, giving him all my attention. I knew that was a seed for disaster.

Jiyi unlaced my bodice and removed it, leaving me completely naked. Then he moved behind me to cup both my breasts in his hands. Not willing to be left out, Tai climbed onto the bed as well, closing his large hands around my ankles; another possessive gesture.

I shot him a look and Tai immediately loosened his grip. I was not in the mood to be tested this morning. The insolent aristocrat sleeping in the next chamber had tested my patience all week and I was spent.

"He's been pining for you," Jiyi confided, fondling my breasts in a way that had me melting back against him. He tossed Tai a sly look and then bent to speak low in my ear. "He kept on calling out your name while climaxing. I would have scolded him, were my mouth not occupied."

I laughed and Jiyi joined his deeper voice with mine, gathering me close as we shared in the jest. Even the fire in Tai's expression tempered, becoming warm as he stroked his hands up my legs to bring him closer to both of us. They were my chosen concubines, my slaves, but I cared for them. I believed they cared for me as well. Perhaps it was merely a pretty fantasy, but what was all of life if not a dream?

Perhaps it was the laughter that roused Yuan from his bed. He appeared through the curtain a moment later, still dressed in his sleeping clothes, to see me completely naked in the embrace of two men.

Something curled tight within me at the sight of him. His eyes locked onto mine and my heart hammered within my chest. What was this hold he had over me?

The smile faded from my lips and Tai detected the change in me. He looked over his shoulder and immediately his spine straightened. He shifted positions to rearrange himself by my side as he faced off against Yuan.

"Princess Shanyin," Yuan greeted me as if the other two weren't there.

Lazily, Tai draped an arm over my knee and ran his fingers lightly along the inside of my thigh, stopping just shy of my sex. All the while he kept his gaze on his rival. I permitted the small power play and was glad I did when I saw how Yuan's pupils darkened.

Yuan had seen me like this before, laid out between two men as they pleasured me to my climax. I felt no shame then and I refused to feel it now, but deep down, my body still wanted it to be him here with me. Him above all others.

I didn't know if it was the novelty or the challenge of it that excited me. I just knew my flesh longed for his and there was no sense to it.

I will never give in to you. His declaration rung in my ears.

I will never give in…

"Come here."

My throat was dry as I rasped out the command, then held my breath. I had never issued an order I wasn't certain would be obeyed. There was no reason for Yuan to comply; he could simply turn his back and walk away and I would be left, grasping and weak. Tai and Jiyi would be there to witness my defeat. I had given Yuan power over me with that single entreaty.

"Maybe he has never been with a man before," Jiyi offered, amused. I gave him a pinch for it and he grinned, working my nipple between his fingers in return. It hardened to a peak while my skin flushed pink. Yuan watched every exchange, his expression darkening.

I was convinced he would turn on his heel in disgust, but instead he took a step toward the bed. One and then another, slow, but purposeful.

What he did next made my heart stop. I had to be dreaming.

Yuan paused by the edge of the canopy to remove his clothing, letting his tunic drop to the floor and the trousers along with it. When he climbed onto the bed, my sex flooded. Every muscle in my body weakened with desire. Jiyi could feel my response as my flesh grew lush and warm in his embrace. Tai looked at my face before leaning toward me.

He wanted to kiss me. Or rather, he wanted Yuan to see him kissing me. I wouldn't allow it. No man would make a pawn of me.

Breaking away from Jiyi and Tai, I reached for Yuan and pulled him into my arms. The other two still surrounded us as I pressed my lips against his, slipping my tongue into his mouth, my hand into his hair to hold him where I wanted him.

Yuan was hesitant at first. I could taste it in his kiss, but that soon changed. His tongue slid against mine and his breath became my breath. He started to lower me to the bed, but even while my heart pounded and my blood burned for him, I knew he didn't mean to give me what I needed. This was just another show of his resistance—he could endure whatever torment I could devise.

I turned in his arms so that my back was pressed to his chest, my head tilting up and resting against his shoulder. I could see his face from this angle and he could see mine. I could see from the torment in his eyes that I was right. Nothing had changed.

It didn't matter. I had my lovers here to satisfy my every need. I nodded toward Jiyi and he moved between my legs, parting my thighs with gentle hands.

Yuan's hands curved around my waist. I could feel their hot imprint on my skin as he spoke. "Send them away," he said roughly, almost pleading. "You don't need them."

Beside us, Tai made a derisive noise. Even Jiyi circled his thumb against the inside of my thigh, stimulating the pulse point and reminding me of all he could do for me.

"Liar," I told Yuan with a shudder. "You'll only tease me again."

Right then, Jiyi closed his hot mouth over my sex and my back arched involuntarily, my hips pushing against his tongue. He used it like a calligraphy brush, swirling the firm, wet tip of it in luscious and practiced strokes over my folds. I closed my eyes to yield to the pleasure of it.

Yuan's hands tightened on my hips. I knew he had a full view of what Jiyi was doing to me. He could feel my response as every part of me quivered and tensed. And all three could hear me, moaning.

"*Darling*," I murmured. "Yes."

Jiyi rewarded me with a series of soft, slow licks that made me want to weep. At the same time, it was Yuan who was holding me. It was the earthiness of his skin that I smelled and his cock growing to push against the cleft of my buttocks. In a wicked and perverse union, my mind combined them together into one being, created only for me.

Yuan's breathing deepened and he dragged me harder against his body. For a moment, there was a contest of wills. Yuan gripped me tight around my waist while Jiyi moved his hands onto my hips to steady me for his mouth. Ever the peacemaker, Jiyi let his hand wander upward, stroking over Yuan's forearm in invitation.

The aristocrat froze and Jiyi withdrew, though his tongue never stopped working my slit in this most intimate of kisses.

"Darling, if you don't stop, I'll come too fast," I warned, running my hands through Jiyi's thick hair as the pleasure rose higher inside me.

"Then I'll take the time to bring you back once more." His lips brushed my flesh as he spoke, making me shudder. His tongue found the soft pearl hidden in the folds and fluttered over it.

"Yes. Oh heavens, yes. *Right there.*"

I opened my eyes to see Yuan staring at the other man between my legs. His chest pumped up and down rapidly. The lost look in his eyes sent me over the edge and my climax came crashing into me.

Yuan held onto me, absorbing each shudder into his own body as his hard cock throbbed against my lower back, trapped and denied.

"It feels so wonderful," I whispered to Jiyi, to Yuan. Perhaps to the heavens.

Jiyi planted a kiss against my sex while his hands kneaded my thighs lovingly. My sweet slave. But then I felt him leaving me. Tai moved to take his place between my legs. He held his erect member in one hand. It was thick with a broad head, dark with arousal and ridged with veins.

I shook my head while my hips churned restlessly. I hadn't yet come down from my first release and I knew my sex would be swollen, too tight. But Tai paid no heed to me. He knew what this would do to me. And how I liked it when he was a little cruel.

With one hand braced against my shoulder, Tai knelt between my legs. Between Yuan's legs as well as he was mirroring my pose, his legs providing a brace for mine. Tai paused with his organ pressed to my slit. I could barely breathe, waiting for the moment the thick head would breach me.

Then with one smooth thrust of his hips, he drove into me, not stopping when I cried out or when my hands reached out to push against his chest. It was reflex only. My body wanted this invasion, even as a sob broke past my lips.

"Princess?" Yuan's voice was tight with concern. He'd removed his hands from my waist and instead settled onto my shoulders, preparing to defend me, of all things.

"It's good," I moaned brokenly. "So good."

Nothing felt like being filled by a man. And no two men were alike in this. It wasn't just the length and breadth of his cock, but so many things. His weight upon me, the sweat and salt of his skin. His smell. His taste. I'd wanted to know Yuan this way, but this half-measure was all I could have.

I dragged Yuan down to me as Tai began to pump in and out of me in small strokes.

"This is you," I told Yuan in a whisper. I could have the fantasy if I couldn't have him. "I can feel you inside me."

I kissed him, letting the taste of him take over my senses. Yuan returned the kiss hungrily and my flesh closed tight and wet around the cock that penetrated me. I imagined that it was Yuan there, driving himself into me, desiring me too much to stop himself.

Distantly, I could hear Tai groaning, the force of his

thrusts increasing, but I pushed those details aside.

It was perverse and cruel to dismiss him so, but I forgot all that as my climax roared through me, harder and faster than anything I'd ever felt. I drowned in the madness of it, lost.

When I came to my senses, Yuan was no longer kissing me. His body had grown rigid, his grip tight as he fought against himself.

"Leave me, darlings," I said, keeping my eyes shut.

I had meant the command for Tai and Jiyi, but Yuan untangled his limbs from mine and retreated as well. I let him go, my body weeping silently over the loss of his warmth. I lay on my bed and listened to the pulse of my own heartbeat as it gradually quieted until there was nothing left but silence.

Late that night, I was called once again to my brother's palace.

"I saw her," he cried the moment I entered his chamber. His robe was a shambles and his hair wild about his face. One of his concubines cowered in the corner, but she appeared unharmed as far as I could see. I looked to the servants who hovered nearby for some answer, but they were all staring wide-eyed and mute.

"Who did you see?" I asked firmly. When he didn't answer, I took hold of his chin, forcing him to look at me. "Ziye, who did you see?"

"In my dreams!" he blurted out. "She was wearing white. So pale. She said I was wicked and would be dead by the next harvest."

My brother had been afraid of ghosts since he was a boy. He'd seen them in every shadow and cold breeze while I had chased them away for him. But there was no consoling him tonight. Delirious, he called for incense, for talismans. He had a sorcerer and a monk both summoned. He was the Emperor and all we could do was indulge him.

"Light every lantern in the palace," he commanded while we waited for the first orders to be carried out.

I managed to calm him down enough for him to explain how he'd seen our deceased aunt appear before him, the one he'd beheaded because she'd refused to lie down and be violated for his amusement.

"She claimed her death was wrongful, but it was my every right," he insisted. "I am the Son of Heaven."

Yet he wore his guilt plainly on his face. He was ragged with dark circles beneath his eyes. Every noise made him jump.

"In dreams the boundary between the afterlife and our world is thin," he said desperately. "In dreams there are no guards to stop the spirits from coming for me."

By the time the shaman arrived, there was incense burning throughout the room. He chanted and waved his staff while my brother bowed before him, head to the ground. Then he spoke of how our aunt's soul had suffered an injustice and now wandered as a hungry ghost.

"You must appease her with offerings," the sorcerer counseled.

Ziye promised he would. He had an altar set up in the Bamboo Hall that night.

I had more sleeping elixir brought to my brother, this time adding a dose of opium. Ziye finally fell asleep with all the lanterns burning and Bataar stationed immediately beside his bed. The smell of camphor from the burning incense clogged the air.

With a heavy heart, I made the journey back to the East Palace. Once we left the lanterns of the main palace, there was nothing but darkness surrounding the litter. As the carriers made the last turn toward my residence, I thought of my brother and of Yuan. Only a few days ago, I had feared losing one and yearned hopelessly to possess the other.

I was only now realizing that they were both already gone.

CHAPTER NINE

When Yuan came to me midway through the next morning, I made a show of being absorbed in the letters I was writing. He stood there before the desk waiting patiently, or perhaps impatiently, I didn't know. I stared at my brush as I wrote in bold, black strokes of ink.

Had he looked over my shoulder, he would have seen the characters were nonsense. He would have seen my hand was trembling.

"Princess."

He was the first to breach the silence and I looked up to see the scroll in his hands. A heaviness settled onto my shoulders, sinking me into the floor. Let this happen quickly, I begged the heavens.

Finally, I centered my gaze onto his face. An overwhelming sense of longing swept through me. He was beautiful. As beautiful and proud as the first day I'd seen him. My heart had insisted then that he had to be mine. No other conquest was as important as this one.

It was wrong to be so obsessed with a man. This blind desire for Yuan had made me weak. He was just a man: strong shoulders, two arms, two legs. A cock hanging between them; soft or hard, depending on the circumstances.

"Why am I being banished?" he demanded, his anger barely controlled.

My stomach fluttered. I liked him angry.

Slowly, I set my brush onto the holder. "I thought you would be happy," I drawled. "I'm releasing you from my service two days early."

His jaw clenched tight. "So this is punishment."

"I tire of you. I tire of the sight of you. The thought of happening upon you in my brother's court sickens me."

My knees nearly buckled from weakness when I stood from the desk. I had to steady myself with a deep breath. In this act, I had declared myself the victor in our game. He would not be given the opportunity to refuse me and serve out his ten days. I would walk away from Yuan. I would prevail.

"The decree is clear, is it not?" I said. "You are to leave today from the capital. It was courteous of you to stop by to say farewell, but unnecessary. Be gone with you now."

With a bored expression, I retreated toward the back of the room. I could hear Yuan's strident footsteps behind me and my heart started pounding. He was upon me before I could reach the curtain.

Taking hold of me, he pressed me against a column. I could feel his chest at my back. "All of this because I wouldn't give in to your demands?"

His voice was low and dangerous in my ear. My sex flooded with wetness, but I braced my hands flat against the wood and refused to turn around. All I could think of was how he'd kissed me so hungrily the last time we were together. His erection had stabbed hard against my back as I climaxed.

When I didn't answer, I felt him tugging my skirt up. His hand stole between my legs, his fingers slipping immediately into the damp folds of my sex. My breath rushed out of me in a gasp. I closed my eyes and laid my head against the column as he rubbed roughly back and forth, drenching his fingers with my wetness.

There was no denying my body still wanted him, but I couldn't allow myself to hope he'd give in now. He'd played me long enough.

"Rescind the decree," he demanded, pressing the scroll

cruelly against my cheek. Down below, he tweaked my bud between his thumb and forefinger. The effect was devastating and I couldn't hold back the sob that escaped my lips.

"It's too late," I whispered, trembling.

I would not give in. Even as pleasure radiated through me, weakening my body, my resolve remained strong.

Then Yuan did something unexpected. The hand between my legs became gentle, sliding in soothing strokes over the tortured flesh. My heart beat out of my chest as he let the scroll fall to the floor. That left both his arms free and he placed his other hand beside mine on the column. He leaned in and his body curved over mine. Warm breath fanned against my cheek.

"There is one way," he suggested in a sensual tone that sent shivers down my spine. "You can leave as well."

I stared at our hands laid side by side, struck dumb by his suggestion. "With you?" I asked breathlessly.

Below, his fingers worked delicately over my sex, stroking and slipping just inside my folds. "Leave the palace and leave Princess Shanyin behind. Then you can have me in every way."

He penetrated me with one long finger then to emphasize his point. I wanted to laugh at him that he thought his body could be worth so much, but the thrust of his finger inside me awakened an all too familiar yearning. With a sigh, I let him continue.

"What would I be, your wife?" I shouldn't have even asked that question. It gave him too much power.

Yuan's hand stilled between my legs. "That isn't possible."

I swung around and his fingers slid out of me. "You would have me give away my royal position, and not even for the meager protection of your name?"

Yuan remained close and unwavering, trapping me against the column in a near embrace.

"The very thing that you believe protects you, endangers you," he warned.

"I see. You have to cast yourself in the role of my savior in order to fuck me. How tiresome."

My sharp words failed to wound him. Instead his face softened as he regarded me. "I didn't want to care for you."

The ache in my heart was too much for me to bear. How much did he know of my brother's atrocities? Of how volatile the Emperor had become?

"I know being princess puts me in danger," I replied quietly. "I've been in danger all my life."

"But you can escape. You gave Sparrow a choice. Now you can make that choice for yourself."

"Little Sparrow?" I was surprised he even remembered my brother's pitiful concubine.

I had sent the girl to a monastery so she could escape my brother's cruelty, but there was no such escape for me. What did Yuan expect me to do, leave the palace and shave my head? Live the rest of my life in self-denial? I was stupid to have wavered, even for a second.

"I am Princess Shanyin and always will be." I tilted my chin up to meet his eyes squarely. "And you have been ordered to leave the capital."

He held my gaze for a long time, leaning close. For a moment, I thought he would kiss me, but he straightened.

"Farewell, Princess," he said softly.

My chest hitched. I was only imagining the tender look in his eyes.

"This is the last I will ever see of you," I told him without a hint of emotion.

That was how I ended our nine-day dance of seduction. With Yuan walking away while I watched him go.

My spies reported to me immediately after Yuan left the

capital city that same day. He was accompanied by an entourage of servants with all his belongings packed into trunks. I'd found another appointment for him near the coast. I imagined it would be beautiful there with the ocean spread out before him. Maybe he would even think of me during the long journey.

As soon as I was certain Yuan was gone, a sense of emptiness overwhelmed me. I took out the bamboo brush that I'd kept hidden in my sleeve and ran it gently over the inside of my wrist, feeling tears gather at the corners of my eyes.

It was the fine-haired brush Yuan had tormented me with that day at the hot springs. I'd saved it, secretly hiding it in my robe. I imagined his bold hand wielding the instrument now. Teasing me until I wept with frustrated pleasure.

My thoughts were interrupted by a visitor. It was my brother's personal bodyguard, Bataar. He bowed when brought before me and regarded me gravely with his one good eye.

"You told me to inform you, Princess, if there was any more trouble."

At his words, my heart sank. I followed Bataar out to the wagon he'd driven from the palace. There was a single trunk in the back. The kind used to store clothes. Even though he didn't want to obey, I commanded the bodyguard to open it.

A woman's body had been shoved inside, curled up tight. I imagined she was one of my brother's servants or concubines.

"Close it," I said quickly. Bile rose in my throat.

Bataar did as I asked and helped me down from the wagon. "The Emperor strangled her because she resembled the other woman he had put to death," he explained. "Then he told me to get rid of the body."

It would have been pointless to protest that the woman hadn't resembled our aunt in the least. Maybe we were all starting to look alike to my brother.

"Bury her properly," I told Bataar. He bowed again and left to do my bidding.

That night my brother asked me to stay in the imperial quarters with him. He was pale and shaken. I took one of the rooms adjacent to his bedchamber and was woken up in the middle night by his screams.

"She's back! I see her. *I see her.*"

I bypassed the sleeping elixir and gave him opium tea directly. He required two doses before he would calm down enough to sleep. Afterward I lay awake in my bed, shivering even though the night was warm.

Did Yuan truly think I didn't know how dangerous my brother was? With one wild impulse, Ziye could have me beheaded and then weep over my lifeless body afterward. But if I abandoned him, no one would remain to control his murderous whims.

The high-ranking eunuchs didn't care. As long as a weak Emperor sat on the throne, they could do as they pleased. The powerful ministers of the court all feared being the first to be made an example of. Why risk their positions for the lives of a few pitiful concubines and palace women?

Yuan would never know the real reason I'd sent him from the palace. My brother was becoming angry, jealous and violent. Of all my lovers, there was only one he knew by name. And Ziye had already accused me of wanting to run away with Yuan.

If I had gone with him today, the Emperor would have found us. He would cut off Yuan's organ and feed it to wild dogs while Yuan bled to death.

Let Yuan believe I'd exiled him as punishment for refusing me. Men were nearsighted by nature, cursed to only see one side of every story.

CHAPTER TEN

The next morning, Ziye gathered three hundred of his palace women all dressed in white to congregate in the Bamboo Hall. I walked beside him as the procession traveled through the imperial park. The atmosphere was solemn. Not a single word was spoken the entire way.

The white robe I wore reminded me of a mourning garment. The last time I'd dressed in white was for my father's funeral. Ziye had been crowned Emperor shortly after. Had it only been a year ago?

Four shamans were waiting for us inside the building. Ziye had decided one was not enough; he required four. They each wore ritual headdresses and strange clothing with almost a tribal appearance. Together, they chanted a wailing tune that hurt my ears.

Ziye fell to his knees before them and the rest of the procession did the same. The vast hall fit all three hundred of us with room to spare. My brother had ordered his guards to stand back and remain outside. He feared the swords would anger the ghosts—as if his very presence wouldn't upset them.

I bit my tongue and kept all my thoughts to myself. I hoped these shamans were skilled enough to make Ziye believe.

"There are ghosts in this hall!" one shaman proclaimed in a singsong voice. The others echoed his cry. *Ghosts in this hall.*

"We will banish them today so they will no longer haunt the earth."

There was the clang of cymbals and the beat of drums. The

head shaman presented a bow and four arrows to my brother. He was to shoot the ghosts, one in each corner of the hall, and then music would be played to clear out the spirits.

Ziye stood and I could see his hands were shaking as he took the bow. His face was pale and drawn and there were deep circles beneath his eyes. With one look at me, he moved to the center of the room. The shaman pointed to one corner of the room while he chanted away and my brother pulled back the bow and fired the first arrow. Then the shaman repeated the process in the next corner and the next.

With each arrow, my brother seemed to strengthen. He no longer trembled as he aimed the last arrow into the corner. It occurred to me then that Ziye needed to be afraid of something to keep him contained. Maybe this ghost-catching ritual wasn't a good thing.

As the last arrow flew, one of the woman broke away from the sea of white and ran toward Ziye. That was when I realized it wasn't a woman, but a man. One of Ziye's closest retainers. He dragged a dagger out of his robe.

The bodyguards were all outside.

Ziye tried to run. The palace women all scattered, but I was still kneeling on the floor. My limbs wouldn't move.

I watched as the assailant caught up with my brother and thrust the dagger into his chest. The hand holding the blade withdrew and thrust again. My brother slumped over, the front of his white robe stained with blood. The palace women swarmed all around me like a flight of cranes.

White on white on white, then red.

I rose to my feet, my head spinning. My brother's gaze roamed through the crowd until he found me. His eyes were impossibly wide as he stretched out his hand. That was his final expression and his last act. Looking at me, pleading with me for something as he died. Whatever it was, I would never know.

Did we not always say our fates were linked, you and I?

Armed men finally entered the hall, but I realized they weren't my brother's bodyguards. It was Bataar who grabbed me. The sight of his ragged face brought me back to my senses; he was easily recognizable.

"Rebels," he told me. "It's an uprising."

Throughout the hall there was shouting, running, confusion, blood. The imperial guards had stormed inside as well as rebel fighters. I didn't know who was on what side. It looked as if everyone was striking out at everyone else. Women in white lay crumpled to the floor.

There were ghosts in this hall. More ghosts by the moment.

"The Emperor is dead," I told Bataar listlessly, my voice floating in from far away.

He stared at me with his one eye. The clouded one seemed to look past me.

"You must come with me now, Princess." He drew his broadsword and took me by the arm. "This will only get worse."

A rebel faction was gathered outside of the Bamboo Hall, but Bataar and the other bodyguards fought through them. Blood splattered over his uniform and onto me as well as he swung his sword with one arm and dragged me forward with the other.

When we were free of the imperial park I saw fighting had broken out in the palace. I heard the name Liu Yu spoken over and over. One of the uncles in cages, who I had insisted Ziye free.

"Take me to the East Palace," I told Bataar.

"Princess—"

"Do it," I commanded gently.

Bataar cleared the way for me to return to my residence

while the other bodyguards joined up with the palace guards. Their loyalty was to the Emperor, not to me.

I had survived more than one palace coup and I knew what came in the aftermath. Perhaps this was why I found myself so eerily calm while the world burned around me. I could tell that news had reached the East Palace because the servants were frantic when I arrived. Everyone started asking me questions all at once: "What do we do? What do we do?"

"Leave now. Run away," I said, partly because it was likely their only chance of escaping, but also because I couldn't stand their wailing any longer.

I opened all my coffers and spilled my jewels onto the floor of my quarters. "Take it all. Bribe anyone you can to get free."

The maidservants wept. Some of them didn't want to leave and huddled in their rooms. Others filled their skirts with jewels and fled.

"You should escape now as well, Princess." Bataar's rough voice startled me as I stood alone in my dressing room. "While the imperial guard are still fighting."

I smiled sadly at him and shook my head. "There will be no escape for me."

Retainers had already assassinated the cruel and vindictive Emperor. His depraved and immoral sister was soon to follow. This was how old regimes were toppled and new ones propped up. I had seen this happen again and again.

"Do not lose heart, Princess. We may be able to regain control."

Who would have thought that this fearsome beast of a man would harbor such an optimistic soul? Again I shook my head. "It won't happen."

No one would stand up to rally the imperial forces in the wake of my brother's death. Ziye had left no sons behind and his closest adviser had been myself, a more unsuitable ruler than he was. This was the end of our line.

"Then if the princess would accept my service. I would swear my loyalty to her until my very last breath."

The warrior sank to one knee, head lowered. He had been my brother's servant, not mine, yet here he was pledging undying loyalty to me in my final hour. I couldn't help but be touched.

"Allow this servant the privilege of dying in your defense," Bataar requested. I hesitated before reaching out to touch his shoulder.

"That privilege should be ours."

It was Tai who spoke. He came into the parlor with a trail of men behind him. A fist closed painfully around my heart when I saw that they were all assembled together; all thirty of my beautiful lovers.

"Please go, all of you," I implored. "Escape now while you can. I don't want to have your deaths on my soul."

I turned away, unable to look at them. So much beauty wasted. My eyes stung and I couldn't bear for them to see my tears.

At first, no one would leave me. But as news of the rebellion became worse, they began to depart in twos and threes. I wished them all peace and hoped that at least a few of them would survive. I really did care for them—it was hard not to when they had been dedicated to the singular task of pleasing me.

Tai and Jiyi were the last to remain. Bataar had departed with the last set. He was a warrior who deserved to die fighting.

"Go," I commanded my two favorites gently. "Promise me you'll survive and find a pair of pretty and innocent girls to seduce into a blissful marriage."

"But Princess, how can we leave you?" Jiyi's eyes were filled with tears.

"We will stay with you until the end," Tai insisted.

I went to them, kissing each of them tenderly on the lips. "You've given me such great joy. Please leave me to make my own peace with my ancestors. This is my final wish."

It might seem like I was being kind and selfless, but that wasn't true. I couldn't bear having to witness their deaths while I was preparing to meet mine.

They finally turned to go, walking side by side, and I was left alone in the eerie silence of my palace where I had indulged in every earthly pleasure I knew. The only decision that remained was where I would be found when the rebellion came for me.

I considered lying down on my legendary bed, but I didn't wish to sully the good memories I had of it now that my harem was gone. Instead, I went to my flower garden to sit among the blooms and let their perfume surround me.

There are only a few ways a woman can be remembered. History might have immortalized me as a pawn, or a victim. A poor unfortunate princess who was brutalized by the whims of more powerful men. I chose instead to be remembered as a woman of pleasure whose lust knew no bounds. These scars on my back, the nameless men who took me to their beds—it was all by my design, for my own enjoyment. That was how I chose to remember it. This was how I mastered my nightmares.

I would not be haunted by the past. There were no such things as ghosts.

In the end it wasn't men with swords who came for me. Only one lone figure entered the garden and as soon as I saw him, I had all the answers I had been missing.

Yuan came to stand before me while I sat surrounded by clusters of jasmine. My heart beat harder in his presence. My skin flushed and came alive. I must have been deranged after all to still respond this way even when I knew the truth.

"You were part of the rebellion all along, weren't you?" I

asked him.

"Yes."

"Is it over yet?"

"It is."

He didn't appear triumphant as he regarded me. As always, his look was one of turmoil.

"My dear Yuan, you should have simply taken me to bed," I chided. "You could have fucked any secret you wanted out of me."

"No, Princess. I couldn't."

The sincerity in his voice tore me in two. The reason for his stalwart refusal had also become clear. Yuan didn't want to make unspoken promises with his body that he would later have to break.

"How wonderfully honorable of you. Let me guess, is Chancellor Wu also part of the rebellion? That was why you were so mortified when he saw me using you to satisfy my lust. And Liu Shang as well as the other uncles, of course."

Yuan remained impervious to my taunting, but there was no need for him to get angry. He'd won.

"They know that you intervened to spare their lives," he said.

"And I'm sure they will now reward me handsomely for it," I replied with a snort.

He came closer until he stood immediately before me, his shadow blocking the setting sun. "You have been accused of immorality and sentenced to commit suicide."

I hated how he spoke without emotion. I hated even more that he brought tears to my eyes. I would have rather had my death proclaimed by someone I cared nothing for.

His speech became less formal, his tone softer. "Allowing you to take your own life seemed preferable to…the other options."

I laughed, feeling madness setting in. "So this is their

kindness. And you're here to ensure the deed is done?"

Finally Yuan appeared regretful, perhaps even sad. "Yes, Princess."

It wasn't as if I could escape. The entire palace had been taken over. Within the day, the imperial court would be swearing loyalty to a new Emperor.

"Is there any final preparation you require?" he asked quietly.

I looked down at my clothes. For the first time, I realized I was still wearing the white robe from the ghost-catching ceremony, but it had been splattered with blood.

"I would like to change clothes."

He nodded solemnly. Together we left the garden to return to my quarters. All of my attendants had fled or were in hiding, so I went to my wardrobe myself. I ended up selecting the same silk robe I'd worn on our trip to the hot springs and wondered if Yuan even remembered. The gold shawl was still missing. Was it still in his possession? Did he inhale my scent while he brought himself to climax?

"All my maidservants are gone," I told him.

Without a word, Yuan moved to help me undress and put on the clean robe. His touch was impersonal, refusing to linger. His eyes avoided mine.

Even now, he denied me and left me wanting, though I was no longer seeking sexual release. All I wanted was a kind look or a soft touch. I knew I was undeserving, but I was still greedy.

When we returned to the sitting room, a messenger stood there with a tray in hand. A single cup of tea sat on the tray. I didn't have to ask what was in it.

Yuan gestured for the poison to be left upon the table. The messenger disappeared promptly and we were alone once more. There was no need to draw out the inevitable any longer.

"Will you stay until I'm sleeping?" I asked him. When in our brief time together had I ever requested anything of him?

At first Yuan didn't answer. He looked at me the same way he had when he'd said farewell—was that only a day ago? His look was soft, almost tender. "I will, Princess," he said finally, his voice rough with emotion.

"Once I'm gone, will you make sure no one is allowed to cut up my body? Or…or my face?" My voice was so small it was barely there.

"I won't let anyone touch you," he vowed. Then he added, very gently. "I never knew you to be so vain."

I tried to smile. "You called me beautiful once."

All of a sudden, his arms were around me, warm and secure. His mouth found mine and for the first time he kissed me passionately, without reservation. My knees weakened and I sagged against him, returning his kiss with my entire being.

He didn't take me to my bed; to the place where so many other men had served and pleasured me. Instead he lowered me right there onto the floor while I tore at his clothes. Before long, there was a pile of silk surrounding us and his hand was cupped between my legs. I bit into my lower lip to keep from moaning as he eased a finger inside me.

I had to be perverse to already be so aroused, even now at the brink of death. Especially now, but I was. Every nerve in my body was crying out for one more climax, one more perfect moment. And I had waited so long for Yuan, wondering how he would feel when we were joined together.

Reaching up, I wrapped my hand around his cock and watched his face as I stroked him from base to tip.

"I thought about you every night," he groaned. "Every night I spilled desperately into my hand, dreaming of you." He closed his eyes as I worked his shaft. "You weaken me," he muttered. "You weaken me, you weaken me."

We didn't bother with any preliminaries. The last nine

days had been foreplay and our patience was spent. Yuan shoved my hand aside and entered me in one long, endless penetration that left me breathless. I closed my eyes to shut out everything but him. He thrust again and my body squeezed tight around him to hold on to the sensation. I knew it would be this good. Oh heaven, I knew.

In three hard thrusts, he had me coming with stars in my eyes. My back arched so forcefully that I thought I would snap in two.

My only regret was that it had happened so fast when I wanted so much for it to last. As I came back to my senses, I realized Yuan was still hard inside me. He withdrew and I moaned as he pulled out, my body sensitive in the aftermath.

Before I could catch my breath, he flipped me over. With my hands braced against the floor, he lifted my hips and entered me from behind, his cock piercing me from a different angle. I cried out, overwhelmed with what he was doing to me. Each thrust brought me to a new height and soon I was close again.

How could this be? How could I reach orgasm so readily when I knew it would be my last?

I didn't have time for such worthless questions. All I had time for was this. Pleasure had always been my escape. I swam in it now. My time was measured and this was the last memory I wanted to take with me to the afterlife. Not regret or sadness or anguish over the cruelty of fate. I wanted to remember the warmth of Yuan's skin and the indescribable feeling of him deep inside me, fucking, fucking, fucking me into oblivion.

When he first entered me from this position I thought he was avoiding having to look me in the eye, knowing what would have to happen afterward. But that wasn't it. He shortened his movements until they became a second heartbeat, pulsing in and out of me. Then he lowered himself and I could feel his lips pressing against the scars on my back, one after another.

"Please come now," I urged. "Come inside me."

A moment later, he did, spilling his essence deep against my womb as I joined him in a climax that started in my sex but radiated out until my whole body shook and spasmed.

Afterward, the sound of our breathing combined in an uneven cadence and his weight grew heavy over me as we both sagged into the floor. I thought it was done until his hand closed over mine.

"It has to be this way," he said regretfully.

I closed my eyes. "I know."

He wasn't betraying my trust. I had known what would happen, but I wanted him anyway.

Yuan rolled over on his back and I crawled over to curl myself against his side and lay my head on his chest. For a few precious moments, I listened to the sound of his heartbeat.

There was no better time than now, while my body was sated and warm from our lovemaking. I could wait and cling onto every last breath, but for what purpose? That would only give time for regret to sink in.

I rose from the floor and stood, looking down at Yuan. He propped himself up on one arm to watch me. I appreciated how he was put together in clean lines and hard shapes. For the last ten days, I had obsessed about possessing him and now I had, in the most bittersweet of ways. Perhaps I had known Ziye's tyranny would have to come to an end. I wanted to seek my own selfish pleasure until my last breath.

With that one final look enclosed in my heart, I went to the table and picked up the cup. By now, the tea was cold. I lifted it and took the poison into myself the same way I'd approached life: swallowing it whole without looking back.

There was sweetness on top of the bitterness. Someone had laced the brew with honey, a small kindness. It made me smile.

I returned to Yuan's arms then and he accepted me, holding me tight and stroking my hair. Sleep came quickly after that and I didn't try to fight it.

"I'm glad you're here with me," I told him, my words starting to slur together.

"I insisted. I wouldn't leave you to anyone else."

Closing my eyes, I snuggled into him. I willed myself to believe that I really was only falling asleep so I could go without fear. Yuan would be waiting there for me when I woke up and, because there would be no one to tell me otherwise, I convinced myself that he really did love me, just a little bit.

EPILOGUE

In the afterlife, I saw my brother. Ziye was wandering around in an endless gray. I could hear the mumble of voices all around us but I saw no one else. He was still wearing the white robe with a bloodstain at his chest where the dagger had struck. His face was pale and gaunt.

"I'm hungry," he told me.

I looked around, but there was no food. There was nothing. Our family had fostered a tradition of killing one another and there was no one left to light incense or honor us with offerings of rice and fruit. Such was the fate of those poor souls who died without any offspring. Who had been disowned by our families. We were left to wander forever as hungry ghosts.

"I'm hungry," he repeated, his voice sounding hollow and lost. "I'm hungry."

There was nothing I could do for my brother. Desperately, I reached into my chest and pulled out my own heart, still beating faintly, and fed it to him.

Light came in flashes, hurting my eyes. I squinted against it, finally forcing my lids open enough to see something besides gray.

I was wrapped in a large blanket or bolt of cloth. There was a cover over my head and I pulled it away, catching a glimpse of trees overhead and a wagon around me before the cover was yanked back in place.

"Princess, we're still in danger. You can't be seen," a voice whispered.

I thought I knew that voice, but I couldn't identify it through the fog in my head.

As the wagon rolled on, I began to piece things together. I was still alive. There were two men in the wagon with me, one in the driver's seat and another beside me. I wasn't bound, but I could barely move. My limbs were stiff and my stomach rolled as if I were going to be sick.

"It's Jiyi," the voice beside me whispered and my heart nearly burst with joy.

A long time later, the wagon stopped and Jiyi unwound me from the bundle of silk I'd been hidden inside. I had figured out who his companion must be. Tai unhitched the horses and tethered them while Jiyi tended to the fire.

"I told you to leave me," I scolded them as I climbed down from the wagon.

Tai flashed me a crooked smile, cutting through the weariness on his face. "The princess likes me best when I disobey."

I had so many questions to ask them, but all the emotions I'd been holding back flooded into me all at once. I bent over, sobbing with my arms wrapped around myself. I was alive and Yuan…Yuan hadn't sent me to my death after all. The tea had contained a strong sedative rather than poison. Yet he'd played a cruel trick on me by not telling me.

Despite only having spent ten days with Yuan, I understood him so well now. He wanted me to suffer at least the fear of death. There were consequences to my pleasure-seeking, to my selfish neglect of right and wrong. I knew then that he truly did hate me. But that he loved me as well.

"Princess?" Jiyi addressed me tentatively.

I raised my head to see the two of them looking at me, uncertain what to do. They'd never seen me crying before.

"I'm no longer your princess," I corrected, wiping my eyes.

Princess Shanyin was dead. The only life I'd known was gone and I had no sense of who I was or what my life would be like from here. With a deep breath, I took a step toward my two former concubines to discover what this new existence would be.

Book 2: The Enslavement

CHAPTER ONE

I didn't know how much time had passed since I was smuggled out of the palace. My brother was dead, assassinated, and I should be dead as well. Vaguely, I knew that a new Emperor was on the throne and that we had fled away from the unrest of the capital.

For a long time, the days blurred together and I had little awareness of why I was doing the things I did. Even now while I held a needle and thread in hand, sewing two torn edges of fabric together, I didn't know why it had to be done other than it was something to keep my hands busy, to pass the emptiness of the hours.

When I was living in the palace as imperial princess, these answers had come easily. All my needs were taken care of with me blissfully ignorant of the practical details. I simply did whatever caught my whim. I sought out every sordid pleasure I could think of. Anything I wanted was there at my fingertips.

Almost anything. Almost anyone, except Yuan.

The needle wove in and out of the cloth, the silver glint of it catching my eye. I jumped as the point bit into me. Raising my finger to the light, I became transfixed by the perfect drop of blood that formed on the tip. It was a brilliant vermilion, as red as the peonies in my royal garden. Red like the silk banners unfurled on state occasions. Red as the live fire that had consumed our imperial home.

It seemed a lifetime had passed since I had seen such color. I had come from the lushness and grandeur of the palace to this colorless place of browns and grays. My peasant clothing was dyed dark. The walls were bare wood.

The door opened, breaking me out of my trance. Tai Jin leaned against the door frame and regarded me for a drawn-out moment before coming toward me in an unhurried stride.

"Princess," he drawled.

I ducked my head to stare at the garment in my hands. "Don't call me that."

He came to stand before me, swallowing me in his shadow. Tai had always been impossible to ignore, even among a harem of male concubines vying for my attention. He was tall in stature, his shoulders broad. Like all of my concubines he'd been chosen for his attractiveness, but it was more than his strength and beauty that had captivated me. Tai refused to be overlooked.

Tai placed a finger beneath my chin, tilting my head upward. I met his eyes without flinching, though my heart beat faster at the intensity of his gaze.

"What shall I call you then—Shanyin?" His tongue slid sensually over my name. "It sounds so intrusive. So insolent."

It was all insolence. The way he touched me now without my permission. The casual way he ignored my commands. I had let these small liberties slip by in the period after our escape from the palace and there was no taking them back—not without guards and ritual and strict codes of conduct to enforce such order.

Now every exchange was a battle. If I asked him to remove his hand, he could defy me simply by leaving it there. Or if he complied, then I would still have acknowledged his impertinence aloud, giving it life. Instead I stared at him, my eyes locked with his until he removed his touch of his own accord.

His gaze flicked downward. "You're bleeding."

I had forgotten about the needle prick on my finger, but

Tai went onto one knee before me. The action wasn't one of a supplicant. He took hold of me, his thumb secure against my palm, and watched my face while he slid my finger into his mouth and sucked gently. A shudder snaked along my spine. Deep and low in my belly, there was a stirring I hadn't felt in a long time. I snatched my hand away.

He regarded me with an expression that was part amusement and all heat. "How long has it been…Shanyin?"

Everything he was doing—the deliberate pause before my name, his nearness, the shockingly wet caress of his tongue on my skin—turned my insides out, pushing me to somewhere I didn't want to go. My heart was hammering now and my throat so tight I could barely speak.

"Where is Jiyi?" I asked in a voice that was too small.

He was our third, another concubine who had fled with me after the palace coup. In the time since our escape, the three of us had been in near-constant contact. There was no privacy in the small hovel we inhabited.

"Him? I sent him to the market," Tai replied.

I hated how he watched for my every reaction. He had always been that way, but I hadn't taken much note of it when Tai did it for the purpose of knowing what pleased me.

"I've never known you to deny yourself for so long, Princess," he went on. "Never for more than a few nights before summoning one of us. Or two."

Or three. Tai knew, perhaps better than anyone else. He had shared my bed more than any of the others. That intimate knowledge played itself out now in his smile, but his eyes held something decidedly fiercer.

I swallowed at the sudden dryness in my throat. Desperately, I wanted a drink of water, but I would never ask him for it.

"This is not the time," I warned him.

At that, something dark flickered beneath the surface of

his expression. He rose suddenly, taking me up with him. The stool I was sitting on fell aside as I tried to back away, but Tai held me fast. With one arm around my waist, he pressed me against his hard body while his other hand lifted to the back of my head, fisting tight into my hair.

"Are you certain?" he asked in a low growl. Roughly, he pulled my head back, making me gasp. But his next touch was gentle, his lips feathering against my throat. "Are you certain?" he asked again, softer this time. His hand remained clenched in my hair as he kissed my neck.

My emotions were in turmoil even as my skin flushed and warmed to the familiarity of his touch. Tai knew my body. He thought he knew my mind as well, how it liked the occasional rush of fear and daring he provided. But he didn't know me. I was hidden so completely behind a heavy veil of lust and sexual abandon.

This was a frequent game with us, with Tai as my disobediently obedient slave. But he was no longer my servant, I was no longer his mistress and I was racked with confusion. My pulse thundered in my ears and I couldn't think.

"Let me go," I implored, my tone flat. Powerless.

Tai paused for a heartbeat before his grip tightened on me. "Keep saying that," he said into my ear. "Keep saying that the entire time."

He brought me to the sleeping pallet in the corner, pushing me down onto the bamboo mat. It was only marginally padded and I could feel the hard floor against my back as Tai leaned over me. I didn't struggle as he stripped away my clothes, but I didn't help either. Instead, I looked at the light coming in from the window overhead as he pushed aside the linen to leave me naked.

The market was hours away by foot and Jiyi would not be returning any time soon. I was alone with Tai, who I had named for his strength and virility. Despite all the times he'd been in my bed, we had never been alone before. I had never been truly alone in a palace of thousands, with eunuchs and maidservants and guards waiting behind every screen.

I glanced back at Tai as he raised onto his knees. He took time opening his tunic, watching me so he could see in my eyes the knowledge of what was going to happen. Beneath his clothes, his skin was sun-browned from toiling out in the patch of dirt that now provided us with food. Rather than making him appear like a peasant, his bronzed skin gave him a raw, primal look.

When he removed his trousers, he was already aroused. His manhood lifted away from his body, rising to its full length. Tai could see how my breathing had quickened. He likely mistook my reaction as a sign of desire rather than fear. I didn't know myself which one it was.

If I wanted to make any attempt to escape, the time was past. Tai lowered his naked form over me, pinning me from shoulder to hip to thigh. Fear, true fear, rose up from my belly. At the same time, my flesh warmed and molded itself to his body. My pulse skipped frantically.

The sense memory of Tai was strong in me. In my short life thus far, all twenty-four years of it, I had preferred this man over all others except one. But the one...

Yuan. Chu Yuan. His name came to me as sharply as the memory of his hands and his mouth on mine, taking my breath into him as I took his cock into my body. It was the last time I had been with a man. I had been sentenced to death, and the orgasm that thundered through me with that knowledge left me blind in its wake. A devastatingly final taste of life.

Somehow I had cheated death, but I wasn't so sure I had wanted to. I still didn't know.

Tai sensed that my attention had wandered from him and dug his fingers hard into my hip, making me flinch.

"Kiss me," he commanded.

I wouldn't. When he tried to lower his mouth, I turned my head away.

This was a sign for him to do away with any pretense of a slow, skillful seduction. Tai hooked his hand beneath my knee to open me for him. With his other hand, he took hold of his member and guided himself to my opening. Then, without any effort to prepare me, he pushed the broad tip inside.

My body braced instinctively against the invasion. Tai had been the most well-endowed of my harem and his cock had given me so many days and nights of pleasure. It was an instrument of pain now, pushing against the tightness of my inner muscles until I gritted my teeth.

Even when I was fully aroused, Tai always stole my breath away when he entered me. That exquisite mixture of pleasure and pain that could only come from one act. But I wasn't prepared for this onslaught and there was only pain.

This was the one way Tai could completely dominate me now that I no longer had the protection of my imperial status. I feared he would continue regardless of my suffering, but he halted. I opened my eyes to see him staring down at me, always watching.

If his expression softened, it was for no more than a second. Then his intense look returned as he began to touch me. Instead of fondling my breasts, he placed his hand between them. For a moment he remained there, as if feeling for the beat of my heart, before massaging me in soothing strokes up over my shoulders and then back down as if he were once more my patient lover, there for my pleasure alone.

His sex remained inside me while his hands explored my body. "So soft," he murmured, pressing a kiss to the curve of my breast.

I didn't know whether it was his sudden tenderness or simply the strength of memory. Or maybe it was merely self-preservation—my body protecting itself against the intrusion—but my flesh dampened around his hard cock, growing slick and wet with a flood of rain.

Tai thrust shallowly, easing himself inside me gradually. And gradually, my tight flesh yielded and formed a seal around him. He groaned and closed his eyes as he moved his hips in one long thrust that brought him fully into me. For a moment, I was filled with a sense of power. I could still bring a man to his knees and it had nothing to do with being imperial princess. It was because I was a woman and he was a man, and the look on his face as he moved in and out of me was one of pure abandon.

My body remembered this rhythm so well even though I had tried to forget. I was immediately caught up in the thrust of his hips; slow and deliberate to stroke the fire. He could continue all day if I wanted him to. I remembered that too.

I still didn't want this…but the truth was most of me didn't care.

And soon, as Tai thrust deeper, I didn't know up from down or yes from no any longer. My body had stopped fighting and my limbs were soft and without any will.

"I waited for you," he said, his voice rough with desire. "Every night…I waited for you to call for me."

He continued to fuck me while he spoke. His eyes were half-closed, absorbing the raw pleasure of flesh against flesh. "'Make me forget,' you would say. And I would have."

With his hands, he spread my legs wider, pushed into me deeper until I could feel nothing but him. I bit my lip to keep from moaning.

"Say it now," he commanded. He reached his hand between us and the tip of his finger brushed over the tiny sensitive bud of my sex.

I shook my head even as pleasure streaked through me, rising from that single point. It had been so long since anyone had touched me like this. The sensation was a hundred times stronger than I ever remembered it being.

He stroked in an endless circle, and a moan escaped my lips. I couldn't help it. Closing my eyes, I arched my back as the pleasure rose in me and consumed me, causing every muscle to tighten in anticipation.

"Say it, Shanyin."

His demand came to me from some far off place. I was spiraling toward climax, floating, letting my mind wander to the last time…the best time…

A sharp tug on my hair brought the pleasure to a cruel halt and my eyes flew open. Tai's gaze bore into me. "Are you thinking of him?" he asked in a low voice.

When I didn't answer immediately, he pulled harder, his hand tightening into a fist in my hair.

"Yes," I gasped.

There was no question who he meant. Tai had been the most favored of my concubines, but there was one man who I had wanted more than anyone. Unlike my slaves, Yuan had refused me and that made me want him even more.

Tai's expression darkened and my heart thudded with fear as well as an echo of desire. For a moment, I'd allowed myself to slip beneath his will. Tai was no longer my servant, taunting and challenging me, but always obedient in the end. He was dangerous now, as dangerous as any man had ever been to me.

His manhood was still embedded deep within my sex. I could feel his body growing rigid with anger and my first instinct was to beg him not to hurt me. But that was never our game…and I didn't know how to beg.

Deliberately, Tai withdrew his hand from me. He resumed his thrusting, slowly and with purpose, with no further attempt to pleasure me. I was relieved—it would end now. Gradually his thrusts increased in intensity. I could see the sheen of sweat gathering over his brow. I could smell his skin, a rich dark scent like the earth.

As his eyes held on to mine in challenge, I suddenly realized I was wrong. He was still intent on fucking me to orgasm. As if he would conquer me in this way.

His hips ground into mine, stirring an unwanted pleasure deep within me. My flesh grew even damper, bathing his organ in fluids. I knew he could continue like this without tiring for hours if he wanted, pushing me to one climax after another. Tai knew my body. Heavens above, he knew what it liked…but he didn't know my mind.

I shook my head sharply at him, fighting against the growing pleasure. It was a small thing to deny him while my sex held the length of him tight, but it became everything. Our battleground.

With a growl, he pushed hard into me. Then harder, yet still I refused him, fighting against my release though my flesh was aching for it. Finally, his entire body clenched tight as he succumbed before I did. His essence pulsed hot into my depths as his thrusts grew weaker, fueled only by the remnants of desire.

He pulled out of me then and rose to his feet. With his climax, Tai's anger seemed to have dissipated. He wore a satisfied expression as he pulled his trousers back on while I sat up to gather the edges of my robe around me, covering my breasts. I had never shown any shame before, but I felt too naked now. My victory, if it was that, had been a thin one.

With a grin, Tai discarded his tunic and picked up the one I had been mending. He put it on and smoothed a hand over his front. "Thank you, Shanyin. It fits perfectly. Just like you."

Jiyi returned to the farming hut later that afternoon. Tai and I were both sitting at the table, occupied with weaving out a new thatch for the roof, when the door opened.

Our other companion had an amiable way about him and an expressive face that easily danced between playful and serene. One look at us and his mouth tightened.

I had run a washcloth over my face and tidied my hair back into a knot, but it didn't matter. Jiyi knew immediately what had happened. He entered the room without greeting us and placed a half-empty sack into the corner. Walking up to us, he took a palmful of coins from his belt and put them on the table, staring at Tai the entire time. Tai met his gaze without flinching and something passed between them.

It was always that way with them, able to speak without speaking. They had both been favored concubines in my harem. I knew little of what happened within those walls, but I'd often summoned them together to my bed. There was a rhythm and an interplay between them that had always excited me, both harmonious and contentious at once.

It didn't excite me now, though my pulse did jump as Jiyi broke his stare with Tai to look to me. "Princess," he greeted with a nod before going to wash his hands.

No one touched the coins on the table. In the tense silence, I grappled with a feeling I'd never experienced before. In the past, I'd enjoyed their bodies, together and individually, without a thought to the other. They were both unquestionably mine.

But now this silence held the sting of betrayal.

Jiyi had his back to us as he stood by the washbasin. He was slightly shorter in stature than Tai, though still tall and lean. My lovers had been selected for their beauty and Jiyi had been my poet, my scholar. At least I imagined him so. But he had no clever words now to ease the rift between us.

We ate our evening meal with little conversation, though the heat building between the two of them became suffocating by the end of it. I wanted to retreat back into the corner, but they wouldn't let me.

Tai caressed his thumb from my wrist down my hand when I left it resting on the table. Pulse racing, I immediately snatched it away and kept it in my lap for the rest of the meal. When we stood at the end, Jiyi placed his hand to the small of my back. The touch wasn't a sexual one, but my skin flushed as my thoughts spun.

They weren't making love to me with these small attentions. It was language between them that I couldn't interpret. The scroll had no knowledge of the ink placed upon it.

Had it always been this way and I had simply been blind to it? All I cared was that they brought me pleasure and fulfilled my every desire. Maybe they hadn't been making love to me even when I'd lain between them. Their hands and mouths on my skin had served a dual purpose.

Yuan had told me once that no man would tolerate his woman with another. I had haughtily disagreed with him. My lovers were my slaves and had no choice, but maybe they had never truly belonged to me. Maybe I had belonged to each of them, broken up into so many pieces I could never find them all again.

"It's time for bed," Jiyi said gently.

I always slept alone on a pallet beneath the window while Jiyi and Tai retreated to the corners. Then darkness would descend and I could be unseen and alone for that space between dusk and dawn. It was all the privacy I could have.

Tonight, I thought they might come to me. Tai had broken through an unspoken boundary when he'd thrust into my body.

I lay on my pallet with my heart beating and my stomach tight, waiting. What would I do if they did seek me out? I didn't seem to have the strength in me to command their obedience as I once did. If I couldn't master them, they would master me.

But they didn't come. I eventually drifted off to sleep and awoke some time later to the sound of voices outside. The stars were visible through the open window above me.

"I didn't plan it that way. You know our princess." Tai, haughty and unperturbed.

"I know you better." Jiyi, hurt and angry. "Maybe I should go away. Leave the two of you to each other."

"With the army still scouring the roads?"

The next part became muted. I rose and peeked out the window and saw the two of them locked together beneath the moonlight. Tai had Jiyi pressed against the wall, caught in a rough kiss. Desire unfurled in my belly at the sight of them; strength against strength cast in dark shadow.

I had always suspected the two of them were lovers, given their ease with each other, but I'd never seen them. In my bed they had always been focused on me. Tai's hand curved around the back of Jiyi's neck in a gesture of dominance I knew well. Jiyi held Tai's face in his hands. It was too dim for me to see either of their expressions, but the push and pull of their bodies revealed the story. There was passion there, anger and torment. I heard Tai moan as the kiss deepened. The low, guttural sound resonated against my spine.

The sight of the two men kissing stirred me in a way Tai's fucking had failed to do earlier. I had felt removed then. Distant. Yet here, as a secret observer, I was strangely more connected.

The Shanyin that I was would have continued to watch without embarrassment, as if these two beautiful creatures were on display for my enjoyment alone. But this was not my palace. They were no longer part of my harem, so I sank back down onto the pallet and closed my eyes.

I couldn't close my ears, however. I listened to the rumble of their voices, rough with passion. In my mind, that one kiss went on forever as two muscular bodies writhed and thrust together, seeking release. Then a grunt, the hiss of a breath expelled, and a strangled sound that could have been either pleasure or pain. Likely both.

Tai and Jiyi were all that was left of the hundreds of slaves and guardsmen and attendants who had served me in the palace when my brother was Emperor. Now everyone who once claimed to be a loyal subject had denounced us or faced execution as traitors. It had been the same way when my brother had first taken the throne.

At least I was finally free of that cycle of power and corruption, of blood and death. I was no one of any importance. No one worth killing or worth dying for. I was nothing.

CHAPTER TWO

We had found the hut abandoned. The small plot of land around it had become overgrown. The former inhabitants were either deceased or had left it. We would never know, but no one came to claim it so we stayed.

There was a lake nearby, hidden behind a line of trees. I sat beside it the next morning with my feet bare in the grass, and looking at the ripple of sunlight on the water for answers.

I knew it was Jiyi who approached from his gait alone. He always moved lightly, easily. Even his touch on my shoulder felt natural. He slid his hand along my arm, his fingers intertwining with mine as he settled down in the grass beside me.

"Princess Shanyin."

The way he said my name was like a warm breeze. "You shouldn't call me that. It's dangerous."

"Then I'll only call you that when we're alone."

He turned to me and smiled. Whereas Tai possessed a rough, rugged handsomeness, Jiyi was classically beautiful. His mouth was subtly curved. His high cheekbones tapered down into a sculpted chin.

"I heard the two of you last night," I said.

For a moment he was taken aback, but then he accepted. It was impossible to hide anything among us while we shared this small square of earth.

"He wants to claim us both, doesn't he?" I stared out to the water once more, feeling Tai's weight over me while my body both fought and yielded to him. "I imagine this is what he's always wanted."

"Tai is different out here. Something changed in him."

I wasn't so certain of that. "You must have all despised me for enslaving you."

Jiyi regarded me with eyebrows raised, then his lips quirked. "There are far less pleasurable forms of enslavement."

"You didn't hate me, even just a little?"

In one smooth motion, Jiyi pulled me closer and rolled me beneath him. His hips set against mine with just enough pressure to anchor me to the grass, but not make me feel trapped.

"Princess," he admonished. "One cannot hate just a little. That is not how hate works."

That teasing smile was still on his lips when he kissed me. The caress of his mouth on mine was warm, sensual and inviting. It was easy to accept. Easy for me to return the kiss.

When he lifted his head, I was breathing hard. Still, I clenched my hand into the front of his robe and dragged him back down. I felt his laughter as our breath mingled. I wanted to swallow it and take it inside.

With Tai, everything was a battle. With Jiyi, every moment felt like a gift. As he untied my sash, I tugged at his belt, still laughing. I was too distracted to do a good job of it. In the end, Jiyi had to do it himself while I lay back in the grass to watch.

"Why?" I had to ask as he removed his robe. "Because Tai had me yesterday?"

The sun was above him, casting his face in shadow. "No, Princess. Because you want me to."

Instead of lowering himself back over me, he shifted downward and parted my thighs with gentle hands. I sighed, knowing what came next. My skin tingled with anticipation and my sex grew damp, even before the first touch.

Each heartbeat felt like a century, but Jiyi didn't make me

wait too long. He lowered his head and touched the delicate tip of his tongue to my sex. I moaned, lifting my hips upward in offering, and he tasted me again, swirling in a small circle that made my limbs turn to liquid.

After that I lost track of time. I lost track of self. He licked me slowly, easing me toward climax. I splayed my fingers into his hair.

"Faster," I moaned.

He refused to comply and my moans turned into sobs. His tongue slid over my sex as if Jiyi had all the time in the world. As if my release were inevitable.

Every muscle in my body wound tight. The slow build was exquisite torture, but Jiyi was skilled. He could read my desire in the pulse of my blood and the flex of my body. Just when I despaired that it wouldn't happen, that I was no longer capable of giving myself over, Jiyi slid a long finger into my tight passage and I came in a flash of white light, hotter and brighter than the sun.

Finally I opened my eyes. When I was able to take my first breath, Jiyi's face was above me. His gaze locked on to mine as his organ penetrated me, longer and thicker and so much more satisfying than his fingers.

His look was tender and I felt the pang of it deep inside, deeper than any cock could reach.

"Come inside me," I murmured to him.

It was old habit; me granting him permission just as when I'd held complete dominion over his body as well as my own. He reached his climax in a few long thrusts, holding on to me the entire time.

Afterward, we embraced one another in the grass with our clothes crushed beneath us.

"I tried other times to touch you," he said, looking upward into the clouds. "Your arm or your hand. Even your hair. You never noticed, Princess."

He was right. I didn't remember any of it. But now I could feel the sun warming my skin and hear the wind over the water. The grass was green and the sky blue, penetrating the edges of my gray world. I turned to Jiyi and bit him lightly on the shoulder. It was gratitude.

He held me tighter. "For the last month, it was as if you weren't here." When he turned to me, his expression was haunted. "As if you were still wandering in the afterlife. I was frightened."

"I wouldn't have done anything to harm myself."

"But you did."

The words slipped into me like a cold knife. When the rebels had taken over the palace, I had been condemned to death. A cup of poison had been brought to me and I'd swallowed it without hesitation. It had been my decision.

In truth, the cup had not been filled with poison, but that didn't remove the choice I'd made. I'd embraced death. It wasn't a decision one was meant to come back from lightly.

"It had to be Tai who brought you back, didn't it?" he said bitterly. His arms around me had gone stiff even though they held the shape of an embrace. "I don't have it in me to be as cruel as you require."

"He didn't hurt me," I insisted.

Jiyi released me abruptly and pushed himself up into a sitting position. The shadows from the trees danced over his naked body.

"Tai didn't hurt you?"

I gasped as he grabbed me by my wrists and dragged me up beside him, holding my arm up in front of my face. "Can't you see?"

For the first time, I noticed the bruises on my wrists; the imprint of Tai's grip as he held me down. The scratches on my thigh.

"Where else?" my voice was barely a whisper.

"Here." Jiyi caressed his fingers gingerly over the side of my neck. "And here." My bottom lip where Tai had ravaged me with his teeth. And that Jiyi had kissed so tenderly only moments earlier.

"You can't even see yourself," he said quietly.

I had thought Jiyi astute when he came home and knew immediately what had happened. But in truth, Tai had done all he could to leave his mark on me. And he had wanted Jiyi to know.

"You know how Tai is. The games he likes to play," I said, retrieving my tunic from the grass. I summoned a smile, my Princess Shanyin smile that no one could shake. "And I'm known to like a rough touch."

Jiyi's eyes narrowed for just a moment. "Not from me, Princess," he replied slyly.

I started to put my clothes on, but Jiyi intervened. His hands teased over me as he dressed me, lingering over my breasts, the narrow curve of my waist. We were back in our old selves, the princess and her beloved concubine.

He still wanted to be my slave. It was the only way we had been and knew how to be. There was comfort in that.

The truth was I hadn't felt any physical pain with Tai. All I recalled was that he had tried to exert his will upon me, not merely sexually, but edging into something more dangerous. I had recognized it, known it inside my bones as the darkest sort of fear.

Jiyi was right—Tai had awakened me.

We made one last attempt to straighten our clothes, but it was futile. My tunic was stained with dirt and grass. There was no way to keep secrets between the three of us.

Before we broke through the line of trees, Jiyi grabbed me once more to steal a kiss.

"I can make you forget him," he promised as his lips brushed mine.

"How?" I laughed. "The three of us are together from the moment we wake up until we fall asleep."

His eyes flashed with heat. "No, not Tai. *Him*."

He pressed my back against a tree and I closed my eyes before his mouth descended. Jiyi didn't even say his name, yet indeed my body was yearning for him. For Yuan. For the one who consumed my last days as princess.

CHAPTER THREE

Even though I had possessed a harem of thirty handsome and virile male concubines, I had still wanted Chu Yuan from the very first moment I saw him. He had presented himself at my brother's court as a mid-level official with a good name. I still remembered how he looked in that first moment, standing there with his back straight and chin lifted to the point of haughtiness. His shoulders were rigid with propriety and genteel sensibility. I wanted to strip all of that away and fuck him until we both could no longer stand.

That wasn't so long ago. I had only known Yuan for ten days before my death. I should call it my first death, my false death, but some of it was very real. Though I lived, the scars could not be erased.

I was not meant to die peacefully as an old gray-haired grandmother in her sleep. I was the daughter, the sister, the niece of tyrants. Yuan's family was the sort that made kings and destroyed them just as easily. His line would continue and thrive while we who sat upon the throne offered up our necks as sacrifice.

Yuan's was the last face I had looked into as I believed my life to be slipping away. I wasn't angry at him, or at fate. There was nothing to be angry about. Only a sad resignation that I would no longer feel the warmth of life and the pleasures it provided.

Yuan had been involved in the uprising that had condemned me to death. In the end, he hadn't let me die, but he didn't tell me I was to be spared, either. I had been forced to face those final moments of reckoning before death.

Yuan had held me in his arms, to comfort me in my last moments—or so I had thought. He also gave me the most powerful orgasm of my life; one that wrung out every muscle in my body and drained me dry.

I didn't know what I felt about Yuan now, but he was still in my skin. We were still connected. The fate between us unfinished. When I closed my eyes, I remembered the way his flesh had filled me so completely. Tai and Jiyi could sense his essence lingering in me. Yuan was a ghost lover who would haunt every bed I occupied from here until my true death.

And I still didn't believe for one moment that I would go peacefully.

"I may be here with my hands in the dirt, but I'm no peasant. The difference is that I know it. In here," Tai thumped his chest twice before taking another swig of wine. He looked down at his cup. "This stuff tastes like piss."

"Yet you've swallowed half of it," Jiyi teased.

Jiyi and I both chuckled, exchanging a knowing look between ourselves. Tai caught the not-so-secret glance and scowled.

We had all had too much to drink. Jiyi had brought back two jugs of millet wine from the market. It was wasteful to squander it all on one night, but it felt good to indulge ourselves.

"So it's the two of you now, hmm?" Tai accused. "Co-conspirators, hand in hand."

He drank again, perhaps too deeply.

Tai certainly knew about our tryst by the lake, but he never spoke a word of it. For the last few days he'd maintained his distance. Some sense of balance had been restored between the three of us, but I knew it couldn't last.

"You've had enough wine, friend," Jiyi said beneath his

breath.

Tai raised the jug to his lips and, with a defiant glare at Jiyi, tipped it back.

"There's no need to fight," I chided, laying my head down against Jiyi's shoulder. I was warm and sleepy and floating outside of myself. "Besides, you were always my favorite, Tai."

Jiyi pinched me hard on my arm in retaliation. I giggled as I swatted away his hand. It was almost like we were back in the palace, without a care.

Tai's gaze heated as he watched the two of us. "Come here and kiss me then, Princess."

A cold silence took over the room.

"Have you earned it?" I returned haughtily, emboldened by the drink.

In the palace, Tai would always push against the boundaries. In moments like this, I had to seize control back quickly, lest he come to think that he had any power over me, but everything was different now. I had no palace guards or my Emperor brother to protect me. All I had was myself.

I expected Tai to challenge me, but instead he extended the wine jug. I accepted it and took a drink that burned down my throat. I didn't like the taste, but I liked what the liquor did to me, warming my belly and making me larger than I was, if only for the moment.

"There she is," Tai remarked quietly, watching my every movement. "I was wondering where you were hiding."

"I'm right here." I tried to return to our earlier playfulness, but the moment had come and gone.

Tai regarded me for a long time, lost in his thoughts. With every moment I grew more tense, waiting for him to reveal some grand scheme.

"It's time for us to leave this place," Tai declared.

"Why?" Jiyi spoke up first. "We have everything we need here."

"Everything *you* might need. I need more than this pitiful hut and a patch of dirt."

"Where would we go?" I asked. "We have no money and if the Emperor's forces discover us, we'll be killed."

I felt no particular attachment to this hut, but it was hidden away and we had managed to survive so far. The silver Tai and Jiyi had smuggled from the palace was long gone. Over the last months, they had bartered and sold away the few other items they'd taken.

Tai's grave expression unnerved me. "We should leave this place and find someone loyal to Emperor Ziye's regime, someone with influence and wealth."

All the warmth fled from me. "My brother and I have no allies left in court."

My brother had been killed by an assassin's knife. There was no benefit at all in remaining loyal to a dead sovereign.

"There's always someone plotting against the throne. You'll always be valuable to them," Tai argued.

My spine stiffened. "You want us to ingratiate ourselves to traitors and insurgents? So we can be beheaded alongside them?"

Jiyi sensed the tension building and reached over to massage my neck, trying to soothe me. "It seems a very bold plan, Tai. Perhaps we should put more thought to this before acting."

"I don't want any more thought put to it," I told them harshly. "The two of you don't realize how much I shielded my palace from the turmoil of the imperial court."

Tai's jaw clenched. "So the lowly concubine should stay in his place."

"You don't know how dangerous it is playing with politics," I replied, agitated.

"And you avoided it at all costs, preferring instead to close your eyes, my Princess," he sneered.

"You must stop calling me that—"

"Why?" Tai stared down at us. "Because you've given up?"

"Because Princess Shanyin is dead."

A cold shiver ran down my spine as I said it. I was courting ill-fortune by speaking of myself as if I were already in the grave, but Tai needed to abandon this notion that we could return to the life we once had.

"My uncle Liu Yu has seized the throne and declared himself Emperor," I said. "And my uncle hated my brother and me. Every official will want to get in his good graces and would gladly sacrifice an imperial princess to do so. I know how these people think." My lips twisted. "I'm one of them."

"Oh, Shanyin." Tai smiled bitterly, shaking his head. "I'm one of them as well."

My argument died in my throat.

"Yes, Shanyin. To you, your *mianshou* were nothing but pretty faces and strong bodies for your enjoyment."

He used the term the palace had adopted when referring to my concubines. Beautiful faces, they had been dubbed.

Guilt weighed me down as I looked from Jiyi to Tai. It was true that I had never considered who they were or where they had come from prior to being given to me as a gift.

"When your father was Emperor, my father was one of his chief advisers," Tai went on. "But then Ziye took the throne. Over a single disagreement in court, my father was condemned as a traitor and executed. His heirs faced the choice of death or castration and banishment. I chose castration."

His eyes burned into me and I wanted to shrink into the floor. My younger brother had singlehandedly destroyed Tai's family.

"The man had the knife against my cock when the Emperor's procurer came by seeking suitable concubines for the princess's harem." His laughter rang hollowly in my ears.

"Imagine that. One slice of the knife and I would have had nothing left to please you with."

The night of drinking ended in an uncomfortable silence, with the three of us retreating to our separate corners. What more was there to say?

I woke up much later as a knot was pulled tight around my wrists. All of the oil lamps had been extinguished, and I couldn't see anything in the darkness. I tried to roll away, but strong arms held me fast, pressing me back into the floor.

"Jiyi—"

A fist tightened in my hair, cutting off my cry for help. It was Tai's voice that spoke in my ear.

"He won't come for you."

My heart pounded frantically. Either Jiyi had been sent away or Tai had bound him as well.

"Let me go, Tai."

Instead of answering, Tai undid the belt of my tunic. "It doesn't bother me, you know. The two of you."

He opened my tunic and tugged my trousers down. I tried to kick at him, but he merely caught my leg in his strong hands and pinned me with his weight. My legs were forced open by the width of his hips.

"I always suspected you preferred to have Jiyi there when I was in your bed to act as your shield. Jiyi poses no threat to you—unlike me."

My head was clouded in a fog of wine and fear. Though I thrashed and tried to push him away, all of my struggles amounted to nothing. With hardly any effort at all, Tai positioned himself over me, his body fitted against mine to immobilize me.

"And everyone knows that Princess Shanyin can't be satisfied by a single man."

"If this is revenge for what my brother did to your family—

"

"That is all in the past, my darling. This is between you and me."

I gasped for breath as Tai took hold of my bound wrists. With one hand, he pulled them high over my head. The position both pinned my arms helplessly to the floor and lifted my breasts. His mouth descended to close over one nipple, sucking hard before scraping his teeth over the sensitive peak. I jumped, startled, and my pulse pounded. The urge to escape took over my body even as pleasure flooded my sex.

This is what Tai always did. Confused me so I didn't know whether it was day or night anymore. I wanted to claw my way out and flee, but I also wanted him to fuck me so hard I'd forget how to escape.

He was just as unforgiving to my other breast, rasping his tongue over the hard nipple until I sobbed.

"Tai," I whimpered. "Tai, please don't—"

"I won't," he promised too readily.

His fingers dug into my wrists while his other hand reached between our bodies. He found my sex and his fingers slid momentarily over the sensitive nub before slipping into my folds. I moaned brokenly, unable to control myself. I hadn't known how wet I'd become until his hand moved over and into me. Inside, my muscles closed over his long fingers, pulsing and squeezing tight.

"I won't until you beg me," he amended.

He bent his head again to kiss the side of my neck. His hand continued its exploration, while my hips rode his fingers, seeking a deeper, fuller sensation.

This was punishment for what had happened earlier. I'd contradicted him and now Tai wanted to dominate me by taking the one thing I'd refused him. He wanted my release, my body's complete surrender.

This is only my body, I told myself as his fingers worked

me into a frenzy. If I come, it will be for myself. For my own pleasure.

It didn't matter to me what Tai wanted. I wouldn't play the game by his rules. I wouldn't—

I cried out as he held my outer lips open and centered his finger over the tiny pearl of my sex. With the smallest of motions, he drove me higher, mastering me.

When I came in a rush of breath, his mouth moved from my neck to clamp down over my lips. His tongue pushed into my mouth as my inner muscles spasmed and pulsed.

There were no more entreaties or quiet commands. He kissed me until there was no breath left in me. Helplessly, I returned the kiss, unable to stop myself. While my body writhed in orgasm, I tasted him. I smelled the sweat of his skin and arched myself desperately into the hard press of his body. There was no denial—this orgasm belonged to Tai. No one else could make me feel this way, wracked with torment while I shuddered, completely lost to the pleasure he dragged out of me.

But Tai wasn't done yet. He turned me over and only then did I realize he had long ago stopped holding my wrists down. His hands ran over the muscles of my back, kneading softly near my spine. Then his mouth followed the same path. For a moment, his touch was almost soothing. Just as my heartbeat began to steady, Tai pushed my face against the pallet and bit hard into the back of my neck, sending a riot of sensation cascading to every nerve in my body.

"Say you're mine," he commanded as my heart beat out of my chest.

I tried to shake my head, struggling against the grip of his hand. He took my earlobe between his teeth. I braced myself, expecting more pain, but Tai nibbled and sucked gently. A shudder ran down my spine and my toes curled tight.

"You're mine, Shanyin."

His voice was low and urgent this time. He covered me with the length of his body. His knee wedged between my legs to hold them apart. "Say it."

My hands were still held above my head. I bit into my arm to keep from moaning when I felt his fingers parting my damp flesh once more. After coming once, my senses should have been dulled. I should be too satiated to be roused so quickly, but I was wrong.

Desire flowed hot through my veins, and my heart beat out an even more desperate rhythm. Something about the way Tai worked me seared away all my shame, all my doubts. I didn't trust him the way I did Jiyi, but Tai took me to a darker place where I didn't care anymore.

When Tai stroked me, I became nothing but nerves. When he penetrated me with his fingers, I sobbed aloud and moaned his name into the crook of my arm.

His body stilled and I felt a sigh of triumph against my neck. He'd heard me. His shaft thickened, pushing against the cleft of my backside.

"You're mine."

"No."

"*Yes.*"

He sank his fingers deeper into me. Then he pulled out and gripped either side of my hips, lifting them as he positioned himself. The angle pushed my head against the floor and I tried to brace myself onto my elbows, but my arms were still tied.

A moment later, I felt the broad tip of his organ parting my sex. He slid back and forth, bathing himself in my fluids before centering himself and pushing into me.

I cried out once more, "No...*no.*"

I had to say the words. I needed him to hear the denial because it was only my body he was claiming. It was just sex and...it was indescribable. His cock penetrated so deep, filling me completely. I was powerless against his thrusts as I let go of all resistance, allowing myself to feel everything.

And Tai did not hold back. I continued to deny him my complete surrender so he drove into me relentlessly, raising my hips higher to give himself access.

I was so, so grateful for the darkness. Not because my head was bowed to the ground, shoved against my bound wrists, or because my ass was in the air. I was grateful Tai couldn't see my face flushed red and my mouth gaped open. My eyes were flooded with tears.

And throughout all of it, my body was crying for release. Tai reached between my legs, working me roughly until my orgasm came in a rush. I gasped and bit down hard into my bottom lip.

I wanted to sink into the floor, but Tai wouldn't release me. His thrusts continued. Harder now, shorter. He still hadn't climaxed. Silently I begged for him to come so it would be over.

He brought me to another shuddering climax, but by now there was little pleasure in it. Only a brief, hollow sort of relief as my muscles unwound. Only after he had absorbed every last spasm did he finally allow himself to come inside me, thrusting so deep that our flesh melded into one. I knew then that this was his revenge. My surrender. My enslavement. And I would never be free of him.

CHAPTER FOUR

After Tai's organ slipped out of me, I collapsed exhausted onto the floor. Sometime later a blanket was placed over me, but I was too far gone to even stir.

The next thing I was aware of was the sensation of light through my eyelids. Groggily, I opened them. I lay on my side as the morning sunlight streamed in through the window. My body was still sore from Tai's merciless fucking.

I started to close my eyes again when a shadow fell over me. My pulse raced as I twisted around, but it was only Jiyi who stood looking down at me.

Without a word, he bent to untie my wrists, then lifted me with the blanket still around me. Tai was nowhere to be seen as Jiyi carried me from the hut and into the trees toward the lake.

His face was unreadable, but his arms were strong and secure around me. I reached up to touch my hand to the tight line of his jaw and his expression softened just a little.

When we neared the water, he cast the blanket aside as well as his shoes before stepping into the lake fully clothed. The water was cool and I shivered as I sank below the surface. Jiyi held on to me. Soon I was floating with my arms around his neck.

"You were there last night, weren't you?" I asked him.

"Yes."

Sunlight reflected from the water onto his face. Despite his lighthearted nature, Jiyi had deep, thoughtful eyes that tended to take on a somber look.

"Why didn't you stop him?" I wasn't angry at him, but Jiyi was always so protective of me. I had assumed he must have been restrained or incapacitated in some way.

"Did you want me to stop him?"

I had no answer. There had been few boundaries between the three of us in the bedchamber. The lines that had once existed were erased completely.

"Are you cold?" he asked.

"A little."

Jiyi held me closer. "Take a deep breath and close your eyes."

I did as he asked and heard him inhale before lowering us both below the surface until my head was submerged as well.

I didn't know how to swim, but the water was shallow and I felt no fear with Jiyi holding me tight. It was as natural for me to trust him as it was for me to fight against Tai.

Still underwater, I opened my eyes and saw his face close to mine. It was a colorless world beneath the surface, free of sound and weight. A moment later, I was lifted into the air once more. Surprisingly, I wasn't cold anymore.

"Your body acclimates to the water faster that way," Jiyi explained.

Setting me on my feet, he removed the rest of his soaked clothing. We bathed in the lake, letting the water wash us clean, before returning to the shore. Jiyi retrieved his clothes and wrung them out, arranging them out to dry. Then we lay down as well, curling together in the grass with the sun warming us.

We didn't make love then, though it would have been the most natural thing to do. Instead we lay face to face. Jiyi was a pleasure to look at. His features were smooth and well-defined, and the corners of his eyes swept gracefully upward. Phoenix eyes, the poets called them.

He reached over to touch his fingertips to my lips. In many

ways the caress was more intimate than a kiss.

"What was your name before you came to the palace?" I asked him.

Jiyi smiled. "I don't remember. I like your name for me better."

He was being coy, but I let him. "What was your life like back then?"

"I wasn't as high-born as Tai." The mention of Tai's name brought a momentary chill to the air. "My father aspired to be a scholar and a poet, but couldn't manage to be any more than a writing tutor to the local merchant families. One day the Emperor's retainer noticed me and offered service in the palace. My father considered it a great honor."

"But you must have known you wouldn't be an imperial scholar."

"I thought I would be serving in the Emperor's harem," Jiyi said with a laugh. "His sister is much prettier."

The devilish look he gave me made me giggle. In moments like these, it was easy to believe I could fall into an idyllic cycle of pleasure and decadence here, just as I had enjoyed in the palace.

Tai would punish and torture me every night, trying to force my surrender. Jiyi would soothe and banish all my fears when morning came. It wouldn't matter where I was as long as my body and mind remained in a state of sexual arousal and satisfaction, blind to any consequences.

But it wasn't that simple anymore. Perhaps it never had been.

I had tried my best in the palace to stay away from the schemes and intrigues that wove through the halls. When my brother had taken our uncles captive, I'd persuaded Ziye to release them, hoping to end the bloodshed. But I couldn't save us from our fate. One of those very uncles had come back to seize the throne and sentence me to death.

"You must know what Tai wants to do is dangerous," I told Jiyi. "I can't ever return to that life. Everyone believes that Princess Shanyin is dead and that's how I must remain."

"Tai was always ambitious, trying to gain favor," he replied gravely.

I had never thought of my concubines that way. Among the Emperor's concubines, every woman attempted to climb the ranks by giving birth to the Emperor's children and potential heirs. My lovers were there for purely for my enjoyment — or so I had assumed.

"We could leave, just you and I." Jiyi looked troubled as he suggested it. "I would do that if it was the princess's command."

So loyal and caring. And as skilled a lover as any woman could want. Why couldn't Jiyi make me burn the way Yuan did? Or even Tai, for that matter? I must be as immoral and depraved as they said. I needed to know pain to enjoy pleasure.

I laid my hand over his in the grass. "You love him, don't you?"

For a moment, Jiyi looked open and vulnerable, but then his eyes gleamed with mischief. "But I love you more, Princess."

The day continued as if nothing had happened. Tai and Jiyi worked the fields, digging yams from the earth and tending to the other vegetables. When I tried to help, they wouldn't let me.

"We must keep your fair skin out of the sun, my love," Tai said.

The endearment, tossed out so casually, made my pulse jump. When I brought water to both of them, Tai's gaze lingered on the rope marks around my wrists. Hastily, I pulled my sleeves forward to cover them.

He knew exactly what he was doing to me. I retreated into the hut to sleep. I'd had little rest the night before and if this continued, I didn't know if I would ever sleep again. I would make myself ill staying awake and jumping at every sound as I waited for Tai's approach.

In the afternoon, Tai left to take a walk alone through the woods and the wild notion crossed my mind that I could escape. Jiyi had suggested it, hadn't he?

But the thought of leaving left me physically ill and I couldn't even take the first step. When Tai returned, I was exactly where I was when he'd left.

There was little conversation that evening over supper. We sat on the floor around a raised wooden slat that served as a table. The fare was humble, boiled yams and greens. Half a jug of wine remained from the night before, but we all wisely stayed away from it.

Partway through the meal, Tai spoke. "It occurred to me that I didn't get to hear you beg."

Beside him, Jiyi concentrated on his meal as if nothing had been said.

Did Tai think I could be unsettled so easily? My reply was equally calm. "You never will."

His gaze darkened as he regarded me. "Are you certain?"

My heart pounded as I recalled the last time he'd asked me that question. I knew he was already plotting how and when he'd try to prove me wrong.

"I don't belong to you or to anyone," I told him. "If anything, you belong to me."

Tai snorted at that. He and I stared at one another like two tigers circling. Neither of us flinched, neither of us looked away. He was the first to break the silence.

"We are no longer who we were, Shanyin. Jiyi may still be yours, but I'm my own man now."

"Enough, you two," Jiyi admonished.

Maybe we were both wrong. After all that had happened, the three of us were bound together in some unspeakable fashion. I needed them, but they needed me too.

"I brought you a gift," Tai announced as if we hadn't just been locked in a contest of will.

He went to the corner to retrieve a small bundle which he placed before me. Pushing my supper aside, I untied the cloth to reveal a block of pale green jade, carved into the shape of a phoenix. It was my imperial seal, used to sign official documents in the palace. I remembered the weight of it. The seal had required two hands to lift and apply my mark.

"If you go to some warlord, claiming to be a lost imperial princess, who would believe you? But this will support your story."

Silk robes, jewels, any of my other belongings could be easily duplicated, but the official chop contained my name. It appeared on all of my communications with my family and could be identified as uniquely mine.

"Is that all you brought back with you?" Jiyi asked pointedly.

The two men exchanged an unreadable look. "Yes, this is all. The rest has been sold off."

When the rebellion had broken out, I had emptied out my trunks and told the servants to take as much as they could carry. Tai and Jiyi had fled with a collection of valuables they had gradually sold off for food and supplies. Apparently Tai had held on to the jade seal for a greater purpose.

"You were already planning this before you even left the palace," I said, incredulous.

Tai looked proud at my acknowledgment. "Our families have watched regimes come and go, have they not?"

My brother Ziye had only ruled for a year. Before that, our father had been Emperor for only ten years. Each change brought about death and more death.

Tai came to look over my shoulder. "You know that an Emperor's rule is most vulnerable at the beginning of his reign. Now is the time to seek out opposing forces."

Had his father plotted rebellion against my brother in the same way?

"Throw it into the lake," I said, rising to put some distance between me and this relic of my past life. "I have no taste for this sort of plotting."

"Of course not. You never had a mind for the hard decisions," Tai agreed. "So let me make them for you."

He rested a hand on my shoulder, his thumb touching the bare skin of my neck. "Let me take care of you," he entreated in a low voice that had no place except the bedchamber. "You know I would never harm you, Princess."

His hand at the back of my neck felt like an iron collar even as he tried to seduce me with his words and the sheer power of his presence.

I met his gaze directly, knowing Tai would pounce upon any sign of weakness. "I don't know anything anymore."

CHAPTER FIVE

I awoke to the weight of a hand in my hair, stroking down the length of it gently. Stubbornly, I kept my eyes closed to feign sleep.

"Shanyin." Tai's voice was low and husky. "Look what you do to me."

I didn't have to look. I could hear the rustle of cloth. Something warm and satin-smooth brushed against my cheek. I felt a teardrop of moisture against my skin before the head of his organ nudged against my lips.

"Take me in your mouth," Tai instructed gently.

His hand paused on my hair to cup the back of my head. I could have resisted until he forced the issue by pulling my head back and thrusting inside. Tai would have me completely at his mercy then, helpless. I couldn't allow that.

I ran my tongue over my lips to wet them. My heart beat dangerously fast.

The broad tip of his sex pressed against my lips. Gradually, Tai slid inside, widening my mouth until my jaw ached. He could be cruel or kind, but even when Tai tried to be gentle, his size was in itself a form of cruelty.

"Shanyin." He moaned my name as he slid in farther. "Look at me."

I didn't want to. I didn't want him to see the tumult of emotions in my eyes. When I didn't comply, his hands closed around either side of my face, tilting my head upward while his cock pressed against my tongue.

My eyes fluttered open and immediately locked on to his.

He let out a shuddering breath and his organ grew even harder and thicker, blocking my airway. He thrust shallowly; once, twice, moaning with each invasion of my mouth.

Tears stung at the corners of my eyes while Tai's expression was caught between torment and ecstasy. There was a time when I had loved the way he made me feel. When these games were nothing but games, and they'd excited and driven me to exquisite heights of pleasure.

Now that I held nothing over him, the danger was still there as well as the dark thrill of anticipation, but there was nothing to hold back the shame or the humiliation. Or the helplessness.

I moaned in protest as he pushed deeper, nearly sobbing from how he had me pinned. Tai exhaled sharply and his entire body trembled, momentarily overcome.

I still had power over him.

It wasn't something I suddenly discovered. It was something I decided in that moment.

I raised my hands up to take hold of his hips. Tai's gaze clouded as I pulled him toward me, drawing him deeper into my mouth. It was the tiniest motion, half a finger's length more that my mouth worked on his cock, but Tai's head fell back. I slid my lips up and down in a slow, building rhythm, watching as the cords of his neck stretched tight and sweat gathered over his brow.

Tai had both of his hands on my face, cradling it, urging me onto him faster, but I continued at my own pace, working my tongue against the sensitive underside of his organ. He groaned as I sucked his cock harder, but not hard enough. His body vibrated with need.

This was our new battle. My blood heated as I dug my nails lightly into his hips to hold him captive. I watched Tai's face as he gave in to what I was doing to him.

How had I forgotten this part? The real reason I favored

Tai above the others. Watching such a physically impressive man succumb to something as base and simple as sexual ecstasy was a thing of beauty. All it took was the smallest flutter of my tongue, and every muscle in his body strained.

Tai ran his hands through my hair, moaning my name. His hands tightened convulsively at the nape of my neck, but I was the one in control. Wetness pooled between my legs.

At that moment, a palm came to rest at the small of my back. Jiyi. His touch both soothed and aroused me as he ran his hands down the length of my spine. Tai opened his eyes to acknowledge Jiyi's presence. It was the first time the three of us had been together like this since escaping the palace. The feeling was as different as it was familiar. We were no longer who we were.

Jiyi's touch curved down over my backside, parting my thighs as his fingers dipped into my sex and stroked gently over the slick petals. Pleasure arced through me, weakening my limbs, and I made a soft sound around Tai's cock. In response, Tai bucked his hips, nudging his organ against my throat. I braced a hand against his thigh to control the penetration, while Jiyi's fingers inside me quickly erased the moment of discomfort.

If it could only stay like this; the three of us entwined and the pure pleasure of our bodies.

Tai was ready to come. I could taste his essence on my tongue, a scattering of rain before his release. Beneath my hands, his muscles were clenched tight.

But he pulled out before reaching his climax. His hands were rough and impatient as they hooked beneath my arms. Lying back, he lifted me onto him, willingly putting himself beneath me while I straddled his hips.

I was surprised he would relinquish control over to me so readily, but was the position truly one of submission? I was the one giving him satisfaction, bestowing it onto him while he lay back to accept. There was no answer to that. There never would be. I sank down onto him, closing my eyes to savor the moment as his cock filled me completely. We both moaned at the raw pleasure of it.

I rode him slowly, concentrating on the feel of his flesh inside me as I leaned forward with my hands braced against his hard chest. The angle put the perfect amount of pressure against the bud of my sex and soon I became centered on that feeling, grinding onto him to bring out more sensation.

When I opened my eyes, Tai was looking not at me, but over my shoulder. "Remember?" he asked, his voice rasping.

Tai and Jiyi rarely spoke to one another when they were in my bed. In part, it was to indulge one of my favorite fantasies. I liked to imagine they were part of the same lover, four hands and one mind intent on satisfying me. As Jiyi came up behind me to kiss my neck, his gaze was fixed on Tai.

Remember. Apparently that one word was all Tai needed to communicate his intentions. Jiyi left us momentarily and when he returned, I also remembered. Panic rose up to take me by the throat.

Jiyi placed a hand to the center of my back once more, but this time his touch was firm. His other arm rounded my waist as he bent me forward. Tai's arms immediately closed around me. In the haze of arousal and fear, I couldn't even form a protest as I felt the trickle of oil flowing down into the cleft of my buttocks.

My body tensed, causing my inner muscles to squeeze Tai's cock harder. He made a sound of satisfaction deep in his throat. By now, my pulse was racing and my breath came quick and shallow as if I were fleeing for my life. It was like a dream. My legs wouldn't move while my mind sought desperately to escape. It was like a nightmare.

Beneath the fear, there was the feel of Tai inside me and Jiyi's wonderful hands kneading my lower back to relax my muscles. His fingers slipped between my cheeks to rub oil into the hidden opening there.

I did remember. It had happened nearly a year ago. The hour was late and we were full of wine. Tai and Jiyi were new lovers to me then and I wanted to explore anything and everything they could give. They hadn't asked for my permission to take me that time either—it had simply happened in one inevitable step after another, pain and pleasure melding into one until two cocks penetrated me at once. I had screamed so loud in my release that the entire palace had awoken.

Afterward, when I could think again, I decided they would never be allowed to do it again. And they had never dared...until now.

Jiyi's fingers pushed past the ring of muscle in my back passage and the shock of it stole my breath. Closing my eyes, I shook my head, but Tai dragged me against him to capture my mouth in a kiss. Below, his hips thrust upward into me. At the same time, Jiyi pushed his oiled fingers deep, widening my passage. Preparing me.

If I commanded him to stop, would he? But the same thing happened here as had happened before. I'd had no wine this time, but I was drunk on the things they were doing to me. My body had become greedy for more, in any way that I could have it.

I cried out at the penetration of a cock into my ass. Jiyi wasn't as large as Tai, but he wasn't small either. He tried to be gentle, but it didn't matter. Tai already filled me from below and Jiyi worked himself into my back passage. I was stretched beyond pain and split asunder.

Jiyi began to thrust shallowly behind me, each movement fucking me onto Tai's cock which had become harder and thicker than I'd ever felt it. Pinned between the two of them, there was nothing I could do but accept. I belonged completely to them in this position and I couldn't bear it. That was why I had forbidden it, but all my commands and edicts were thinner than air.

I was no longer mistress over them. And heaven and earth, my body loved it.

An animal sound expelled from my lips, an endless string of grunts with each thrust. Tai squeezed my breast hard as the orgasm was wrenched out of me, more powerful than any I'd ever known. I came screaming with my legs splayed out helplessly between my two lovers. My face contorted with unbidden and sordid pleasure.

Tai watched every moment of it, his eyes blazing.

"This is better than hearing you beg," he said before spilling his hot seed into me to bathe my insides.

Jiyi came a moment later, collapsing on top of me. I could barely breathe. It would be fitting if this was my end, with my pitiful body crushed between them. Jiyi rolled off me a moment later and tried to gather me tenderly into his arms, but I wasn't fooled. He had turned from an ally into a traitor.

I stared down at Tai, whose eyes were half-closed. He and Jiyi were indeed two halves of the same whole, just as I'd always fantasized. His organ slipped wetly out of me and I was left emptied, gutted.

Silence descended in the aftermath. Even the birds in the surrounding forest seemed to have quieted. I dressed without looking at either of them and retreated to the corner beneath the window to breathe in the fresh air.

Tai went to ladle a drink from the water bucket and retreated to sit at the opposite corner. He leaned his back against the wall and stared at me, no longer as triumphant as he had been when I was shuddering on top of him.

Jiyi brought me a cup, but I ignored him. "Your scheme will lead to our deaths," I said to Tai.

This was what everything revolved around—Tai's bid to take over our actions. The sex was merely a screen behind which the shadow puppets played.

"You were never one for any sort of plan, Shanyin," he retorted. "All you ever wanted to do was close your eyes."

"And lie on my back," I finished for him. "Perfect for being your slave as well as your whore. That's what you want, isn't it? A princess in your palm who you can sell out in return for influence."

"What would you rather have? The three of us staying here in the muck and dirt, fucking until our hair turns gray?"

"And our teeth fall out," I returned snidely.

His eyes flashed at me. If Tai had thought coercing me would make me docile, he'd been mistaken. Each sexual boundary we breached brought back the Princess Shanyin I had once been. That Shanyin felt no fear and no shame. She embraced depravity with lewd enjoyment.

"Every official and aristocrat wants me dead, darling. You'll find no one to lure into your trap."

"Why don't you just tell her?" Jiyi interrupted.

We had overlooked him in our bitter exchange, but he moved to stand between us now. "You never told her about the letter."

Tai's jaw clenched.

"What letter?" I asked.

He met my gaze, his eyes hard and unwavering. And said nothing.

"What letter?"

"I burned it."

Deep within me, I knew who had written this letter. Only one person could bring out such hatred in Tai.

"Lord Chu Yuan gave us a message," Jiyi confirmed.

Suddenly my cold heart was beating again.

"Look at her." Tai ran a hand through his hair in agitation.

Untied, it fell over his eyes in a look that was unkempt and sensual. I went to stand over him and willed him to look up at me. He did eventually, but his jaw was set with defiance. "Just the mention of that bastard's name and you look like a blushing maiden," he said with disgust.

My eyes narrowed onto him. I looked like a fallen woman who had been fucked on the floor by two men at once.

"What did the letter say?" Outwardly, my tone was one of command, but inside my stomach fluttered nervously.

Tai shrugged. "I never even looked."

He was lying. Taking hold of his chin between my thumb and forefinger, I tilted his head back. "What did it say?"

Tai was stronger than me and easily capable of swatting me away, but a slow smile twisted his lips. "You are so beautiful when you're like this."

"Lord Chu Yuan intended to meet up secretly with us once we were free of the palace," Jiyi said. "But we didn't go."

"That would have meant death for sure," Tai argued. "He and his rebel faction had just ordered you executed."

I let go of Tai and turned away, trying to sort out my thoughts. Tai was right. It would have been dangerous for them to trust anyone, especially one of the leaders of the uprising, but I could barely breathe as I realized Yuan had given me a final message. I had been so certain he wanted nothing more to do with me. Though he had spared my life, I was dead to him.

But the mere existence of that letter meant I had been wrong. Yuan hadn't abandoned me.

Tai stood and came forward. He caught me near the wall, bracing his arms on either side of my head to cage me in. Behind him, I saw Jiyi rise to come to my aid.

"Stand back," Jiyi warned. "Let her breathe."

"We're only talking." Tai dismissed him without a look and turned his attention back to me. "Don't you see how perfectly suited we are? I was never meant to be your slave, Princess. I was meant to be your equal." He leaned in closer. "That bastard Chu Yuan is no higher born than I am. And he never could satisfy you the way I do. Your maidservants were very clear on that."

My maidservants? "You were spying on me."

What foolish creatures my brother and I had been. As Emperor, my brother had recruited young men for me based on their beauty alone, not realizing who he let in. Yuan had been a part of the rebellion that ended our rule. Tai was the son of an enemy.

"We can't escape who we are," Tai continued. "You sensed from the start I wasn't like the others, didn't you? That's why you let me do these things to you."

I started to deny it, but he pressed me against the wall as he bent his head to capture my mouth. I tasted bitterness in his kiss and the sharp bite of anger that had been there, in one way or another, since the first time we met.

There was one person Tai hated more than Yuan. It was me.

I twisted out of his grasp. The jade chop in the corner caught my eye and I grabbed it before fleeing from the hut. It was heavy, but I hugged it against my chest and kept on running through the fields. Behind me, I could hear Jiyi calling my name, but I didn't look back, not even for a moment. If I stayed, Tai would keep on punishing me for making him a slave. It would never end.

By the time I reached the woods, I was already out of breath. At first no one came after me. Tai and Jiyi didn't believe I could ever leave on my own. I knew nothing of where we were or of how to survive outside the palace. For the last month I had depended on the two of them...or had it been months?

"Shanyin, come back inside."

Jiyi was marching through the fields. Of course he would be the one to try to bring me back. Amiable and even-tempered Jiyi, who could charm the moon if he set his mind to it.

I turned and ran as hard as I could, fighting the pain in my legs and the tightness in my chest. At the edge of the lake, I stared into the water, remembering the colorless world without sound beneath the surface.

The snap of a branch behind me roused me from my trance. I lifted the block of jade high above my head and hefted it toward the deepest part of the lake. The treasure seemed to hover in the air, pale green over dark water, before it plunged deep. The ripples radiated outward toward the shore and I turned to run once more.

When I looked over my shoulder, the lake had shrunken to the size of a small puddle. A figure in gray came up beside it and dived beneath the surface. How quickly he assumed I had gone under.

That was the last time I glanced behind me. Soon I was lost in a blur of trees, rock, grass. I stumbled over a fallen log and crawled into the hollow inside. There I lay as still as I could, listening to the chirp of crickets and the song of the woodland birds. My heartbeat sounded like thunder in my ears and I pressed my hand into the layer of moss that had grown inside the trunk, breathing in the verdant scent.

I closed my eyes then and tried to absorb the cool air into my skin. There were no voices outside. No shouts. Still I was so filled with fear that I stayed there, hiding as the hours flowed by and the light outside faded into night.

Never had I been so completely alone. The desire to crawl back to safety overwhelmed me, but I had gotten myself lost. Perhaps on purpose, perhaps not. When evening came, I longed for Jiyi's warm embrace around me. Or even Tai's. It was tempting to be held at all, even if it was with an iron grip.

Now I was hopelessly adrift.

The two of them might think I had escaped to find Yuan out of some foolish romantic notion. I had been so completely fixated on the handsome aristocrat while the kingdom was falling to pieces around me. But I didn't have to run toward a new destination to run away from an old one.

Tai and Jiyi were the last remnants of my palace life. It wasn't easy leaving them. No easier than it had been to swallow poison. In the end, all it took for me was a moment's decision, the closing of my eyes, and not stopping myself when I started to fall.

CHAPTER SIX

I was first drawn to the Floating Happiness by the painted lanterns which hung warm and pink from the eaves. The drinking house sat on stilts over the river and a zigzag bridge spanned the water from the opposite bank. The sharp angles of the design were meant to ward away wandering spirits who could not navigate corners. I hoped no ghosts followed me as I stepped onto it.

Soft music came from inside and ladies dressed in silk graced every window, smiling with their painted lips.

The owner of the house was Madame Lin Lifei who knew who I was the moment she saw me. She didn't know my name or that there was even a Princess Shanyin, but she knew my story, or at least enough of it. It was the story of many a fallen woman.

My cold night lying in the woods had been followed by a string of cold nights as I wandered. The clothes I wore were ragged and filthy. There was dirt beneath my nails and my hair was knotted and tangled. Madame Lin sat me down in her parlor and poured me a steaming cup of tea. I cradled the smooth porcelain in my hands to breathe in the delicate fragrance. It smelled of jasmine flowers, a sensual and decadent perfume.

"My entire family was killed by bandits," I told her.

It was true. The insurgents who assassinated my brother were indeed thieves. They stole his throne, our palace, the entire kingdom.

Madame Lin nodded, though she was unimpressed. "It is clear from your speech and manners that you come from a good family. What is your name, little one?"

"Give me whatever name you wish, Madame."

She smiled at me. Within the week, I was sitting at one of the windows like a freshly cut flower.

There is a distinct difference between a whore and a courtesan. A courtesan was trained in music and art. She moved with elegance and excelled at witty banter and conversation. A courtesan was a companion whose role was multi-faceted and complex: stroking egos, soothing tempers, interpreting poetry. A man was meant to fall in love with a courtesan, if only for an hour, whereas a whore's primary role was to provide sex.

I was most certainly a whore, though Madame Lin insisted we call ourselves courtesans.

Floating Happiness wasn't a palace. It was merely a cheap imitation of the things that signaled elegance. Art scrolls done in a pedestrian hand hung on the walls. We pranced around in silk robes that were worn at the seams. The drinking house gave the barest illusion of wealth and luxury, which was fitting considering I was only a faint shadow of my former self.

"Come in here, Autumn Rain," Madame called out to me from her parlor one evening.

There was already a Spring Rain among us so Madame chose Autumn for me to mock my advanced age of twenty-four. She had thought I was younger when taking me in. Apparently being disheveled and covered in mud made one appear more youthful.

There were four other girls under Madame's care. The youngest was fifteen and the oldest eighteen. They looked to me like kittens, so fresh-faced and new.

Inside her sitting room, Madame lounged beside a well-dressed gentleman. His silk robe was dyed with expensive colors, indicating wealth.

"Meet our honored guest Lord Wu Chien."

He appeared to be just shy of thirty years. Not strikingly

handsome, but certainly not plain either. He had a slight bend in the bridge of his nose and the left side of his mouth was set lower than the right, giving his smile the look of being crooked. These small features gave him an imperfect yet compelling appearance.

"A new girl," he remarked pleasantly.

I bowed my head while glancing at him through my lashes. Called him Lord Wu. All the things that were supposed endear me to him, though I mainly did them because Madame Lin was watching me with the eye of a hawk.

"Autumn Rain can hardly be called a girl," she drawled. "But she is very worldly and perhaps suitable for your requirements."

I raised my eyebrows at her and she slid a coy look back at me.

"And what would your requirements be?" I asked our visitor directly.

"Yes, tell her."

Madame Lin was practically draped over Wu Chien and enjoying herself immensely. He indulged her, stroking her hand as he spoke to me. "I am looking for someone skilled in the art of the bedchamber."

"Like flower arrangement?" I asked blandly.

He choked back a laugh.

"See what I told you?" Madame said, her eyes glittering. "Insolent. No wonder someone took a lash to her back."

I pressed my lips tight to keep from baring my teeth. Madame and I could trade barbs as much as she liked, but my scars were a private matter. She'd seen them when I was in a bath and they were another mark against me in her eyes. Who wanted to pay for a courtesan who was scarred? It ruined the illusion of perfection.

"I need a woman with experience. Someone who knows how to arouse and entice a man," the gentleman, who perhaps wasn't much of a gentleman at all, went on. "Not some fresh and innocent flower."

I smirked at him. "Don't be fooled by our darling Spring Rain. Madame Lin has sold her virginity at least twice this week to different buyers."

"You are certainly not shy," he acknowledged.

"And you have no shame," I returned. "Should we start right here, then? Madame seems to be quite entertained. Will she stay and watch?"

My blunt tone was an attempt to hide my irritation. I didn't like Madame Lin's mercenary attitude or her constant measure of what she considered my assets and my shortcomings.

"Actually, Madame Lin told me you are quite clever, able to converse with anyone on a variety of subjects," Wu Chien said.

"I said 'too clever,'" Madame corrected.

"Indeed." Wu gave her arm a warning squeeze and she immediately quieted. He beckoned me to the seat across from them. "Tell me, Miss Autumn Rain, how do you go about enticing a man?"

I snorted. "I don't. I worry about my own pleasure and he worries about his. Somehow the two align. The language of sex isn't a difficult one."

His eyes glinted. "Unlike flower arrangement."

I didn't smile, but I did look him over from head to toe for the first time, considering what he might be like in bed. I admit, his odd behavior had me mildly curious.

He noticed my attention. Of course he noticed.

"What if the man is someone who you feel no attraction to? How do you see to your own pleasure then?"

I narrowed my eyes at him. "Do you ask so many questions in bed?"

"What if he's hideously ugly?" he pressed.

"I simply put out the lanterns."

Once more, I glanced down the front of his robe, wondering if he was hiding some disfigurement beneath the expensive silk. His questions had taken an odd turn.

"Do you pretend?" he asked, undaunted. "Put on a convincing show of cries and moans?"

Even Madame Lin seemed to be getting a little uncomfortable at this point. She squirmed in her seat and made a show of adjusting the rings on her fingers.

"I find it easier to discover something desirable in the situation rather than putting on a show. Much more pleasurable as well."

For a long moment, he stared directly at me as if he too were weighing some asset he hadn't named.

"I want to see," he said finally. Then to Madame, "I want to see how your Autumn Rain seduces and beguiles a man."

I didn't know what mad scheme Wu Chien had in mind or what sort of perverse thrills he desired. We made arrangements to meet the next evening, though he paid for my time for the entire day.

I spent the morning pondering what he could possibly be planning, using each question he'd given me as part of a riddle. Perhaps Wu was unable to perform and sought an experienced bedmate to entice him? Or was he injured in some way? Did he engage in some sadistic practice? Perhaps that was why Madame Lin had so gleefully brought up my scars.

I tried to ask Madame Lin what his story was, but she was purposefully vague. Perhaps he was free enough with his coins for her to not ask questions.

"Wu Chien is an important patron," Madame Lin reminded me nearly ten times that day. "Just make sure you please him."

"It's not as if he's a demon with two cocks," I retorted after being pestered one too many times.

I wasn't afraid. Anyone who could hurt me was dead or far from this little town with its wine house brothel.

As evening neared, I prepared myself with a bath. Afterwards, I applied a touch of perfumed oil to my throat and a red tint to my lips. My hair was arranged in a romantic style.

I had been at the Floating Happiness for two months now. Despite the way Madame Lin and I nipped at each other, I wasn't unhappy. I wasn't the best of prostitutes. Patrons fawned over Spring Rain and Fragrant Orchid and the other kittens. They were sweet and wide-eyed and flirted with ease.

The slightest attempt at being charming and coquettish made me feel like a wooden marionette. Still, I was not without admirers. Those who did take me to bed weren't disappointed and neither was I. They were distractions for the evening, someone new to explore and discover.

None held the same power over me as Yuan or Tai or Jiyi. Or the line of other men who had been in and out of my bed when I was princess. Some of them I'd chosen, others I hadn't.

And I never imagined my former lovers' faces on my patrons. If anything, I hoped to erase the imprint of their flesh on mine.

Madame Lin had warm wine brought to the bedchamber and I lit the lanterns around the room. Then I waited.

When the curtain finally stirred, I knew immediately it was not Wu Chien. From the shadow, he was much taller, his shoulders twice as broad. A hand pulled aside the curtain and my limbs froze. My breath came out shallowly as a wave of dizziness hit me.

I knew him. And I knew exactly what spectacle Wu Chien wanted to witness.

The man before me had only half a face. Most of the left half had been gouged out and scarred over, including his eye which was covered by a milky-white film. His arms were like tree trunks, his chest like an ox's. Fearsome in every way.

He was Bataar, one of the fierce warriors my brother had enlisted to be his personal guard. His name was a barbarian one and he looked the part. The sight of Bataar would scare demons away, my brother had joked.

Bataar had been ordered to stand back the day my brother was assassinated. He'd rushed into the throng too late, but managed to fight through the insurgents to escort me to my palace. There, he had offered to die defending me. Me, the depraved and immoral fox-whore of the old regime.

But I hadn't allowed the warrior that 'privilege' as he'd called it. I thought for sure he was killed in the rebellion, but Bataar was here and his face was unmistakable.

In the palace, I'd barely been able to look at his ruined face, but I regarded him openly now with a hand over my mouth at the shock of seeing him. He'd been brought here as a joke for Wu Chien's amusement and likely Madame Lin's as well. They were probably spying on us from some peephole.

They wanted to watch me service the ugliest man they could find and derive pleasure from it, as I'd so brazenly said I would.

Bataar was staring back at me. "My lady," he began brokenly. "I'm sorry for frightening you."

"No, you—you don't frighten me." I lowered my hand from my mouth.

He smiled wanly. "That's kind of you to say. What's your name?"

He didn't recognize me.

I was thinner and my complexion was darker from being exposed to the sun, but I realized it wasn't that at all. Just as I'd found it difficult to look at him, Bataar had barely looked at me in the palace. His eyes had always been lowered, with nothing more than a brief glance toward me only when etiquette allowed it.

"They call me Autumn Rain."

"Pretty," he replied gruffly. "You're pretty too."

His manners were so rough. The Floating Happiness was a brothel, but this room was staged to look like a lady's chamber and Bataar appeared uncomfortable in it.

"Should I put out the lanterns?" He moved toward the nearest one and it looked as if he would crush the paper bamboo frame in his broad hands.

"No, leave them."

Bataar stopped where he was. "It might be better for you with the lanterns out."

My heart broke for him. In the palace, I had surrounded myself with beauty so I could pretend ugliness didn't exist.

"I don't mind scars," I told him. "I have them as well."

Turning away, I lowered my shawl to reveal my shoulders. The wooden floor creaked as he approached, and my breath caught when his shadow engulfed me. The sheer size of him intimidated me more than his scars did.

At first he merely looked at my back. When he finally reached out to touch me, his palms were rough, but his touch so very gentle. "Who was it that put a whip to you?"

"My father, for disobedience."

It was a lie, which is why I said it so easily.

When I turned around, I was nearly up against Bataar's chest. He was staring down at me with the strangest look on his face.

"You...you look so much like her," he said in a halting tone.

My stomach churned. "Who?"

"Someone I used to know."

I didn't want Bataar to recognize me. Not that I feared he

would endanger me, but I wanted to be someone else tonight. I didn't want the burden of being Princess Shanyin.

I took hold of Bataar's wrist, needing both hands to circle it. "Come," I said gently as I led him to the bed.

Bataar sat back and began to remove his boots. I moved to help him as he undid his belt and removed his tunic. Underneath he was pure muscle and sinew. A warrior through and through.

There were more scars on his chest and back. How many battles had he survived? How many men had he killed with his own hands to be here, at this moment?

I bent to undo his belt and heard the name I dreaded spoken aloud.

"Shanyin."

My heart stopped. I looked up at him, a question in my eyes.

"The woman you remind me of," he explained. "It wasn't her name, but that was what they called her. You're prettier than her, though. Now that I've taken a closer look."

I bit back a smile. "You don't have to flatter me."

"I'm not. And you are."

He removed the rest of his clothing and lay back, completely filling the bed. His organ lifted straight up, fully aroused.

I slipped out of my robe and climbed on top of him, straddling his wide hips. There was no need to tease or beguile. Bataar was a straight and honest man. Such artfulness would have been mockery to him.

His eyes drank in the sight of my body without shame before focusing on my face as I took him inside me. Then he closed his eyes as I began to move, grinding my hips in a slow circle that fed my own desire.

I could have closed my eyes as well and imagined him as someone else. Bataar's body in itself was pleasing; densely muscled with his sex hard and pulsing inside me. I could have conjured up one of my past lovers or I could have smoothed out his features in my mind, imagined him in a better light.

But I kept my eyes open to look at Bataar for the first time without pity or discomfort. How could I be embarrassed now? We were both stripped bare while I rode astride his manhood.

He smelled of the stables. Of leather and earth and grass. His hands settled onto my hips, easily spanning my entire waist. They were rough hands, callused, with nails that were blunt and cracked. He held on to me, but didn't use his grasp to drive me onto his cock. Instead this fierce killer lay still, allowing me to take him at my own leisure.

I watched Bataar as I claimed him. The lines of his face relaxed, replaced with a look of abandon that fed my own desire.

Bataar's features would never be anywhere near handsome, but there was a raw sort of beauty in the masculinity of his body. It was one that had been cut and torn and battered, but never beaten.

I wasn't surprised when sensation began to gather and build inside me. I had always been particularly sensitive, deriving pleasure with ease. But I was surprised when my chest began to tighten and my throat closed up. Tears fell onto my cheeks as I climaxed.

The squeeze and spasm of my inner muscles brought Bataar to the edge as well. His hips thrust upward, hammering him into me until his release took him.

"Did I hurt you?" he asked immediately afterward.

My body was still caught in the aftermath of release. It took me a moment to focus on him. Bataar was looking up at me with concern.

"No, you didn't hurt me," I replied, still startled by my reaction.

"Then why..." He reached up to my cheek to catch a tear

against his knuckles.

"Oh, that happens sometimes."

Which was a lie. I'd never been moved to tears during sex. At least not these sort of tears, as if I'd been turned inside out.

Roughly, I brushed the rest of the tears away and climbed off Bataar. Silently I dressed with my back turned to him while he did the same. When he was done, he came up behind me.

"Autumn Rain, may I come see you again?"

I wished I had the courage to face him, but I didn't. "If you can," I said as brightly as I could.

He left then with little in the way of farewell. The deed was done. What reason did he have to stay?

The bodyguard was the first link I'd seen to my former life. He was proof that world of decadence and depravity had existed. My eyes had filled with tears because I was happy he had survived. I thought for certain he had been killed, as so many of the palace guards must have been.

Bataar was an honorable warrior who had wasted his loyalty on worthless masters—my brother and I. At least he hadn't wasted his life as well.

CHAPTER SEVEN

I woke to the sight of Wu Chien standing over me. I shot up, fear curling in my stomach as I pulled the blanket around me.

"Miss Autumn Rain, it's time to go," he announced.

He reached for me, but I shoved his hand away. "What are you doing here?"

Wu Chien had likely been watching Bataar and me from some peephole last night. He had seen more of me than what was revealed now in my linen shift, but I didn't care. He was uninvited and that fox-whore Madame Lin was doing this to deliberately toy with me.

I pushed past Wu and tore through the corridors searching for that woman. Madame was sitting serenely in her parlor sipping tea, apparently waiting for me. "Autumn Rain, be a good girl for your new master."

My insides knotted. "What do you mean?"

"I sold your bond to Wu Chien. You belong to him now."

The entire morning was like being thrown in cold water. I blinked at her. "You can't sell me. You don't own me."

"But I do." Madame reached for the scroll beside her and opened it. "See, you signed yourself to me when you started work here at the Floating Happiness."

Of course, I hadn't. Of course, it didn't matter.

"Oh, Autumn Rain," she sighed theatrically. "So worldly, yet so naive. You always glided around here like an empress, better than the rest of us. But you were a good investment after all— you fetched a good price in the end. Now off with your new master."

Two men entered the room. They were the thugs Madame used to wrangle drunken and unruly guests, and they waited by the door with menacing stares. Wu Chien looked on curiously as the confrontation unfolded. It was conceivable that I could make enough of a scene that he no longer wanted any part of the bargain, but that would still leave me in the hands of this witch.

In any case, I would not be dragged from this place by peasant hands.

I turned on my heel and strode toward the door. The two thugs started toward me, but I waved them away with an imperious air. By some miracle, they stood back, looking confused. I was a whore, but in my bones I was still princess.

"Should I dress before we go?" I asked Wu Chien.

He smirked at me, the left corner of his mouth smiling, the right corner in a frown. "I would prefer it."

"So what is it?" I asked once we had embarked on our journey to an unknown destination. "Am I to be your concubine? Your servant?"

"I believe you would be a poor choice for either of those," Wu Chien replied.

He drove a horse-drawn wagon while I sat beside him, holding a bamboo parasol to shield me from the sun. My palm was sweating against the handle, but I did my best to appear calm. Though I felt no particular attachment to the Floating Happiness, I had known what to expect—or at least I thought I did.

"One doesn't go searching for a woman experienced in the bedchamber to be his wife," I remarked dryly.

He laughed aloud at that. "A shame really, isn't it? But you're not meant for me, Autumn Rain. To my great regret."

Wu Chien had a direct and open manner about him, but it

was impossible for me to let down my guard. There was something dark hidden behind his easy smile and the way his eyes lingered on my face unnerved me.

I tried to consider what possibly lay ahead, but Madame Lin was right about me. I had no knowledge of the world outside a palace or a brothel. With my heart pounding, I considered trying to escape as we left the town behind. But where would I go?

"Your master has perverse tastes, then," I suggested flippantly.

"The Governor isn't my master. And as to his preferences, I've never been invited to witness his exploits in the bedchamber," he replied with a gleam in his eye. "But I'm certain he'll make use of your skills."

So I was being sold and then handed off like a goat or a pig. With a deep breath, I tried to calm myself. There was nothing to do but wait and see where fate would take me next. And if this Governor turned out to be a sadistic madman—he wouldn't be the first I'd encountered.

"You were pretending last night, weren't you?" I looked over to see Wu watching me with a serious expression. "You imagined that beast was someone dear to you. Otherwise how could you bear having him inside you?"

I bit my tongue to keep from snapping back at him. "He was no more a beast than any man."

"His scars didn't frighten you?" he pressed on. "I found him in a roadside tavern. Even dogs would run away in fear."

Lowering the parasol, I turned my shoulder to Wu, pointedly staring at the road. His interest in the matter was nothing but lurid. "I don't see why it matters to you."

Bataar didn't need me to defend him. I would never see him again, but it was rude for this stranger to pry and prod at him.

"I'm curious. One single act, yet so many ways to

accomplish it. So many little variations, all unique."

"Oh, so you like to watch from afar."

He smiled wickedly. "Not too far. But I do admit, it's difficult to focus when one is in the center of things, surrounded by sweat and skin."

I shifted in my seat, but there was no escape. Wu Chien's face had become flushed and his eyes glowed with excitement. Maybe it wasn't only the Governor whose tastes were perverse.

"Talking of details is rather tiresome," I said dismissively. "It takes away the mystery of it."

"Ah, but you understand me perfectly. The mystery is what fascinates me. Did his ugliness excite you? Things that repulse some women will cause strong arousal in others."

"This conversation is becoming obscene."

Wu ignored me. He was speaking faster, caught in a rapture. "Your desire last night wasn't feigned, was it? You looked quite genuine. There's nothing more beautiful, more exquisite than a woman at that point of complete surrender."

"Lord Wu!" I interrupted sharply. "I will not answer any more of these questions."

There was little that offended me, but Wu Chien's manner of interrogation made my skin crawl. I'd had strangers invade my body, but Wu Chien was trying to insinuate himself into my mind.

My hard words appeared to shame him. He fell silent, blushing all the way to the tips of his ears. "I apologize for my excitement, Autumn Rain. It's rare that I can find someone to share my thoughts with. A woman who won't shy away from such talk."

I was far from flattered. He meant someone who couldn't chastise him for his impropriety. Someone who didn't have the power to escape it. Who better to reveal his sordid fantasies to than a prostitute?

"Let us enjoy the scenery in silence for a while," I suggested, though it consisted of dirt and more dirt. I lowered my parasol and angled it to form a barrier between the two of us, praying that our final destination wasn't too far away.

Four or five hours passed before we reached the Governor's mansion. The residence was located on high and surrounded by green hills. As we approached, I appreciated the breadth of it. The complex must have spanned several courtyards, housing servants as well as direct family.

I could see a city in the valley down below, but the complex was isolated on a high vantage point. I might have appreciated the luxuriousness of it if my heart wasn't pounding so hard.

At the brothel, I was for sale but I belonged to myself. Now I belonged to some nameless, faceless man, procured for the specific purpose of warming his bed.

The servants who met us at the gate allowed us inside without challenge. Wu Chien seemed to be a familiar face among the household. They greeted him respectfully while all I received were curious stares.

A woman stood in the garden. From her face and hands, she appeared young though her hair was pinned in the style of a married woman. The Governor's wife, I assumed.

"He isn't home," she told Wu Chien coldly as we approached. "He was called away suddenly."

"Then I shall have to leave her to your care."

The Governor's wife refused to look at me. I took a more careful assessment of her now that we were close. A man might be the head of the family, but women ruled the home, they said. His wife would have nearly as much power as the Governor in determining my comfort or misery.

Her robe was dark in color and embroidered with red

peonies. Two combs adorned her hair, holding it in place. She would have been pretty if her face wasn't twisted into a scowl.

"What should I do with her?"

"Whatever you see fit." Wu Chien handed over to her the scroll documenting my sale along with a wooden case covered in black lacquer. "I'm certain the Governor will be pleased with his gift once he returns."

Wu gave me a nod in farewell before departing. I sensed it wasn't the last I'd see of him, but I had more pressing concerns. The mistress of the house finally deigned to meet my eyes. The sight of me caused her mouth to press tight and her eyes narrowed like a snake's.

"Come," she said brusquely, turning on her heel. "We serve no purpose standing out here and staring dumbly at one another."

From her speech, I immediately placed her as high-born. Aristocracy, most likely. She was also younger than I. I doubted she had been married for long. She was awkward in her own skin, but made up for it with her sharp tongue.

I followed my new mistress into the inner recesses of the great house. She put me into the hands of the head servant. Old Jie put me to work immediately scrubbing the floors of the walkway in the inner courtyard. For the next several hours, I was on my hands and knees with a bucket of dirty water beside me.

I would have preferred at that moment to have simply been bought for sex. Being bedded was certainly more pleasurable than doing servants' work. Less demeaning as well.

No one spoke to me, or came to check on my progress. By the afternoon, I was only halfway done with the courtyard and my back was sore. I stood up to stretch and caught the sight of the Governor's wife through an open window. She was in a sitting room with a scroll in her hands, reading intently. The lacquer box that Wu Chien had handed over lay in front of her on a low table.

She glanced up and I quickly bent once more to my task.

Supper was brought to me by one of the other servants. The middle-aged woman said little as she handed over a bowl of gruel. I ate alone, sitting beneath the eaves as I watched the sky darken over the courtyard.

It was late in the evening when I finished my task, but still no one came for me. By that time the house had gone quiet, but I didn't yet know where I was supposed to spend the night. When I stood, every muscle in my body complained. I was unaccustomed to labor and there was an ache in my lower back that would not go away, no matter how much I attempted to stretch and knead at it.

Hours had passed since I'd last seen the Governor's wife, but I returned to the window of her sitting room hoping to find her. The thought of having to beseech someone for the simple necessities was humbling, but I wanted so much to curl up somewhere and rest after stooping and crouching for the entire day.

The sitting room was empty, but the mysterious lacquer box was still there on the table. Glancing about, I saw no one and curiosity got the better of me. I went inside and sat upon the padded seat, enjoying the comfort for a moment before reaching for the lid of the box.

My eyebrows rose upon seeing the contents. There was the scroll I had seen the Governor's wife reading with such concentration earlier. Beside it lay a collection of phalluses of various size and shapes arranged in a row.

Some were realistic depictions, fashioned to follow the natural shape and curve of a man. The jade one even had raised veins in the stone to mimic an erect organ. I couldn't resist running my hands over it, admiring the artistry.

Other examples were more fantastic in nature. I picked up one that had been carved out of rosewood and polished to a shine. There were a series of bumps along the length that would pleasure a woman in ways no man could, once inserted inside her.

Perhaps the Governor's wife wasn't as tight-lipped and proper as she seemed. Then again, people's private selves rarely aligned with their public ones.

"What are you doing in here?"

I looked up to see the woman glaring down at me while my hand was wrapped around a wooden phallus. I replaced the item with as much dignity as I could and closed the lid.

"I was looking for the servant's quarters."

"This is my private parlor." Color rose high on her cheeks. "You have no business rummaging through it."

Rising, I attempted a bow, feeling awkward as I did so. "I apologize, *Furen*."

"This is my house and servants must be taught their place."

As her voice pitched higher, I was reminded of a child throwing a tantrum. Reaching for a vase on a nearby stand, she sent it crashing to the floor where it shattered. I stared at the pieces, dumbfounded.

"Old Jie! Come here." Her gaze remained pinned on me until the head servant appeared. "This clumsy thing has broken a precious heirloom. Take her outside and beat her."

My mouth parted in shock, but no words came out. The elderly servant called for two others and, before I could protest, I was dragged out into the center of the garden and pushed down to my knees.

The indignity of it was impossible to bear. I wanted to cry out that I was innocent. Or that I was sorry, even though I was innocent. Then I remembered all the times I'd had servants beaten for similar infractions: a broken comb, a stain on my silk robe, or once for placing a bowl of soup before me that was so hot I burnt my tongue.

I wanted to laugh. I wanted to cry.

Instead I bit down hard onto my lower lip as rough hands pulled my robe down to expose my back. The first lash brought tears stinging to my eyes. I tried to close them as the second blow came down over my shoulder blades, but darkness only made pain worse.

I am a princess! A small voice tried to cry out from deep inside me, but underlings had no voice. I tried to swallow my sobs as the switch struck me again and again. My back was on fire, but the shame was worse than the pain.

It had been years since anyone had dared to raise a hand to me. *Never again*, I'd vowed. *Never again.* But what did I know? When my brother became Emperor, he'd had those bastards executed. I didn't even have the strength now to vow vengeance on the spoiled bitch who was responsible for my present torment.

Finally the beating stopped. I was allowed to pull my robe back over my shoulders to cover myself, and I did so while tears spilled down my cheeks. Even that small motion drew more pain across my body.

Old Jie took me to the dark corner where I was to sleep. There I was left alone to curl up as I'd wanted to, but now with the welts on my back to keep me company into the night.

Wiping my face with my sleeve, I balled up as tight as I could, trying to disappear inside myself. For the first time in a long time, I conjured up my former lovers in my mind. Tai was there. I had him holding the switch to administer my punishment only to pull me into his arms afterward and fuck me until the pain turned to pleasure. That had never really happened. I wouldn't let anyone, let alone my slaves, hurt me like that, but I worked hard to force the fantasy over the sharp edges of reality.

Jiyi was there next to soothe my aches and pains with his gentle hands and mouth.

And finally Yuan. The handsome lover who my body had only known once. Yuan was there, strong and solid beside me, to hold on to me and rock me gently to sleep.

CHAPTER EIGHT

The next day I was sweeping out the rooms in the front of the house, my back still throbbing, when the Governor's wife came at me. I shrank at the sight of her, my hands gripping the broom tight.

"What are you doing here?" she shrieked.

I could have reported snidely that I was doing exactly what I was told to do, but I remained silent. How quickly I was learning the ways of servants.

"Come here. Quickly."

She grabbed my arm and started to pull me alongside her, but I tore out of her grasp. "I can walk."

For a moment she stared at me, stunned at my tone. I headed out toward the garden. By the time she caught up with me, the Governor's wife was out of breath, but she didn't slow down. She led me to the rear courtyard, ushering me through a doorway.

"Stay here," she commanded.

I looked around. She'd shoved me into a storage room without windows.

"Don't you dare come out." She shut the door, leaving me in darkness.

With a sigh, I sank down to the floor and let my head sink into my hands. From the mutterings and stirring on the way back here, I'd gleaned that the master of the house had returned. Wu Chien should have known better than to hand me over to a jealous young wife, but he'd had no reason to concern himself with me.

If the brat was so worried I'd steal her husband's attention away from her, why didn't she just dismiss me and send me wandering off to nowhere? Not that the sight of me would seduce a man. I was dressed in the same brown house robe as the rest of the servants and I shuffled around stiffly like an old woman, trying to move my back as little as possible.

I ended up dozing for minutes, maybe an hour at a time. No one came by with food or water so I was parched when Old Jie finally came to let me out.

"What hour is it?" I asked.

"Almost sundown."

He appeared put out rather than concerned at having to deal with me. I was placed this time in a small chamber and given tea and a simple meal of rice and vegetables which I devoured before sitting back to look at my surroundings.

It was much better than the storage closet. At least there was a more comfortable sleeping pallet and a blanket. There was also a window that opened out into the courtyard. If this was to be my prison, at least I could catch a glimpse of sunlight and breathe in fresh air.

Was I truly resigning myself to being prisoner? What would Princess Shanyin have done? Seduce her guards and the Governor before ordering the petty Governor's wife to scrub the floors. It was a fanciful dream, but I had no taste for seducing the elderly Old Jie. I had no desire to bed the Governor either, a bureaucrat who needed secondaries to procure prostitutes for him.

The Governor was likely old and impotent himself. Suddenly the request for a woman skilled in the bedchamber took on a new light, which left me sick to my stomach.

I fell asleep lying on my side while plotting a half-hearted escape. I was still drifting in and out of sleep when I was awoken by a scream. My heart raced as I sat up. Another scream cut across the courtyard, loud enough to shake the heavens. Strangely, no one in the household stirred.

The answer to the mystery came quickly to me. More cries came, muted this time, along with a masculine voice, low and urgent. I couldn't hear the words, but I didn't need to. Apparently the Governor wasn't impotent. If anything, he seemed rather vigorous in the bedchamber. The noises died away quickly after that.

The next night, I was awoken by the same scream, but the episode was briefer this time.

The third night, the screaming never came. Instead there were raised voices, shouting, the sound of a woman weeping.

I started as a door slammed. It was impossible to close my ears to the drama that was unfolding and I imagined the worst. Maybe there was still time to escape.

Maybe the Governor's wife would want to come with me.

Surprisingly, I was let out the next morning.

I was given a list of chores to complete and I was almost grateful for the activity after having done nothing but stare at four walls for the last few days. While dusting in the main parlor, I caught my first glimpse of the Governor.

He was at the far end of a corridor and in conversation with one of his retainers. I paused, partially hidden by a wooden screen, to look at the man who ruled over this household as well as the entire commandery.

The Governor was turned away from me so I couldn't make out his features clearly, though he appeared tall in stature when framed by the hallway. Not old as I'd imagined, but broad in the shoulder with a posture that spoke of confidence.

He must have sensed my gaze on him because he turned to look down the corridor. I ducked behind the screen with my pulse racing, feeling like a coward. Some instinct told me I wanted to keep as much distance between this man and myself as possible. The very air inside the household grew oppressive while he was there.

I encountered the Governor's wife as well. For most of the morning, she sat in the rear courtyard with a silk handkerchief and embroidery needle in hand, saying nothing to anyone. She met my eyes with a cold stare when she saw me, but I stared right back at her until she looked away.

That afternoon, instead of a list of chores, I was given time to take a bath. The other servants brought hot water to fill the tub in the bath house and I steeped in it, reveling in the warm caress of the water over my skin. I never imagined a simple bath would feel like such an indulgence.

Afterward, I was given a salve for my back though the pain had faded. The robe laid out for me was also of noticeably finer cotton than the drab tunic and trousers I had worn previously.

Such small luxuries did not come without a price. It was easy to guess the reason behind this sudden change in my treatment. Perhaps Wu Chien had informed the Governor that he'd safely delivered me to the mansion. Or the Governor had decided he required my services.

My suspicions were confirmed when I was brought to a larger room, one with a proper wooden bed raised off the floor. I sat down on it and contemplated my change in fortune. I wasn't ready to declare whether it was better to be under the Governor's hand or his wife's, but I would have my answers tonight.

As the sky darkened, my skin warmed with vulgar anticipation. The man I'd spied in the corridor was able-bodied and strong. He could still be a monster inside—from the way his wife screamed and wept whenever he visited her, the Governor certainly seemed to have a cruel streak. But there were many levels of cruelty, some of which were not entirely unpleasant.

I lay down on the bed and let the night wrap around me. Tonight I would know whether the Governor would master me or I him. The uncertainty made my heart pound and my palms sweat. My sex dampened as I considered the upcoming battle, which only proved how wanton I was. I hoped the Governor wouldn't be too easy to seduce.

For all my speculation, the Governor didn't come for me. Once more, I heard the moans and murmurs of the bedchamber floating across the courtyard. The Governor was certainly a man with a strong appetite for sex. The interlude went on for a long time tonight, the sounds of lovemaking dying down only to start up again. By the time the sobbing started, my eyelids were drooping closed.

I drifted off, feeling unfulfilled and strangely envious. Since that one night with Bataar, my days had become empty again. Empty and colorless and void of any sensation to pique my interest. Sex was an infusion of heat and formless emotion in the purest sense.

When the door to my room opened some time later, that early haze of desire had faded. The room was cold and the mansion completely still. I sat up with a startled gasp as I stared at the dark figure in the doorway. The Governor.

When he closed the door and came toward me, I knew he had been drinking by the sway in his step. I froze as he stood beside the bed, unable to see his face or anything else about him in the darkness.

Leaning over, he braced one hand against the bed frame, right beside my knee, but not touching me. Then he paused, breathing in and out slowly, balanced on the edge of some decision. I had a decision to make as well.

I couldn't run and the Governor could easily overpower me. My breath grew shallow and my throat dry with desire at the thought of this man taking me while I had no knowledge of what he looked like. It didn't matter who he was or who I was.

Reaching out, I curled my fingers into his robe to pull him to me. I could at least claim this; our first touch. The dance would begin now, the push and pull of sex. The giving and taking.

Immediately his hands closed over mine and he pushed me onto the bed. He pinned my wrists tight against my heaving chest as he loomed over me.

"Don't move. Don't say anything," he warned, his voice strained. The roughness of it sent a shudder down into the pit of my stomach.

Blind as I was, I couldn't anticipate what he would do or whether he regarded me with desire or disdain. All I had was the language of our bodies, which always became confused in the storm of emotions that accompanied sex. I could barely breathe as my muscles tensed.

He reached for my sash and fumbled at it, trying to work the knot loose. I didn't dare help him. Instead I lay as still as possible, just as he'd commanded. I could hear him snorting with impatience, and the smell of rice liquor on his breath washed over me.

I closed my eyes out of instinct, straining to read some intention in his clumsy movements. He was drunk. He would be impatient, perhaps rough. I remembered the shouting over the last few nights and prayed he wouldn't become belligerent if he failed in the act.

Finally the sash came loose and he opened my robe. I was naked underneath. No underclothes had been provided, which I had taken as another sign the Governor had intended for me to be available to him tonight.

He took hold of my breasts roughly, but the moment his hands touched my skin, something changed. There was no greedy, mauling of my flesh as I'd expected. His touch became careful, almost tender. I could hear his breathing deepen above me. He took in a long breath and held it as his hands moved in slow circles; caressing, kneading, exploring.

The Governor was studying my body. I had no other way to describe it. There wasn't a sound in the room but our breathing, which tangled together in two discordant streams. His thumbs rubbed over the hard peaks of my nipples and my back lifted from the bed. He held onto me and firmly pressed me down against the hard surface to remind me. *Be still. Be silent.*

I obeyed, sinking back as I willed him to continue. His hands returned to cup my hips, angling them upward. One hand withdrew only to return lower against my thigh. I let my legs fall apart while I held my breath.

Find me. Please find me. Touch me.

He did find me. His fingertips brushed over my slit and I heard the catch in the Governor's breath when he discovered the wetness there. He laid himself alongside me, fully clothed, and his mouth closed over my breast, tongue working me gently. Down below, he slipped a long finger into the folds of my sex. I gasped and let out a helpless moan, unable to contain myself.

"*Quiet.*" It sounded almost like a plea. Warm breath fanned against my nipple. His fingers penetrated and stroked me, setting me alight. He wanted me to come quickly and I wanted nothing more than to obey.

I dug my nails into my palms to will myself to remain still. The Governor's fingers fluttered over my bud mercilessly now while he sucked my nipples into his mouth. I wanted to writhe and squirm and buck my hips with abandon, but I wasn't allowed. My head moved from side to side, silently begging. If this was a battle, I had lost. I would do whatever it took as long as the Governor didn't remove his hands from me.

The climax crashed over me like a wave, hard at first, then

soft. Hard enough to take my breath away, then soft as my body continued to spasm in waves. I bit down on my lower lip to remain silent as the orgasm took me over, leaving me trembling.

Afterward, the Governor's fingers withdrew and he lay over me as if spent. Tension still rippled through his body and his breath was labored. He wasn't yet fulfilled.

Once again I reached for him and once again he trapped my hands, not allowing me to touch him. I was confused. What had he done every night that had his wife screaming and begging for mercy? All he wanted of me was that I remain passive and willing.

He lay there for what seemed like a long time while my passion cooled and I began to drift off once more. Before leaving, he pressed his face to the side of my neck. I thought he meant to kiss me there, but he took in a deep breath, inhaling the scent of my skin into himself, before getting up to leave.

CHAPTER NINE

The Governor's wife made a point of crossing my path in the courtyard the next morning.

"Remember you're just a whore, bought and paid for," she said through her teeth. "Easily replaced."

I kept on walking. As far as insults went, her words slid off me like the pelt of cold rain. A moment's annoyance and nothing more.

There were no floors for me to scrub that day and I was allowed to wander the grounds at my leisure. I hid near the front of the mansion, waiting for the Governor to appear. It was late in the morning when he finally did.

A groomsman brought a horse out. A moment later, the Governor himself appeared and I shrank behind the shrubbery. His back was turned and I allowed my gaze to roam over him, committing the shape and size of him to memory so I had an image to hold in my mind in the dark. I could remember every touch of those strong hands on my skin. How I'd shuddered and writhed beneath them.

And it was only the beginning. My mouth grew dry imagining what he would do to me tonight.

The Governor came to me once more in the dark, but at an earlier hour. I wondered if he had been waiting for the sun to set as I had been.

I saw his silhouette against the doorframe for just a heartbeat before he closed the door and I was blind once more. But in that one glimpse, I knew where to find him.

I went to the Governor and reached up to touch his face, running my fingertips along his cheek and down the line of his jaw. I didn't know his age or whether he was handsome or ugly. Whether he had kind eyes or hard, cold ones. I suppose it didn't matter.

He endured that one touch before taking hold of my wrists. His breathing deepened as he walked me back to the bed and lowered me onto it. His hands were gentle, but firm as he pressed my arms onto the thin padding, positioning my hands on either side of my head.

"Don't move. Don't say anything."

The same command as before. The Governor wanted me to make myself an empty vessel. The frightening thing was, I wanted to do it. For him. Maybe there was peace in being empty. I could get rid of all that was rotted and worm-eaten inside me. I could be new again.

Pushing up my robe, he slipped his fingers between my legs. His breathing deepened when he discovered I was already wet. He shifted to reposition himself, and removed his hand from my sex only to replace it a moment later with the warm caress of his mouth.

Throwing my head back, I fought to keep my hips still as his tongue licked into me. He did it again and then again, stroking over my delicate bud until I sobbed. The moment I did, his mouth left me and I wanted to weep. Once more he changed positions.

"Quiet," he reminded me. He found my hands where he'd left them and held them down with his own before pushing his hard cock fully into me, not stopping until our hips were locked.

I had to bite into his shoulder to keep from screaming as I took all of him, all at once. He grunted with pain, but his member swelled inside me and his thrusts became more fervent, rubbing against some hidden source of pleasure that made me unravel until there was nothing left except the sensations he drew out of me. Though it had only been days, it felt like an eternity since someone had filled me so completely.

The taste of his skin lingered on my tongue and I could smell his scent all around: cedarwood and sweat. As he continued to fuck me, I could no longer obey his command for silence. Small cries escaped my lips, each one a plea for him not to stop. To never stop.

The Governor clamped his hand over my mouth. It made it difficult for me to breathe, but I didn't care. I was coming. The orgasm centered at first on my sex, then radiated throughout my body as I screamed into his palm. He was killing me. He was killing me.

I was so blinded by my own pleasure that I didn't realize the Governor had come as well until his organ slipped wetly out of me. Even so, he wouldn't let me speak. As soon as he removed his hand, his mouth crushed against mine in a kiss that stole my breath, my voice, and the last shred of my will.

This wasn't over between us, the kiss promised. His cock was momentarily spent, but his desire hadn't cooled. Dear heaven, he was hungry. A thrill shot through me, spreading to every limb.

When his tongue slid over mine, the taste of him brought back some yellow-tinted memory. I tried to grasp on to it, but it slipped through my fingers. Had anyone ever kissed me like this before?

After we broke apart, he remained close, his forehead pressed to mine while his breathing gradually slowed. Then he fell asleep over me. His weight crushed me into the bed, but I liked the feeling of being held so securely. I wanted to stroke my hands through his hair or run my nails over his back, something soft and sentimental to prolong the moment, but I held back.

For whatever reason, the Governor didn't want to be touched. He didn't even want to hear my voice. With the lanterns extinguished and the night surrounding us, I could be anyone.

My suspicions were confirmed when the Governor stirred above me much later. He pressed his lips to the spot between my neck and shoulder.

"You're exactly as I remembered," he murmured before leaving me alone with my own ghosts to tame.

CHAPTER TEN

The Governor's wife ambushed me the next morning, pouncing on me the moment I stepped out into the courtyard. Her eyes were swollen and her face was wet with tears.

"It's all a trick, isn't it? A whore's trick."

I stepped back defensively, but she refused to let me escape. The woman advanced on me and tore at my clothes, calling me names. Whore, witch, fox-demon.

With my hands raised, I tried to fend her off, but there was nothing I could do to fight back. She was the lady of the house and the Governor's wife. One word from her and I would be thrown out like a beggar.

"*Furen*, everyone can hear you out here."

"She-demon!" she spat at me and I wondered if she had gone mad overnight. She was the one who was acting like a demon. "Everyone should know what a liar and whore you are."

I grabbed her then and forced her into my room, shutting the door behind us. Then I turned around and slapped her across the face as hard as I could.

"Calm yourself!"

For a moment, she could do nothing but stare at me, stunned. Her hand hovered over the cheek where I'd struck her, but it was as if she was afraid to even touch it. Half her face glared red.

I had done it to calm her, but also in retribution for the insults she dared to hurl at me. I shouldn't have let her provoke me like that. This one slap could be the end of me.

Her eyes burned fire, but instead of lashing out, she doubled over. Fresh tears poured over her face. "You pretend with my husband, don't you? You must pretend to enjoy the way he shoves that thing between his legs at you. I tried to bite my tongue and endure it so many times, but I can't."

She glared at me hatefully through her tears. I felt a moment of pity for her, but not too much. No matter how many times the Governor came to my chamber, she would still be his wife while I was little better than a servant.

"I don't have to pretend. Our bodies hunger for each other," I told her, feeling my cruel streak rise to the surface. This was the same woman who'd had me beaten in front of all the servants. "But you shouldn't be so surprised. Men are supposed to respect their wives, as they say. Love is meant for courtesans and concubines."

I left her then, shutting the door on her while she stared at me, red-eyed and mouth gaping. My hands were shaking as I hurried away.

Despite my boastfulness, I wasn't the Governor's concubine. I was his whore and the rule for any mistress or consort was to promote harmony and goodwill toward the first wife. At least on the surface. No man would tolerate such bitter rivalry and turmoil beneath his own roof.

Was I deliberately trying to get cast out? After only two nights, the Governor, or at least the idea of him, had taken hold of me like no other lover. I wasn't some innocent, to be won over simply because a man could fuck me to orgasm. With the Governor, I wanted to lose myself in his desires at the cost of my own. As long as he kept on making me feel alive.

With my pulse pounding, I went to the main courtyard where the Governor's study was located. In my heart, I sensed my time here was already over. The Governor's wife would recover enough to have me punished for my insolence before throwing me out onto the dusty road. The Governor would procure a new slave to lie spread out and obedient before him.

A servant was carrying a tray of tea toward the study. I intercepted the boy, taking the tray from his hands. "I'll bring this to the Governor."

He stared at me, uncertain what to do. I had no established status within the household, but by now every servant in the mansion knew how the Governor had shared my bed.

"The tea is getting cold," I warned. "I better go in now."

The boy nodded, looking between me and the door of the study. Finally he relented and scurried off while I tapped twice against the wood.

"Come in."

That voice. Even from the other side of the door, with space between us, that voice found its way deep into me.

I opened the door to see the Governor with his head bent over a paper on his writing desk. It was the first time I'd looked directly at him, in daylight. Even though I couldn't see his face yet, my palms began to sweat.

What could I hope to accomplish here? I would see my lover's face for the first and last time. I'd say farewell to him, the only word he would hear me speak.

He was writing out some decree, holding up his sleeve with one hand as he worked the brush with the other. Thick, black hair was pulled up into a topknot, but a section of it fell over his forehead, hiding his eyes. His fingers were long, but too broad to be considered elegant. The sight of them touched up against an unbidden memory.

The brush moved furiously over the paper. His movements were restless, agitated, and he appeared to pour all his frustrations onto the black characters he slashed over the page.

My heart started pounding. I knew those hands. Not just in the dark and on my skin. I knew that posture, the tilt of that chin—the Governor looked up then and the tea tray slipped from my fingers to crash to the floor. I barely noticed the hot water splashing over my slippers to scald my toes.

Yuan was staring at me, a frown cutting deep into his brow. The Governor had transformed into Lord Chu Yuan, the man who had haunted my dreams all these months.

I turned to flee. It was all I could think to do.

I had conjured Yuan from my memories. That was the only possible explanation. Yet behind me, I heard him calling my name. *Shanyin.*

I fumbled with the door, needing to escape. The moment I opened it, a hand shot forward to slam it shut. The hairs on my neck stood on end. I could feel him right behind me, caging me in. The silk of his robe brushed against my shoulder blades.

"Turn around and look at me, Shanyin."

I turned, but kept my eyes averted. I was trembling hard.

He took my chin in his hands to tilt my face upward. My gaze locked on to those dark, serious eyes and my knees weakened. I had to lean against the door for support.

For a moment, all we did was look, taking each other in, to the smallest detail. Then he cupped my face in his hands and brought his mouth onto mine. With the kiss, I knew without a doubt it was Yuan. My once lover. My destroyer. My savior.

The kiss continued, deepening and taking on an edge of desperation as if I were as dear to him as his next breath. I was so used to Yuan holding back, refusing to show the full measure of his passion, but he held nothing back now. He kissed me until I could barely breathe and my flesh and bone melted away. If he hadn't held on to me, I would have crumbled to floor.

He broke for only a moment before capturing my mouth again. With one hand he worked the front of his robe open.

There were so many questions I wanted to ask him. How had he become Governor of this remote commandery? And he had a wife now. When had he married?

And after the palace coup, had Yuan truly wanted to find me?

With a hand pushing my legs apart, he opened and entered me in one powerful stroke and all my questions disappeared. My leg curved around his hips while my back pushed against the door. Down below, Yuan pumped in and out of me in short, tantalizing strokes, claiming me as his.

I closed my eyes then to once again cast myself in darkness. There I sensed all the things I had felt before, but couldn't fully grasp. Vaguely, I had recognized the taste of him, the smell of his skin. And the way Yuan touched me was like no other. My body must have known all of this deep inside. I had fallen so quickly for the Governor.

I was falling again now as Yuan made love to me in broad daylight. My eyes flew open to latch on to his as a climax crashed through me, breaking me into a thousand pieces.

"You're exactly as I remembered, Shanyin," he said with a moan. "Exactly as I remembered."

Book 3: The Fulfillment

CHAPTER ONE

An hour had passed since I had been reunited with Yuan, who at one time had been both my savior and my downfall. We lay on the floor of his study with my body draped languidly over his. My limbs molded to him like warm wax after all the things he'd done to me. It was a long time since either of us had said a word, but it was Yuan who finally broke the silence.

"This isn't love."

Yuan regarded me without blinking as he declared his lack of feeling. As always, I was stricken by the stark beauty of his features. The fierce arch of his cheekbones and the strong and unyielding jaw. Bones of jade. He was every bit the proud nobleman I remembered.

The front of his robe was still open and I drew a lazy pattern over his bare chest with my finger. "I'm heartbroken."

He propped an arm behind his head to look up at me. We'd come together so urgently there hadn't been time to fully disrobe. Yuan had backed me up against the door and entered me while we both stood. The grind of his hips had pinned me upright.

Afterward we collapsed in the exact place we found ourselves now.

"I thought about you constantly after you disappeared." His tone held a note of reproach, as if I'd had any control over my fate after being smuggled from the palace. "I would see you out of the corner of my eye; in the curve of a woman's throat or the way she held herself. Or I'd hear the sound of your voice. But then she would move or speak and the fog would clear. Every time it wasn't you, I would be left hollow and disappointed."

He tilted his head now as he looked at me, as if to be certain that I wasn't another illusion. Leaning down, I pressed my lips to his shoulder. I heard his voice above me, hollow like the echo from an empty well.

"But this isn't love. It's lust. A fixation."

He didn't have to convince me. For the last two nights, he had come to my room without knowing who I was to make full use of my body. His gaze was aimed over my shoulder as he spoke now. His pose was relaxed, spent, but I ran my hand down over his stomach and his sex stirred once more.

"I've taken you over a hundred times, losing myself into the emptiness of my own hand," he confessed. "It's unhealthy to surrender your essence so fervently to a ghost."

Though his skin was hot, his words rang cold. They sent a shiver down my spine. I wasn't superstitious, but I had come so close to death at his hands that I was afraid to speak of it aloud. I was also afraid to admit that I had thought of him too, but not for sexual gratification. I'd sought out his memory for comfort.

"You can take me again now," I offered without shame.

His eyes became lidded as my hand closed around his cock. Even when not fully aroused, Yuan was thick and heavy in my grasp. He hardened quickly, watching the rhythmic movement of my hand as I stroked him.

When he was ready, I opened my robe and climbed onto him, straddling his hard thighs. With my fingers I placed the swollen head of his sex at my entrance and felt a new wave of desire take me at that initial contact, when sensation was still a delicate thing. Skin to skin.

I looked up to meet his eyes before sinking down onto him, letting my back arch as I took him fully inside. His pose hadn't changed from our conversation to this moment of joining. Even as I lifted and lowered myself to feel the smooth glide of his sex into me, he didn't move. He remained reclined, head back with his eyes shielded and jaw set. A spectator.

My robe was undone so I pushed the last of it from my shoulders and cast it aside. His breathing deepened at the sight of my bare skin. We'd only known each other in complete darkness for the last two days, with him slipping clandestinely into my chamber only once the lanterns were out.

I had control in this position and I took advantage of it, taking him as slow and as deep as I wanted to, grinding my hips at an angle to pleasure myself.

Yuan reached out a hand to caress my thigh, spanning it easily with the breath of his palm. The touch was as slow and unhurried as my rhythm on his cock.

"You're like a spring down there. A river." His hand moved to where his flesh penetrated mine. With fingers splayed, he slid his hand between us, framing the juncture of our bodies. As if he could take possession of our union. "You're always ready, aren't you?"

I ground my hips against him, rubbing the pearl of my sex against his hand. Yuan had always been so restrained around me that hearing him speak so openly aroused me even more.

"For you," I murmured. "Only with you."

Overcome, I reached for his face, wanting to touch him in some way beyond where our bodies were joined. Yuan caught my wrist to hold me back, even as his cock stirred inside the tight clasp of my body.

His black eyes glittered. "I don't believe that."

There was no reproach in his tone. Yuan knew who I was. I made no other attempt to touch him aside from where he wanted me. He lay back and watched as I rode him, seeking out a rhythm that would satisfy both of us. His posture remained relaxed to accept my gift. He may have dreamed of taking me, but he was content here to be the one taken. I could only detect his arousal in the quickening of his breath, and the faint tension that hardened the lines of his face. The effect heightened his beauty.

When my climax rushed through me, I squeezed my inner muscles around him and rode him hard. He did find his release, but while I trembled and shuddered above him, Yuan remained still through his crisis. His jaw tightened momentarily and there was a slight jerk of his hips as I felt the hot pulse of his seed inside me. Some unnamable emotion flickered across his eyes like lightning.

In the next moment, the flash of heat was gone, and Yuan lay beneath me, unmoved.

I sensed Yuan's eyes following me, making my skin tingle as I retrieved my robe.

"I'm not an illusion," I assured him as I turned away to dress myself.

His gaze unnerved me. There was a time long ago when I had been vulnerable, but I'd built a protective shell around me. Now I reveled in my nakedness. My body was a vessel for my own pleasure.

Yet my skin prickled as I straightened the layers of my clothing before Yuan's searing gaze. I had been given a flowing robe of embroidered silk which set me apart from the other house servants who wore drab tunics in gray and brown. Despite this small mark of favor, I was still in every way a slave.

When Yuan and I had first come together, I had been Princess. My brother ruled over this land as Emperor. Now I'd been brought to this mansion as a bonded servant. As much as Yuan stirred my blood, the very soul of me warred against being dragged under anyone's hand.

I sensed his presence behind me. For a long moment, he said nothing. Only when his hands closed around my waist was I assured his body was still hungry for mine. His robe remained open as he pressed his chest to my back. His warm breath tickled against my neck.

"You better go, Shanyin. I won't be able to resist if you stay."

I shuddered as his lips moved over my skin. He drew me into his arms even as he told me to leave.

"You must have important responsibilities as governor," I murmured, glancing over at the desk.

A scroll was laid out over the surface. Yuan had been writing before abandoning his work to come to me. His brush had fallen onto the paper, leaving a splash of black over the pristine white. The official decree was ruined. It thrilled me that I could have such an effect on him, making such a controlled man forget his duties.

He followed my gaze. "Yes, responsibilities," he echoed before capturing my earlobe into his mouth and sucking gently.

A bolt of sensation shot down my spine and settled deep in my belly. My toes tingled as he nibbled on me. His arms held me tight in contrast to the indifference he'd shown while I rode upon his cock.

"But I've wasted half the day." Just as quickly, he let go of me and stepped away to straighten his clothes.

"Wasted?" I purred as he returned to his desk.

His expression was set in stone. "You have always had a way of making me forget, Shanyin."

Lover's words, but spoken with such bluntness that they were hard against my ears. He returned the ink brush to its stand and cast the ruined scroll aside.

"You'll come to me tonight, then." I cringed as soon as the entreaty left my lips. These weren't the words of a seductress, assured in her own power. They certainly weren't the words of a princess.

He raised an eyebrow at me. "Maybe. Maybe not."

I straightened my spine, matching the sudden stiffness of his posture. "If you were to come looking, you might find me already gone."

"Oh?" he looked only mildly interested. Hot one moment, cold the next. I knew this game. It was the same one he'd subjected me to when we'd first met.

"I had an argument with your wife before coming to you."

"That is not surprising. The character for trouble is two women under one roof." Yuan retrieved a blank scroll and calmly began a new notice.

It was more than an argument. She had confronted me in a near rage and I'd struck her. It was unforgivable by any measure.

"When did you come to be married?" I asked.

"Three months ago." Yuan's head remained bent as he spoke.

Shortly after the palace coup. "Your wife seems to be from a good family."

"She is."

I was accustomed to being despised, but certainly not ignored. "Was she the long-lost love you were pining after?"

Finally he glanced up at me. "My first intended is no longer alive. I told you as much."

"I forgot."

I could feel the spark of the old battle between us igniting. The round against the door and then again on the floor was merely an exchange of courtesies. Now our weapons were drawn. My blood stirred at the promise.

"You should know Mao Mei is the Emperor's niece by marriage."

Which made her some distant sort of cousin of mine. "You have the ill-fortune of being matched with princesses."

His jaw hardened. "Apparently it's my fate."

Something lurked beneath his gaze, a darkness I didn't remember. I could feel the hairs on the back of my neck rising.

"Does she know who I am?" I asked.

"She knows you're a courtesan, brought into the household to fill a particular need." Yuan folded his hands before him and regarded me with a superior air. "It is best that she continue to think of you as nothing more. Make no mistake—my wife is the lady of this house. Go make your peace with her."

CHAPTER TWO

There was a hint of perfume in the hall. The slightest wisp of something delicate and feminine which signaled a presence outside the door not too long ago.

I didn't need to seek out Yuan's wife. She was sitting beneath the viewing pavilion as I stepped out into the garden. An embroidery frame rested in her hands and she was focused on pulling a length of red thread through green silk.

Her gaze slid over to me as I passed through the stone circle of the entranceway. I imagined her outside her husband's study, listening to the sounds of our lovemaking. Watching the murky rise and fall of our shadows through the paper window.

She was angry, though she tried to hide it. I could only see her agitation in the grip of her fingers on the silver needle. The tight press of her lips. She was younger than I, and not as experienced with controlling her emotions.

"*Furen*," I greeted, keeping my gaze steady on her as I ascended the stairs of the pavilion.

Mao Mei lifted the tea cup to her lips and took a sip, taking her time. The pale skin of her cheek was smooth and unmarred. I hadn't hit her hard enough to leave a mark, but the damage was done. A pervasive and heavy silence hung between us.

I stood to await her response. Without a word, Mao Mei set the cup back down and turned her attention back to her embroidery. I had to admit that Yuan's wife was much prettier than I. I'd never considered myself a beauty. The men who called me so did it only for flattery's sake—except Yuan.

But Mao Mei was a classical beauty. The picture of elegance. How pleased Yuan must have been on his wedding night to see this lovely creature was meant to be his wife. Lovely and cold.

Maybe they were a perfect match.

I tilted my head in not quite a bow before turning to go. "Farewell, then."

"You like what my husband does to you," she interrupted, her tone cutting.

By the time I stopped to face her, my smile was in place. It was the sort of smile only a woman could give another woman. The smile of a rival who had the upper hand. "I do. He's quite skilled."

Her top lip curled, showing the barest glimpse of white teeth. "Whore."

I let my smile widen slowly. She could call me any number of unflattering names: whore, witch, fox-demon. The words she spoke were irrelevant. All that mattered was that she was compelled to speak and I was secure enough in my advantage to remain silent.

I even bowed to acknowledge the insult graciously, to sink the knife in further. Yes, this lowly whore shows the great lady the respect which is her due. Mao Mei knew where I'd spent the entire morning. Her imagination in these matters might be limited due to her youth, but she was a newly married woman. She knew enough.

"I'm actually grateful," she continued, pulling the needle through the cloth with a snide look. "My husband has a considerable appetite when it comes to the bedchamber. At least he has another warm body to put his greedy thing into so I can finally get some rest."

"Then we are in agreement, you and I," I goaded.

Her mouth tightened. "Perfectly so."

She was deceptively delicate in appearance with her snow-white skin and wide-eyed, peach-blossom features. Now that I knew of the royal blood that flowed between us, it was no wonder we clashed.

Yuan had told me to make peace with his wife. He didn't know us women. We could perform all the correct actions and say all the right phrases, while each word cut like a knife.

"Remember this, Autumn Rain." She called me by my courtesan name as she jabbed her needle into the embroidered hummingbird at the center of the cloth. "No matter what favors my husband bestows upon you, I'm the mistress of this house. You're nothing but a second hole."

Up until her vulgar outburst, I was starting to feel sorry for Yuan's young wife and how outmatched she was in this contest. In another life, we could have been kindred spirits. Now I felt no pity for her at all.

"I would never presume to take *Furen's* place," I said with utter politeness. "A cold bed must be a hard place to sleep."

Anger flashed in her eyes, but she managed to keep her composure.

"You're only here because I allow it," she warned. "Enjoy your affair, Autumn Rain. But step out of line and I'll have you thrown out of my house. You'll be the prettiest beggar in the kingdom."

My stomach knotted as she spoke, though outwardly I gave her nothing. Everything Mao Mei said rang true. I might have once outranked her once, but I'd had everything stripped away. As mistress of the house, she held power over me and over Yuan as well due to her familial relationship with the Emperor. I needed to find a way to placate her, not goad her, but it wasn't in my nature to bow down to anyone.

Not even someone who hated me, yet held my fate in her hands.

Yuan did come to me that night. Instead of extinguishing the lanterns, he moved around the room lighting more of them. White orbs flickered around us, bathing us in a warm light. He met my eyes as he lit the last one and my pulse skipped. In the next heartbeat, he was crossing the room to sweep me up in his arms.

Without pause, he laid me down on the bed and pushed a hand beneath my skirt. With any other man, such an action would have seemed clumsy and rough, but there was a confidence to Yuan's touch that promised I would feel exactly what he wanted me to feel.

He parted the outer lips of my sex and stroked in between the petals until my eyes rolled back. I sank like water onto the bed, formless, without any will of my own. His long finger penetrated me. His cock followed soon after, claiming me in one hard thrust.

Hard and throbbing, he plunged into me as if he'd spent all day dreaming of this moment. His thick organ parted my lips and invaded my flesh as my body tightened around him to hold him to me.

I willed myself to come for him. I willed him to take me there and he did. Oh, how he did. My body convulsed in waves as his arms enclosed me, the full press of his weight anchoring me to the bed. With any other man I would have felt confined, but with Yuan I was held secure in his embrace.

"Beautiful," he murmured, his voice rough.

My eyes opened to the sight of Yuan watching me. He was strikingly handsome, the look in his eyes so intense that it hooked deep into my soul just like the first time I'd seen him. His mouth came crushing down over my lips, heating my insides even though I'd already come.

His cock remained hard as it slid in and out of me, finding a new rhythm for us as my body writhed beneath him. Soon I

231

was panting once more with my legs hugged tight around his hips.

I was so used to Yuan denying me, denying both of us that it was a revelation to see him so uninhibited. He held onto my hips as he plunged into me again and again, grinding, urging me toward release. Sweat beaded on his brow.

Reaching between us, his fingers found the bud of my sex and soon I was falling deep, thinking of nothing more than my own climax.

My muscles clenched tight while he fucked me and I cried out, startled at the quickness and the intensity of my surrender. My entire body throbbed as the orgasm sliced through me.

I sank back onto the bed, and Yuan's cock slowly slipped out of me, leaving me hollow.

"This is how it should be," he murmured. His hand closed possessively around my breast. "You don't know how it feels, Shanyin. To be able to finally touch a woman like this, like I've been longing to. And to have her respond so sweetly."

He could have been talking of any woman, but he pinched my nipple lightly between his thumb and forefinger. I moaned and my back arched helplessly. His eyes burned as he watched me, and my sex flooded once more.

His mouth closed over my other nipple, sucking gently to reawaken my senses before scraping lightly over the swollen peak with his teeth.

I screamed. Heavens, he was tormenting me. My body was exhausted from his fucking, while his hands and mouth aroused me to a new fervor. Overcome, I cried out his name. I knew who Yuan was now as he took me. It made the sensation a hundred times more intense.

"This is how I remembered you," he murmured. His palms closed over my breasts, the touch momentarily soothing. "Insatiable."

His eyes glinted wickedly as he pushed inside me once more. He was the insatiable one. I winced as the sensation became unbearable, edging over into pain.

"Are you sore?" he asked gently.

I nodded and he bent to kiss my neck just below my ear. The tenderness of it gutted me. His thrusts in and out of me slowed, though he didn't stop.

A whimper escaped my lips. I wanted to please him, but my body was aching and so sensitive. He had taken me five times since that morning, each time riding me hard as if he owned me.

Perhaps he did. Perhaps I wanted him to.

Yuan stopped abruptly and withdrew. I sucked in a breath as his cock slid out of me. Even that brief motion was painful. When he reached his hand between my legs, I shrank away out of reflex and held my knees together.

"It's too much," I complained.

I never thought I'd be the one refusing him.

Yuan closed his hand around my knee and squeezed lightly. "My tongue is soft," he assured me, opening my legs as he lowered his head between them.

He was intent on bringing me to orgasm once more, and I had no will to fight him. I laid back, my arms and legs limp, as Yuan touched the wet tip of his tongue to my sex.

Pleasure shot through me and my muscles tightened, but even the pressure of his mouth was too much for my sensitive flesh. I inhaled sharply and lowered my hand to his head to hold him back. My fingers twisted into his hair.

"I'll be gentle," he promised, bracing a hand against my thighs to keep my legs from closing.

Before I could refuse, he bent to touch his tongue to me once more, gliding wetly over the soft pearl and teasing along the folds. Yuan licked me slowly, not increasing the pressure as the pleasure built throughout my body.

I was coming again. My release was sharp and bittersweet and it wrecked me, leaving me sobbing. Yuan drank in my surrender, absorbing every last shudder into his mouth. His tongue never ceased its gentle stroke over me until I begged him to stop.

Afterward, he moved alongside me to gather me into his arms and I let my head fall on to his shoulder, exhausted. I could taste the salt of his skin beneath my lips and his masculine scent surrounded me. His arms were strong and muscled, yet capable of such tenderness that my heart wept.

I collapsed against him and let myself soak in all that had happened, every little thing Yuan had done to me. He was still hard. I could feel his length pressing hot against me he held me close, but when I reached down to take him in hand, he stopped me. My body was wrung out beyond pleasure, beyond pain. I'd been taken apart piece by piece and left in pool of raw sensation.

"Why did I fight you for so long?" he asked against my hair. "When pleasure was right before me for the taking? What greater thing is there in life than this?"

His words warmed me and I wondered if I was merely dreaming. This was not the Yuan I'd known. This was a dream lover I'd conjured from my memories.

Brushing my long hair back, Yuan rolled over me so he could look down into my face. I could see him clearly now, with the warm glow of the lanterns surrounding him. His face was cast in dark shadows and something struck me about him. A hardness around his eyes and his mouth that made him a stranger to me.

I realized then that he hadn't yet come, despite bringing me to climax again and again. He was still denying himself by preventing his own release.

"I should have learned a lesson from you, Shanyin." He kissed my throat and then my shoulder. "You're shameless."

Perhaps I was shameless. Depraved, even. But the way Yuan kept on emphasizing it left me unsettled.

Don't be like me, I wanted to warn him. Not like me.

Yuan rolled me onto my side, positioning me as if I were a puppet. And I let him. I was too exhausted to fight. My body was molded clay in his hands as Yuan lifted my leg and slid into me.

"Is this all right?" he murmured into my ear, his cock moving slowly in and out even before he had my answer.

Though his skin was hot against mine, though his words warm, I sensed a coldness deep inside him. I nodded listlessly as his hands moved up to cup my breasts.

"Shameless," he echoed, his teeth grazing the side of my neck as his hips continued their slow torment. From this position, his weight didn't press directly onto my sore flesh. Even though I wanted desperately to rest, my body still responded, shuddering in his embrace.

His words were both a compliment and an insult, just as his fucking provided both punishment and pleasure. I managed to come one final time, faintly, the sensation far removed from my center. Only then did Yuan give himself over to his own release, spending into my exhausted body.

His organ slipped wetly from my sex as it softened. It was no longer a weapon of my undoing.

Finally, with him lying still beside me, I was allowed to fall away into sleep.

CHAPTER THREE

He reached for my hand and brought it down between his legs. His manhood stiffened as he pressed my fingers against him. I couldn't resist cupping the hard ridge through the cloth and listening to the hitch of his breath.

We were shut away in the privacy of the litter. I could slip my hands beneath his robe and fill them with the thick length of his organ. Or I could take him into my mouth and suck him until he forgot his own name.

Yuan would promise me things as I pleasured him; tell me I was beautiful, even declare I was a goddess. None of it would mean anything. A man's body was easy to command in the moment, and hardly a triumph when it served his own desires so perfectly.

My triumph was always in how I took my own pleasure, and in that respect Yuan had proven himself a generous lover. Yet why did I still feel unfulfilled? Yuan had brought me to the point of ecstasy again and again until I'd begged him to stop. I'd dreamed of such nights when we had been apart. I'd yearned for him until my very soul ached with loneliness.

I removed my hand from his cock. "You seem to surrender this body quite willingly now. I don't think it even belongs to you any longer."

His eyes darkened dangerously. "What do you want? My heart?" he asked in a mocking tone. Yuan sat with his shoulders straight and head lifted; power and authority in his very demeanor.

"Keep it." My own pulse was pounding. "What would I do with a man's heart anyway?"

"That's good to know." He settled back into the seat, smoothing his robe back in place. "Because I have no heart, Shanyin."

The proprietor of the inn that night scrambled to prepare rooms for us. Our entourage took over the entire establishment, including the stables. Servants were sleeping in the storerooms and the woodshed. Even the main room was taken up by Yuan's soldiers.

I was to sleep in Yuan's room. No one batted an eye.

As we finished up our dinner in the main room, the door opened to admit a familiar face. One that I was less than happy to see.

I hadn't seen Wu Chien since he'd brought me to the Governor's mansion over a week ago. The nobleman grinned crookedly as he entered. He was unable to smile in any other way. Half of his mouth permanently drooped downward. Despite that slight flaw, his face wasn't unattractive, but there was something unnerving to me about the look of the dissolute young lord.

Wu came directly to us and sat down without being invited. "I see you're enjoying my gift," he said to Yuan.

As if Wu ever had me in his possession to give. I narrowed my eyes at him, but Yuan's expression remained blank.

"Lord Wu," he greeted.

"Governor." Wu Chien was still grinning.

"How is your father?"

Wu shrugged. "Alive. At least, last I heard."

I gathered his father was someone important, though it mattered little to me. Even when I was in the imperial palace, I avoided politics as much as possible. I had thought to stay out of danger that way, but in the end it hadn't mattered.

"She's quite a treasure, isn't she?" Wu went on.

Yuan raised his wine cup to his lips. "I find the arrangement suitable."

"You can always tell the women who are high-born, cultured beauties whose families have fallen upon hard times. Pretty commoners and peasant girls can be taught to pour tea and play instruments, but they're pale imitations. It's the fallen women who make the best courtesans. Elegance with the perfect note of tragedy." He fixed his lurid gaze onto me. "In the tea room as well as in bed."

My first instinct was to tear him to shreds. First with my words, but if those didn't suffice, then my nails. Instead I made my face pleasant and blank and kept my eyes lowered; fading into the background as a good courtesan should.

"No longer hungry, Autumn Rain?" Lord Wu taunted.

Beneath the table, his foot stretched out to caress mine as if we were secret lovers. I would have kicked him except it would have created a scene. Yuan glanced at me as I stiffened.

"I'm very tired, my lord," I murmured. "If I may retire with your permission?"

Yuan nodded curtly and Wu followed me with his eyes as I stood to go. I heard Wu's laughter as I retreated toward the private chambers.

"So even the most stalwart of men can't resist a beautiful woman…"

Once I was shut inside the chamber, I could breathe again. In the brief time I'd spent with Wu Chien, I'd found him to be an annoyance. He was nosy and pried into all manner of things that were none of his concern.

The chamber was a small one with a bed against one wall. I lowered myself to the bed, lying on my back as I stared up at the ceiling. I wasn't there long before the door opened.

Yuan entered, closing the door quietly behind him. He didn't turn to face me. The stillness of the room unnerved me, but it was as if we were at an impasse. Neither of us wanted to be the one to break it.

"Did you give yourself to Wu?" he asked finally.

"This is what concerns you?" I asked in disbelief. "He procured me from a brothel."

Yuan did turn to me then. His face was a mask, his expression smooth and composed. "That isn't an answer."

I rolled onto my side, propping myself onto my elbow to see him better. "I took many men to my bed, darling, but not Lord Wu."

Wu apparently preferred to watch.

Yuan began to undress while I watched, fascinated. His movements were slow, his hands steady. All the while he continued in an even tone, "I don't like knowing you were subjected to other men."

"Other men?" I had to laugh at that. "When you first met me, I commanded a harem of thirty lovers."

His hands paused on the edge of his outer robe and he fixed his gaze onto me. He seemed to war with something inside him before continuing. "I feel responsible this time."

I raised my eyebrow questioningly, but he didn't elaborate. He'd bite off his own tongue before admitting he felt in any way bound to me, but I knew how Yuan's mind worked. He'd saved my life after the palace coup by switching the poison I was ordered to take for a sleeping potion. That act of defiance on his part connected us together.

Why had he saved me? His motives had to go beyond desire and lust, though we had plenty of both between us.

"Still so honorable," I purred at him. "So full of duty and tormented with guilt. Do you know I went to the brothel madam myself to offer my services? It was better than being hungry and cold while I wandered the dusty roads of this broken kingdom."

Yuan continued removing his outer robe as well as his underclothes. My breathing deepened as his magnificent body revealed itself. He really was beautiful, in face as well as form. I swallowed as Yuan stepped out of his trousers and cast them aside.

His manhood jutted from him, already erect and suffused with blood. I was reminded of the first time he stood naked before me. I'd commanded him to remove his clothes and had seen evidence of his arousal then as well. No matter how unaffected Yuan seemed on the surface, I knew his body wanted mine.

"You should know that the only thing you can be held responsible for are your own actions, Yuan," I said quietly. "My choices are always mine and mine alone."

His eyes became shuttered at that, the pupils growing black as a muscle ticked along his throat. He stopped at the edge of the bed to look down at me. "Take off your clothes, Shanyin."

His voice was thick with desire. I could feel my own sex dampening, the outer lips swelling and opening.

"You take them off," I replied insolently.

The only thing that happened against my will was being sold off to the commandery governor, who had turned out to be Yuan. It may seem like this was fate, that it was good fortune, but as much as I desired Yuan, I hadn't chosen him as my master and some part of me continued to rebel against that.

It would take more than that small defiance to anger Yuan. He climbed onto the bed and took hold of my ankle. Heat radiated from that single contact all the way up my leg to center itself at my sex. He pulled me down to him at the same time he stretched up to align his body with mine. Soon I was pinned by his weight and every pulse point in my body was alive.

He didn't bother undressing me. His hand stole beneath the skirt of my robe, pushing aside thin layers of silk as necessary until his fingers slid against the smooth, slick folds of my sex. I gasped as he stroked, softly at first and then rougher. My head rolled back as I became lost in the decadence of it, and I felt his mouth against my throat to claim me. I could fight all I wanted, but whoever controlled my pleasure controlled me.

At least for those brief moments.

His hips pushed forward, driving his organ into me in one long stroke that made my eyes close and my toes curl. His second thrust filled me completely, driving the breath from my lungs. For a moment, he paused, sheathed to the hilt. My inner muscles clenched around him, holding onto him as my heart pounded. I knew he could feel my pulse against his chest where he was pressed to me. I knew he could feel it in the throb of my flesh surrounding his cock.

When I opened my eyes, Yuan was directly above me. Still watching me with eyes full of ice and steel as he thrust into me in a controlled and relentless fashion.

"What changed?" I asked him breathlessly. He had spent so much time denying his own urges and not giving in to my demands. What had changed to remove his inhibitions?

He didn't answer. There was something perfunctory about the way he'd removed his clothing and climbed on top of me. A sense of inevitability.

It didn't matter. The end result was the same. Yuan's hard cock was fucking me toward orgasm and my body wanted this more than it wanted food and water. Or even air. I was still sore from yesterday—I was starting to believe I would be perpetually sore—but the pain receded as age-old rhythm and instinct took over.

I clung to his shoulders as my sex clenched. Silently, I willed him to let go of the hard shell that kept him away from me, even while he fucked me so thoroughly. He finally did let go, his face clouding with desire as his arms closed tight around me. One settled at the back of my neck, the other sank low to curve around my buttock, lifting me to him as he sank deeper into me.

"Come, please come," I pleaded softly, as my body convulsed and tightened around him.

He did, closing his eyes as he lost himself inside me. At least we could be together in this. The pureness of this moment.

CHAPTER FOUR

"He's coming with us?" I watched the next morning as Wu Chien approached our caravan with the reins of his mount in hand.

"He goes where he pleases," came Yuan's reply before he turned away to complete preparations for the journey.

Wu's gaze settled on me from the front of the caravan and a lazy smile spread across his lips.

There were few men I couldn't stand. Wu Chien was one of them. I ducked inside the carriage, happy to be out of the glare of the sun as well as Wu's leering gaze.

"Are you friends with that know-nothing?" I asked when Yuan joined me in the litter.

His expression remained mild. "His father and I share a common interest."

"What business could he possibly have on this journey?"

Yuan arched an eyebrow at me. "What business do *you* possibly have?"

Heat rushed to my face. I was only here for his pleasure, wasn't I? How easy it was to forget that I was no longer Princess and free to make demands. I had never been good at biting my tongue, high-born and fallen woman that I was.

"The Elder Lord Wu received a high-ranking appointment in the new Emperor's court. He wishes for his son to become involved in administration as well, so I indulge him."

I smirked. "All this talk of honor and justice. Your rebellion was fought for power and position, like any other."

"So it would seem," he conceded darkly.

Yuan turned away, presenting me with the stark lines of his profile. His manner was unreadable, evasive. As I watched him, something locked into place in my mind. The Elder Lord Wu, a high-ranking official of the rebellion. Minister Wu.

My stomach twisted. Wu Chien's father was one of my bitter enemies in the imperial court. Chancellor Wu had taken part in the uprising that had overthrown my brother's reign and sentenced me to death.

The blood drained from my face and my fingers went to ice in my lap. "Does Wu Chien know—?"

"He doesn't know who you are," Yuan replied soundly.

"If he found out, they'll come after me."

"If he found out, it would be dangerous for both of us."

How could Yuan be so calm? Wu Chien had only known me as Autumn Rain from the brothel house. No one there had known I was Princess Shanyin. The one person who had come close was a former palace guard named Bataar. Wu had been watching through a spyhole as I bedded the swordsman.

Sex. All that Wu was interested in was the sex act. I prayed he never made the larger connection.

"You can't bring him with you," I insisted. "It's too dangerous."

"Won't it raise questions if I refuse him now? Let him be. That know-nothing, as you called him, will tire of this task and wander off before seeing it to its end."

I sat back with a huff, agitated. I'd never liked Wu Chien, but now he was dangerous. Yuan should know better than to keep such a snake around, waiting for him to bite.

"So what is this all-important task you've been sent on?" I asked sullenly.

Yuan shook his head, dismissing the matter, but I wouldn't let it die. "You can't tell me it's not important."

"It's not important. To you," he added when he saw my lips part to protest.

We both fell silent as the carriage rolled on toward its mysterious destination. His shoulder pressed against mine, but other than this touch, we remained distant. It was easy in the heated moments, when passion had me in its grip, to believe that Yuan and I were one. That the walls between us had been destroyed and we were both raw and vulnerable. But what held true in the dark, while skin to skin, wasn't true in the daylight.

"Why are you so agitated, Shanyin?"

"Don't call me that."

Yuan went on, regardless. "No one was better at being willingly blind than you. If you didn't want to see something, then it just didn't exist."

What was I supposed to tell him? That I had changed? That I had become afraid?

"So I'm just here as a diversion, to entertain you while I keep my mouth shut?" I challenged.

Yuan looked away, his shoulders stiffening. "I don't know why I brought you with me." It was a while before he spoke again. When he did, his tone sounded forced. "Of all people, Shanyin, I thought you might understand."

"Understand?"

"What it's like to live surrounded by darkness."

As the journey continued, Yuan grew quieter. I knew something was weighing on him. Whenever I asked what he had been tasked to do, his eyes would become shuttered and his mood unaccountably dark.

"I brought you with me so I wouldn't have to think of such things," was all he would say.

Our caravan made its way up into the mountains. The roads disappeared, leaving nothing but a trail that faded here and there, only to pick up some distance later. Yuan had sent out scouts to ride ahead, and each night he conferred with his soldiers before coming back to our tent.

When he returned to me each night, I took him under my care. I poured wine and engaged him in idle conversation; all the things I supposed a courtesan should do. I didn't try to pry any more information from him about the nature of his duties to the Emperor. I, more than anyone, understood the need to take in life's pleasures in the moment.

"This must irritate you, having to perform the duties of a servant," Yuan said one evening.

My hands were on his shoulders as I tried to work out the knots in them. It was a never-ending battle, but I enjoyed the wiry strength in his muscles as I dug my fingers into them.

"It amuses me," I purred.

There was no mistake that I was the worst slave in the world, but Yuan was willing to tolerate my disobedience, my insolence. I practically required servants of my own to wait on me.

As we traveled up the mountainside, his mind was preoccupied. He still wanted me as a distraction, but sex seemed to require too much focus for him. Instead he held me at night, while I said nothing. It was too difficult to control my thoughts when there was nothing but silence and the sensation of Yuan around me, holding me so tight that he was holding me together.

I was afraid of what I might say to him in those moments.

Better that he fuck me until I had no thoughts. Then there was nothing to cry out but his name as I beseeched the heavens.

"Tell me what happened after you escaped the palace," he suggested this night.

His shoulders were just starting to relax and I could hear from the deepness of his voice that he was beginning to get drowsy. I rubbed my hands over his neck, kneading in small circles at the base.

"There isn't much to tell. There was so much confusion. I was smuggled away from the palace by two of my concubines."

I didn't like to think of those moments; that harsh awakening when I realized I wasn't dead, but still in danger.

"They were supposed to bring you to me," Yuan said. He bowed his head as I ran my fingers along his scalp, sighing deeply.

"Well, they're quite disobedient, those two," I said dismissively.

Inside, I felt a pang in my chest. I hadn't seen Tai and Jiyi in so long. Most likely I would never see them again. They were now relegated to the long list of names and faces who had come and gone in my life. One day…one day Yuan would join those ranks as well.

"They wanted you for themselves."

I almost thought Yuan might be teasing me, but his tone was dark and serious.

"Perhaps they did," I murmured absently. "But I left them as well and then I wandered around lost. Until I found you."

I'd added the last part lightly, as an afterthought. I'd tossed it out with my usual carelessness, but Yuan straightened. I could feel all the tension I'd fought to ease away creep back into his shoulders.

He turned to face me. "Shanyin," he began, his voice rough with emotion.

But it was a beginning with no end. He said nothing more as I stared at him, waiting desperately for the next word. The way he said my name could mean anything. It was a question, a declaration, a warning all at once.

His hair was untied and fell to his shoulders, giving him a wild, raw appearance that made my heart race. I didn't know what to do, and it was killing me, this stillness between us as we took measure of one another.

I leaned toward him. I meant to seduce him, to drag him down onto the rug and let yin and yang and nature do the rest, but my approach was more hesitant than I intended. Yuan met me partway, his hands sliding into my hair as his palms cradled my face.

When our lips touched, I felt my very essence pouring into him. It frightened me. I'd given him too much, but there was nothing I could do about it. He was kissing me. I was kissing him back. Tenderly, as if it weren't merely our lips that touched.

It wasn't what I wanted at all, but his hands took over mine when I tried to reach for him. He was holding me back, willing me to let go, and let things unfold in their time.

I'd never kissed anyone so slowly, letting it be an end in and of itself. I always became impatient and demanding, but this time I let myself linger as I learned his taste, the texture of his mouth, the feel of his hands in my hair. I closed my eyes to inhale his scent.

All the while, dangerous thoughts spilled into my head. Yuan only wanted me to gratify his sexual urges. He told me I was like a poison that had infected him. He fucked me senseless as a way to forget.

But he was lying. He was lying, the kiss told me. This was what was real.

I broke away, panting as I struggled to gather my wits. He looked confused as he stared at me.

"Shanyin—"

"Don't call me that." My voice broke. I shrank away from him, letting my hair fall over my face. I didn't want him to see me like this.

When we'd first met, Yuan was haughty and self-righteous. So full of pride, and I had wanted nothing more than to master him. To possess him. Now we didn't know what we wanted from each other, and that left too much room for foolish dreams.

When I turned around, Yuan had composed himself. He stood, as tall and proud and impenetrable as ever. For a long moment, we did nothing but stare at one another, locked in a battle neither of us knew how to win.

He turned to go without bidding me farewell, and I didn't call after him. We said nothing, nothing at all to one another.

CHAPTER FIVE

The next day took us high into the mountains until we disappeared into the shrouded mystery that was the summit. The cliffs rose lush around us and a fine mist caressed my cheek when I opened the curtain to peer outside the transport.

It felt as if we were in a sacred place; a place of pilgrimages and private meditation. The entire party seemed to recognize this without saying. The caravan continued in silence. Even the horses plodded on docilely, heads bowed.

Yuan hadn't ridden with me in the carriage that day. I could see him astride his horse at the head of the party, back straight and head high. A hitch gathered in my chest. He presented a majestic sight.

I had to wonder why women became so fixated on powerful men. Even a woman who didn't want to be captivated. A woman like me who had everything to lose.

My mood darkened immediately after. The scoundrel Wu Chien rode alongside him. I could see them exchanging words.

I knew Wu and a hundred others like him. They were hangers-on, grasping at the elbows of those in power. There was a time when I was the most powerful woman in the land—or at least the imperial court. Cronies and admirers were as thick as flies; each one vying to make the dubious crawl to get closer to the throne.

Then there were the marriage proposals. Bureaucrats, generals, noblemen. I had scoffed at them all. I much preferred the company of my harem. They were there only to please me.

By mid-morning, we reached a plateau where a grand villa rose up from the surrounding rock. I was surprised to see such luxury among the verdant hills. The residence was empty except for a few servants who lived there like hermits to maintain the grounds. Apparently the villa was one of the Emperor's remote retreats.

The servants greeted Yuan as if he were royalty and the party was quickly installed within the chambers. Yuan didn't stay long, however. After a cursory inspection that everything was in order, he prepared to ride out.

I watched him from the corner of the courtyard as he gave the order to prepare the horses. His guards departed to carry out his command and he was left alone. Yuan turned to look at me then, as if he'd known I was there the entire time.

Everything stilled around me. For a moment, I became locked in this place and time with him and I couldn't move. I could barely breathe. What was this hold Yuan had over me? I could deny sovereigns and generals, but not him.

He was wearing a sword at his side and his robe was as dark as night. Though I knew he'd at one time served as a soldier, I'd never seen him with a weapon before. A chill swept through me and I wrapped my arms around myself. It was more than the cool mountain air or even the sight of a blade that made me shudder. It was Yuan's eyes. They were flat as they looked at me. Dead.

When he left the courtyard, I had the urge to run after him. Imagine that. Me, running after Yuan like a lovesick maiden. And what would I do? What would I say?

Stay, don't go.

I didn't even know where he was going. Instead, I turned to retreat into the house.

For the rest of the day, I tried to find ways to distract myself. I ordered a hot bath drawn to try to banish this chill that had settled into my bones. Soon I was sinking beneath the steaming waters of the heated pool in the bath house. The scent of star jasmine surrounded me and the combination of herbal oils tingled against my skin, cleansing away all the worries and ills that clung to me. Laying my head back, I closed my eyes and imagined myself melting away until I was like the mist floating over the water.

"Beautiful."

My eyes flicked open. I saw Wu Chien through the haze of steam. He was reclined against the entranceway, his arms folded in front of him. Obviously enjoying the show.

"Wu," I replied coolly. It would have been too much of a victory for him were I to act startled or offended.

"You're a fascinating woman, Autumn Rain." He pushed away from the wall to saunter over. "You become so lost in yourself that nothing else exists."

"Why aren't you with the others, Wu Chien? Are their pursuits too strenuous for you?"

My attempt to challenge his manhood only earned a laugh from the playboy. "Not to my taste," he replied, coming over to kneel at the edge of the pool.

He trailed a hand into the water, his fingers dipping just below the surface. Even though he was at the opposite side of the bath, that touch felt invasive, as if he were reaching toward me. A shiver ran down my spine. I sank the tiniest bit lower into the bath to try to reclaim the heat.

I was hardly shy about my nakedness, and Wu Chien had spied on me having sex with a visitor to the House of Floating Happiness before procuring me for Yuan. Yet something about Wu's demeanor set my teeth on edge.

"I've decided that you're not exactly beautiful," he drawled.

I arched an eyebrow at him. "Oh?"

"Not on first glance. But there's something about you that draws the eye. I can't stop thinking about you. How magnificent you looked astride that demon at the brothel—I couldn't look away."

"Fool," I muttered, far from flattered. "I know your kind. Every month it's some other fallen flower you're in love with."

He laughed at that. "Perhaps. But for now, it's you Autumn Rain. I want to know everything about you."

"Maybe you should have made your advances before handing me over to the Governor."

"That's incidental. You don't belong to him. He hasn't laid claim to you." He met my eyes pointedly. "Nor you to him."

My stomach churned. Wu was correct that this arrangement could very well be temporary. I wasn't Yuan's wife or officially accepted into the household as his concubine. I wasn't certain I wanted to be either.

"What does that matter? I certainly won't ever belong to you," I retorted.

"Ah, see, I have no need to possess you." He straightened and moved closer along the edge of the bathing pool. "I just want to know what dark thoughts float inside that head of yours."

"Dark?"

"Oh yes." His piercing gaze settled on me. "Dark and deviant."

Now it was my turn to laugh, but it was strained.

"What I want to know is your story. What exalted family line did you hail from? Were you raised a sheltered, fresh young flower? What was it like, being plucked from the garden?"

His eyes were alight as he tried to pry into my secrets. I realized that this was sex for him, a penetration deeper and more invasive than flesh into flesh. I might as well have been sucking his organ into my mouth, as excited as he was.

"A woman is more alluring when she keeps a few secrets to herself," I said evasively.

"I think you must have been quite high-born, my lady. I can tell just by the tilt of this chin." He reached toward me, but I swatted his hand away. "Yes. So superior. Proud."

"This conversation is getting tiresome."

"Indeed." Wu straightened to sit with one knee raised as he regarded me thoughtfully. "I do get bored quite easily and you're the only mystery I've found that interests me in a long time."

Wu was the son of a powerful minister, one who could easily bring about my death a second time if I was discovered. I considered telling him some elaborate lie, but the more tales I spun, the more Wu would have to entrap me. It was better to bite my tongue and wait for him to lose interest.

"I've left my past life behind," I told him.

"Oh? Because your past doesn't seem to have left you."

"What do you possibly mean by that?"

"Two men came by the Floating Happiness the other day. Humbly-dressed, but well-mannered. Gentlemen, by the look of them. They seemed to be searching for someone."

I went still beneath the water. Wu didn't fail to notice.

"Ah, your lovers, then?" The tip of his tongue darted to the corner of his mouth, and his eyes glowed with delight. "Oh yes, an innocent heiress debauched by her tutors."

He couldn't be further from the truth. If anything, I was the one who had initially debauched Tai and Jiyi when they were forced into servitude as my concubines. But then they had returned the favor tenfold.

"I have many admirers throughout the kingdom."

"Well, I think I'll be able to find these two admirers for you," he said, savoring my torment. "They might not be as tight-lipped as you are, my dear. I think I'll do exactly that."

I let out a breath. "What do you want, Wu?"

Gradually his smile widened. "I want something to chase away this boredom, Miss Rain."

"So you want to bed me while the Governor is away?"

"Oh no. Something better than that." His expression grew dead serious and his breathing deepened. "I want to see you lose yourself. I want to watch you die that little death once more."

My heart skipped a beat. It wasn't possible that my sex was swelling at this demand.

"I want to watch you achieve satisfaction right here, without any walls between us. I've hardly thought of anything else since the first time I witnessed it. The way your eyes closed and your mouth fell open, helpless with pleasure. But you were turned away, I could only see part of your face."

He sounded agitated at having been denied, and my throat grew tight. Instinct told me Wu Chien wasn't the sort of man to force himself on a woman. His tastes were very particular.

"And in return?" I demanded.

"Oh, you *are* a whore," he rasped, unaccountably aroused.

I scooped up a palmful of water and splashed him with it. Wu flinched, water dripping from his face as his gaze darkened. For a moment, I feared he would drag me from the water and take me right then and there, but his hunger was held at bay.

"Perhaps I can be persuaded not to pursue your past any further," he proposed softly. "If you can keep my thoughts from wandering."

I couldn't have him hunting down my former concubines.

"All you wish to do is watch?" I asked, my throat dry. I should have known better than to appear open to negotiation.

"Touch yourself," Wu commanded, his eyes lighting in triumph.

I swallowed as I let my hands fall from the edge of the bath to sink down beneath the surface of the water. Wu's expression hardened and a muscle twitched along his jaw. My heart pounded just from watching him. Wu wasn't an obviously handsome man, with none of the hard symmetry and masculine beauty that Yuan exuded, but there was an intensity about him that drew my gaze. Even though I didn't like him.

Keeping my eyes on him, I let my hand fall between my legs. My chest heaved beneath the water and I could barely catch my breath. What was this dark appeal Lord Wu seemed to have? His hands clenched into fists at the edge of the bathing pool, willing me to continue.

My sex was throbbing even before my fingers brushed against my flesh. I dipped slowly into the wetness between my legs. I was slippery with my own arousal, a different sort of fluid from the surrounding water.

Wu knew the moment I'd reached my sex. He exhaled harshly, his pupils growing large and opaque. When his lips parted, I wondered about the deformity of his mouth. What had caused one corner of it to droop slightly? I stared at him as my fingers circled the tiny nub down below. The half-frown made it seem as if he disapproved of my wantonness, but his eagle-eyed focus said otherwise. My lower muscles shuddered and tensed as I played with myself.

Every part of me was connected by silken threads to my center. The bath water started washing away my fluids, but I dipped two fingers into my sex to draw out more.

"Who are you thinking of?" Wu asked, his voice rough with passion. "Are you thinking of Lord Chu?"

"No," I whispered. "Only of you."

"Liar."

It was the truth. I didn't need to trick myself with fantasies when Wu's lurid interest held me captive. My head fell back against the edge of the pool, still looking up at him. My fingers moved quicker now, and lighter. An invisible fist clenched around my insides and every part of me wound tight as I yearned for release.

Lord Wu came closer to lean over me. My vision centered on him as my mouth fell open, panting as I spiraled toward climax. Suddenly, his hand shot out to grip me by the back of my neck. I gasped, but he didn't kiss me. Nothing as mundane as that. His piercing gaze remained fixed on my face.

I rubbed my fingers frantically over my sex to push myself over the edge at that very moment. A guttural sound lodged in my throat as my body jerked beneath the water, sending a wave over the bath that soaked Wu's robe.

My mouth was locked open as the last spasms shuddered through me. All the while, I was face to face with Wu, his iron grip holding me in place. I couldn't have looked away if I wanted to. He devoured every moment of my rapture with his eyes.

It was obscene.

I had come as hard as I would with a man's cock thrust inside me. Maybe harder—there was no intrusion of another person's flesh to distract me.

"Thank you, Autumn Rain," Wu said, his tone suddenly deep and formal.

There was no gloating or smugness to his demeanor. Gradually, he let go of me and stood. Lord Wu left the bath house as quietly as he came while I remained in the water, muscles lax and leaden, willing the pounding of my heart to calm.

CHAPTER SIX

Yuan didn't return the next day or the next, and I was starting to count the hours.

I spent the days wandering the villa. Occasionally, Wu Chien would engage me in a game of chess out in the viewing pavilion overlooking the mountains.

"This is the way of the concubine. The long wait," he said, when he saw how distracted I was during one match.

I captured his general to try to shut him up. "You're an appallingly bad player," I retorted.

"You distract me," he said with a leer.

The young lord stretched across the table toward me, but I snatched my hand away, disturbed by the heat that shot through my arm. Wu's gaze told me he had other ideas of how we could be spending our time. I couldn't look at him anymore without thinking of how he'd watched me so intently, willing me to come for my own enjoyment. And for his.

As much as I disliked Wu, there was no greater aphrodisiac than a man's unfettered interest.

"Why not play a little?" he asked lightly. "No one would ever know."

I gave him a slanted look. "Do you think I care if anyone knows?"

"Even Chu Yuan?"

My pulse raced at the mention of his name. He wasn't my master, but I couldn't deny he'd always had some claim over me. Even when he hadn't wanted it.

"He knows I've been with other men." I affected a smug look. "I'd wager he likes me more because of it."

Shameless. That's what Yuan kept on whispering while he thrust into me, wasn't it? Yuan loved how shameless I was. The thought was starting to leave me cold.

Wu smiled. "Well, then—"

"No." Then in response to his raised eyebrows. "I'm not bored enough for that."

"Don't be so quick to judge, my dear. Lord Chu is at the center of a kingdom in turmoil. He rules over a broken house. His time may be shorter than we know."

For the first time, I detected a hint of anger beneath his careless exterior.

"I didn't mean to offend—"

"Oh, I think you did," he interrupted sharply. "You know my name is nothing to sniff at and you, my dear, may find yourself looking for a new master."

Yuan had been gone for so long and now Wu's warning tied my stomach into knots. I wanted desperately to ask about the trouble he hinted at, but I wouldn't give him the satisfaction.

I shuddered to think that this could be my future. Going from one lord to another for protection. It would never be Wu, but he had reminded me of one thing. His father was powerful and dangerous to me. I was on the verge of wounding the young lord's pride and I had to bring this conversation back.

"I care little of names," I replied lightly. "They're very easy to forget in the dark when one has the right skills."

Wu smiled slowly. "And how you must wonder what skills I truly possess."

The secret look he gave me did make me wonder. I still detested him, but the pounding of my heart told me I could dislike someone and still feel a hidden thrill at the thought of

259

them. I was sick with worry and my will was weak. Somehow, I knew Wu would have ways of distracting me, mind and body. That burning gaze all but promised it.

It had always, always been my way to seek escape from all that was trying and unpleasant. Apparently in that respect, I hadn't changed much at all.

As curious as I was, I didn't succumb to Wu Chien's sly form of seduction, and went to bed alone that night thinking of Yuan. Was I starting to feel bound to him? It was impossible. He'd done nothing more than pleasure me a few times, no more than the most favored of concubines had done over the year my harem had been in service. But the way I felt when he held on to me stole my breath away. When I was with him, I could let go of myself.

Late into the night, I heard the sound of footsteps in the adjoining chamber. They were too strident to be a servant's or even Wu Chien sneaking into my quarters. I sat up and shoved my feet into my slippers. Pulling a thin robe over my underclothes, I rushed into the adjoining room.

A single lantern had been lit and shadows danced in the room. It only took me a moment to locate the figure in the far corner. Yuan. Yuan had returned. I knew it was him by the breadth of his shoulders and the rigid set of his spine.

"Are you all right?"

His back remained to me, his head bent. "Go to sleep, Shanyin."

"You're hurt."

"I'm fine."

As I approached, I saw he had plunged his hands into the wash basin in the corner, but was making no effort to scrub them clean. They hung from his wrists like pieces of meat.

I hazarded a touch to his back with my palm settling flat beneath his shoulder blades. He tensed at my touch. Every muscle in him was coiled and ready to spring; whether to flee or to attack, I didn't know. I could feel the heavy rise and fall of his chest beneath my fingers.

When he didn't lash out at me, I let my hand travel across him to his arm. My touch remained on him the entire time, reminding him where I was and that I was there. With him. My hand trailed over his shoulder and I allowed myself to venture closer. My stomach lurched when I finally saw what he was trying to wash away.

Yuan's hands were caked in dark stains. Blood, no longer red, but a brown, rusty color having dried onto his skin. His nails were black as if dipped in ink.

I should have been afraid. My heart was certainly pounding in fear and my throat tight with it. The man before me was a stranger.

But I had grown up surrounded by ruthlessness. I knew what the face of wickedness and cruel depravity looked like, and it wasn't this. My hands dipped into the water to close over Yuan's much larger ones. Silently, I began to scrub. At first, his hands were as unyielding as the rest of him, but gradually the blood started to clear away. Yuan came back to life to help me in my task.

The nails were harder, but I tried to clean them as best as I could. "I'll get a washcloth."

His hand clasped over mine for a brief moment before abruptly letting go. Gingerly, I lifted his hands from the water and reached for the cloth. He held his hands out before him, as if he were afraid of his own touch as I dried them.

Taking Yuan by the elbow, I directed him back onto the padded bench in the parlor and sat him down.

"What happened?"

He shook his head grimly. "It's better you don't know."

Whatever it was, it was devouring him from inside. His eyes were haunted, staring through me rather than at me, and he looked drained of his very soul. A hard and empty shell. I placed my hand against his chest to feel for his heartbeat. It was still there, steady and strong, and at my touch something flickered in his eyes. I ran my hand down the plane of his stomach, pausing with my hand on his belt.

Finally, his eyes met mine. He nodded.

I undid his belt. Working quickly, I opened his robe and pulled aside layers of cloth until my hands caressed over bare skin. His member lay limp and heavy against his thigh. I would have been surprised to see any life to it when Yuan was empty of all emotion.

Gently, I took his length in hand, careful not to graze him with my nails. I was used to seeing his organ jutting upward, a sign of virility and power. This was the most vulnerable I had ever seen him. He rarely showed any sign of weakness before me, not even when I was imperial princess and he had been brought before me as a servant for my pleasure.

Yuan sank against the seat, his head falling back. He closed his eyes as my hand stroked over him. His organ twitched beneath my hand, recognizing my intentions. I traced the shape of him from head to shaft to root with my fingertips, reveling in the velvet softness of his skin. Tension gathered in his muscles and his jaw hardened. His hands curled into fists beside him.

I rubbed my thumb over the smooth head, feeling him firm immediately to my touch. A moment later, I lowered my mouth to it, caressing him with my lips, my breath. Above me, I could hear Yuan's breathing deepen. I stroked my hand over his shaft, which had hardened enough for me to have something to hold onto. I did it once and only once, enjoying every emotion that flickered across his face. At least he was no longer cold and formless. There was heat in his blood now.

I went to my knees and insinuated myself between his thighs. This was a position I'd never liked—kneeling like a slave before a man. I'd only endured it enough times to know I didn't enjoy it, even in play.

But it was different now. Yuan groaned above me as I pressed a firm kiss to his swollen head. The sound vibrated low in his throat. Guttural. Pleading.

He wanted the wetness of my tongue, the hard pressure and suction of my mouth. I parted my lips to lick him, teasing just beneath the swell of the dark tip. His hips churned, but I used my hands to hold him still.

Only when he obeyed my touch did I finally allow my lips to part. I slid him into my mouth, swallowing his length slowly, taking as much of him as I could. Yuan was fully aroused now and it was impossible for me to take all of him. Slowly I pulled my head back, my tongue licking against the underside of his cock as I withdrew. He rewarded me with a moan that made my insides churn.

I may be no better than a slave now, but so was he. We both were powerless together.

I sucked him deep into my mouth, reveling in the taste of his skin, the smooth, flawless texture. With Yuan it wasn't a chore to pleasure him. As he filled my mouth, my sex swelled and opened with yearning.

His hips started pumping, pleading for more. More heat, more wetness. I sucked him hard and his body strained upward. Every part of him belonged to me in that moment. I grasped his thighs and pushed them open before drawing him in so deeply that his swollen head nudged against my throat.

He gasped and his breathing grew shallow and strained. There was no rhythm left to it.

If I allowed Yuan to lose his essence into my mouth, he would have been alone in his pleasure, caught in his own world while I was left unfulfilled in mine.

I let him slip from my mouth and ignored his grunt of protest. Instead, I climbed onto the bench, my knees straddling his hips. The swollen folds of my sex opened as I parted my legs wide and centered myself. I could feel my wetness bathing the head of his cock as he slid into place. Then I lowered myself onto him, using my weight to drive him up and deep into me.

It was *wonderful.* Indescribably wonderful to feel him inside me.

Yuan's eyes opened as I seated myself fully onto him. For a moment, all we could do was stare at one another, face to face with nowhere to hide. That last thrust had driven the breath from me and I couldn't seem to find it again. His mouth was close to mine, but we didn't kiss. I wanted to…but I didn't dare. It would have been too much.

It seemed an eternity before I could gather my wits enough to lift myself, just a few inches before sliding back down. Oh heaven, the way his cock pushed against my womb. Pain and exquisite pleasure.

His arms encircled me as he watched me ride out my pleasure. His expression was far from indifferent now. His eyes were black and endless. His sensuous lips were full. They parted as if to say something, but no words came out. Instead Yuan slid his hand between the press of our bodies and there was nothing else to say.

I closed my eyes as the tip of his finger brushed against my bud. All the while, his cock filled me. I shifted to angle my center against that touch point, and pleasure shot through every nerve and vein.

We came like that, with me in his lap and his arms holding on to me. I opened my eyes as the tide rose, and caught the moment Yuan's expression glazed over. His essence spilled hot inside me as he lost himself. I followed soon after, clinging on to him as the wave crashed over me.

Afterward, we collapsed. My body was still trembling when I wrapped my arms around him to hide my face against his neck. In the sultry haze that surrounded me, I whispered something to him as I drifted off to sleep. One part might have been his name. The other part I must have been mistaken about.

This couldn't be love. There wasn't anything or anyone in this world I loved anymore.

CHAPTER SEVEN

In the morning Yuan was gone.

I woke up in a cold bed, entangled within the covers. Only the nakedness of my body and the dampness between my legs told me Yuan hadn't been merely a dream. He'd returned to me, but where was he now?

I wandered the villa, finding it as empty as before. Where were Yuan's captains, his soldiers?

A maidservant finally came to relay that I had been summoned to Lord Wu. The young girl blushed furiously as she delivered the message before slinking away.

Curious, I went to Wu's quarters. He had been given an entire private area in the main part of the mansion, smaller than Yuan's section by area, but still spacious. I knocked on the door and was bade to enter.

Inside, I found Yuan and Wu drinking wine. They poured for themselves, having sent all the servants away. Though it was just before noon, the two looked as if they'd been enjoying their cups since the break of dawn.

"Autumn Rain."

Wu held up his wine flask cordially, but I ignored him to fix my gaze onto Yuan. He was staring straight ahead, drinking from his cup while purposefully not acknowledging my presence. On the low table before them lay a collection of discarded wine flasks and a chess game that appeared to have been forgotten.

"You summoned me?" I asked Yuan.

"I was the one who asked for you," Wu interrupted. "It was hardly an occasion without our celebrated courtesan."

He gestured to the pillow between the two of them. Warily, I seated myself at the low table. Yuan had yet to speak a word to me. Despite having fallen asleep in his arms, he was as cold to me now as when we'd first met.

"I was worried about you," I told him, ignoring the fact that we weren't alone.

Yuan set his cup down. "I don't need you to worry."

"What happened last night before you returned?"

"Nothing you need to concern yourself with."

I stiffened. Apparently Yuan intended to be a bastard to me unless we were fucking. Wu watched our exchange with great amusement and I refused to provide him any more entertainment by going into theatrics.

Wu smiled crookedly as he leaned over to fill my cup. "There is something interesting I've noticed about you, Autumn Rain."

A shudder ran down my spine. He wouldn't dare speak of the incident in the bath house. Yuan remained silent beside me and I steeled myself for the worst.

"Despite being an elegant and refined courtesan, you never pour the wine. Or the tea." Wu sat back and set the flask deliberately in front of him. "I find that absolutely fascinating."

I stared at my recently filled cup and then over to Yuan's empty one. Wu wore a smug expression as he continued. "It's said that the most accomplished courtesans can seduce a man with nothing more than a gracefully turned wrist while pouring a drink for an admirer."

"My admirers apparently didn't come to drink," I returned smoothly.

"Ah, but even the most humble prostitute knows enough to serve her master."

The look he gave me then was full of challenge. I lifted my cup to drink. Though my hand was steady, my fingers were cold with fear. I was ever aware of Yuan's rigid presence beside me, but he said nothing.

Wu suspected I was something more than I pretended to be. But all courtesans pretended to be something they weren't. They pretended to be in love.

"There's an easy explanation, of course." Now the playboy's eyes glittered. He was enjoying my discomfort. "Lord Chu Yuan is completely smitten with you. He's lost all sense of propriety to become your willing slave. I wouldn't have thought it possible, as proud as he is."

The two men regarded one another, exchanging an unreadable look that tied my stomach in knots. What had they been discussing in the hours before I was summoned?

"Autumn Rain is unlike any other woman," Yuan remarked. "If you spent one night in her embrace, you would understand her allure."

The words themselves weren't out of place for two friends exchanging taunts over cups of wine, but Yuan sounded disturbingly clear-headed. The look he gave me stopped me cold.

Wu was the only one in the room smiling. "You should know that your master here is quite accomplished in the art of courtship."

Hearing anyone referred to as my master made my blood run hot, but I bit my tongue. This was Wu's game. He spent his time scrutinizing and spying, reading every little reaction. He knew what got under my skin.

"There was a time when Yuan and I divided the flowers of the Jiankang pleasure quarter between the two of us." Wu's gaze lingered on me. "And for those pretty girls who couldn't decide who they preferred, we simply shared."

For a moment, I swore I had heard wrong. There was little that shocked me, very little I hadn't tried in my many sexual exploits, but this was Chu Yuan, who prided himself on honor and respectability.

"The pleasures of youth," Yuan intoned.

"Seems like yesterday." Wu's smile no longer reached his eyes. What showed there was something much more intense.

Because I was so inept at being a servant, Yuan moved to refill his cup himself and raised the wine to his lips. "You're welcome to her," he tossed out before drinking.

My heart slammed against my ribs. Outwardly, I remained completely still, though far from serene. Was this Yuan's way of deflecting suspicion from me? Was he trying to convince Wu Chien I was really nothing more than a slave bought for his pleasure?

Maybe that was all that I was. The thought made my skin go cold. My vision swam black before me.

Wu's laughter rang in my ears. "Tired of her already?"

"Hardly."

His answer did nothing to reassure me. My hands twisted in my lap as Yuan reached up to brush back a strand of hair from my face. "But there's something you've probably realized about Autumn Rain. She can never be satisfied by a single man. Right…my love?"

Slowly, as if moving through water, I turned my head to look at Yuan. His eyes were flat as he regarded me. Emotionless. It was as if last night—as if all our nights—had never happened.

"An obedient concubine knows her place," I replied woodenly.

"Does she?"

His voice was soft, but sharp enough to tear my soul in two. His thoughts had never been more hidden to me. What was he truly trying to accomplish? Was this some sort of test of my loyalty?

"Well then, it will be an interesting evening," Wu said.

"Why wait?" Yuan looked to me. "I can see how the thought of it already has her flushed and feverish."

With anger, I wanted to shout at him. And shock that he would hand me over so readily.

Perhaps it was a test. A test to see if he really held any power over me. If what happened last night mattered more to me than it had to him. A test to see if Princess Shanyin had truly changed.

I would most certainly show him I hadn't. Yuan had no claim to me, especially when he didn't want it.

"I see no point in delay," I stated firmly.

Yuan looked over at Wu. "See? Exactly as I told you."

Wu didn't gloat. Instead he reached for my hand, taking it with care as if my bones were made of glass. "Come, my dear."

He led me to the wide daybed at the other end of the sitting area. My breath caught in my throat. Right here? I glanced over to see Yuan refilling his cup and leaning back to watch, his arm draped casually over the seat.

Yuan had seen me with my concubines, I reminded myself as Wu removed my clothing. I had forced him to watch me being pleasured by two men at once, one with his cock inside me while the other used his tongue to bring me to ecstasy. But I had been in control then. Now my heart was beating frantically. I was filled with fear and uncertainty. I was in Wu's hands now.

He made quick work of my clothes. Disrobing me was merely a preliminary. The tease of it held no allure for him. Finally he laid me naked onto the daybed and stood over me.

"Do you know why I find you so intriguing?" he breathed.

"I don't care why." I closed my eyes, shutting him out. I tried to shut out Yuan as well, but I could still sense him there, watching us.

"It's because you know, my dear." Wu sounded closer this time. "You know that this has nothing to do with love. Or affection."

I flinched when his hands closed over my breasts. His thumbs tweaked over my nipples roughly and I gasped, gritting my teeth to steel against the flood of sensation. A moment later, his mouth was on me, wet, warm. Soothing over the sensitive peak.

My back rose against my will, bowing so sharply I feared I would break. Wu caught me with both his hands then and used his teeth. I sobbed brokenly, his puppet. And Yuan was witness to every moment, watching another man bend me to his will. He'd wanted this to happen.

So he would know I didn't belong to him. And I would know he didn't belong to me either.

The pain was so sharp I wanted to curl up against it, but Wu was pulling my thighs apart, opening me to him. I slitted my eyes open and saw him standing between my ankles at the end of the seat. He held a lacquer case, which he opened to reveal a set of smooth round jade marbles polished to a shine. Each pale green orb was the size of a quail's egg.

A red thread connected the orbs. The end of it was woven into an intricate knot ending in a long tassel. He dragged the silken end of it over my sex, a light, tickling caress that made me squirm.

"Like the plum rains," he murmured, dragging the end of the tassel over the head of my little pearl. The tip of his fingers played over my swollen entrance. "Is she always like this?"

He'd lifted his head to direct the question to Yuan. I didn't dare look in his direction. Not when he could see the evidence of my arousal glistening on Wu's hand.

I was wet with desire. Aching for release. Despite my mortification at being cast aside, despite my turmoil at being so used, my body still wanted what it was due. Sex, heat, and fulfillment in every way. Nothing else mattered to it. I was exactly as Yuan said…shameless.

There was no answer and Wu returned his attention to me. This time he rubbed one of the jade marbles over my slit, coating it in my juices before gently pressing it inside me. One by one, he fed the stones into my passage. My sex quivered at the intrusion. I could feel my inner muscles tightening around the jade and threatening to push them out.

"Keep them inside," Wu commanded, gentle but firm. I don't know why I obeyed. Lord Wu had noted how disobedient I was, yet my body responded to his slightest touch. How quickly I became enslaved by pleasure.

He straightened and looked down between my legs. The red thread protruded from my slit, and I moaned as the jade marbles rolled with each throb of my body. Slowly he took off his robe, his eyes locked on to me the entire time.

When he was finally naked, my gaze strayed downward. Even from where I was lying, I could see he was fully aroused. His organ was slightly shorter than Yuan's, but thicker. The head of his cock was broad and blunt and it practically vibrated with anticipation.

"You look surprised." He ran a hand up the inside of my leg, inching closer to the edge of the seat where my center lay open and vulnerable. "Did you think I only cared to watch?"

I don't know what I thought, but I swallowed hard and waited.

"Ah, you thought me incapable of performing such duties." I could feel his longest finger inside me as he pressed the smooth orbs deeper into my tight passage. My inner muscles clenched involuntarily against the intrusion and Wu's eyes glazed over. "I'm more than capable, my dear."

With the jade marbles still inside, he guided his cock into me, pushing into my quivering channel. I looked over to see Yuan watching, his face a cold mask, as I was penetrated by another man. As I was taken, cheeks red, lips parted. Yuan clenched his hands into fists and his gaze filled with smoke and fire. The sharp rise and fall of his chest could have signaled desire or anger, but he did nothing to stop what was happening.

Wu pushed deeper into me, taking me in inches, and a sense of foreboding crashed over me. What's done was done. There was no turning back.

I could feel the tiny orbs sliding against my sensitive walls as Wu filled me with his cock. My flesh molded itself around the intrusion, clenching and unclenching in spasms as the jade moved around inside. The effect was indescribable. I closed my eyes to try to take account of what was happening to me.

"It's good isn't it?" Wu murmured huskily.

I opened my eyes to the sight of the young lord standing between my legs, thrusting slowly in and out of me. He was in a grip of passion, his eyes lidded and lost. The round orbs rubbing against his cock must have added to his pleasure as much as it did mine.

Before we had begun, part of me had hoped I wouldn't enjoy this. My body would finally tell me it had made its choice. But the truth was, I couldn't deny how good this felt. Wu had captivated me despite my intentions. And now I wanted Yuan to watch him fuck me senseless.

Wu was doing exactly that. With his organ still embedded inside, he lowered himself over me, shifting the angle of his penetration as well as how the tiny pearls moved and rubbed against my slick passage. My head fell back as my breath came out in gasps. Heaven, it was more than good. Unable to stop myself, I sobbed out my pleasure.

By the time he laid himself over me, he was grinding the bud of my sex with each exquisite stroke. I threw my arms around him and dug my nails hard into his back, knowing no other way to react to what he was doing to me.

"I know a hundred different ways to fuck you." His voice was low and rough in my ear. "Ways you've never imagined. After I'm done, I'll know everything there is to know about you."

There was nothing to know, except that he was going to make me come. He was making me come now, and I squeezed my eyes shut as the orgasm raged through me, turning me inside out. It shouldn't have felt like betrayal, but it did. I thought of Yuan watching as Wu broke me and I cried out in a riot of emotions: frustration, abandon, ecstasy.

Throughout it all, Wu continued fucking me and I continued wanting it, my hips pushing up to meet him. My legs wrapping around his hips to drag him closer. Yet shame tainted every moment of it. For the first time, I was ashamed of how much I loved this.

When Wu finally stopped, we were both breathing hard. I opened my eyes and through the haze of sex, I saw that Yuan's seat was empty. He'd abandoned us—at what point, I didn't know. I'd been too caught up to care.

"Well, Autumn Rain," Wu panted. His body glistened with sweat as he lifted himself off me. "How shall we indulge ourselves next?"

I squeezed my eyes shut, no longer caring. Yuan was gone. We were each complicit in this, pushing each other to this point. Now he couldn't bear to look at me.

"I suspect you might like being tied down," Wu went on.

Taking me by the wrist, he stretched one of my arms over my head and then the other, before wrapping a length of silk around both wrists. Then, lest I mistakenly assume the silk was only for show, he pulled it tight enough to make me wince.

My eyes opened to the sight of Wu looking down at me with adoration. "Yes, I think I'm right about that," he said breathlessly.

His cheeks were flushed and his eyes alight. The powerful orgasm had left me drained, but it seemed to have invigorated him. He attached the silk tie to the foot of the bench, stretching my arms cruelly overhead before fixing them in place. I was left with little movement should I try to struggle. Then he went to work securing my ankles.

Throughout his ministrations, I lay docile and accepting. My limbs were like a wax doll's which Wu Chien moved and placed wherever he liked. The true struggle was inside me and it had little to do with him. Inside I was breaking into tiny jagged pieces.

"Oh, Autumn Rain. You really are fearless," he said with admiration as he finished attaching the opposite ankle. Each foot was stretched toward a corner of the bed, which forced my legs obscenely open. Wu stood between them, completely at ease in his nakedness as he stared down at me.

"The thing about noblemen such as Chu Yuan is they spend their time divided between many different pursuits: archery, poetry, the study of the classics. But a wastrel such as myself? I've studied only one thing, my dear. Would you believe the study of sex and all of its facets can take several lifetimes to master?"

My breath quickened as he climbed onto the bed, lowering himself to all fours as he reached toward my sex. The pearls were still inside me. Wu looped the red thread around one finger and tugged gently. My inner muscles clenched in small spasms as the orbs were withdrawn, a faint echo of the climax that had rocked my entire being not long ago.

He lifted the string and I could see that the red thread was soaked and the pearls glistening. Wu discarded them before lowering himself back onto his elbows. My swollen sex was open before him. I tried to still my thoughts as he stared at me, but to my dismay I felt a new flood of moisture gathering at my center.

"You look exactly like an orchid," he marveled with a shuddering sigh. "A pink orchid drenched in morning dew."

I gritted my teeth as he touched his tongue to the delicate knot of flesh. My hips lifted of their own accord. There wasn't any use fighting it. My body knew what it wanted, what it liked. And my mind—my mind told me that Yuan was already gone and there was only one way to forget the pain of how easily he'd handed me over.

"Does the Governor like to taste you like this?" I could feel Wu's hot breath fluttering over my sex as he spoke. He licked me again, tracing his tongue all along the edges of my bud before circling the exquisitely sensitive head.

A fist closed around my heart. "Don't talk about him. You can do anything else you want, but don't talk about Yuan."

Wu lifted his head in surprise. He brought himself up until we were nearly face to face. His body hovered above mine with his weight balanced onto his hands.

"Oh, my dear Little Rain." He stared at the tear that slid from the corner of my eye and down my cheek. "You love a man who doesn't love you," he realized solemnly.

I shook my head fiercely, but with my hands tied, I couldn't brush the tears away. Another one fell. And another.

"We can stop," he offered quietly.

It could have been an elaborate game, but I could tell by his eyes that it wasn't. What madness was this? The bastard Wu could sound so kind and sincere when Yuan couldn't even be honest with me or with himself, even while fucking me.

"Tell me to stop and I'll untie you," Wu said.

A tear had strayed to the corner of my mouth. I tasted the salt of it before looking him directly in the eye. "Don't you dare stop. Don't you dare."

For the next hours, until the oil lamps burned low, Wu was good to his word. He teased and tormented and pleasured me in ways I had never thought of. My cries of ecstasy turned into one long, never ending moan. Then later, I became so exhausted there wasn't any sound left in me. I fell silent and limp, but Wu continued on tirelessly.

Throughout it all, I tried to exorcise Yuan from my mind. I had had lovers before him and I would go on having lovers after him. What was he to me?

But each time I tried to cut him out, my heart lay open and bleeding once more. I tried to hide the pain behind a veil of pleasure, but with each shuddering climax, I punished him and I punished myself. Even if there was no sense to it. Even if he'd never know or care.

By morning, both Wu and I were exhausted. He'd untied me long ago—many of his tricks were better performed when we both had our hands free. I lay curled up in a sleepy bundle on the bed while he was sprawled on his back beside me.

"Do you know sex is believed to be one of the gateways to immortality?" he said. "The cultivation of yin and yang and circular breathing and"—he yawned—"lots and lots of practice."

"Go to sleep, Wu," I muttered.

"Ah, you're still thinking of him."

I didn't answer because I was. Yuan had remained inside me, mind and body, even while Wu had pleasured me.

"Sometimes harmony can only come about through discord." He raised himself onto his elbows while I regarded him skeptically. "There's so much more we haven't explored…if you're looking to lose yourself."

"What exactly are you proposing?" I was willing to indulge him, given how many times he'd satisfied me throughout the night.

"I suspected from the beginning you had a taste for pain. Why else would you have these marks on otherwise flawless skin?" His voice dropped low as he reached out to trace one of the silvery lines on my back.

I shrank from his touch and pulled myself up to a sitting position.

"I can do that for you, if that's what you want," he offered, unperturbed. "I can be as cruel as you need me to be."

His breathing had deepened. The very thought had him aroused once more and I watched as he reached for the discarded sash that had bound my wrists. He wound it around and around his hand in anticipation.

"No." My robe was too far to reach. We'd been together for hours, yet only now did I feel truly naked and exposed. I pulled the blanket up to shield myself as drowned memories threatened to push to the surface. "I don't want that."

"Oh." His face sank with disappointment. "Well, then. Perhaps you could do the same for me?"

CHAPTER EIGHT

It was mid-morning when I finally left Wu Chien's room. I returned first to Yuan's quarters to find them empty. A search of the rest of the villa yielded the same. He was gone.

I was starting to panic when I heard the sound of riders approaching. I went to the front gate to see who it was and discovered it was the garrison that had ridden out earlier that week. They were visibly haggard and travel-worn. Yuan wasn't among them.

"Have you seen the Governor?" I asked.

A man who I assumed was the captain stared back at me. It was the first time I'd addressed them personally and the soldiers looked at me as if I were a fox that had started talking.

"We lost him several days ago," the captain replied.

"But the Governor came back. He's here," I protested.

The man frowned at me. "When?"

"Two nights ago."

The soldiers went on to explain that there had been a battle. They were vague on the details of with whom and where, but Yuan had disappeared in the thick of it. Afterward, they had scoured the area for him, assuming he was injured or dead, but they'd been unable to find his body.

A shudder ran down my spine. I wasn't usually superstitious, but an eerie feeling settled over me. Yuan was nowhere to be found—what if I had only seen his ghost? The last two nights could have been nothing more than a waking dream.

I continued searching for Yuan, almost frantic. When I didn't find him in the villa, I left the sanctuary of the walls to scan the surroundings. The morning was overcast as it always was with the clouds so close. The grayness of the sky made the grass and vegetation clinging to the granite cliffs more vibrant. Cool air filled my lungs, chilling me straight to the bone.

Surrounded by the silent mountains, I was keenly aware of the churn of my emotions inside me and the desolation that always followed sex. The hotter the fires burned, the colder I felt afterward.

Finally I saw the dark figure beside the viewing pavilion overlooking the cliffs. With my heart in my throat, I ran to him.

Yuan stood near the edge. A few feet beyond him, the mountainside dropped off into nothingness. I shouted his name, but my voice was swept up by the howl of the wind. He remained with his back to me. So still.

Desperately, I called to him again as I neared. Finally he turned toward me, his face registering surprise as I rushed to him.

He caught me in his arms as I lunged forward. "Shanyin—"

"What are you doing out here?" With trembling hands, I dragged him away from the ledge. "I couldn't find you anywhere. I was so afraid—"

"You were with Wu. I could hear the two of you through the walls," he said grimly. "I couldn't stay any longer."

I struck him in the chest. "But you gave me to him!"

Yuan regarded me impassively. "You wanted to go."

I wanted to scream. Cry. Raising my hand, I struck him hard across the face. The sharp crack rang out against the stillness of the mountains.

He stared at me. His eyes were no longer cold and flat. They were burning. I glared back just as heatedly at him. My hand stung from the impact. A faint red welt was forming over his cheek, but it wasn't enough. I couldn't hurt him enough at that moment.

With tears blurring my vision, I raised my hand again, but he caught my wrist this time. Yuan dragged me against him and then into the pavilion while I called him a bastard, an animal, a demon. Any name I could think of.

Madness unraveled inside me as my screams split the air. My back hit against the stone table just as Yuan's hands closed over my shoulders. His grip tightened painfully, and I stared up into his face, that portrait of masculine beauty that had once captivated me. It was broken now, twisted with anger and loathing.

His hard frame pressed against me and I waited for him to push me back onto the stone table. To shove my skirt up and force himself inside my body. He'd torn me apart in every other way. We would commence destroying one another.

Suddenly strong arms surrounded me. I felt a hand at the nape of my neck and my face was being pressed against his chest. I could hear the beating of Yuan's heart, like thunder as he held on to me.

"I am," he muttered. "I am a demon. I am a monster."

My body sagged against Yuan as the fight drained out of me. I circled my arms around his waist to embrace him. At that moment, it was as if we were desperately holding the pieces of ourselves together. If either of us let go, we would fall apart.

"You're not a monster," I whispered back. "I know monsters. I call some of them kin."

Monsters didn't destroy themselves the way Yuan was doing. We sank down to the ground, huddling together beneath the pavilion with the gray mountains surrounding us.

Still holding me, Yuan told me about the Emperor. About the purges, the executions of anyone who had ever stood against him or who might stand against him in the future.

"All of his brothers," Yuan ground out. "The youngest was only nine."

As sick to my stomach as I was, I wasn't surprised. This was the uncle who had my brother assassinated. Before that, my brother had executed many of our uncles and imprisoned the rest. My family did nothing but turn upon itself, again and again.

He bowed his head and took a deep, shuddering breath. "I came here to hunt down a small faction holding out in these mountains. We found them in the caves, cold and hungry. Some of them begged. The others fought like wild animals. We slaughtered them all."

I put my arms around his shoulders, feeling small and inadequate. I wished I was large enough to wrap myself around him and enclose him completely.

Instead I took Yuan's face in my hands. "Our royal blood is poisoned. Infected. Let us kill each other off if that's what my uncles insist on doing."

His expression had become grim. "The Emperor will either have me killed or take me down with him."

"He won't." Yuan was strong and honorable. Even the most wicked of rulers needed good men. "All you have to do is survive these dark times. Protect your own and survive."

Silently, we stared out into the mountains, holding on to one another. The tranquility of the setting cast everything into sharp contrast. Yet at the same time, I felt small amidst the grandeur. My troubles were insignificant.

"It's beautiful here," I said, though even speaking it aloud seemed to break the peace.

Yuan breathed deeply before replying. "Sometimes I dream of a place like this, far from the imperial court," he admitted. "Then I could be forgotten."

I was beginning to understand how he had become governor of a remote commandery. He wanted to get away from the corruption of the imperial court, but he hadn't fled far enough to escape the Emperor's notice.

"My uncle trusts you. He thinks highly of you."

Yuan regarded me for a moment before replying. "We knew each other long before he became Emperor."

I had to laugh at that. Bitter laughter that broke the stillness of the surroundings. I had brought Yuan into my bed and attempted to seduce him, never bothering to discover how close he was to my enemies.

"I deserved my fate, then."

Yuan looked thoughtful. "My path is set, but you can escape. There must be some place far away where you can find your peace."

Oh, how presumptuous of him. Still trying to save me from myself.

"I'm already at peace," I said, agitated.

"We can't remain like this forever. The Emperor will inevitably summon me back to the capital, and I can't have you by my side. You can never be my wife, Shanyin."

His words were like a knife in my heart. "I'm very fortunate in that respect. Your wife doesn't seem particularly happy."

Yuan looked as if I'd stricken him across the face once more. I turned away and refused to meet his eyes. It seemed peace between us could never last for long. As soon as we spoke to one another, it was broken.

We returned to the villa in silence. We were better together when we said nothing.

I led Yuan to the bath house and lit the fires beneath the pool to heat it. Yuan undressed me himself, stripping away layer after layer of silk, before we sank together into the steaming water of the bathing pool. Then we took turns washing one another, massaging our tired and aching muscles.

Yuan paused to drag me closer. He reached up to brush back a strand of hair that had fallen over my face and his fingers stroked a path around the shell of my ear. My pulse raced so fast I couldn't think.

"You've always done whatever you wanted to do, haven't you Shanyin?" he said gently. "I used to take that as evidence of how corrupt and immoral you were. Left to your own ways, you and your brother would destroy this empire."

Just like that, the warmth drained from my body. It still hurt inside to think of my younger brother and his descent into madness. And I had followed him down with my eyes wide open.

Yuan went on, uncaring or oblivious to my pain. "I thought I was fighting on the side of justice, but the new Emperor turned out to be just as corrupt and twice as bloodthirsty. No one's hands are clean." His gaze became distant. "Certainly not mine."

So this was how honorable men reacted when dragged into depravity. "You're alive and I'm alive. And we're both here."

He frowned as he regarded me. My words certainly hadn't soothed his conscience, but I was lying naked in the arms of a lover, with breath in my body and blood in my veins. For me, there was no other truth and no other peace.

Yuan was right that I was immoral. I commanded handsome men to my bed, didn't I? I willed them to fondle and tease and fuck me without remorse. If sexual acts could bring down an empire, then surely I would be the one to do it.

"There's nothing for you to do but live your life," I told Yuan. "Tyrants will come and go. They bring about their own deaths in time."

It was cold-hearted of me, but if Yuan needed to know only one thing, it was this. This was madness and there was nothing he could do about it but lock his soul away and keep it somewhere hidden.

I had fought against the darkness by shamelessly pursuing the pleasures of the flesh. I lost myself in sexual gratification while those around me hungered for blood and power. Was my choice really so deplorable?

In many ways, Yuan was still an infant, keeping his heart out where it was so vulnerable. The demons of the world would claw and tear at it.

The water was still warm when he took me into his lap. With my knees on either side of his hips, Yuan lowered me down and his organ entered me beneath the surface of the water. I closed my eyes and let myself sink fully onto him until he filled me completely.

I kept my eyes closed as I moved over him, feeling the warm thrust of his flesh into mine. He groaned, the sound between pleasure and torment. It was all mixed up for him— sex and death and despair. It was all mixed up for me as well. It always had been.

"Shanyin, open your eyes. Look at me."

I was afraid to, but I did so anyway. Yuan was watching me. For the first time since I'd found him again, his expression wasn't distant and haunted. He was here with me, mind and body. If I wasn't certain before, I was now. My heart was suddenly too big for my chest. Everything felt tight and constricted and it was impossible to take even a single breath without realizing it.

I loved him.

There was little room for us to move in the bath. Yuan raised his knees up behind me, creating a wall I could lean back against. With my hands on his shoulders, I rocked gently back and forth onto him. Water splashed over the sides with each movement, but we didn't care. We just looked at one another as the pleasure rose slowly between us.

Yuan lowered his hand between my legs to touch me. Once he found the precious little pearl, he barely moved. Instead his hand remained close, letting me seek him out with the motion of my hips. His cock remained hard while I slid back and forth on it, finding a rhythm that seemed to suit both of us.

It was the quietest I'd ever been while fucking. I didn't even know if it was fucking. It was so…gentle. We were hardly doing anything for it.

My climax built slowly with the tightening of my inner muscles. I knew that Yuan could sense it because his eyes darkened. He took hold of me with both hands, pulling me onto him as he thrust upward. It was the smallest of movements, a slight pumping of his hips, but it was enough. I let my head fall back. His knees were there to support me as my release washed over me in a warm wave.

It took a harder rhythm to bring Yuan to his peak, but he came a few minutes later, spilling his seed into me. Afterward, we reached for one another at the same time, and Yuan held me against his chest, stroking my hair. His skin was hot and damp, and I placed a small kiss onto the raised shape of his collarbone. All these little details. I wanted to remember them forever.

"Shanyin," he murmured.

I let out a sigh and held him tighter.

"Shanyin, I want you to bear my children."

And then everything went cold. Yuan could sense the change in me and pulled away to look at my face. His expression was full of concern. He truly did care for me. Perhaps not as a wife, and not as a concubine, but as something more.

I wanted to look away, but we'd chased and feinted and dodged each other so often over the last days that I had no will for it anymore.

"I can't have children, Yuan."

A stinging sensation gathered at the bridge of my nose and I bit my lip to hold the tears back. I had thought...I had thought it didn't matter to me.

"I thought you knew," I said quietly.

How else would an imperial princess be allowed a harem of concubines? When royal blood was so important?

Yuan looked so broken that it tore my heart out even more. "When I found you again, I thought...I didn't believe it, but I thought you must have been a gift from heaven. A gift when I had fallen so low that I didn't deserve one," he choked out, overcome.

He bowed his head and I tried to reach out to him. Yuan let me pull him into my arms, but it was impossible to recapture the warmth we'd had only moments earlier. If I had known it would be gone so quickly, I would have held on tighter.

Yuan clung to me as if I were the strong one. "My wife can't stand for me to touch her, Shanyin. Because of what I've become."

It was the closest I'd seen him to tears, but none fell. He just took all the pain inside himself and held onto it.

"She's young," I began. "You both need time to discover one another."

Yuan shook his head and my words trailed off. I didn't know what to say to him. For once, I wished I wasn't cold and soulless and empty. Then I would have something more to give.

"Mao Mei detests me. She's frightened of me. I touch her and she goes cold."

While I was always warm and more than willing. My temples throbbed and I could feel a headache forming inside my skull. I hadn't felt one like this since my days surrounded by the treachery of the palace. I squeezed my eyes shut to try to will it away.

"Time," I insisted firmly. "Every woman is a mystery. You'll discover her in time."

Finally, Yuan nodded. He kissed me, sighing deeply. "You *are* a gift, Shanyin."

How wrong he was. If he wasn't so broken himself, he would be able to see that I was and always would be a curse.

He kissed me again, more urgently this time. I returned the kiss, letting my lips linger on his. He tasted both bitter and sweet.

Yuan wanted to make love again, either to heal the sudden rift between us or to forget the troubles that plagued him. But the water had gone cold around us, and a chill was setting into my skin.

Gently, I untangled myself and we both rose from the bath to wrap ourselves in loose robes. Yuan reached out to hold me again once we were dressed and I accepted his embrace for only a moment before telling him we should return to our rooms.

The entire time, I knew I was pushing the man I loved away. I was willing him toward the woman who would take him from me, and provide him with a future that I could not.

CHAPTER NINE

Mao Mei was waiting at the front gate when we returned to the mansion. Yuan left me to go to her and she bowed low as he approached, the dutiful wife. As a woman, I recognized all the signs. Her robe flowed sensuously over her curves like water and her hair was laced with flowers. She was pink and perfect, her cheeks as rosy as a spring peach. There was not a wrinkle on her face, no frowns or cross looks. Certainly not a poisonous glance in my direction.

I wanted to tell Mao Mei she didn't need to work so hard. She had a claim over Yuan and I had none.

But I didn't have a chance to say anything to the mistress of the house or her husband. Yuan took her graciously by the arm to lead her inside while I was left to find my place with the rest of the servants.

That night I slept alone in my barren room. The bamboo walls were thin and I could hear Yuan in his wife's chamber. There was no screaming or sobbing this time, just soft little noises that stabbed into my heart. Tiny little jabs with a sharp needle.

I supposed it was no worse than what Yuan had endured when Wu had had his way with me. The affair with Wu seemed like it had happened a hundred years ago. The scoundrel had all but ignored me on the journey back, which suited me fine. I had unwittingly accomplished one of my goals by sleeping with him—the aristocratic playboy was no longer interested in prying into my past.

The rustling and moaning went on for a long time before the house fell silent. Even so, I continued to toss and turn. It was nearly morning before I finally drifted off, but even then my slumber was far from peaceful.

I hadn't dreamt in a long time.

I returned to the imperial palace in my dreams, but the palace as I had known it before the rebellion. In the dream, I didn't have my own private palace or the army of maidservants and eunuchs who used to attend to me. I didn't have my beloved harem either. Instead, I was a concubine in the Emperor's harem. One of hundreds of young women.

In the main hall, there was a collection of tiles with our names on them. At night, the Emperor would turn over the tile of the one he wanted brought to him. My tile had never been turned.

I only ever saw the Emperor from afar when he was sitting on his throne. He looked exactly like Yuan, heart-wrenchingly handsome. We all vied for his attention, but each night I went to bed feeling empty and frustrated. If he would only choose my name, I would be able to capture his heart and hold on to him forever. Even though I was still untouched and a virgin, somehow I knew things about how to please a man. Secret and wicked things.

But the Emperor never did pick me. He never even looked my way.

I woke up, still yearning, laughing at the absurdity of the dream. Laughing and crying.

The next day, I was nothing but skin hanging over my bones. I would have slept until noon if I was allowed, but I was summoned before the Governor's wife. I went to the garden feeling my eyes were weighted down with iron. My movements were sluggish and without grace.

Mao Mei drank her morning tea beneath the pavilion. I caught one look at her smug expression and couldn't help but wonder what Yuan had done with her last night. She might be a young and a nervous new bride, but Yuan was not without patience or skill. Or stamina.

She let me stand outside in the sun for a long time, continuing to drink her tea in small little sips like a bird.

"You don't look well this morning," she remarked, quite triumphantly.

"I didn't slept much last night or throughout the journey."

Her eyes narrowed on me, trying to discern whether I intended some other meaning in my words, but I was too tired to play along.

"Well, we have no further use of your services, Autumn Rain," she announced.

Though I had been expecting something like this, the news still struck me hard. My chest squeezed tight. "Is the Governor aware of this?"

"My husband defers to me in all such matters," she replied disdainfully. "After all, I was the one who acquired you for him."

I went still, staring at her in disbelief. Mao Mei lifted a scroll from the table and held it out to me. "As a dutiful wife, I saw that he had need of a companion in the bedchamber, so I asked that Lord Wu find me a suitable woman to keep him entertained. So my husband has little to say in the matter of whether you stay or go. You were always here by my grace."

I had underestimated her authority in the household. My legs felt heavy as I moved toward her, stepping into the shadow of the pavilion. I paused with my hand on the scroll as our gazes locked across the piece of paper that had recorded my sale.

From close up, I could see the dark circles under her eyes that she had covered up with powder. Her lips were pressed tight, and she wavered as I continued to stare her down.

Mao Mei was afraid of me. She might have royal blood in her veins, but it was faint. She had not been raised surrounded by power and corruption as I had been, which meant she was fortunate. She had been spared from political intrigue...until now.

"The Son of Heaven has married you to Chu Yuan to keep him bound in servitude," I told her. "The Emperor only values you for the hold you have over your husband. If you can't bear Lord Chu a son, the Emperor will have you replaced."

"I don't need advice from a whore," she snapped.

In that, she was absolutely wrong. But I wasn't trying to manipulate her or play on her fears. "Be patient. The inner workings of women and men, yin and yang—they naturally sort themselves out," I said with a sigh. "Your husband is a good man. Or he wants to be. There are not many men like that left in this kingdom."

I could have been more specific in my advice than "yin and yang," but I wasn't kindhearted by nature. I pried the scroll from her slack fingers and left her in the garden to return to my room. It wouldn't take long at all to gather my belongings. I'd come to the mansion with nothing but the clothes on my back. I'd be leaving much more behind. My heart, my hopes.

All I wanted to do was sit inside with my eyes closed and linger for a little bit longer. Yuan had come to me in this room, before he'd known who I was. I wanted to believe that even in darkness, our souls had somehow recognized one another. That there was truly fate between us.

But fate was not enough to keep two people together or grant them happiness.

Protect your own and survive, I had counseled him.

For his line to carry on, Yuan needed sons. And Mao Mei was the Emperor's niece. My uncle had put Yuan in an elevated and trusted position from the start. Some day he would return to the imperial capital and I would not be able to follow him. Sooner or later, I would have been forced to go.

But I had foolishly hoped it would be much later.

"Can you show me?"

A voice came from the doorway, quiet yet dignified. I turned to see Mao Mei hovering at the threshold. "Show me how you seduce my husband."

It would have been cruel to laugh at her, so I didn't. Instead I rose to go to her.

"You want to watch me with your husband?" I asked coolly.

She swallowed and took a deep breath, looking quite young. "Yes. I have books, but—" Mao Mei straightened her spine and lifted her chin with a haughty air. "The writings aren't very clear."

I had to admire her audacity. After dismissing me, she still dared to ask me for this favor. Well, we were distant cousins after all, even though she was unaware of it. Our bloodline had no sense of propriety—or boundaries.

"Come with me." I moved past her and started toward the garden.

"Now?"

Despite her surprise, Mao Mei followed obediently along beside me. Yuan had always come to me at night. I had never been inside his private chamber and neither had his wife, apparently. When we entered, I saw that Yuan was still asleep beneath the canopy.

His chest was bare and he had one arm thrown over his head. Dark hair fell about his shoulders. My heart cracked just looking at him. Strong, yet so vulnerable. Completely unaware of the two scheming women hovering nearby.

I gathered myself and directed Mao Mei behind the silk screen. Then, with a deep breath, I approached the bed. Kneeling beside the wooden frame, I touched him gently on the shoulder.

Yuan started awake. "Shan—"

"Shh…" I hushed him before he could say my name out loud. His wife still didn't know who I was and she could never know. "Don't speak, my love."

He looked up at me sleepily as I climbed onto the bed. "I missed you."

There was no teasing or boyish charm. Just a deep sincerity in his eyes that made my heart flutter.

Yuan didn't know his wife meant to send me from the house. I could tell by the way he reached for my hand as if we were long-time lovers. As if we would be lovers forever. I swallowed back tears as I placed my palm over his heart.

Mao Mei must have been quite confused, spying on me from behind the screen. This wasn't seduction. For a long time, all I did was look down at him. And him at me.

This would be our last time. Yuan didn't know it yet and I wouldn't tell him. What use was it? He'd have to abide by Mao Mei's wishes regardless and then I'd have the pain of being forced out, not by a jealous woman, but by Yuan himself.

So I didn't care if she found our coupling instructive. I didn't care if she was bored to tears. This moment was mine.

"What's the matter?" Yuan asked, frowning suddenly.

I shook my head. "Nothing."

"You look…solemn all of the sudden."

"I missed you as well, darling."

I ran the tip of my finger down his nose. It was meant to be playful, but Yuan wasn't convinced. He started to sit up, but I pressed him back down to the bed with a sly look.

"We'll have to be quiet about it. I had to sneak in past your wife. Do you know she patrols the courtyard like a guard dog?"

I thought I heard a muted sound behind the screen, but Yuan was focused only on me as I ran my fingertips lightly over the part of my robe. The faintest curve of my breasts could be seen through the silk. My hand rested there and stroked absently while I watched Yuan's breathing deepen and his eyes go dark.

I'd never prided myself on being a seductress. I rarely had to seduce anyone, and those men I did lure to bed wanted power more than sex. Sex, I rarely withheld. Power? Always.

This was the first time a man had cared to look at me so intently when I wasn't doing something as overt as stroking a hand over his cock. It was as if Yuan wanted to understand every bit of me, even the parts that couldn't be stroked and teased and fucked for his pleasure.

I was becoming maudlin. Reaching up, I pulled the long, silver pin from my hair. Yuan's gaze filled with smoke and fire as I shook the length of it loose, letting it fall over my shoulders. He let his fingers curl into the dark mass as I slipped my robe from my shoulders. I was nearly undone when he pressed his hand to the nape of my neck, tilting my eyes up ever so gently to meet his.

What was he doing? What were these small touches and tender gestures? Maybe he did know I was leaving after all.

No, he didn't know. Yuan was merely watching me, watching my reactions. I was telling him in small and invisible ways how I wanted to be touched. Even when I was completely disrobed, he still didn't reach for me.

"Take me now," I whispered.

His warm gaze pierced my heart. "There's no hurry."

"But I'm impatient."

That, he had to believe. I was Princess Shanyin, wasn't I? I was insatiable. Shameless.

Yuan gave an odd smile and sat up, taking me into his arms. For a moment, I thought we would continue now, as we always did, but he bent his head to my ear as he pulled me close.

"Tell me what's troubling you." His lips grazed my earlobe, sending a shudder down my spine. "And then I'll make you feel better."

My pulse skipped. This was progress.

"You know there's no need for words." My breath came out in gasps as he nibbled the side of my neck.

"Tell me anyway."

His touch had grown firmer and bolder, his palms shaping the contours of my body as he ran his hands over my hips. His fingers stole to the inside of my thigh to stroke gently over the sensitive skin.

"There's only one thing I need," I murmured.

At that moment, his fingers dipped into the folds of my sex to seek the pearl inside. His arms caught me as my head sank back and my hips rolled forward. This part I knew. I knew it very well.

Yuan slid a long finger inside me and I gasped. I could feel my inner muscles squeezing over his knuckle, becoming slick and swollen with the penetration. He lowered me onto the bed, using his weight to anchor me while his hand continued its magic.

The first time he'd made me come was with his hand. Yuan had refused to kiss me. He'd refused to touch me anywhere else but my sex and only because I'd ordered him to.

Useless sentimentality. I dragged his mouth down to mine and kissed him hard, trying to make up for all the moments we would no longer share.

He sensed the desperation in the kiss. Once more, he stopped to stare at me questioningly.

"I need you inside me. Now," I pleaded, then bit my lip to keep from sobbing. "And hard."

It was artless, but true. I needed him to be rough with me. I needed him to fuck me so I could center myself on that sensation, on the feel of his relentless cock turning me inside out. Otherwise I would keep slipping away into faded memories.

His mouth closed hot around my nipple and I whimpered as sensation shot through me. I knew what this was. He was showing me, promising me there was more to come. Yuan started moving into place above me; hips over mine, his weight resting on his elbows. The head of his organ pressed against the opening of my sex, and I closed my eyes to wait for the inevitable moment of penetration.

But Yuan didn't thrust into me, filling me as only he could. He was still angled over me when I opened my eyes, but his attention had wandered. Yuan was looking out from the bed to stare at his wife.

Mao Mei was standing very close with a handkerchief twisted in her hands. Her eyes were open wide and a natural flush stained her cheeks.

At first, I was certain she was there to stop us. My blood boiled at the injustice of it. I knew she was jealous. Vindictive, even. But what could she hope to accomplish by catching us in the act, or at least pretending to? I had practically dragged her into Yuan's bed chamber.

The hand around her handkerchief closed tighter and I noticed the tremor that ran along her arm.

The young Mao Mei wasn't angry. She was frightened.

Yuan sat up, turned toward Mao Mei and then back to me. As he caught my eye, an understanding passed between us.

Yuan extended a hand toward his wife. "Come."

It took a long time before Mao Mei was willing to approach, but as soon as she settled herself beneath the canopy, Yuan reached for her.

I was left alone. Just moments earlier, I was being held in my lover's arms as he prepared to take me and now I was a secondary. An underling. Yet I'd agreed to this. Mao Mei could give him a son while I could not. Mao Mei could stand by his side while I would have to remain hidden.

Yuan removed her silk robe while she cast her eyes downward shyly. I could see how she affected him, this innocent creature who belonged to him alone.

What could possibly cause a rift between them? From what I could see, Yuan was not merely attentive to his lovely wife, he truly desired her. And Mao Mei was neither cold nor unwilling.

Mao Mei's breasts were small, but perfectly formed, and her hips were surprisingly full. Men didn't have an opportunity to see their wives before their weddings nights. Yuan must have been pleased to find such unexpected sensuality beneath a demure exterior. She was every man's dream. Even as a woman, I found myself wondering what her skin would feel like. Would she blush so prettily when Yuan thrust into her?

When Yuan bent to kiss her breasts, Mao Mei folded her arms across her chest. He said nothing about her withdrawal, and moved to kiss her shoulder instead. She hazarded a sideways glance at me over Yuan's shoulder. She had meant to watch us, not be part of the union.

Strange how I was the one able to read her intentions here. It was me she implored with those pretty eyes, and not her husband.

I went to Yuan, sliding my hands over his lap. The bed was grand enough to fit all of us, though intimately so. Mao Mei remained beside us and I met her gaze as I took her husband's organ into my mouth.

Her eyes went wide. They were phoenix eyes, with the corners lifting prettily. Her lips parted and she caught her lower lip in her teeth, watching with rapt attention as I swirled my tongue over the smooth head. Yuan ran his hand through my hair, exhaling slowly. His grip settled against the back of my head, the touch light, but unmistakably possessive. I kept my attention on Mao Mei.

She was breathing hard. Her gaze was fixed onto me, not wanting to miss a moment as I took Yuan deeper. Bracing my hands against his thighs, I sank down until the tip of his cock nudged against my throat. The small pain brought tears to my eyes, but Yuan groaned above me, undone.

Mao Mei was unable to look away. She could see how much he wanted what I did to him and how much I loved it in return. I could feel the folds of my sex plumping, yearning for attention.

Yuan lay back onto the bed with his hand extended to Mao Mei. His other hand was still tangled in my hair to hold on to me. Emperor of his domain.

He circled his arm around his young wife and bent his head once more to the soft curve of her breasts. When his mouth closed over her nipple, she whimpered in surrender. I was transfixed by the way her body moved, writhing against him while her head wrenched back. A mix of emotions played over her face. Aroused, I sucked Yuan harder and felt the shudder that went through him.

Mao Mei bent to whisper something into his ear, blushing. Gently, Yuan pulled me up. His organ glistened as it slid from my mouth.

"Lie back," he commanded quietly.

I did what he asked, my heart pounding. My legs opened naturally for him and he moved between them while Mao Mei crowded closer, her eyes bright. Tentatively, she touched a hand to my knee and parted my thighs further. I supposed she'd never seen herself. She focused her attention between my legs, directly onto my sex, and I felt myself skin burning.

Boldly, she reached for Yuan's organ and guided him into me. She gasped as he entered, her voice mingling with my own shuddering sigh as my body yielded to accept him. The look of concentration on her face held me captive as I was stretched and penetrated. I was suddenly more aware of myself and of all the sensations down below. The softness of her hands soothed my sensitive flesh even as Yuan's cock sank fully into me, making my insides clench tight.

Mao Mei caught me watching her and looked away shyly. Yuan stilled above me and tried to reach for his wife, but she curled herself away from his embrace. Instead she repositioned herself so she could see between my legs to where Yuan and I were joined. He twisted his hips to accommodate her as he slowly lifted and lowered himself over me, starting the sacred rhythm that would take me above the clouds.

"It doesn't hurt?" she whispered to me.

I let my head fall back, breathing heavily. "No. It's wonderful."

Her hand moved between us. I could feel her fingers along my entrance. My cunt was stretched taut with Yuan's cock embedded inside. The sensation of Mao Mei exploring my sex made me throb with need. If only she would touch me *there*, on the tight nub where my entire being was centered.

Instead, her curious fingers moved over Yuan's cock and then back to me. "What does it feel like?"

I looked up at him. Yuan's dark gaze bore through me. I was aware of him inside me in a way I'd never experienced before. "It feels like he's a part of me," I choked out.

He crushed a kiss to my mouth, his tongue invading to capture mine. The angle brought his thrusts deeper into me, bringing me to pleasure at a different angle. I closed my eyes, overcome. I forgot Mao Mei's curious gaze, forgot her soft, questing touch. I forgot everything as the rhythm and pressure of Yuan's body took me over.

At the critical moment, I did feel a touch directly onto my precious pearl. I didn't care who it was. I clung to Yuan as the soft caress coupled with his relentless thrusting, brought me to my peak. The orgasm seared through me like lightning, burning away everything in its wake.

Afterward, Yuan moved away sooner than I wanted him to. I was left emptied as he reached for Mao Mei, kissing her passionately. For a long while, I kept quiet to watch them. Mao Mei response was both innocent and sincere as she clung to him. Soft moans of pleasure punctuated the silence as I closed my eyes and let myself sink into the bed, spent.

CHAPTER TEN

"I wish you would make peace with my wife," Yuan told me while at his desk later that day. His head was bent over some official document.

"But didn't you see how affectionate we were with one another this morning?" I asked sweetly.

He glanced up, eyebrows raised. "Sex does not equate with peace with you."

Unable to argue, I wandered to the corner of his desk, my fingers playing at the surface of it near his elbow. Despite their passionate kissing, Yuan and his wife hadn't engaged in a second round of lovemaking after he and I had finished. Mao Mei had instead retreated to her private chamber and had remained there for hours.

At least she seemed to have forgotten that I was banished.

"Go see to her," Yuan said, still absorbed in his work.

"It's cruel to expect me to mediate between the two of you."

He stopped and eyed me sternly. "You're both women."

His tone told me these were women's matters and I should handle it for him. How very convenient. When I didn't immediately go do his bidding, he set aside the decree and reached for me, covering my hand with his larger one.

"This has to be the way of it," he said gently.

This time, I could hear the disappointment that weighed down his words. The regret. I was seeing Yuan through different eyes.

"I know." Mao Mei would always stand between us. I was far from gracious, but I wanted him to think well of me.

"Shanyin—"

"I'll go."

I stopped him from whatever explanation he meant to say and headed for Mao Mei's quarters. He was wrong to assume I had any better ability than he to soothe her. I lacked a woman's softness or compassion.

To my surprise, she opened the door immediately when I tapped on it.

"Autumn Rain," she greeted, her eyes bright. "Come inside."

I had expected her to be scandalized and sulking, but Mao Mei was far from it. She led me to her sitting room where I saw a lacquer case had been laid out in the center of the table. There were scrolls and books scattered around it.

"I've been trying to understand, but the books only write about clouds and rain and internal energies flowing," she explained as I glanced over her collection.

"They're written by men," I told her singularly as I seated myself.

She took the seat beside me, suddenly becoming shy. "That was wonderful this morning." Color rose to her cheeks. "I couldn't see how a woman could find the act enjoyable, but I thought it must be to some women. All these books…and the pictures."

I looked over at one which showed a young woman lying naked in a garden with her lover entwined around her. Her red lips were parted in ecstasy. Most likely Mao Mei had been sent off to her marriage bed with little more than a few pictures and whispered words with her husband, and the forces of nature expected to provide the final instruction.

"This is an impressive collection," I remarked.

"I asked Lord Wu to bring them for me."

I couldn't imagine how she'd managed that—though I now realized she had also asked Wu to procure her husband a concubine as well. I had a newfound admiration for Mao Mei. She wasn't one to remain passive and accept her fate.

Curiosity was killing me. "Did you and Lord Wu ever…?"

"No. *Never.*"

Of course Wu hadn't offered any of his services to her, though I doubted he'd be unwilling if she'd asked. Mao Mei was *Furen*, an aristocrat's wife, and deserving of more respect.

"As accommodating as Lord Wu has been, there are things I couldn't speak to him about. Things of a personal nature." Her blush deepened.

"Is there something you wish to ask me?" I offered with a sigh.

Mao Mei shifted closer, her voice dropping to a near whisper. "Does it hurt at all when my husband pushes himself inside you?"

"Only the good kind of hurt," I answered, which made her frown. I wasn't particularly skilled at this and sex *was* confusing.

"Is it ever difficult for your jade gate to open up?" she pressed on.

She was using vague, poetic terms, but it wasn't because she was shy. This was the only language she had on the subject. Perhaps this was even the first time she'd spoken the words out loud.

"Not when your body is prepared for it. There are many ways. Touching, kissing—"

Mao Mei hung on my every word with her eyes wide and eager. After at least three months of the marital bed, she couldn't be so completely innocent anymore. Certainly Yuan knew how to pleasure a woman and ready her for him. A sudden thought came to me.

"Has your husband ever been inside you?"

She bit her lip and immediately looked away. "We've tried many times, but…"

Her voice faded. I remembered the feel of Mao Mei's soft fingers exploring my passage as Yuan penetrated me. She had been fascinated by how I had opened and stretched to accept him.

If the conversation hadn't been intimate enough before, it now became luridly so. "What does your husband do before he tries to put his organ into you?"

"All the things you've mentioned. More." She ran her tongue over her lips, becoming accustomed to speaking openly. "He does the same things I saw him doing with you."

The last part sent a small pang through my chest, but I pushed on. "Does he use his tongue?"

She blushed a darker shade of red. "Yes."

"Down there?"

At that she could only nod. My own sex flooded at the thought of all the things Yuan could do with his mouth on me.

"Is he a good lover?" Mao Mei asked meekly. The look on my face was apparently enough of an answer.

It was a unique experience, being able to speak so candidly about a lover. In my harem, my two favorites had also been with one another. At times our conversation had bordered on such intimacy, but never quite like this.

"Do you like it?" I continued.

She looked flustered, barely able to sit still in her seat. "You mean his tongue?" she asked, her voice cracking.

"His tongue. His lips. His fingers. Teeth."

She paled. "Teeth?"

I gave a little shrug. "The rest of it then."

"I…I do. It feels nice."

"Have you ever reached your climax?"

LILIANA LEE

I knew I didn't have to explain too much. Mao Mei was an avid reader and she had to have wondered about that great mystery. High tide, the clouds and the rain, thunder and lightning.

She ran her tongue over her lips nervously. "Would I know if I had?"

"You would know." I rose from the seat and went to her. "Lie down."

At first she only blinked at me.

"Lie down," I commanded with a teasing laugh. "This is what you're dying to know."

With a shy little smile, she reclined on the padded seat and my heart ached at the sight of her. So young and fresh and eager. Different from me in every way. How Yuan must cherish that about her.

She tensed when I reached beneath her robe, and I immediately stopped. "Are you afraid?"

"A little," she admitted.

"There won't be any pain, good or bad," I assured. "Just breathe. Closing your eyes might help."

Mao Mei nodded and did just that, exhaling slowly.

"Keep breathing," I said, moving my hand up along her leg.

I parted her thighs gently and her eyelids fluttered as I ran a fingertip gently along her cleft. Her hair was light there, as soft as a peach. I wasn't a stranger to another woman's body. In the palace, there had been a maidservant here and there who had been summoned when I was feeling adventurous, but being with another woman had never excited or satisfied me as much as being with a man.

But this situation was different. I wasn't here to seek my own pleasure so I found myself in strange waters. Mao Mei also seemed to trust me. She expected me to guide her. It was a little bit daunting even though I rarely felt intimidated by matters of the bedchamber.

At first, I did nothing more than run my fingertip gently over her outer lips, just over the slit. Men rarely spent enough time there, stroking at the gate before being beckoned inside. They usually wanted to rush in and skip to the end game before properly setting up the board.

I could hear Mao Mei's breath quickening.

"I'm going to touch you, but I won't go inside," I told her. "Just breathe."

Careful of my nails, I parted her folds and laid a fingertip over her pearl. She was only a little damp, not very aroused at all, so I kept my exploration very light. Just so she was aware of what was there.

"Does Yuan touch you here?" I asked, though I knew the answer.

"Yes." Her reply was more breath than voice. "You call him by his given name?"

Once again I was reminded that we shared the same man. As hard as it was to forget, I always seemed to find a way to distance myself from the truth. It would be impossible after today.

"We're lovers, my dear. I've called him all sorts of things, none of them proper. Now focus."

She fell silent, properly chastised.

"He puts his tongue here, as you say," I went on. "And licks and strokes you. And it feels nice, as you say."

When she nodded, I could sense her growing wet against my fingertip. Dipping gently into the pool of moisture, I slicked it over her little pearl, bathing her in her own fluids. Mao Mei's lips fell open with a sigh. The play of emotions across her face was a beautiful thing to watch.

"Why does he stop, then?"

Her brow creased. "Because I ask him to."

"Why? You like it, why not let him continue?"

My finger circled tighter over her bud. The muscles throughout her body tensed and her voice was pitched high when she answered. "I don't know. It starts to feel…strange."

"Strange? You mean confusing?"

"Yes. I suppose. I don't know."

I smiled. "It is all very confusing, my dear."

I eased up on her, changing the motion of my fingers as not to wear her down. A small gasp escaped her lips. "Your hands are so much softer than Yuan's."

Oh, don't think I didn't miss that little power play. The reclaiming of her husband's name. But I let that insolence slip by. Mao Mei was really at my mercy now, straining toward the barest touch of my fingers.

Men were so much easier to bring to pleasure, and their reactions so much easier to read and comprehend. To watch a woman discovering her way to pleasure was incredibly arousing for me.

It was like putting up a mirror before myself. I'd never seen what I looked like when I was aroused. This was what Yuan saw whenever he made me come.

"You love this," I murmured. It was undeniable. Her hips were churning restlessly, and her chest heaved with each labored breath. Her skin practically glowed.

When Yuan had told me Mao Mei couldn't stand his touch, I wondered whether she was able to become sexually aroused at all, but I had that answer very clearly in front of me.

"Why not let this go on?" I slid my fingers directly over the tiny bud of her desire and watched her body tremble. "Why would you ever want this to stop?"

She moaned as I took her higher. Dear sweet girl. I was getting heady with my own power. This was a hundred times better than when I'd first brought Yuan to orgasm.

"It…it starts to feel not as good," she gasped. "I worry. I worry that I'm not doing the right thing."

"You worry about what Yuan wants? That he's getting impatient or that he's not pleased with you?"

She nodded, her head moving from side to side restlessly as I worked that precious pulse point. I considered slipping my finger inside her, and even stroked lightly over her slit. A shudder traveled all along her body and her thighs tensed. It could have been excitement or fear. Or both.

In the end, I decided against it. Mao Mei was already so close to coming.

I moved up alongside her, raising her skirt as I kept my hand between her legs. There was enough room on the seat for me to curl up beside her, and I laced my fingers into her hair, caressing against her scalp. Heavens, I loved it when Yuan pulled on my hair before I was about to come. Just hard enough that I knew he was there. Mao Mei loved it as well. Her mouth fell open, panting. If I had kissed her then, I knew she would have welcomed it.

But I didn't dare. I didn't dare speak or do anything to disrupt her. Down below, the tip of my finger continued in an endless circle. Feather-light because she was so sensitive now. Faster with the rise of her pulse.

Her skin smelled like flowers and she was so soft. I wanted desperately to see what Mao Mei looked like when she gave herself over for the first time. I wanted to be as close to her as possible when it happened.

Finally, her expression pulled tight. Her lips rounded with surprise. There was no doubt what was happening.

I did kiss her then. I couldn't help myself. My lips captured hers, and she sobbed brokenly as her sex flooded my hand.

The chamber books were filled with visuals of climbing mountains and dying deaths. Reaching the pinnacle of perfection. Clouds. White clouds everywhere. Enough poetry to perfectly confuse. But now Mao Mei knew the truth.

We didn't break the kiss even when she came down from the clouds. With a little sigh, Mao Mei pressed her soft lips to me. Her tongue slid over mine. Shyly. In gratitude.

"Elder Sister." She'd taken to calling me that in the last hour since I'd given Mao Mei her first orgasm. "Do I seem normal down there to you?"

She remained lying on the daybed, though considerably more relaxed. Also considerably more eager.

I'd untangled myself shortly after our kiss had ended, embarrassed at how easily I'd been swept up in her youthful desire. Pleasure was pleasure. There was no yin or yang to it and it was addictive, the strongest of spirits. I returned to my position at the end of the lounge, with her bare feet curling beside my lap.

"Normal?" I echoed.

She stared at her painted toes. "Yuan says I won't open up to him. I try to lie back and relax, just as you told me to, but my gate remains closed. I fear that my…my cave is just too small to accept a man."

I pressed my fingers against my temples. Not having grown up with sisters or with a mother's instruction, this conversation was new to me. "We should find some old and experienced maidservant to explain this all to you."

"No!" She shot up in alarm. "Please, Elder Sister. Everyone will know…"

It wasn't surprising Mao Mei hadn't confided her troubles to anyone. She was surrounded by servants while she was a princess. We kept our secrets close. What she needed was some old busybody *amah* who had known her all her life to instruct her, but obviously there was no such woman here.

"It's shameful enough that the servants can hear us," she went on. "They know something must be wrong. They haven't seen the blood on my sheets from our wedding night. They see how withdrawn and angry my husband has become."

"Stop worrying so much about what the servants think. Or what your husband thinks, for that matter," I said with a sigh. "His anger is due to something else entirely."

She narrowed her eyes at me. "Are you so certain of that? And how do I stop worrying? He's my *husband*."

I was taken aback by her rebuke. It was so easy for me to focus on my own pleasure. That was the one gift sex had always given me: the ability to close the window to the rest of the world.

"I want to please him," she said sullenly. Defiantly. "Will you tell me now that it should be easy to please a man? That it's the most natural thing in the world?"

"No, I won't tell you that." Gently, I laid her back down. "I'll tell you more about yourself instead."

Though she was agitated, she stilled when I pulled the layers of her robe aside and lifted her skirt. Her eyes clouded when I put my hand between her legs once more. She liked my touch.

"All those pretty words," I murmured, feeling gently along the seam of her flesh. "Jade gates and cinnabar caves—they don't mean anything. We're not empty down there, waiting to be filled. We're flesh and blood, with a passage that is willing to give a little, depending on the circumstances." Mao Mei opened her legs as I parted her swollen lips with my fingers. "When a man puts his organ inside of you, he has to push part of you aside to do so."

She held her breath as I touched against her opening, tensing just as she'd done the first time.

"How many years are you?" I asked softly.

"Eighteen. Is that too old?"

I smiled, with a shake of my head. "No, not too old."

It had been so long since I'd been a maiden. I'd been young, younger than Mao Mei even, but I still remembered the fear. There had been pain, more pain than there should have been. And sadness too.

That was as far as I'd let myself go back. I hated thinking of the past. I just had to remember enough to try to understand.

"You're frightened when Yuan tries to enter you. But every woman is frightened," I told her in a soothing voice. "Even if she's a young bride and he's very handsome and she wants it to happen."

"I…I do want it," she admitted in a quivering voice.

It was evident from the collection of scrolls and writings scattered on the table that she wanted it. Perhaps too much. Along with the writings, Wu had also provided her with phalluses carved of jade, of wood, and even ivory. They came in all sorts of fascinating shapes. Yuan probably had no idea how much his wife was dedicated to consummating their marriage.

I had stumbled upon her collection of phalluses shortly after arriving at the mansion. In her shame, she had me beaten for discovering her secret. Maybe I could forgive her for punishing me now…just a little bit.

"Are you still afraid?" I asked, probing her entrance lightly.

"Not as much."

Though her sex was damp from the earlier stimulation, no new wetness formed to ease my way. Mao Mei was very far from excited.

Maybe it had been a trick of my body. I had discovered long ago that I could react to fear and pain with arousal. And it was just another step to transform that storm of emotions into desire.

Desire was not one clean line. It consisted of many fragmented brushstrokes, brought together to form a whole.

"Are...are my yin energy points closed off?" Mao Mei asked.

I snorted which earned me a glare.

"I don't know anything about the mysteries of yin and yang," I said, duly chastised. "But let's see about you."

Removing my hand from her, I reached for a porcelain vial painted with a yellow orchid on the table. It was a strange choice. The orchid was such a lonely flower. I opened the stopper and poured a few drops of fragrant oil over my fingers.

This time, Mao Mei tilted her hips toward me. I could see how much she wanted to know these answers as well.

She was tighter than I expected. The muscles of her womanly channel were nearly rigid.

"Breathe," I murmured.

"I am," she whispered, her face twisted with despair. I could see she was ready to cry. She had been so full of hope.

I hushed her, probably being firmer than I should have been, but she quieted. With two fingers, I spread oil over her inner folds, parting them bit by bit until I was able to insert the tip of my smallest finger inside. Her muscles clamped like a vise around me.

Withdrawing, I smoothed her skirt back down over her knees and sat back, lost in thought. The dilemma was easy to see. Yuan couldn't penetrate his wife. He could please her in other ways and she could undoubtedly please him, but if he couldn't slide his cock into her, they would never be able to produce children.

For a man, the solution was easy. Another concubine, another wife. For Mao Mei, there was no solution. Her value depended on her ability to give birth to a son. There would be nothing for her but heartbreak.

I was interrupted from my reverie by a sob. Mao Mei was sitting up with tears streaming down her face. She had her arms hugged around her knees, pulling herself into a tight ball. "I don't do it on purpose," she choked out.

Appalled at myself, I rushed to her side. "I'm so sorry. I didn't mean to forget you."

She shook her head, overcome. I tried putting my arms around her which felt very strange.

Mao Mei buried her head against my shoulder. "Is there any way, Elder Sister?"

What did I know? I didn't know anything. "Of course there is. Of course there is."

I stroked her hair and told her it would be all right. My lover's wife, my enemy's niece—I whispered and I rocked her the way I imagined it was supposed to be done. After a while it seemed to help, for her and for me.

Yuan was waiting for me in my chamber when I returned that evening, something he'd never done before.

"You were in there for a long time today," he said jealously.

"We had things to talk about," I replied with a shrug. "Women's things."

I helped him out of his robe and brought him to bed, while he regarded me with a wary eye. "I thought undressing me was beneath you unless it served your purposes."

"This does serve my own purposes. You're very warm."

Begrudgingly, he put his arms around me. "Is my wife still upset?"

"You should ask her."

I yelped as he pinched me lightly on the rump. "Is everything all right?"

"It will be," I relented. "But I'm very tired, darling. You'll have to have your way with me while I lie here. I may fall asleep in the middle of it."

He kissed me hard then, a kiss that was full of passion, but not desire. My heart opened to him even more. When we broke apart, it was only for him to gather me into his arms. We shifted about restlessly for a few moments before settling in. I knew Yuan was agitated at my coyness, but I placed a secret, hopeful kiss against his shoulder as I curled up against him.

Yuan had been in darkness. So had I. There was no way for me to bring him out of it. We weren't those people to each other.

But maybe there was still a way for us to find the light.

CHAPTER ELEVEN

Mao Mei wasn't my lover. Over the next months, we explored and practiced and devised different methods of readying her for taking a man into her body. We weren't lovers even though I brought her to orgasm, even though I allowed her to touch and explore my body when she asked. She wanted to know how Yuan liked to have me, how I liked him best. I had never thought of the answers before she'd asked these questions.

"With him cradling me in his lap," I told her, surprising myself. "With us both facing each other while he's inside me."

"Does it feel best that way?"

"No," I admitted, laughing. "Not at all."

There was no leverage in that position. Yuan couldn't thrust deep or hard enough, but it was still my favorite. There was a lot of laughter between Mao Mei and me those days. I'd rarely laughed in the palace. My heart had always been too shut away and afraid.

Mao Mei asked once if she could put her mouth on me. She wanted to know what I felt like inside when I came. I could barely breathe as I consented to it.

Her touch on me was light, tentative. So much softer than any man's. She slid her finger inside me before she even touched me with her mouth.

"You're always so wet," she marveled.

"It's easy for me."

My voice was as thick as sugar syrup, lower in my throat than I'd ever heard it. With Mao Mei, we used steam baths to soften and relax her muscles, and oils to gradually work her womanly passage open. She could accept my fingers easily now, and the smallest of Wu's toys when properly prepared.

I needed no such preparation. For me, all it took was the thought of sex or the slightest touch. This time, all it took was the whisper of Mao Mei's breath over my flesh and I flooded with arousal.

She kissed my nether lips tenderly before opening me. Then all trace of uncertainty disappeared. I wondered how long she'd thought about this.

When Mao Mei's tongue slid against my soft pearl, I closed my eyes and it was as if a warm lake had poured its waters over me. I didn't imagine she was Yuan or any other man who'd ever tasted me. It was impossible to pretend. None of them felt like this.

"You have a heartbeat in there," she told me after I'd come, writhing against her mouth. I screamed when it happened and feared that I had scared her, but her eyes were soft and dream-like as she gave me her report. "And you tighten and squeeze in so many different ways."

Mao Mei wasn't my lover. She was something more.

Yuan did remain my lover, coming to my bed and taking me to heaven with his cock deep inside me. Holding me afterwards. He visited Mao Mei as well, but I wouldn't allow him to penetrate her. Not yet. They both accepted my rule, and the cries coming from their chamber were good ones now. No more weeping.

The three of us never joined each other in bed after the first time. I wasn't sure why. It just didn't seem to fit what we were becoming. We each of us had our own mysteries we wanted to keep intact. I jealously guarded my time with Mao Mei as much as I guarded my time with Yuan.

When Mao Mei and I weren't practicing the art of the bedchamber, we sat in the garden or in her parlor. Yuan had an impressive collection of books and scrolls—apparently it was a love of his that I didn't know about. I would read through books of poems and epic tales while Mao Mei worked on an embroidery pattern.

"Elder Sister," she said one day as we were lounging in her sitting room. "I'm sorry for calling you a whore before."

I turned the page, unperturbed. "I am a whore."

"No, you're not." She said, very seriously. I looked up from my book to see her watching me intently. "I knew from the beginning that you were educated. The way you speak sounds like—"

"What do I sound like?"

"You sound like me," she finished, looking embarrassed.

A pit formed in my stomach. Of course we sounded alike. It was a combination of learning and diction and dialect. We'd been raised similarly. We were both princesses.

Sooner or later I would be discovered. How would the Emperor, the very man who had sentenced me to death, feel about his niece receiving instruction from the great whore herself?

I was being paranoid. Shaking my head, I pushed those thoughts away and returned my attention to my charge. I was starting to think of her a little bit that way. I'd never had a student. Or a sister.

"Do you think you're ready?" I asked her, changing the subject.

Without fail, that grabbed her full attention. "Do you think I'm ready?"

Mao Mei had wanted to for weeks now, but I'd held her back. I could tell Yuan was getting anxious as well. His gaze would stray to her from afar, hungry and heated.

"I think it's time," I said, feeling a bittersweet sense of hope. I wasn't enlightened enough to be beyond jealousy. "It's time for your wedding night."

On the chosen evening, I sent Mao Mei to take a long, luxurious bath and went to Yuan in his chamber. The bed was strewn with flower petals and the canopy veiled with pink curtains to create a romantic air. It was as if tonight was indeed their wedding night.

I reached out to touch the curtains, my chest hitching. The material was translucent, as delicate as air, as thin as dreams.

"What are you doing here?" Yuan came up behind me.

I turned around, smiling crookedly. "Dulling your sword."

He was freshly bathed, his skin clean and smelling of cedar and spice. My pulse beat faster as he neared.

His eyes glinted. "I don't need my sword dulled."

Backing him toward the sitting room, I gave Yuan a playful shove and he toppled onto the lounge, sprawling back onto his elbows. He watched me with a smile playing on his lips as I climbed over him.

"Oh, you don't now?" I straddled him, still clothed. "I see how you've been looking at Mao Mei all week. Like a tiger about to devour a rabbit."

"I can control myself," he protested.

I rose to work his trousers open while he took it as an opportunity to slip my robe from my shoulders so he could fondle my breasts. Freed, his manhood thrust eagerly into my hands. It only took a few moments more for me to move layers of silk aside and center myself. Closing my eyes, I sank down slowly, letting my weight pull me down onto his hard cock.

The liar. He was harder and thicker than I ever remembered. I seated myself fully onto him and heard the sharp pull of his breath. His hands curved around my waist possessively as his hips jerked upward. Three, maybe four thrusts later, he was already spilling deep into me.

When I opened my eyes, Yuan was grinning wider than the Yangtze River, albeit sheepishly. I didn't even feel the need to taunt him.

"I can go again. Right now if you wanted me to," he insisted.

I was certain he could. Yuan was as hungry as an untried youth tonight. Every muscle in him vibrated with it. "Save yourself for the main course later."

When I started to climb off of him, he stopped me. I felt the muscles of his abdomen tightening as he sat up. The movement pulled his organ out of me, the sensation of him withdrawing enough to make me shudder.

He wrapped his arms around me. "These have been good times, Shanyin. Very good."

"They have been," I echoed quietly.

Some of the best days I could ever remember. But then why was my throat constricting so tight I could hardly breathe? I closed my eyes when he touched a hand to my cheek.

"Mao Mei isn't you," he said, his tone as tender as I'd ever heard it. "She never will be."

"But I'm not her either."

It felt so good right now, with Yuan holding me tight. Even though Yuan and his wife had big plans for tonight, even though I'd been the one to orchestrate them, I didn't want this moment to ever end. I was never a particularly noble or self-sacrificing person. Was it so surprising that I wanted to keep the best parts of Yuan to myself?

I truly wanted them to succeed. I'd even selected this chamber. Yuan's quarters weren't tainted by memories of past failure and I knew it was important for Mao Mei to not dwell on all that had happened before.

"Your wife will be waiting for you," I said, using the excuse to climb off him and smooth out my skirts. I caught Yuan eying my back as I pulled my robe over my shoulders.

He finished righting himself, and once again Yuan stood before me, impeccably handsome and distinguished. "I have to thank you for all you've done for us."

"What have I done? I haven't done anything."

But he wouldn't let it go. Yuan stared at me, his gaze dark and piercing "You're an intriguing woman, my princess."

Why did it still pierce me so deeply to hear him call me that? Because I would always be a princess, with all the sins and entitlements my rank had given me.

"I'm an endless mystery." I waved at him dismissively. "Now I really must fetch your bride."

The scoundrel caught my hand before I could go. "I'll never know all your secrets, will I?"

"A woman always has to keep a few secrets close," I teased, fighting against a growing sense of emptiness inside me. "But I'll grant you one on his auspicious occasion."

He didn't bat an eye before speaking. "What are those scars on your back?"

"One of my many uncles." I answered quickly enough, and with a steady voice as well. "He was punishing me for...for being my father's daughter."

Did he know I had forbidden my harem to speak of the scars? They had obeyed my every command, treating me as if I were unscathed and beautiful. Yet despite having such accommodating and virile lovers at my service, I had wanted Yuan. An outsider who wouldn't bow to my every whim. He wouldn't let me forget either.

"You know I would protect you from them," Yuan offered solemnly. "From your uncles or anyone who dared to harm you."

I turned away from his look of concern. This wasn't the time to dredge up dark confessions. This was supposed to be a happy night for bride and groom.

"I'm not afraid of them anymore," I told him with more than a little bravado. I'm more afraid of keeping Mao Mei waiting. She'll be getting more anxious by the minute."

I left Yuan's quarters to meet Mao Mei in her chamber. Her maidservants had dressed her in yellow silk, embroidered with a pattern resembling birds in flight. Her hair had been perfectly combed and pinned with jewels, and her lips painted an enticing shade of red. The pink flush on her cheeks, however, had nothing to do with makeup.

How many hours had we spent practicing with various oils and implements? All in preparation for this moment. Her hand trembled as it slipped into mine.

"We're sisters, aren't we?" she asked me as we crossed the courtyard.

"Yes," I replied haltingly. "I suppose we are."

"Always?"

She stopped our progress to await my answer. The sky was just fading into evening, and there was a gentle breeze flowing through the garden. In the dimly lit area, the blackness of her eyes seemed endless. Her lips were painted cherry-red, highlighting the luminous quality of her skin. She appeared almost otherworldly in that moment.

I squeezed her hand tight and placed a kiss on her forehead. "This night belongs to you and your beloved. Think only of that, my darling."

The warm glow of the lanterns greeted us inside the bridal chamber, and Yuan's eyes lit up the moment he saw Mao Mei.

She blushed furiously beside me. When I moved to guide her forward, she wouldn't let go of me. "Please don't leave me, Elder Sister!"

The two of them had spent many nights together exploring each other's bodies. I had told her tonight would be very much the same except they would be letting their lovemaking take its natural course.

Yuan held out his hand to her. "My wife," he said, his voice heavy with emotion.

Though I knew Mao Mei wanted him, her hands went to ice. She gripped me as if her life depended on it. Yuan shot me a questioning look.

"Come to the bed," I instructed.

She allowed Yuan to put an arm around her waist as he led her into the sleeping area. He bent to whisper something in her ear that I couldn't hear, but it made her smile. I hovered at the edge of the room as Yuan undressed her.

I shouldn't have worried about Yuan's part. He was a skillful lover. With me, he would pin my wrists as he thrust into me. Bite my neck as I came—all things that drove me wild. But with Mao Mei, I saw how utterly patient and tender he could be.

My heart ached as he kissed her lips, taking his time as if the sun and moon would wait. He undid the pins in her hair one by one. Once Mao Mei's hair fell loose around her shoulders, Yuan straightened and removed his clothing. The muscles of his back rippled in the firelight. My breathing slowed as I watched their dance.

When Yuan started to lower Mao Mei onto the bed, she stiffened and her eyes immediately darted to me. It made sense that she would rely on me. I was present for all of our practice sessions, easing one phallus after another into her tight flesh.

Hesitantly, I stepped forward. Just seeing my approach seemed to relax her, so I went to the bed. There Yuan reached out his hand to welcome me. Though I took it, I didn't undress or move to lie down beside them. I merely squeezed his fingers once before letting go. Yuan likely needed to be reassured as much as Mao Mei.

"Remember to breathe." I took up a position beside her head and raised it onto my lap.

We had done this nearly a hundred times, but this time Yuan's organ was waiting to enter Mao Mei, and she knew it, which seemed to change everything. She was as tense as she'd been weeks ago.

Gently, I stroked my hand through her hair. "Close your eyes. Just think about how good it feels."

Yuan lowered himself between her legs while I continued to soothe her. I watched in fascination as Yuan parted Mao Mei's folds and his long tongue slid in between, licking gently along her slit. Gasping, she grabbed onto my knee and held on as if I were the only thing keeping her from being swept away.

I'd never seen what he looked like doing this. I'd always been caught up in my pleasure, impatient for my deliverance, but now I could see why Wu Chien often loved to just watch. It was an entirely different kind of pleasure, sweet and forbidden, and unclouded by my own physical sensations.

I stopped Yuan with my hand on his shoulder. He understood immediately.

"Lie on your back," I told him.

He did so, his hard cock rising like a tower from his hips. I reached for Mao Mei's hand to help position her, but at the last moment, turned her around to face away from Yuan. He still frightened her a little, didn't he? This way he could enter her without her having to worry about every emotion that flickered across his face.

The muscles in Mao Mei's legs flexed as she lowered herself onto his organ. Immediately she hit a point of frustration when the head of his cock failed to breach her entrance.

"It takes time," I hushed her.

Bending between Yuan's legs, I took his member in hand and gently pushed him into her. Meanwhile, I licked gently at her little bud. Gradually her rigid muscles relaxed and the swollen tip slid inside.

"Shanyin."

Yuan ground out my name, forgetting himself in a moment of passion. I could almost feel his cock as if it were thrusting into me. My sex flooded as if it was me he was penetrating. A moment later, he cried out Mao Mei's name as he slid farther into her. I doubted she heard him. She was in her own world, focused on all the things that were happening to her body.

Caught up, I bent and teased my tongue gently over her sex, following the line of where Yuan's cock stretched her wide. I stroked a wet trail between Yuan and Mao Mei, cock to cunt, closing my mouth over both of them. The shocking intimacy of it made my sex clench like a slippery fist.

What wouldn't I have given for Yuan's cock inside me? For Mao Mei to touch me with her delicate fingers?

Yuan opened his eyes and peered at me over her shoulder. The heat of his gaze slammed into me like a summer wind. His sword was far from dull. He had more than enough stamina to satisfy his wife and then slide hard into me immediately afterward to give me what I wanted. He had been waiting so long for this moment that I'm certain he would go all night.

But I needed to leave. As long as I stayed, I would overshadow Mao Mei and this night was meant for her.

I kissed her lightly on the pale skin of her inner thigh before rising. Yuan was embedded inside her now, thrusting so very slowly. His arms were thrown around her, holding her tight, while Mao Mei's eyes were open and filled with wonder and ecstasy. The sight of the two of them took my breath away, yet left me lonely all at once. I pulled the curtains closed over the bed before turning to leave.

I stood by the withered peach tree out in the garden, listening to the sounds of lovemaking coming from inside the bedchamber. My mind was a tangle of emotions. I was happy for them. I was sad. My skin was still flushed and my body aroused.

Yuan's words came to me. *Mao Mei isn't you. She never will be.*

She wasn't me, but she was close. We shared blood, no matter how distant. She was a princess as I had once been.

As the cool air washed over me, darkness set in. I don't know why these memories would come to me now, when I had buried them for so long. I don't know why I let them inside. I held on to the trunk of the peach tree as they poured into me like black water.

Me, kneeling in the courtyard, arms held as I was whipped. My little brother forced to watch. No, we didn't know where my father had fled to. After a while, I don't think my uncle or his commanders cared. They simply turned and walked away, conversing about horses as the soldiers surrounded me.

That day had been endless. I closed my eyes so there was only darkness and sounds. Faceless men above me. Hands holding me down to claw at my robe, rending the silk apart.

When I dared to open my eyes, more soldiers had surrounded my brother. One of the men struck him across the face and I could see blood spilling from his mouth. They were ready to kill him…or worse.

Ziye was just a child. Perhaps I had only been a child then as well, but that was no longer true from that moment.

"Stop," I commanded.

The men stared at me. Stared at my nakedness as I rose to my feet. They may have had swords in their belts, but they were still nothing but slaves and servants to me.

"Come here," I told them.

In the end, they left my brother to come to me. I didn't need to close my eyes this time. I wanted to remember when it came time to seek vengeance.

When my father took the throne, all of those vermin were beheaded. And when Ziye became Emperor, he continued his own string of executions.

Now another of our uncles had taken the throne. Our line seemed to have an endless supply of tyrants, no matter how much we slaughtered one another.

When my brother's thirst for blood had grown, I couldn't fault him. I had wanted vengeance too, hadn't I? Protect my own and survive, I'd told myself while we were imprisoned. We survived and as Princess Shanyin, I commanded every man who entered my body. They pleasured and served me as I wanted to be pleasured. They belonged to me in every way.

I came back to the present in a very different courtyard. A more tranquil one. The bedroom voices rose before falling silent and a moment of surrender and peace descended. My chest swelled—I was a part of that union. Perhaps it was the only way I could find happiness; through the fulfillment of another woman's dreams. Mine were too broken.

There was no better time to go than now, while Yuan and Mao Mei were one. While I had some measure of peace. My body was still warm from their bed, the touch of their skin was still on my fingers. And the memory of Yuan hard inside me, his hand on my cheek and looking at me fondly. Mao Mei calling me sister.

Mao Mei wasn't me. She was Yuan's wife, while I was never meant to belong to Yuan or any man.

I untangled myself from the branches of the peach tree and moved toward the gate, leaving the courtyard empty and still except for the swinging of the lanterns in the night.

CHAPTER TWELVE

The sun was nearly at its zenith when I heard the distant sound of hoof beats. I veered off the road, moving into the surrounding woods, and kept on walking. I wandered aimlessly through trees, through grass and brush.

I had reached a field of yellow flowers when I heard the sound of a voice behind me. It was a familiar voice, one I knew too well and that pierced immediately into my heart.

"Shanyin!"

He called the name twice and still I didn't answer. There was no Princess Shanyin anymore.

"Shanyin, stop."

This time a hand closed over my shoulder to whip me around. I stared up at Yuan's face, which was more beautiful now than when I had first seen him. I knew him now. There were creases that didn't exist before. The frown lines around his mouth and eyes were more defined, but I understood the reasons behind them. I was a part of his story.

Right now he was angry beyond words. He could do nothing but stare at me with his eyes blazing.

"Why?" he demanded.

"I can't stay," was all I could say. I turned once again to go, but he grabbed me hard. I could tell he wanted to shake me.

"Why now? When things have been so good?"

His expression softened and I wanted so much to reach out to him. "What happens when my uncle summons you back to the capital?"

He frowned. "I said I'd protect you, Shanyin. That isn't why you're leaving."

A lump formed in my throat. Why wouldn't he just let me be? "You have everything you could possibly want now. This is how it was always meant to be between us."

"Do you know Mao Mei has been crying all morning?"

"Then go and comfort her." Yuan didn't realize how cold I could be. He looked at my blank expression, at a loss. "In a month, you'll all forget."

"I didn't forget you." He moved closer, enclosing me in his shadow. I could smell the familiar mix of cedarwood and sweat, and I wanted to fall into him and let his scent envelop me.

"Remember?" His voice dropped low, tempered for me and only me. "I couldn't forget you after you fled the palace."

"But that wasn't love," I returned bitterly, his own words coming back to haunt me.

His eyes widened. "Is that what this is about?"

"No, it's not." Agitated, I pushed past him. Why did I even mention something so ridiculous?

When he grabbed me this time, I fought back, struggling against his hold. We tumbled into the grass and suddenly his mouth was on mine, his hands tangled in my hair. He kissed me until I melted into him.

"This isn't just love, Shanyin." His voice was rough with emotion. "This is more."

My heart was beating too fast. His face filled my vision and his body pinned me to the grass. Still I shook my head, brokenly.

He didn't argue. Instead he kissed me again, parting my lips with his and sliding his tongue into my mouth. This wasn't a tender or loving kiss. It was a kiss meant to do one thing. A shudder ran down my spine as he tasted me and his hand stole beneath my skirt, pushing through layers of silk until he found the wet mouth of my sex.

"Is this the only way to get through to you?"

My vision blurred as he stroked and opened me.

"Do you only believe how much I need you when I'm inside you?"

He was relentless, his fingers plunging deep, making me gasp with the roughness of his invasion. Yuan knew I liked it rough.

He pushed my legs apart with his knee and opened his robe. Without a trace of elegance between us, he entered me there in the field, crushing me into the grass. I moaned and wrapped my legs around him. Nothing else felt like this. No one else did.

"I'll do this every day if this is what it takes to keep you," he swore, his voice rumbling deep in his throat. He fucked me hard, pushing deep so I had no choice but to feel his need and the desperation and longing in every thrust.

He was turning me inside out, sending me hurtling toward orgasm. Panting, I reached up to touch his face. The proud and defiant face that had first seduced me.

"Tell me once again that you love me," I whispered.

It was both a command and a plea. He gathered me tight in his arms, moving endlessly into me. The scent of crushed grass and wildflowers surrounded us as the pleasure rose to an unbearable peak inside me.

As I came, I heard him call me by the very first address I'd heard from his lips. By what I would always be to him.

"I love you," he groaned as the fire consumed us both. "Princess."

EPILOGUE

I was still falling. Falling into a new life. Falling into happiness.

Within two months, Mao Mei confided that she was pregnant with their first child. She came to me first, with her eyes shining, before even speaking to her husband. As I watched the child grow within her, I experienced hope and fear and love like no other, through her eyes.

Yuan continued to visit both me and his wife, though not together. As I'd said, Mao Mei and I weren't lovers. We were something much more precious.

Yuan did get called to the capital more and more, but when the day came that Yuan was summoned permanently back to the imperial court, I would be by his side. No one knew better how to survive intrigue than I. In the meantime, the mountains were high and the Emperor was far away. Mao Mei was growing pink and round. Yuan walked around the mansion proudly, as if he were an immortal. There were nights when he fucked like one, leaving me exhausted and happy in his arms.

We still kept my identity from his wife. Perhaps one day I would tell her the truth, though I suspected she knew more than she admitted.

As to the princess I had once been, I did have one reminder. It was unexpected, in the form of visitors to the Governor's mansion while Yuan was away. Mao Mei, as *Furen* of the manor, welcomed the two distinguished gentlemen.

They announced themselves as gentleman scholars, and claimed to have known Yuan. They wished to come by and pay their respects. Mao Mei had tea brought for them and engaged the two in conversation while I listened from behind a painted screen to voices I hadn't heard in a long time. Voices that had become imprinted deeper into me than I had ever realized.

The two visitors didn't stay long. I closed my eyes to listen to the polite exchange of conversation, thinking of all the nights we'd shared. I didn't need to forget the past anymore. I was no longer afraid of it.

In the end, I hazarded one glance. I couldn't help myself.

The sight of my former concubines brought tears to my eyes. Tai was as haughty and handsome as ever while Jiyi beside him remained smooth-tongued and charming. I disappeared back behind the screen with my hand pressed to my heart as it beat as loud as thunder inside me.

When they finally stood to leave, a shadow lingered beside the frame. Even in silhouette, I recognized who it was. Jiyi stopped to press his hand against the paper panel. Lightly, lest it tear apart. From the other side, I placed my fingertips against his, feeling just a hint of warmth through the thinnest of barriers, before the two of them departed.

AFTERWORD

Chu Yuan was an aristocrat from the Liu Song Dynasty. Apparently quite handsome, he caught the eye of the infamous Princess Shanyin while at her brother's court. Though she already had a harem of thirty concubines to serve her, she became enamored with Yuan and wanted him for one of her prime faces or *mianshou*—a phrase that was first coined to refer to Shanyin's male concubines. Yuan was given to Shanyin by the Emperor, but he refused to submit to her sexual advances. After tempting him for ten days, she released him.

The surprising thing is that I didn't make this up. *The Obsession*, the first book of the Princess Shanyin saga, largely follows the historical record. With the exception, of course, of what happens in the bedroom.

After a bloody coup, Yuan became an important official in the next administration and went on to survive the reign of several despotic and bloodthirsty rulers, outlasting the Liu Song Dynasty to serve in the early Southern Qi Dynasty. He had many sons and eventually died of old age. The Princess Shanyin of historical record was forced to commit suicide years earlier after her brother was assassinated. Her crime? Immorality.

There is no record of Shanyin and Chu Yuan ever seeing each other again after their ten-day affair. But what if…

Wanderers at the House of Floating Happiness

A bonus short story

CHAPTER ONE

Her name was Spring Rain. He first saw her in the window of a local pleasure house called the Floating Happiness, a fitting name as it was elevated on wooden stilts, giving the building the appearance of rising gracefully over the water. With a smile and a few well-placed compliments, Jiyi had drawn Spring Rain away from the watchful eye of her den mother and swiftly into his arms. Out in this remote bend of the river, the brothel fees weren't as expensive as in the capital, but female companionship certainly cost more than he had to his name.

She was a lovely creature. Her skin flushed pink beneath the mid-day sun as they ran through the wild grass together. They were hand in hand, giggling as they veered from the footpath to leave the town behind.

By the time they fell on to the grass in some hidden part of the woods, he was already half in love with her. He had a poet's heart after all, quick to surrender and constantly shifting like the moon.

He rested his hands upon her supple thighs. With a sigh she yielded to him, and he was completely smitten. It didn't matter that he knew nothing about her beyond the sound of her laughter and the feel of her soft skin. These feelings would fade as quickly as they came, but they were oh so sweet in the moment.

Jiyi was filled with a sense of lightness as he parted Spring Rain's legs. She was young and vibrant, and he wondered what lovely noises she'd make when he brought her to climax.

"We don't have much time," she told him in sultry whisper.

It wasn't really a protest. He smiled. "I won't take long."

The moment he pressed his mouth to her, Spring Rain let out a little helpless moan. His first taste of her sex rushed to his head as well as between his legs. He explored her with his tongue, tracing along the folds of her sex in long slow lines before sinking deeper to circle the pink pearl at her center.

To him, every peasant girl, every scullery maid was a hidden goddess, and never more so than in this moment. The moment before the surrender. When he knew all of a woman's secrets, yet none at all.

Spring Rain's fingers curled into his hair, tightening to the point of pain. Oh, she was completely his now. His cock grew harder as he swirled his tongue in delicate circles. She tasted like rain, warm and fragrant. Perhaps he was being sentimental. She was his first woman since the princess. Since Shanyin, the woman who had been the moon and the stars for the last year.

His beloved. His mistress, but when he had her like this, his tongue between her legs and her body ascending toward heaven, she was the slave. But it was Spring Rain who pleaded with him now, crying out in soft, incoherent sounds. Her legs shuddered beneath the tight grip of his hands.

He flicked his tongue faster, increasing the pressure ever so slightly. There was an art, a delicate balance to pleasing a woman. Her flesh was swollen now, that little nub exquisitely sensitive and demanding the utmost attention.

Men were easier to bring to satisfaction. Women were a constant mystery. Too rough and he would lose that delicate thread of desire. Too light and he might infuriate her to the point where she'd push him aside in favor of her own fingers. Or another lover.

But he was the only one here. He knew the moment Spring Rain was coming. Her breath hitched and her body tensed and bucked. Only then did he slide a finger inside her to feel the spasm of her inner muscles.

He drank in every moment of her climax. When she started to come down, Jiyi parted his robe to ease himself into her throbbing flesh. He was rewarded with heat and tight, damp flesh that welcomed him into heaven.

Jiyi let himself go quickly with selfish abandon, thrusting hard to ride himself toward release. Beneath him, Spring Rain was perfumed softness. He pressed a kiss to her throat so she wouldn't feel neglected. Immediately after, he let the rhythm take hold of him and carry him like a wave toward the shore. Suddenly he was spilling into her, grinding his hips to milk every last drop of sensation from their coupling.

With his release, a buried thought was pulled to the surface. He was no longer a slave. His pleasure was his to claim once more.

"The men who come to the house aren't like you," Spring Rain complained.

She was nestled against him while they lay in the grass. The afternoon sun filtered in through the leaves overhead in spots of light and dark.

"Oh?" Jiyi asked, content to lay back and let the warmth of their lovemaking linger. If there was time, they might go again, but he was in no rush.

"They're old and fat." She stretched out languidly, like a well-kept cat. Her toe brushed playfully against his calf. "So rarely young and handsome like you."

"Because young and handsome men are often so poor."

"Liar." She tweaked two fingers into his side, making him jerk.

A brief tussle ensued involving limbs becoming entangled, and giggling and a kiss or two. Spring Rain really was a pretty girl. Her robe was disheveled and strands of hair fell loose from her tortoise-shell combs. A gift from a patron, no doubt.

"I am poor," he stated soundly once he had her settled once more in his arms.

He was reluctant to let go of this stolen embrace. She was a flower house girl, a prostitute, and he was a former concubine. Yet this moment was their own.

"I can tell you're no peasant," she insisted.

"Oh?"

Reaching into the opening of her robe, he fondled Spring Rain's breasts. She filled his palm nicely and her nipples hardened at his touch.

"You're more than you seem. You sound cultured, like Lord Wu—" She sighed as he gave one pink bud a gentle tweak. "Or Autumn Rain. Even when she was cursing, she sounded like a lady…"

Her voice trailed away when he circled the pad of his thumb over her nipple. Her breathing quickened, and she arched her back, offering herself. How could one possibly refuse?

"Autumn Rain," he remarked absently before closing his mouth over one delicious peak and sucking gently. Once he had her moaning, he switched to the other.

"We don't know where she came from…she just appeared one day…*oh, heaven…*"

The light scrape of teeth there. The tiny shiver that ran down her spine made his cock thicken once more. Vaguely he took note of what she was saying about this Autumn Rain. He would have to ask more about her later.

Much later.

"I'll be late—" Spring Rain gasped as he eased two fingers inside of her. "Madame Lin will have me beaten."

Undeterred, he planted a kiss between her breasts while he slid slowly in and out of her swollen sex. "And mark this beautiful skin?"

Spring Rain's head fell back, exposing the vulnerable curve of her throat as she lost herself in the rhythm of his hand. He bent to devour her breasts once more.

"I'll be punished for certain," she moaned, but made no attempt to leave as her damp flesh convulsed around his fingers.

CHAPTER TWO

"The princess was here, I'm certain of it," Jiyi insisted the moment he was through the door.

Tai had just put his brush to paper when his companion returned to their shared lodging. The corner of a merchant's storeroom, to be correct. He sat on the floor with a low writing table set before him.

"More news from your brothel girl?" Tai kept his head bent to his task, and focused on keeping his brushstrokes controlled and even. It had been a long time since he'd written anything. Service in the princess's harem hadn't required such skills.

"Her name is Spring Rain," Jiyi said defensively.

Tai looked up to see him slouched onto a wooden crate, his back resting against the wall. His robe hung loosely from his shoulders having been carelessly tied, as if he'd just returned from another one of his trysts. Considering they'd only been here a week, Jiyi had worked his charms quickly.

"So you're in love with her now?"

His companion slanted him a sideways glance. "A little."

"You fall in love with anyone you fuck." Tai turned back to his writing. Idle chatter wouldn't get them out of the desolate situation they found themselves in, but a formal letter of introduction would. Even if it was a forgery.

"Does that include you?" Jiyi challenged.

Tai paused with the brush poised over the paper. He needed focus to do this properly while Jiyi was apparently in a mood for a fight.

Though Jiyi's pose remained languid, his hard gaze was fixed onto Tai. When they'd first come together in the princess's harem, Jiyi had adapted to their peculiar situation, and seemed almost happy with his place as a slave. Tai on the other hand had rebelled against it. His upbringing had been in a noble family, as heir and eldest son.

But Tai had come to learn Jiyi wasn't so easy to bend to his will.

Calmly, he set the brush aside. "Is there something you wish to say to me?"

Jiyi glared at him, his eyes narrowing dramatically. "You drove the princess away."

"Shanyin does as she pleases." Tai's mouth twisted. "She always has. She's a tyrant, just like her Emperor brother."

Her *deceased* brother. Until they had found rumor of her in this town, Tai had wondered if Shanyin's spirit had gone to join his in the afterlife. The thought had left a hollow pit in his chest, though he'd never admit it.

"She was a butterfly," Jiyi protested.

"She was a fox demon."

"Yes." Jiyi's jaw hardened as he stood to come forward. The harsh shadows gave his face a grim appearance. "She was all of those things, but she was ours. And we were hers. We were all intertwined, like mismatched threads in a tapestry."

Tai snorted. Jiyi fancied himself a scholar and a poet.

"Why bring this up now?" Tai asked.

"We should find her. We should see if she's safe."

Tai moved away from the desk and rose to face Jiyi. Standing, the two of them were nearly shoulder to shoulder with Tai slightly taller. He outweighed Jiyi as well. Though he was visibly larger and stronger, the two of them had wrestled at times in the boredom of the imperial harem. What Jiyi lacked in strength, he made up for in patience and guile. His companion knew how to wait for the right moment to strike.

They had wrestled in other ways as well, in the dark with their bodies slicked with sweat. Mouth to mouth.

It was a relationship borne of the harem. Of long days in isolation, the endless nights surrounded by others like them, chosen for their beauty in face and form. Tasked with being ready to perform on command, but threatened with death if they were to touch any of the maidservants who attended to the princess.

"I wanted to return Princess Shanyin to the life she deserved," Tai remarked.

"You wanted to use her for your own gain, but she wouldn't allow it." Jiyi glanced down at the unfinished letter. "She didn't want any part of your games of power and treachery."

"They're hardly games," Tai replied coldly.

To him, these schemes meant survival. They were also the only means of regaining a shred of what he'd lost. His family, his name. Honor.

"I'm not ready to disappear into the dust, fucking some common whore as a diversion."

He'd meant to wound Jiyi with the insult, or at least snap him out of his sentimental stupor, but the other man merely grinned. It was more a baring of teeth than a smile.

"Was I part of your plan?" Jiyi asked, his eyes glittering in the dimness. "Or merely a diversion?"

He could have claimed their bond had been nothing more than strategy. Jiyi had quickly become a favorite. With his aid, Tai had been summoned to the princess's bed night after night, the two of them tasked with pleasuring her until her screams of surrender echoed throughout the palace.

After being stripped of all rank and honor, Tai had once again risen to an elevated position. So be it if it was for being the most prized stud in a harem of thirty male concubines. It was really no different than bowing and scraping before an Emperor, his head on the ground and his ass in the air.

"I don't know what we are," Tai said quietly.

There was no use lying. Jiyi knew him, at least the man he had become, better than anyone. They had been together for the transformation—from an aristocrat to a pleasure slave and now a fugitive—all in the course of one year.

"But I know who I am," he continued. "And I won't disappear. I won't stay in hiding."

Jiyi's expression softened. "There's no one left to seek revenge against, Brother."

Tai's stomach knotted and every muscle inside him tensed. The anger that remained trapped inside him threatened to boil to the surface. There was a time when he had wanted revenge against Princess Shanyin, the woman who had caused him to be enslaved. He had wanted to see her on her knees, to see her surrender beneath him, mind, soul and body.

But she was too strong to give herself over, and he'd lost a part of himself to her even as he tried to dominate her.

Shanyin might be gone, but his fight wasn't over. The ghosts of his past were far from appeased, and there were always new enemies to be made. Anyone who stood in his path was his enemy. At this moment, it was Jiyi—who was looking at him now, no longer with scorn, but with warmth and even possibly concern.

"The past is the past," Jiyi said, reaching up to take hold of his arm. Though it was a brotherly gesture, heat coursed through Tai's veins.

They hadn't touched one another sexually since Shanyin had run away. It was if she had been a bridge between them. With her gone, Tai had assumed that need had disappeared as well, but now he wasn't certain.

Jiyi's eyes darkened as well. They were standing close, almost touching with shoulders back and chests puffed out. Like two tigers circling close…or like something else entirely.

If they closed that gap now, if the embraced or grappled or whatever it was, it wouldn't be out of pent up desire or affection. Or even boredom as it had been at times in the harem. It would be about power and a question of who truly held it over the other between them. The answer might destroy whatever they had left.

"The past is not the past," Tai said gravely. "Because there's nothing tying us together any longer, yet we're still here. And our struggle isn't over."

He went to visit the Floating Happiness that evening as Jiyi suggested. They arrived together, masquerading as scholars traveling the countryside. The visit would cost them a few precious coins from their meager stash, but Jiyi argued that if they wanted to re-establish themselves into society, they had to start somewhere.

"Lying bastard," Tai said through his teeth the moment they were seated in one of the parlors.

Jiyi grinned at him, a real grin this time filled with amusement at Tai's expense.

This was no pleasure house inhabited by trained courtesans, filled with music and conversation. No scholars or officials frequented these parlors. This was a brothel thinly veiled in threadbare silk and a worn layer of lacquer. Sure enough, there was the infamous Spring Rain arriving to pour watered down wine for them.

Jiyi had never actually set foot in the place, but that didn't prevent him from drawing the house girls who swarmed around him like wayward butterflies around a flower. Within the hour, Jiyi was dedicating verses to them in turn while they giggled and cooed about him. Even the den mother, Madame Lin with her lips painted in a glaring vermilion tint, seemed utterly charmed.

Tai hooked his hand around the wrist of one of the quieter girls, and led her to through the curtain to the adjoining room where he toppled her onto his lap. She braced her hands against his chest to steady herself as he anchored her legs on either side of him.

"Sir—"

He wrapped his hand around to the back of her neck, tilting her eyes up to meet his. "Your name?"

"Orchid," she whispered faintly.

"Orchid," he echoed, guiding her hips downward. Her mouth parted with a soft gasp as he penetrated her. Moving his hand between their bodies, Tai drew a slow circle over her sensitive opening until her sex dampened, easing his passage. Still, her eyes widened as he angled his hips to push deeper. Then he centered his thumb on to her swollen bud, teasing lightly.

The courtesan's gaze darkened and glazed over. He tightened his grip on her neck, watching her pulse jump beneath pale skin of her throat. Down below, her damp flesh squeezed tight around his shaft. Orchid was yielding to him, body and mind, and Tai reveled in it.

There was no more need for words. With his hands, he urged her into a rhythm, riding his cock while those pretty wide eyes stared into his. Was little Orchid truly this demure, or was it merely an act? It didn't matter. It suited his needs for the moment.

It was pleasurable enough, this routine fucking. Flesh against hot flesh. Sensation building at the base of his spine as his vision began to cloud. It would mean release and relief, but it was only nominally more satisfying than the pressure of his own hand.

His mind drifted to her. To Shanyin. Before becoming the princess's concubine, he'd bedded a few courtesans in pleasure houses and brothels. They all had names like Orchid and Lily, with silken skin and perfumed sheets. Sex had been like an hour in the clouds.

But Shanyin had shown him the meaning of decadence and raw pleasure. There were times he came so hard he thought his bones would snap.

He was coming now. Just a spasming of his body and a momentary release. The spilling of his essence, lost and gone. But he'd lost himself long ago to the cruelest of mistresses. Like all of the other slaves in Shanyin's harem, he'd clamored to please her, but he'd had a plan and purpose. What was his purpose now?

Orchid's voice reached him through the haze. "Please sir," she choked out.

It was a plea borne of pain, but more than pain. His grip was too tight, yet she clung to him, flushed with arousal as she rode him. With a hard look, he took hold of her hips and brought her down fully onto his shaft, grinding up into her. Orchid sobbed and sank her head against his chest as the orgasm wracked her body.

Even before she was done, his mind was elsewhere. Raised voices could be heard outside the room and the sound of running. Tai lifted Orchid off of his lap and cast her aside. Righting his robe, he entered the hallway just as a thin, waifish creature plummeted into him.

He caught the girl by the arms just as Madame Lin rounded the corner. The brothel madam was flanked by a gray-haired woman holding a bamboo switch and a thug who looked to be hired muscle.

"Please, my lord." Black hair fell over her face as she pleaded with him. "Please, my lord, I don't belong here."

"You do now," the old grandmother spat, pointing with her switch. "Get back here and do as you're told."

The girl ignored her captors and clung to his arm. Her grip was surprisingly strong, and he could sense her strength elsewhere as well. In her very being as she stood beside him.

"My lord, I come from a good family. My father was an administrator in Jiankang."

She looked up at him and finally her hair fell away from her face. The first thing he noticed was a cut that ran from her left temple just down to the edge of her cheekbone. The skin around it was angry and red, still unhealed.

The second thing he noticed was that she was startlingly beautiful. The mark on her face seemed to accentuate rather than detract from her beauty. He might have looked away from her after a brief glance, but the cut irresistibly drew his eye back. It undoubtedly ruined the stark and elegant symmetry of her features, but without that mark, her appearance was almost too perfect.

Something tugged at his chest as he stared down at her, though outwardly he showed nothing. Her father was an official as in he was no longer in such a position. Either he'd been stripped of his title or had met some other misfortune. It wasn't uncommon in these troubled times. Tai's family had met with a similar fate. His family name had once been one of the most respected in the imperial court.

But that was two reigns ago. The wheels of power turned quickly as of late. Heads fell fast.

Even though this girl was thin, her skin was luminous and her hair dark and sleek. There was a fullness to her cheeks indicating she'd been well-fed and well-kept. She was fallen nobility, like he was.

Had she somehow sensed their similar upbringing? Was there some hint of his past in his manner or bearing? That was impossible. There was nothing about his appearance that set him apart from the rest of the peasants in this dusty settlement. She was just desperate.

"Please help me," she implored, tears gathered at the corner of her eyes.

Tai hardened his heart at the sign of weakness. She had to be stronger than that if she wanted to survive.

"Forget who you were," he advised coldly.

He didn't need to shake his arm free from her grasp. Her fingers fell away listlessly, as if drained of every last drop of hope. As Madame Lin's minions came to take hold of her, Tai reached out one last time, suddenly loathe to be separated from this frightened creature who didn't even have a name. He only caught the edge of her sleeve, but for a moment they were connected once more.

"But always remember," he added in a low voice.

It was a futile gesture. The girl only met his gaze for the barest of seconds before turning away. Her hair fell once more over her face, shielding herself from this world she had been thrown into. Even after she was dragged into some inner chamber of the brothel, the memory of her eyes, dark and pleading and desolate, lingered with him.

There was nothing he could have done. Even if his family hadn't been stripped of status, even if he hadn't been made into a slave, Tai still wouldn't have been able to take her away from Madame Lin.

The girl would survive. She would have to transform and become stronger and harder than she'd ever known was possible, but she would do it. There was simply no other choice.

A new fire began to burn in the pit of his stomach, fueled by anger at his own helplessness, but also by longing and ambition.

Jiyi and he would stay here. They would establish themselves as respectable gentlemen — they certainly possessed enough knowledge and experience to do so. They might find Shanyin or they might not, but it didn't matter. And Jiyi was right about one thing.

Revenge wasn't what he was after anymore. Tail would never again feel lower than a bunch of hired hands at a dingy brothel. Tai would find his own way back into the life that he'd been born into, fighting and clawing his way up if he had to.

There was simply no other choice.

Jiyi and Tai's story continues…

Go to http://www.lilianalee.com for more information and to sign up for updates.

ACKNOWLEDGMENTS

Thank you to my awesome production team: Jodi Henley, Julia Ganis, and Dana Waganer for embarking on this adventure with me. And special thanks to Shawntelle Madison for all the extra hand holding.

ABOUT THE AUTHOR

LILIANA LEE writes erotic stories set in exotic worlds. The Princess Shanyin series is her erotic debut.

Liliana also writes romantic and speculative fiction as Jeannie Lin.

She can be found online at http://www.lilianalee.com. Go to website for more information and to sign up for updates.

CPSIA information can be obtained
at www.ICGtesting.com
Printed in the USA
LVOW08s2324250117
522220LV00001B/116/P